ACCLAIM FOR
JOHN WESTERMANN AND
LADIES OF THE NIGHT

THE HONOR FARM

"A wry, street-smart, bare-knuckles, behind-bars brawl that bears up under a thick plot and a large cast of dirty denizens. . . . It's difficult to tell the schemers from the scammed as Orin Boyd, a proud Vietnam vet blessed with equal helpings of brains and brawn, takes on all comers. . . . Fans of the police procedurals of early Wambaugh and late McBain will delight in the gruff sensibilities of Westermann's heroes and the unregenerate sleaziness of his villains."

—*Kirkus Reviews*

"A dagger-sharp, edge-of-your-seat thriller guaranteed to keep the pages turning. Westermann just keeps getting better."

—Stephen Solomita

"Westermann delivers another gripping police thriller."

—*Chicago Tribune*

"Westermann, who worked twenty years as a Long Island cop, brings plenty of colorful detail to the novel and to Boyd, who's smart, funny, and not above taking the law into his own hands. The pacing is relentless, and the uncovering of secrets old and new will keep readers glued as they're plunged into a Long Island that's way beyond Levittown."

—*Publishers Weekly*

Also by John Westermann

High Crimes

Exit Wounds

Sweet Deal

The Honor Farm

JOHN WESTERMANN

Ladies of the Night

POCKET STAR BOOKS

New York   London   Toronto   Sydney   Singapore

A Pocket Star Book published by
POCKET BOOKS, a division of Simon & Schuster, Inc.
1230 Avenue of the Americas, New York, NY 10020

Copyright © 1998 by John Westermann

Originally published in hardcover in 1998 by Pocket Books

ISBN: 0-671-87126-9

First Pocket Books paperback printing December 2000

10   9   8   7   6   5   4   3   2   1

POCKET BOOKS and colophon are registered trademarks of Simon & Schuster, Inc.

Cover design by Jesse Sanchez

Printed in the U.S.A.

This book is dedicated to the men and women of the Freeport Police Department below the rank of captain.

Thursday, Oct. 24

chapter 1

IT WAS THE HEIGHT OF THE SILLY SEASON.

Deputy Nassau County Executive Elizabeth Lucido stood at one end of the bunting-covered dais, wishing she were almost anyplace else. Elizabeth was thirty-five, with conservative curves on a tall frame, her brown-black hair swept back in a braid. She wore a gray suit, white blouse, and pantyhose, and gold appropriate to her position. Her party, the Republican party, had just needlessly introduced its current slate to its biggest contributors. The white politicians arrayed to her left were waving at the oft-fleeced faithful, graciously accepting their applause.

Twelve-year veteran County Executive Martin Daly was to head the ticket again. A red-white-and-blue banner overhead proclaimed that Daly had the Experience for the Millennium. It had been Martin Daly's own idea, this particular strategy: suggesting to the populace that he was the candidate best able to face the future, simply by aging in office.

Martin Daly's problem was, it wasn't working.

Though he was only fifty-five, approaching his prime to hear him tell it, people were getting sick of him.

This year the Democratic party challenger, Jackson Hind, was running neck and neck with Daly, nevermind the Democrats hadn't won a big race in Nassau County in thirty years—largely due to the opposition of the remarkable Republican machine, currently owned and operated by its legendary chairman, Seymour Cammeroli.

Chairman Cammeroli had mashed his pasty face between her breasts when Elizabeth had first entered the South Shore steakhouse, then whispered up at her earring, "You mark my words. This fucking clown could blow it for everyone."

"This fucking clown" meant Martin Daly, of course, the tall, arrogant candidate with the ever-darker hair, and lines in his face that cried yachtsman. (The other county-wide candidates resembled, in one way or another, John Gotti: sharp suits, slicked-back hair, salon tans, body-builder postures. The men, too.) Last year Martin Daly had grown so full of himself he had announced for the governor's race, much to the dismay of Seymour, who needed him at home. The ill-considered effort had fizzled, and Daly had quietly withdrawn, saying, alas, his loyalty remained with the taxpayers of Nassau County.

Elizabeth watched the big phony fight back tears as he waved at his cheering supporters. His second wife, Kymberly Scallia-Daly, stood next to him, drunk and disheveled, smirking as usual. Next to her, his Gen-X son, Marty Junior, slouched as if the applause embarrassed him, which it should have. The painfully thin district attorney, Arthur Prefect, and a cluster of minor potentates fanned out from there.

Elizabeth Lucido figured she could ruin half of them, knowing what she knew of their sorry lives, their sordid hobbies, their endless ambition for the free lunch; and yet legions of developers, tobacco lawyers, and health insurance executives stood behind thousand-dollar chicken dinners, cheering these bums as if they were truly the people's servants. It was a system that used to enrage Elizabeth when she was fresh from Columbia Law; she had worked so hard and sacrificed so much only to earn the opportunity to sell her soul. Now she made allowances for twists in logic and decorum. Maturity, she called it. Something in the water. Everybody knew the unexplainable happened with remarkable frequency on Long Island; bimbos shot housewives, nut-jobs riddled commuter trains, predators stalked the Internet, and planes fell from the sky; nothing you could do but clean up and shrug.

A three-piece band struck up "Happy Days Are Here Again," and Elizabeth decided that she'd had all the maturity she could stand. She nudged her immediate neighbor on the dais. "You think he'll need me for anything else?" she said through a frosty smile.

The burly white cop with the slick-shaved head said, "No," through his own phony grin. "Nothing that can't wait until morning. Or next freaking year."

Lieutenant Robert Rankel was grumpily enduring a rough divorce, with twins away at separate private colleges. He had been Daly's bodyguard and driver for eons, and normally, he could sit through anything. These days his patience seemed stretched. "Getting tired of this horseshit, Bob?"

"Wouldn't matter if I was. You got any idea what textbooks go for these days? Not to mention spring break in London for two. Good Lord, have times changed. Spoiled brats."

Elizabeth knew Rankel would likely be out until dawn on a night like this, piloting Martin and Kym around the circuit, in those sap-knuckled driving gloves Martin so adored, fetching drinks and holding coats, discouraging dissent in their immediate area, light duty for the ninety-eight grand Rankel had made last year. An essential expense, Martin called it, allowing him to move among his people without fear.

A crock of donkey shit, Police Commissioner Frank Murphy had called it, but the spending item passed anyway, because an expenditure like that wasn't Frank Murphy's call.

Elizabeth had seen the recently appointed police commissioner earlier, at the bar, hoisting scotch on the rocks and telling war stories, pressing his own pounds of flesh. Elizabeth considered the sandy-haired Murphy a class act among these bad suits; one of the few officials she knew who so far had maintained a degree of independence from the party, with principles beyond "What's in it for me?" Murphy had left the restaurant scant minutes after Emerald Society bagpipers had wailed Martin Daly's arrival, well before the fifty-fifty raffle, a slight that would not be ignored. They were down in her book to have lunch next week at the Beach Café in Long Beach, where they would stare at each other over wine; and leave feeling good about the world.

"I'm out of here, then," Elizabeth said to Rankel. "I've got an early start tomorrow. Make my apologies."

"I only wish I could go with you."

While the back slappers high-fived the ticket, Elizabeth slipped away from the dais and made her way to the front door. She found her claim check in her pocket along with a business card a young committeeman had pressed on her during the cocktail hour.

Outside the restaurant the evening air smelled of grilled steaks and salt and rain. "Honda Prelude," she said to the car-park girl, imagining the chaos facing the poor kid later, when all those drunk public officials left at once. "Blazer," they would bark in unison, "black, four-door, with a TV antenna, big tires." Of course many wouldn't know their official plate numbers, and who could blame them. They parked in numbered spaces outside their municipal office buildings; this problem only arose at off-site fund-raisers, and everybody eventually got matched up, usually by whipping out their cell phones and calling their secretaries at home.

Elizabeth had refused a company car-and-driver as a matter of style, and because she strongly suspected more than a few hid eavesdropping devices. She waved to the pickets who lined the sidewalk opposite the restaurant, some holding signs, wearing gas masks, mugging for the Minicams. A couple even waved back. DALY STARVES ELDERLY, said one big sign. THE MORAL MAJORITY IS NEITHER. The car-park girl whipped the black Honda to a halt at Elizabeth's feet as the demonstrators chanted, "Daly dyes his hair."

"They're right, you know," Elizabeth said as she handed over a five-dollar bill. "About the hair."

The car-park girl regarded the demonstrators. "Who's Daly?"

"Nobody special."

"Thanks for the tip."

Elizabeth locked her doors and rolled away from the hoopla, exhausted at the end of a long day during a long campaign—all for the hearts and minds of the few eligible voters who still troubled themselves to turn out. All that money they had spent, for a dozen years now, and the girl had never heard of Martin Daly.

Elizabeth's pulse quickened as she considered the possibility that she and Jackson Hind had a chance to personally orchestrate the collapse of the last great political machine in America.

And that, she thought, was why this particular Puerto Rican had gone public in the first place.

HER REDBRICK RANCH ON A CRAMPED SIDE STREET OFF COVERT Avenue in New Hyde Park was dark when she pulled into the driveway. Elizabeth wondered if she had forgotten to set her timer-lights. That would be like her, during a hot race, dropping the details of her life in favor of Martin's agenda.

Across the street, Miss Wentzel was at her living room window, peeking through the blinds, keeping her eye on the neighborhood, watching over her fellow spinster. You never knew these days, what with drugs and AIDS and guns.

Elizabeth waved, and Miss Wentzel waved back.

Elizabeth lugged three policy manuals and her brief-case into the modest house. She kicked off her heels, dropped her books on the kitchen counter, checked her answering machine. There was a message from her mother, reminding her to take her vitamins, suggesting a brunch date for Sunday, her treat. As if Elizabeth had a spare Sunday in October, as if she wouldn't be walking a swing district. There was a plea from her administrative assistant Lisa Tibaldi to remember her breakfast meeting at the Marriott with the mortgage bankers. A short message from Jackson Hind, who seemed to be calling from a bar: "Why aren't you home yet? I can't stand thinking of you among those swine."

She put her feet up on the kitchen table, next to the phone. The thought of calling her mother drained her. Better to call Mom tomorrow, with cheer in her voice. Probably the same was true for Jackson. And it didn't hurt that he was aching for her. Not one bit. These were days to be savored, not rushed. She would have kept a journal had she not feared it falling into enemy hands. More than once she had imagined facing the rat-faced District Attorney's grand jury, being perp-walked from the courthouse to the outhouse. She had battled back the fear.

The world was bigger than Nassau County, warmer than New York.

Jackson had taught her that.

Then Elizabeth heard his signature knock, and a smile creased her face. She walked to the door in her stockinged feet and stood on her tiptoes. Through the beveled glass she saw the back of his head, and she knew he was making sure he had not been followed.

Friday, Oct. 25

chapter 2

G OOD GOD, HE HATED BEEPERS. IF THIS WAS PROGRESS, thought Police Commissioner Francis Murphy, leave him most emphatically out. Murphy apologized to his mostly elderly neighbors and slid from his usual pew in the back of the old brick church. He had been baptized here during the prosperous years on Long Island, when almost everyone lived in a new house, worked for a defense company, and bowled on Friday nights. Then the cold war had ended, and Fairchild and Hazeltine and Grumman began shrinking and dying. The best jobs were suddenly government jobs, and those were hard to get. People moved away, or made do with less. Murphy remembered when there was still a place called Limbo.

He had prayed that Friday morning for his fiancée's continued happiness, and he had prayed for his younger brother, Wally, as always. He had prayed for the poor and the sick. Now he prayed this persistent beeping was not bad news, the coin of his realm.

At the rear of the church he dipped his fingers in holy water, turned, kneeled, and made the sign of the cross, then stepped from the sanctity of St. Luke's Church into the dawn bustle on Fairhaven Boulevard.

He unlocked his gray Crown Victoria and climbed behind the wheel, whipped out his cell phone and dialed Captain Jake Posner, who ran Frank's office for him. Jake also ran the Police Department Favor Bank and Rumor Mill. He always knew who owed whom, who was screwing whom and in what combinations, who was drinking too much, or misbehaving when they did, intelligence that could usually wait until after nine o'clock. Jake "the Snack" picked up the hot line on one ring, a civil service record of some sort. "Commissioner Murphy's office," he said. "Captain Posner at your service."

Murphy grumped, "Can't a man visit his Maker without you—"

"Elizabeth Lucido was kidnapped, Frank. Sometime last night."

"No. Stop."

"From her house, it looks like. Artie Prefect is already on his way."

"To make matters worse," said Murphy.

Once a third-rate probate lawyer, Artie Prefect was now the District Attorney of Nassau County because he was also the husband of Chairman Cammeroli's mustachioed sister, Rose. He more than doubled his public salary doing real estate, wills, and divorces for the faithful. Prefect knew he was detested and enjoyed it. His attendance was subtraction by addition at any type of scene.

"You got Elizabeth Lucido's address?" asked Jake. "Well, of course you do."

Murphy stared through his windshield at the church and grimaced. "And people say children are cruel."

"Now you know," said Jake. "Best be ready for it. And what was once an isolated tragedy has just become an epidemic if, God forbid, we don't find that Elizabeth is dog-sitting or something. Two big-shot broads. Poof. Gone. From their houses. And if they ain't safe, nobody is. And this on the heels of a very shitty summer."

That summer, Frank Murphy's first as Police Commissioner, Nassau County had suffered a crime wave of almost biblical proportions. First the movie-plex stickup dominated the news, then a bloody drive-by in New Cassell. A German nun visiting the Long Beach waterfront was raped.

Then, in September, Mrs. Todd Whitcomb III, the outspoken leader of the Republican Women's Caucus, disappeared without a trace from her Old Westbury estate. That case remained open, at a stone-cold dead end.

"I'm on the way," said Murphy. "Maybe I can beat the vultures there."

NASSAU COUNTY HOMICIDE DETECTIVES MAUDE FLEMING AND Rocky Blair caught the squeal on the last of their graveyard shifts, just hours from a long weekend off. They saw the early arrivals standing on Elizabeth Lucido's front stoop as Rocky parked their unmarked black Plymouth outside the jumble of emergency vehicles.

Rocky was a blue-blazered hulk, a thirty-year-old weight lifter with a flattop haircut. He said, "Looks like no sleep today, eh?"

Maude Fleming didn't answer as she shoved open the passenger door and climbed out. She was forty, gay, going on her seventh year in Homicide. Maude dressed like a CEO for her gruesome duties, this clear dawn in a gray pinstriped suit and black pumps, mascara and a slash of red lipstick. She and Rocky shared a barber.

District Attorney Prefect pulled in behind them, tapped his horn lightly, and saluted through the windshield.

"Just remember," Maude told Rocky over the roof of their car. "We don't work for that jackass."

Maude and Rocky got things rolling in no time, the first duties at a crime scene. Maude ejected the spectators and set the truly needed workers to their tasks: the crime scene photographs, the sketches and measurements, the search for fingerprints, the painstaking collection of clothing and carpet fibers, hair, semen, and blood, should any be present. Maude was playing this case as a homicide until someone proved to her otherwise. This was just a bit too familiar to the one unsolved case on her résumé: Barbara "Babs" Whitcomb III. As always, Maude would supervise the gathering of evidence and the questioning of witnesses, and Rocky would leg out her theories, a system that worked for them, credit shared equally.

She made him smarter, and he made her tougher. He didn't care that she liked her vice versa, and she didn't care that he lacked the facility to stifle first impressions, that he sometimes said the dumbest things.

Her own particular skill was to focus clearly on gruesome situations, to see—and understand the significance of—details others overlooked because they were squeamish or frightened, or lacked her dark imagination.

"Anybody know if she's dating anybody?" Maude called out.

None of the cops working the search knew about Elizabeth Lucido's social life. She was management; they were labor.

"We find a diary?"

"Negative." A uniform cop pointed to papers on the kitchen table. "Just those."

"Anybody notify next of kin?" asked Maude.

"We were waiting for you guys."

"I'll bet you were."

She and Rocky would notify the next of kin, and soon. Perhaps her relatives had already heard, thought Maude. Perhaps they were already the terrified recipients of ransom demands. Maybe they were afraid to call the cops.

This woman was neat and organized, thought Maude, which was always helpful when investigating someone's life. Except for the papers on the table and the suit jacket thrown over the back of a wooden kitchen chair, the house could have been a builder's model, everything in its place. The living room looked never-used, not a footprint on the thick beige carpet, no, just one, there. Maude showed it to the techs, then lifted Elizabeth's red leather address book from the hallway credenza, certain the bad guy was listed therein, as they almost always were.

"Who reported this?" Rocky asked.

"Across the street," said a uniform. "A Miss Wentzel, who is only around a gazillion years old. She noticed the front door ajar when she got her newspaper in."

"Can she see that far?" Rocky asked, looking out the front door, squinting. "Will she live until the trial?"

Maude Fleming looked up from the address book and said, "I'm thinking sex here. You feeling it?"

"Not yet," Rocky said. "But you know me. Who do you want me to talk to before their stories get polluted?"

"Neighbors on both sides," Maude said, "neighbors behind. Find out who she's friendly with, talk to them. I'll have a chat with Miss Wentzel."

Rocky tapped the walkie-talkie on his belt. "Stay in touch."

Maude smiled at Rocky's broad back as he lumbered out of the victim's house. Not everyone was cut out for this necessary and difficult work, but to her immense satisfaction, she very much was. She could climb inside people's minds, and make their belongings talk. Like her brothers, she could hunt.

Maude turned to the master bedroom. She saw the unmade queen-sized poster bed was mismatched to the other furniture, all likely plucked from roadsides or driveway tag sales. There were pictures of Elizabeth's handsome parents on the dresser, her father a tall Hispanic, her blond Anglo mother. A cherrywood jewelry box, apparently undisturbed. The crumpled white pantyhose on the floor next to the bed. A StairMaster near the window. A big-screen TV. Bookshelves. A small refrigerator containing a can of diet Coke.

The master bathroom held the normal array of personal products. The shower was dry, as were the towels. A single damp condom and its wrapper spotted the bottom of the wastepaper basket.

So much for safe sex.

POLICE COMMISSIONER MURPHY SLIPPED THROUGH THE ONLOOKERS corralled at the curb and was immediately nabbed on the lawn by Arthur Prefect—in his trademark black raincoat on this crisp sunny morning. Prefect leaned close to Murphy and breathed coffee and Winstons in his face. "I'm thinking task force here, Frank. You want me to put off my vacation? You know this is my last workday for a month."

"Thanks, Art. Not necessary. Go live it up."

"Just thought I'd offer."

"I'll mention that to the working press."

Prefect grinned. "I'd do the same for you."

Murphy saluted his way into the foyer of Elizabeth Lucido's house and joined Maude Fleming and the others with their cameras and clipboards. "Any signs she was injured?" Murphy asked Maude, pulling her into the relative privacy of the kitchen. Elizabeth's answering machine and phone had been bagged for evidence; a squad phone connected in its place.

Maude shook her head. "Not so far."

"Doing everything we can possibly do?"

"And then some."

Murphy nodded and watched cops dressed like scrub nurses scouring the house for clues, requesting additional items and information from headquarters on their walkie-talkies. "I saw her last night," Murphy told Maude. "At Martin Daly's fund-raiser. Not a care in the world."

"She a decent person?" Maude asked. "I mean, that's what I always heard."

"A nun in the whorehouse, for this business. We got search teams out? She likes to take long walks."

"Be a pretty long walk, Frank. We got the call around six."

"I was up then," Murphy said off-handedly, as if that fact alone might have prevented this.

"Swimming Fairhaven Harbor," Maude said, "just like every morning. In your wet suit, I'll wager."

Murphy cocked his head at his best detective. "What am I, a suspect?"

"It's part of your legend, sir. Like going to church all the time."

"I have a legend?"

"The start of one anyway."

chapter 3

COUNTY EXECUTIVE MARTIN DALY KNEW DAMN WELL port wine and Cuban cigars were no-nos, as were champagne and sambuca, but he had sucked them down last night anyway, and now he had wino-breath and a hangover the size of last year's deficit. He stood shaking in his white marble bathroom as he fumbled at the knot of his red power tie; and he swore the next time Campaign Manager Mike Barclay beeped him he would scream.

Who cared what *Newsday* said about all those county vehicles parked outside the restaurant last night: They had raised two hundred grand. Mike Barclay could do his damn job, which was to cover Martin Daly's back, particularly on tough mornings such as these. Or they could call Junior for a comment. Or Elizabeth, if things were really dicey. Anybody but him.

Then Daly heard Rankel's tap-tap-tap honk from his driveway, the big lieutenant too lazy that perfect Friday morning to walk his fat ass up to the house and knock. Martin felt strongly that Bob Rankel was less the loyal servant these days than the short-timer coasting to his pension. Martin was planning a change at the wheel after the election. See how the big phony liked working for a living again.

Honk-honk-honk.

"Honey?" Martin called in to his wife. "Would you please wave a stiff third finger out the window, let Kojak know what we truly think of him."

Kymberly Scallia-Daly was flat on their king-sized canopy bed, still in last night's dress, her face behind a frilly sleep mask, her body stone-still. Martin and Bob Rankel had been forced to help her into the house last night, for the third time this election cycle.

Martin leaned into the bedroom. "Honey?"

Only her lips moved. "What?"

"Forget it, Kym. Don't fucking move."

"I won't . . . I can't."

Campaigns made Martin feel as if his life were on trial, and hangovers made him mean. He stormed through the house and out the double front doors empty-handed, growled as he crawled into the backseat of the limo and eyed Rankel in the mirror.

Rankel apologized for honking, then told him that it was an emergency, that Elizabeth Lucido was missing.

"Missing?"

"From her house, they're saying. A neighbor saw the front door open this morning and called 911. The post cop found her car in the driveway, but Elizabeth was gone."

Martin Daly sat back and absorbed this information.

Rankel said, "You want to go to her house?"

"I thought I was supposed to give some kids a fucking plaque."

"That was Mothers Against Drunk Driving. You canceled, of course. Due to the disappearance of a beloved staff member."

"Damn right, I did."

"Elizabeth's house, then?"

"Right. Sure. Drive . . . Jesus."

As they rode down the long driveway from his waterfront estate, Martin Daly pondered how to play his appearance at the crime scene. What would the press be looking for from him? What would Murphy's cops be thinking? Was he in charge, strong, like nothing bothered him? Or touchingly human—a leader for the sensitive nineties and beyond.

Martin Daly thought next about Elizabeth Lucido; and of the masturbatory fantasies of her he would no longer employ. Replacing her at work, however, was another matter. Elizabeth had been a whirlwind, smarter and more experienced in government than anyone in the office, including himself. And he needed to campaign these days, full-time, more than he ever had before, just when he was growing sick of it, because that fucking preppie Hind was so far up his ass it hurt. Even the Democratic chairman, that douche-bag Donald Neville, had been unable to undercut Hind's growing support.

People didn't know. They thought it was all cocktails and blow jobs. Where were they when he was listening to lunatics rave about taxes? Or stuffing one more rubber chicken down his gullet? People had no idea how tough political life could be.

They passed a huge red-white-and-blue JACKSON HIND FOR COUNTY EXECUTIVE billboard, and Daly thought it would serve that spoiled brat right if he did win: Let him suffer the indignities. Then Daly wondered where Seymour's goon squad had been last night, that they had not trampled this new obscenity.

At his fund-raiser, he remembered. Protecting their piddling jobs, their tits at OTB. Kissing his hairy ass, was where they had been. People didn't know. And Martin Daly sure wasn't gonna tell them.

Fifteen minutes later they parked at the end of Elizabeth Lucido's officially crowded block.

"You okay?" Rankel asked in the mirror.

Martin opened his eyes. "Processing her disappearance, Bob. Nothing more."

Martin waited for Rankel to open the back door for him, then stepped out into the bright autumn sunshine. He noted that Rankel had hung his gold lieutenant's shield on his breast pocket, as if the big putz were actually investigating the case.

Martin put on sunglasses, thinking that he was starting to hate cops, even though they fed his coffers and gave him their endorsements. If he won this time, they weren't getting jack-shit for raises, let 'em whine all they wanted.

FRANK MURPHY WALKED OUTSIDE TO HEAD OFF MARTIN DALY from the cops inside who still had work to do. Murphy thought Daly looked hungover behind his sunglasses, as he had every right to be after a big night out; and Bob Rankel didn't look that sharp himself. " 'Morning, Martin," said Murphy. "Bob."

Bob Rankel saluted smartly, for show; Murphy returned it.

Murphy took a deep breath and began to explain the situation, until he noticed Charlie Hotchkiss, *Newsday*'s longtime political correspondent, pressing up against the barrier, watching them through binoculars. "Hang on," said Murphy. "Charlie Asskiss is lip-reading. Right, Charlie?"

Charlie put down his binoculars and wagged his finger. "No name-calling, now, Frank," he yelled.

Murphy turned his back to the sidewalk.

Daly said, "Maybe I should go say hi to Charlie a second."

"Before we know what's going on?"

Daly frowned but stayed where he was, then nodded, meaning back to the update. Murphy told him what little they knew.

"Okay. How long till closure?"

"I don't know."

"Any ransom requests?"

"We're still hoping."

"Jesus. Any connection to Babs Whitcomb?"

"None that I can see," Arthur Prefect offered as he squeezed into the conversation, "other than all the obvious parallels."

Daly said, "Oh, hi, Art," then turned to Murphy. "Too bad you couldn't stick around last night. I might have needed you. Elizabeth left early, too, though not as early as you."

"You want to dock our paychecks?"

"Don't get smart, Frank. Bad morning for it."

Martin Daly pushed past Murphy and up the slate walk to the front door. Murphy followed, Bob Rankel brought up the rear, and they crowded into the house along a slender corridor roped off by crime scene technicians.

Lieutenant Rankel tapped Murphy on the shoulder, pulled him back to the stoop, confided that Martin was as phony as a three dollar bill, that he was really more upset for what this might mean to his campaign. "Elizabeth is the brains of the operation, make no mistake about it."

"No one ever does."

"On a personal level, Martin thinks she's a stuck-up bitch."

"Martin doesn't like anyone who sees through him."

"Any leads?"

"Maude and Rocky will find out what happened. Make book on that."

"Maude," said Rankel. "Rocky Blair ain't any great shakes."

Murphy thought Lieutenant Rankel had some nerve to crack wise on Detective Rocky Blair. What was he but a bootlicking cabby? Murphy was just about to remind Lieutenant Rankel of this when Martin Daly stepped out the front door and clutched at Murphy's arm. "All we've got, Frank. And then some."

"Of course."

Charlie Hotchkiss yelled out, "Martin! A minute of your time, if you please."

"A wonderful, brilliant woman," Martin Daly yelled back from the stoop. "A valued compatriot."

Murphy said, "You want to try to act like she might be alive? Because you don't know and I don't know."

"Fine, Commissioner. I'll do that. And you solve this . . . this obscenity, and advise me, forthwith."

"We'll do our best."

Martin Daly turned haughtily from Murphy and gave Charlie Hotchkiss the Ron Reagan brush-off, pretending not to hear the next question, happily waving good-bye as he climbed into the back of the car.

Frank Murphy kept his feelings from showing on his face and walked back into Elizabeth's house.

chapter 4

Murphy said, "So, you still think there's a sexual angle here?"

It was already nine-thirty, and they were drinking bad coffee in Elizabeth Lucido's backyard, catching their breath, trying to see if the case was taking shape. Maude had filled the men in on her chat with Mrs. Wentzel, that a black sports car had parked across the end of Elizabeth's driveway at about eleven o'clock last night. It left before one-thirty. Miss Wentzel had not seen the license plate. The car, she said, had been there before . . . often, but that could be due to Elizabeth's schedule. "I mean, the lady worked nights. That's when my friends stop over."

"Good point," said Murphy.

"Or a political angle?" asked Rocky.

Murphy said, "You mean the reason we got all those wolves out front."

"Maybe," said Maude. "Who knows? We need to go through those papers we found on the table, see what she was working on, maybe something's missing. We need her phone records, here and at the office. We'll need a canvass here tonight. And on. And on. We're looking at a very large job, boss, given the fact that there is so little evidence . . . as in none."

"Just like with Babs Whitcomb?"

"You got it."

Murphy said, "I've got troops on the way."

Maude said, "Thank you."

"Mrs. Wentzel can't narrow that time frame for us?" asked Murphy.

"She says the same stupid movie was on her television when she heard the car start up again, but she didn't bother getting up."

"We talk to Elizabeth's parents yet?"

"Next on my agenda," said Maude. "We need to set up tape, if it's not already too late."

Murphy nodded and looked around. The backyard grass was neatly trimmed, the leaves raked, as empty as a prairie. No picnic table. No chairs. No barbecue. Meaning, thought Murphy, no entertaining. Neighbors on both sides had erected small wooden villages for their offspring to infest when they weren't splashing about in above-the-ground pools. Elizabeth didn't do much sunbathing back here.

Maude said, "This will remind me of Babs a whole lot more if we don't get a ransom demand soon."

Rocky held up his hand and said, "And I still say Babs took a slow boat to China to get away from her dorky husband. Which means, I think our record's still perfect."

Maude Fleming dug in her pocket and showed them the business card she had found in Elizabeth Lucido's suit jacket pocket, which had been flung over a kitchen chair. "Anyone know this guy Norman Keller? From the party."

Murphy said no, not offhand. "Ask Junior Daly. He knows these wing nuts. They hang on his every word."

"Scary thought," Maude said.

"Anything else you need?" Murphy asked.

"Nope. We're on it, and we'll stay on it."

Murphy said, "Good. 'Cause this one's got ramifications."

"Frank is right," Maude said, turning to Rocky. "Have someone go seal up her office."

"Roger that. Good idea."

Out front dogs were barking. Murphy and Maude walked around the house and greeted the K-9 officers, then watched as each of three highly trained German shepherds was given a sample of Elizabeth's clothing from her laundry hamper. Each dog, in turn, tracked the scent from the front door, around the side of her house and through her backyard, then the neighbor's yard on the next block north. The trail ended at the curb, where each dog whimpered and moaned.

"Okay, let's tape this area off, too, and get down on our hands and knees," Maude said. "We got a bigger scene than we thought."

Yes, thought Murphy. That is probably true.

"CAN WE TALK TO YOU?" FRANK MURPHY SAID TO THE WOMAN in the house directly behind Elizabeth Lucido's. "I'm Police Commissioner Murphy, and this is Detective Maude Fleming. We'd like to ask you a couple of questions."

"If you'll tell me what happened. I'm dying to know."

"We're not sure yet. Which is why we need your help."

Maude and Murphy were invited inside by Mrs. Eve Margolis, an overweight suburban mother of three. Eve Margolis told them she had been sleeping in her bedroom with her husband last night, the windows open, the television off, from eleven o'clock on. Odds were, Murphy thought, Elizabeth had walked or been carried or wrestled within feet of their home and yet they had heard nothing. Their children heard nothing. They woke up and were shocked to see police on the block behind them.

"You know if she used a landscaping service?" asked Maude. "We didn't find a lawn mower."

"My son Jeremy cuts it, does her other yard work. She's a very busy woman."

"Tell us about Elizabeth's social life," said Maude.

The men, Eve Margolis said, waving her hand, they came and went. Fancy cars. Plenty of late nights.

"Do tell," said Maude. "Were they loud or—"

"Oh, no, Detective. Not at all. The men who came by were not Puerto Ricans." Eve Margolis laughed. "When

I said fancy cars, I didn't mean souped-up Chebbies. Elizabeth was always hobnobbing with the high and mighty. We could never figure out why somebody so important was living in our neighborhood."

"Really."

"I'm not saying this about the men to put her down. Is that what you people think? We were all trying to find her a nice husband and—"

"You have any idea who might have wanted to hurt her?"

"None. Like, not a clue. Tell her parents we're all praying for her."

Murphy smiled and looked at his watch. Maude caught his gesture and nodded. It was already ten-fifteen on a Friday morning, and there were millions of things yet to do, including that talk with the parents. They had wasted time enough on this bigot.

chapter 5

ELIZABETH LUCIDO'S PARENTS LIVED ON A STEEP HILL in Port Washington, in a new brick colonial on a wooded road that dead-ended at a private beach. The lawn was manicured, the three-car driveway empty when the unmarked car pulled into it. Nobody answered Maude Fleming's knock.

There was a polished brass mail slot in the front door, and Maude bent low enough to look through and see envelopes and circulars sprawled on the rich brown carpet.

"Leave a note?" Rocky said when she got back into the car.

Maude pulled the mike off the dashboard. "Leave a patrolman, is more like it, and have him talk to the neighbors, find out the story here. If they don't get home soon, we'll set the tape up from the pole, answer the damn phone ourselves."

"Check."

Maude stared through the windshield, wondering if she was forgetting something. Slipping, things were slipping. The bad guy could already be in touch with the parents. They could be panicking, recklessly deciding to end unbearable suspense.

"Nice house," said Rocky. "Probably too new for Elizabeth to have ever lived here."

"Twenty-one to headquarters," Maude said into the mike. "Have the post car meet us at . . ."

CHARLIE HOTCHKISS WAS AT *NEWSDAY*'S MASSIVE HEADQUARTERS in Melville, staring over his never-pleased editor's shoulder out the window, admiring the dead-straight lines of headstones in nearby Pinelawn National Cemetery. He wore a tired blue blazer and engineer denims. Top-Siders without socks, his thinning blond hair a tad long in the back. He was hoping his editor could not sense his excitement.

Barbara Lasch set aside the pitch and cocked her head at Charlie. "You're a fucking pisser," she said. "A commie-pinko-anarchist pisser."

Charlie remembered when those were considered compliments in the newsroom, before Reagan/Bush and the Creed of Greed. "It's got all the elements, doesn't it?" Charlie said.

"The ones you like, anyway."

"Like a good guy and a bad guy, an arresting beginning—"

"No ending," said Barbara. "Not yet."

"I'm telling you, the good old boys are already ner-

vous. Nobody's answering their phone, everybody waiting to see who done it. Like they expect it to have something to do with them, and they expect it to show up
soon."

"Really? More of that, say, than the desire to suppress
a growing fear that a serial killer is targeting powerful
Republican women?"

"Now who's thinking tabloid?"

"Touché."

"I think the general feeling is: There wasn't much in
Elizabeth's life but politics . . . ergo . . ."

Lasch made a tent of her slender fingers, thinking. She
was young and smart, fresh from salvaging a Providence
daily. Charlie wanted to add his own conjectures to the
weight of the case, but he knew not to bullshit her, to risk
his credibility. Tenure meant nothing these bottom-line
days. Guys who had crossed Barbara Lasch were now
working at weeklies, covering Boy Scout jamborees and
selling ad space from the trunks of their cars.

"This isn't just an excuse to beat Martin Daly's balls
in?" she said. "I mean, is the timing not perfect for you
and your buddy Jackson, or what?"

"I'd be lying if said I wasn't pumped."

She hummed. "The cops saying anything useful yet?"

"They looked like scared little kids."

"Great. What's the D.A. have to say?"

"He's going on vacation."

"So then the news wasn't all bad."

Charlie smiled, waited, and hoped.

"Okay," said Lasch. "It's yours, Charlie. Draw two
reporters and three interns, and give it a couple of days.
Keep me posted, and play it straight."

"You're gonna hear from Martin Daly, if not Seymour
himself, once I get poking around."

"I hear from them every day, Charlie. Now we'll have
something to talk about."

• • •

COUNTY EXECUTIVE MARTIN DALY'S OFFICE LOOKED OUT OVER the vast complex of tan brick government buildings on the Garden City–Mineola border. From his oversized leather swivel chair he could watch the comings and goings at the courthouses, the legislature—places where most of the workers had been appointed by him or Chairman Cammeroli.

This was important because Martin knew almost nothing about the day-to-day operation of the county, nor did he want to know. He learned what to think about issues from party officials. If knowledge was strength, Martin had little.

Still, here, protected by aides and assistants, concentric fence-lines of secretaries, even his dopey son when he bothered to show up, Martin could kid himself that his ignorance was hidden.

But now Commissioner Murphy and those two obnoxious homicide detectives had shown up and just melted his defenses. They were already outside his double doors; and he could hear Frank Murphy saying they wanted to interview him because he was Elizabeth Lucido's boss.

"Send them in," Martin said as he threw the doors open and smiled out at the world. "Anything that I can do to help."

The detectives gave Martin's office the once-over quickly, eyeing up the wall of fame, the plaques and trophies, the casting couch. Rocky Blair smiled, obviously impressed. The tough little lesbian with the mouse-gray crew cut met Martin Daly's inscrutable gaze with her own. Where do they find these fucking babes? he wondered. And how is she not a freak?

"This won't take long," Frank Murphy said.

"In fact, let's go right to it," said Rocky. "You know her best. Who do you think snatched her?"

Martin Daly shook his head slowly as he sat down

behind his desk. "I don't have the faintest idea, Detective Blair. I thought that was your job, to find out."

"It is," said Maude, "and we will."

"Wonderful," said Daly.

"She have many boyfriends?" asked Maude.

"A few over the years she's been here with me. Not many."

"Like how many?" said Maude Fleming. "She's very beautiful, if you hadn't noticed."

Just like you noticed, he thought. Just like you. "Three fellows, that I knew about. Of course I'm pretty certain she didn't tell me everything. Our relationship was professional. She never dated anybody from this office."

"Really?"

"Yes. Really." Martin began to resent the whipsaw questioning, that Maude felt she could pepper him without paying a price. He wondered if she was goading him, if maybe they were recording him. He wondered if he should call for Lieutenant Rankel to sit in. And now this Rocky character was staring at the wall of photographs again, rudely showing Daly his massive back, seeming to concentrate on his son.

"Was she seeing anyone recently?" asked Maude.

"Not lately. No time for that during a campaign. Of course, you always hear snide remarks, but I never paid them any mind." He smiled at Frank Murphy, letting him know.

"Good," said Maude, "then we won't either. You know a guy named Norman Keller?"

"He's a committeeman, from Roosevelt."

"Black guy?" asked Maude.

"White."

Maude said, "Wow."

Martin Daly decided he didn't like this dick one bit, not her hard-ass attitude, not her crew-cut business-chick look. A man-hater. "Is that supposed to be an insult?" asked Martin.

"Not at all," said Maude. "Innocent shock."

"You people don't get paid to be innocent," said Martin. "You get paid to solve crimes. Now do it and do it fast. Murphy, I'm holding you personally and professionally responsible for this mess." He stood up abruptly. "Now I'll walk you folks out . . . unless you've got anything else significant."

"Well," said Rocky. "Actually—"

Maude said, "Seen Junior yet today?"

"You mean Deputy County Executive Daly? . . . No."

Rocky said, "Was Miss Lucido working on anything particularly sensitive for you? A personnel matter. I don't know. Some source of violent conflict."

Martin Daly shook his head: Nothing out of the ordinary, he told them, nothing they didn't see in these august offices a hundred times a week. Certainly nothing someone would hurt someone over. "Of course, I don't know everything that goes on around here. No one possibly could. Right, Murphy?"

"Right, Martin."

Martin walked to his double doors, opened them onto the technobabble of his staff.

"Hang on a second, sir," said Maude. "It just occurred to me . . . to set up a trace on your office phone."

Martin Daly closed the doors. "And why is that?"

Murphy said, "You might get the ransom demand. I mean, who was closer to her? Who can scare up big money faster than you?"

Daly tugged his door open one more time. "Sorry, people. No one taps my phones. But do call me if you need something else. Even money."

chapter 6

HILE ROCKY DUCKED OUT TO PICK UP SCRAMBLED-egg sandwiches and hot black coffee, Frank Murphy and Maude Fleming found a maintenance worker to unlock Elizabeth Lucido's office door.

The office was two doors down the hall from Martin Daly's suite, half the size but still large enough to hold a desk, an eight-chair conference table, and a black leather couch. It looked out on the treetops of Old Country Road, the redbrick upper floors of Winthrop Hospital. Elizabeth's wall photographs were neither as dense nor as pompous as Martin Daly's, though it was clear she knew who was who in Nassau County, New York.

The wide mahogany desk was cluttered with memos and manuals, spreadsheets and faxes, a stove with many pots. Maude sat down and poked through the documents as Murphy watched over her shoulder. Elizabeth's daily planner was in the top drawer, each day's box chock-full of appointments and tasks, with the initials of those she was seeing for each project.

"You'll probably need Elizabeth's assistant to decipher the code," said Murphy. "Lisa Tibaldi. Nice girl."

Maude said, "After we clear her. I like to try these myself anyway, kinda like a crossword puzzle."

The box for today was filled with a breakfast meeting at a bank, lunch with Martin, the afternoon a blank.

Rocky returned with a sack of chow, and the three of them ate late breakfasts at Elizabeth Lucido's conference table. Maude caught Rocky up and then said she was concerned that the victim's parents were still not home. She didn't want them learning of their daughter's disappearance from radio or television, but didn't see how it could be helped. Between bites Maude confessed that she remained baffled, stumped, and frustrated. "I don't even know yet if it's personal or professional or random."

Rocky said he knew what she meant, that this day already felt like a sleep-deprivation experiment, and they had miles to go, that when he was this beat-tired he was even more stupid than usual.

"You're not stupid," Murphy said. "You're thorough."

"Thanks, boss. Not everyone sees it that way."

"Elizabeth Lucido wasn't stupid, either," said Maude, nodding at the cluttered desk. "She had her hands in every facet of this government, from personnel matters to procurement. Who could tell what might be volatile, though, without knowing the players, the history of the transactions?"

"Martin Daly?" said Rocky.

Murphy shook his head. "He really is the hands-off type."

"Just like his dopey fucking kid," Rocky said, laughing, "who still hasn't shown up for work yet."

"Who, then?" asked Maude.

Murphy said, "What was in those papers we found on the kitchen table?"

"I didn't get to them yet."

Rocky asked, "Want me to look at them?"

"I want you back at her house. Gather up all the witness statements from the canvass teams. Interview them, too, see if any of them picked up any vibes. Something that didn't make it to the page. And see how they did with that footprint. Come on, I'll walk you out. I could use the fresh air."

"I'll be along in a minute," said Murphy. "But first get me the Whitcomb file."

● ● ●

THANK GOD, THOUGHT MARTIN DALY: THE DETECTIVES ON the Lucido case were finally leaving Elizabeth's office, hopefully heading back across the street where they belonged. Maude Fleming had Elizabeth's daily planner under her arm, a plastic bag filled with other items. Rocky Blair carried a greasy brown bag. Not a good sign for him, Daily thought, that they were removing items from her office, evidence that what happened might be work related.

Not a good sign at all.

Martin watched them until they rounded the corner, then he trailed behind them down the stairs. At the front door he saw them jumped by a swarm of local reporters.

"Maude! Rocky! What can you tell us about—"

Daly hung back on the stairs as they ducked tough questions politely, as they had been trained to do. Then, in response to a question Daly could not hear, that fucking Blair mumbled something about someone being an oxygen thief.

"Who?" cried out that bastard Charlie Hotchkiss. "Who in there is an oxygen thief? What do you mean?"

Rocky said, "No comment."

"Come on, Rock," yelled a second reporter. "We talking Junior Daly? The old man? Or both?"

Rocky Blair refused to say who he meant, what he meant. But the implication was clear: The Daly Team had been less than forthcoming. Blair was signaling the goddamn horde, Daly thought, telling them he smelled blood in the water, which was all fucking Charlie Hotchkiss would need to hear. Civil service or not, Rocky Blair was looking for trouble. He could be the detective in charge of the shithouse if he didn't watch his mouth. And that dyke, who should know better, was enjoying it. Where was that oily son-of-a-bitch Murphy? Nowhere around when bombs were flying.

And where the hell was Junior? It was almost lunch-time on a payday, and still that hump of a son had not yet troubled himself to park his company car in his designated slot outside. Just for appearances, thought Martin, he ought to be here.

Martin marched back upstairs, past his staff, and into his office. He picked up his phone and called Junior's apartment, got a busy signal. "Shit!"

He speed-dialed District Attorney Prefect's office. Prefect's secretary, Seymour Cammeroli's mother, put him through.

"What do you hear?" asked Daly.

Artie Prefect said, "Nothing yet."

"Which means?"

"They haven't got a clue."

"Put Mama back on."

Click.

"What's up, Mama? Anything?"

Mama grunted and hung up.

Martin was about to hang his head in despair when the phone rang again, this time a loyalist from the bowels of administration, with the best news Martin Daly had heard in months: Jackson Hind and Elizabeth Lucido had been lovers since the spring, when his mysterious slide in the polls had begun.

"You're sure?"

"I didn't see 'em doing it, but pretty sure, yeah."

"Thank God. And thank you."

Hate burned in Martin's chest as he paced the big office, bitterly remembering her look, her walk, the way she smelled, the scent of betrayal. What an incredible bitch! And after all he had done for her, to consort with that WASP motherfucker Jackson Hind.

He wondered what secrets she'd leaked. Jesus. She knew everything, well, almost everything. This was awful. Or maybe it was good. Maybe nothing she had leaked mattered as much as the fact that Jackson Hind was about to go from candidate to suspect.

Martin sat back down and reached for his phone, thinking the race was all but over.

chapter 7

BACK IN EARLY SEPTEMBER, WHEN BARBARA "BABS" Whitcomb III had disappeared from her husband's family estate in Old Westbury, Frank Murphy had been far too busy managing prior emergencies to give the case more than cursory attention. Now, on the heels of a second possible abduction, he sat down at his desk with the file.

Barbara Whitcomb was thirty-seven years old, an acknowledged beauty among the monied set in Nassau, and one of the Republican Party's most graceful—and persuasive—fund-raisers. She had apparently been home alone on the night she vanished. Her husband, Todd—onetime owner of the defunct semipro baseball team, the Long Island Clams—had been in Los Angeles, prospecting a deal to finance a shoot-'em-up cop movie. The maid and chauffeur were getting laid in a Jericho Turnpike motel. Babs Whitcomb had made phone calls to friends and political associates up until nine that evening.

She had plans to ride early the following morning with her sister-in-law, Margie Richmond, of Lattingtown and Palm Beach. Mrs. Richmond found the main house open and empty when she arrived the next morning. All the cars were in their garages. She checked the stables for the woman no one could bring themselves to say a bad word about. The horses were all where they belonged. The woman who loved them was not.

Her clothes and jewelry were undisturbed. A quart of skim milk was souring on the counter.

No ransom demands were ever sent.

No terrorist cells took credit for striking a blow against the Whitcomb financial empire.

The previous six months' phone records and checkbooks showed nothing abnormal or unexplainable, no hint of scandal. Nobody had a motive worth its salt.

Her husband was suitably grieved. The party was suitably grieved. Both embraced the position that Babs Whitcomb was a victim of the random violence that permeates our lawless, liberal society. They held a prayer service and vowed to carry on her good works. Todd Whitcomb filed a claim with his insurance company.

Frank Murphy noted with awe the hours Maude and Rocky had devoted to the case, the huge pile of paper they'd accumulated that said exactly nothing. The only possible reported sighting of the victim had been checked out by the FBI and deemed unfounded, which didn't mean it wasn't accurate.

Maude had worked the money angle hard, even though the husband insisted not a dime was missing. Maude never found anything to show Babs Whitcomb had a stash of her own.

Murphy found that hard to believe. Fifty-fifty, Murphy thought, Babs was alive.

The red phone at his elbow rang, the hot line.

He picked it up and heard out Martin Daly's latest rant.

"I'm sure Detective Blair wasn't talking about you, sir," Murphy said at the first opportunity. "Yes, I know the voters don't know that. All they remember is that you looked ridiculous. Yes, of course, I'll speak to him. . . . No, we don't have anything more yet. . . . Yes, I know it's my ass."

Murphy hung up and rocked back in his big leather chair, thinking Martin was sure getting sensitive. Jackson Hind must be closer than anyone was letting on. Maybe the money was drying up, or flowing in the other direction. Of course, Murphy punishing Rocky and Maude just wasn't gonna happen.

Frank Murphy loved his new job, this dark office, the sense of tradition, of good people doing fine and necessary work over the years, for the most part remarkably removed from political interference, largely on the personal integrity of former police commissioners and their ability to say, "Fuck off, Seymour."

There were portraits on the walls of the previous inhabitants, from Kilbride, to Moses, to Guido, to Magliulo. Frank's immediate predecessor, Calvin Nash, dominated the long wall, a portrait of a face ravaged by choices made in self-interest. Murphy remembered the note he had found in the top drawer of his desk from ex-Commissioner Nash: "Three rules, Murphy, in addition to never ever saying my name to anyone connected to law enforcement. They are: (1) Get yours while you can. (2) Do everything important yourself. (3) Bonifacio from the assessor's office has herpes simplex II. Say no and tell her why." Murphy remembered Miss Bonifacio's inaugural approaches, thinking a man with less information might have fallen. He was sorry Cal Nash had learned the hard way.

Eleven-twenty, his swimmer's watch said. Too soon to bug Maude and Rocky again, and too soon to call his fiancée, Alice, at the bank branch she managed. She would still be digging out from the Friday morning rush, completely uninterested in police department matters.

Tonight, she would say. Tell me everything tonight when you get home. Frank wanted to explain about Elizabeth Lucido before anyone else did. He wanted her to know they were friends who shared information, maybe have Jake tell her the story as only he could, explaining the political necessity of his seeing a beautiful former lover for lunches, drinks, an occasional dinner. Let Jake explain that this was merely intelligence gathering, a chance to predict trends, influence policy, name names. Alice would understand all this, as any girlfriend would.

The door swung open, and Jake marched in with bagels. "I hope Elizabeth's address book's got some names in it besides yours."

"Will you knock it off."

"Seen the *Grunt?*"

"Nope."

Frank Murphy accepted the latest edition of the outlawed employee newsletter and read from the top: "The *Nassau County Grunt* salutes Police Commissioner Murphy for progressive measures long overdue, and believes that our formerly moribund job is finally headed in the right direction. Stay tuned as our ill-equipped and under-manned police department wages an intermittent battle for truth, justice, and the status quo."

Other *Grunt* articles included a medical center spoof called DEATH ON THE CHEAP and a nasty installment of the ongoing cartoon entitled WE'RE RELATED, showing an unshaven Junior Daly with a big-breasted starlet under his arm and a bottle of booze in his hand, driving his county car onto the Shelter Island Ferry. (That summer Junior had been arrested in that tony village for DWI, sentenced to the three-hour class, and threatened with reassignment to Deputy Director of Buildings and Grounds.) This edition's SEPARATED AT BIRTH showed side-by-side pictures of Mama Cammeroli and Vince Lombardi. The *Grunt* arrived maybe once a month, rolling out of county fax machines everywhere, never on any exact schedule. Murphy had been told more than once, "You find out who publishes the *Grunt*, and Seymour will make you a judge."

Murphy's intercom beeped. Murphy's secretary, Mrs. Annie Anderson, a pretty blonde of fifty-something, who was good at covering his back and getting the work done right, said, "Frank? Martin just called back. He said to tell you lunch at the Belle Café. Twelve-thirty sharp, downstairs in the garage."

"Shit."

"Now, now," said Annie. "Me and the vice girls are walking over to the hot-dog truck. Wanna switch?"

"No."

"Wanna talk to any of these reporters yet? Greg Cergol's here. That nice Brendan Higgins."

"Tell them we're proceeding at a vigorous pace."

chapter 8

D ETECTIVES BLAIR AND FLEMING PARKED AT THE CURB in front of the dilapidated gray cottage where Mr. Norman Keller lived. They were down to legwork now, always a bad sign. The day was flying by and they were nowhere. Rocky's report on the results of the canvass had been singularly unenlightening, and Maude's first reading of the papers found in Elizabeth's kitchen had only added to the confusion.

They eyed the dreary premises, the overgrown lawn spotted with wads of fossilized dogshit. The front door was open and loud voices came from inside as they walked up the concrete driveway.

Maude knocked hard on the rusty screen door and peered inside. A wrinkled old woman in a long red dress stood up from her chair in front of a soap opera, and made her way slowly to answer.

"Yes? Who is it?"

"Does Norman Keller live here, ma'am? We're Nassau County detectives, and we'd like to talk to him."

"Norman my grandson?"

Maude showed the woman Norman's flag-embossed business card.

"That's my grandson," she said. "He's not home now. And my husband Norman is dead fifteen years now. What's this about?"

"He working?" asked Rocky. "Your grandson?"

"Why, yes. On your boss's campaign."

"Martin Daly, you mean?"

"Yes, of course. Come in, come in."

"My boss is a guy named Murphy," said Rocky, bristling. "Not that it matters."

Maude pulled the screen door open, and they stepped into a tiny living room decorated with harvest-gold wallpaper and brown shag carpet from the Ford administration. The air was doggy.

"Norman got himself a paying job, too?" asked Maude.

"Not yet. He just got out of college. Here . . . wait."

Norman's nana disappeared down a narrow hallway for a moment, and Maude had time to notice the bungalow was in sorry shape, dust everywhere, that smell. And yet there was time for young Norman to volunteer for a gasbag like Martin Daly. Nana returned with a Hofstra diploma and picture of a plump if not unpleasant boy with brown hair and brown eyes. A softie, thought Maude. A doughboy.

"That's my Normy. And here's his degree."

"I see that," said Maude. "He works lots of hours for Mr. Daly, doesn't he?"

Grandma sighed. "Day and night."

"Late night last night?" asked Maude. "If you know."

"Very late night. They had this big fund-raiser. Norman had to blow up the balloons, then clean up afterwards."

"He sounds like quite a guy, ma'am."

"Single, too," said Nana.

"Interesting. Can we see his room?"

"He keeps it locked. Look." Nana led them to a pad-locked door and shrugged. "He doesn't want me to see his girlie books. Thinks I don't know he has a post office box when we have a perfectly good mailman comes every day."

Maude nodded and handed Nana Keller her business card. "Please have Norman call me when he gets home."

Nana touched Maude's forearm and asked, "Is Norman in some kind of trouble?" in a way that suggested she'd asked this question of detectives before.

"I seriously doubt it," said Maude. "We just need him to clear a couple things up."

"Where's the dog?" asked Rocky. "Out back?"

"We don't have a dog," said Nana. "Not for years."

"WHERE'S KOJAK?" ASKED MURPHY.

Martin Daly explained that Lieutenant Rankel had gone home sick with a flu that morning. "Lazy son of a bitch has a better job than me."

"Better benefits, anyway."

Martin said they would ride to lunch in his personal car, a silver Porsche Boxster he kept parked in the police garage for those occasions when not even Rankel was to know where he was going. Martin, of course, drove this little rocket like he owned the road, which in a way he did. Frank Murphy sat in the passenger seat, his face tugged by G-force starts and turns.

"I love this fucking car," Daly said when they were idling at a traffic light, top down. "All balls, and then some. I wouldn't drive a county piece of shit unless I was, say, you."

Murphy smiled bravely and held on for dear life as they tracked around a forty-degree turn at thirty-five miles an hour, Murphy hoping his revolver, which was wedged between the bucket seat and his right love handle, did not accidentally blast off a chunk of his ass. In front of the restaurant Daly cut the steering wheel, and they flew into the parking lot; Daly stomped the brakes, splattering gravel. "I'm feeling better now," Daly said as he yanked the keys from the ignition. "Blowing out the cobwebs always helps."

"Late night?" asked Murphy.

"Home by midnight. It's just I drank all that sweet shit after dinner."

They took a table near the window and ordered linguine and scallops fra diavalo and diet Cokes, watching with amusement as seven county employees suddenly lined up at the cash register, checking their watches, shocked at how time flies.

Martin Daly said, "Look at those assholes, without the brains to goof off in Suffolk."

This, thought Murphy, from the biggest goof-off in town, except maybe for his son.

Daly said, "So who did this horrible thing to our girl, eh? Who walks into someone's house and just grabs them away? I keep waiting for you guys to tell me she's been found, that she was out jogging and got lost, or slept at some boyfriend's apartment."

Murphy said, "I know what you mean."

"So what's happening?"

"Hard work and waiting."

"For what?"

"Lab tests. Witnesses. A ransom note would be nice. A chance to speak to her parents. Maybe a body."

"Jesus."

"I'm as sorry as you are, Martin, maybe more."

"Any signs this case is related to the Whitcomb woman?"

"We're searching for links."

Daly nodded grimly; and Murphy wondered if this

lunch was merely a photo-op, designed to show those fleeing diners that Martin Daly was in contact with law enforcement, that he was angry and fighting back. Daly usually dodged the spotlight, haunting country clubs, taking his meals in grill rooms.

"I heard some interesting scuttlebutt this morning," said Daly. "From a campaign worker I happen to believe on this sort of thing, Rose Gallo on Task Force 2001."

"Don't know her."

"Really? Big tits? Fat ankles? Used to be in Pre-Planning?"

It always amazed Murphy how many departments and divisions the county had, some he'd never heard of, each requiring a hierarchy and staff, all of them needing cars and cell phones, home computers and fax machines. "What'd she say?"

Daly looked both ways and bowed closer. "She linked that son-of-a-bitch Jackson Hind with Elizabeth . . . romantically, I mean. Said they were real chummy at meetings on some environmental project. Said that when she teased Elizabeth about it, she got flustered."

"Stop," said Murphy, holding up his hand. "The woman is not yet cold—"

"That's what I said at first. But then I'm thinking, he's handsome, smart, rich, downright friendly when he's not chewing my ass. Why wouldn't she date him? Carville and Matalin, only local."

"Loyalty to you is why she wouldn't date him."

"I'm not so sure," said Daly. "Things change. We weren't the same close-knit team we had always been. I even heard her résumé was on the street."

"Stop making things up, Martin. Elizabeth was tired of your act, but she wouldn't ever hurt you. We both know that."

Daly shook his thick head of curls. "I don't know anything anymore."

"Jackson Hind, suspect," mused Murphy. "Wouldn't the press just love that."

"I'm not saying this just because of the election, Frank. Honest. Check it out. What the hell."

"Sure, Martin, what the hell. In fact, I'll take care of it myself right after lunch. Call up young Jackson and ask him if he was schtupping your top aide."

"Don't mock me, Murphy. Not even in jest. There isn't anybody pure here, including Francis Murphy."

chapter 9

THE PARKING LOT NEXT TO THE STOREFRONT HEAD-quarters of the Jackson Hind Democrats was jammed, so Frank Murphy parked near the fire hydrant, in front of the Jamaican deli. A bewhiskered gadfly, Irwin Gold, had a bullhorn outside headquarters and was recruiting new blood from the busy Roosevelt sidewalk. "Lincoln freed the slaves," he cried at predominantly black passersby. "The all-white Republicans want to roll that back, too. Hello, Police Commissioner Murphy. Here to spy on us?"

Murphy winked at him. "Yup. What's shaking?"

"Hind's got you boys worried, doesn't he?"

"No comment."

"I knew it! I knew it!"

Murphy peered through the soapy glass between JACKSON HIND signs and saw the stooped backs of elderly whites in baggy jeans and walking shoes, black house-wives in Reeboks with strollers, graying hippies in Dockers and hiking boots. They were holding fliers, fac-ing a handsome blond man at the rear of the room who was wearing a light tan suit and giving them thumbs-up.

A literature drop ready to go out, thought Murphy. What you do when you can't raise money to buy stamps, which is what happens to all Democrats on Long Island, even those who look like Kennedy cousins. Hind was running on a platform of open government, efficiency, and public employment based upon merit, concepts that were anathema to Seymour Cammeroli and his legion of piglets.

Of course, if Jackson Hind won, Murphy would be fired and Hind would stick his own guy in the job. Still, Murphy had always admired the cut of the man's sail. He eased through the open door, sidled up to the rear of the gathering.

"Now remember, people," Hind was saying, "no mailboxes and no *Newsday* chutes. If nobody's home, tuck 'em in the screen door. I don't want the post office on our backs again—or anyone else Daly orders to harass us. Mark off the folks who want follow-up phone calls. And thank you, everybody. I'll see you all back here at five."

The volunteers briefly cheered their man, then began chatting with each other, choosing up election districts.

This was trouble for Martin, this much enthusiasm. The candidate was dashing, charismatic. Face-to-face with Martin Daly, say, during their televised debate next week, Martin would look like a tired old Russian. A Rhodes scholar who owned his own import-export firm, Hind knew what it meant to risk greatly. He knew what it meant to meet a payroll. He knew what everything meant, just look at him. This was rare, that the race for the top seat would be so close. The minority parties on Long Island tended to send their stars after smaller prizes, rolling over on the big ones. If Jackson Hind won this election, things would never be the same again.

Murphy already knew whom he was going to vote for, and it wasn't that tired old czar Martin Daly. Murphy was registered Republican but voted Democratic, because, like most people, he rooted for the underdog as long as the underdog was not in his way.

The faithful flowed into the streets. Jackson Hind followed them to the door, thanking them, endlessly thanking them, then he saw Murphy and smiled grimly. "Hello, Commissioner. Any word yet on our girl?"

"No."

"Damn."

"When did you last see her?" asked Murphy.

Hind held up his hand, then led Murphy to a tiny rear office with chart-covered walls, a coffeepot, a card table, a phone. "Last night," he said when the door was closed. "At her house."

Murphy's heart raced harder. "What time?"

"From maybe eleven-thirty to one."

"She okay when you left?"

"Of course."

"When did you hear she was missing?"

"An hour ago, when I got here. I have a call in to your office. Isn't that why you're here?"

"No. It isn't. You drive a black sports car?"

"An old black LeBaron convertible."

Murphy nodded, wondering if he ought to stop right there and call for an experienced assistant district attorney. He imagined Artie Prefect in front of a bank of microphones and quivered in horror.

Hind said, "I parked it across the end of her driveway. Did your witness tell you that?"

"You want to tell me what happened?"

Hind said, "Of course. That's why I called as soon as I heard." Hind said they made love, as was their custom, ate some ice cream at the kitchen table, and he left.

"That's all?"

"I certainly didn't harm her, if that's what you're asking."

"No arguments, raised voices?"

"I worship the ground she walks on."

On the wall near the door was a map of Nassau County election districts, some shaded blue, some red. Most blue. Murphy found Fairhaven Harbor, his district. Blue. "Martin Daly knows about you two. He tipped me off at lunch. Said he found out this morning."

"He didn't know yesterday?"

"He says no."

Hind curled his lip. "I'm not sure I believe him."

"Why? Any signs they were on to you?"

"Nothing concrete. A general feeling of paranoia. It was getting to Elizabeth, mostly, but then she had more to lose."

Murphy said, "Let me ask you: Was this relationship purely personal?"

Hind shook his head. "She was helping me with strategy, helping me whip Daly. You need to know the truth."

Murphy recalled Elizabeth's earnest face in café lighting, her eyes twinkling, telling him Daly needed a beating. "Was there anybody else involved?"

"No. Not to my knowledge. No one knew."

"Not Babs Whitcomb?"

"Jesus, no. Man, you guys really are in the dark."

"What was the strategy?"

"Twofold," said Hind. "The first, of course, was constant early intelligence for my spin-team, so I could beat their brains in with facts and figures on everything they proposed. The second was to ignore the crucial core, Martin's core. So Elizabeth began acting like Martin. Like she didn't have to return phone calls or bow to her constituency. Like the years of power had finally rotted her soul. It was working."

"Damn right it was working." Hind had so far done a marvelous job of appearing to know virtually everything about how to run a county better. And people despised

Martin more than ever, including plenty Martin needed. Outside Hind's private office the phones were ringing like cash registers at Christmas, and yet Hind's face said he'd already lost the race.

"What do you need from me?" Hind said.

Murphy told him: "A couple of hours at headquarters, samples."

Jackson Hind volunteered to give hair, urine, blood, shit, snot, whatever it took to prove he had not harmed or kidnapped Elizabeth. He said he would come to headquarters with a lawyer around six, to be searched for bumps, bruises, and hickeys.

"Thanks," said Murphy. "And I'll try to keep things quiet."

"Yeah, sure," said Hind. "Fat chance."

Before Murphy could assure Hind that his homicide squad was relatively tight-lipped, a young black guy wearing a Knicks cap pushed open the door, holding up a phone.

Jackson smiled. "Hey, Dante."

"*Newsday* wants another quote."

"About?"

"Quality of care at the Medical Center."

Hind winked at Murphy. "Tell 'em I wouldn't send my dog there. Tell 'em it's just one more bloated patronage mill—Nassau County's organized grime. Like OTB. Task Force 1999. Task Force 2000. Task Force 2001. The Highway Department. The Byway Department."

Dante nodded seriously and disappeared.

Murphy said, "Seymour won't dig that organized grime slur."

Hind shrugged and said, "We should investigate every one of their family members, too, because they all wind up on the payroll. And when you point it out, they puff out their chests and stick out their jaws and compare themselves to the Adamses, the Kennedys, dynasties carrying a public service gene. Even their dogs have jobs. She thinks highly of you, you know. She wanted to keep you on if I won. . . . Only you, though. The rest suck eggs."

"Each a giant in his field. Just ask them."

Hind said his own party was not much better. "We've got no will to win; that's our problem. Don Neville and friends are happy to live on Election Board jobs, our slots at OTB. You had to see the crap they put me through, just to get on the ballot, a man they can't own. And then they hang his daughter around my neck for good measure."

Murphy laughed. Andrea Neville was twenty-five, maybe. Her Touro Law School diploma was still damp. She was friendless, a family trait. Her race against Arthur Prefect for District Attorney was the quietest in history.

"Her father actually told *Newsday* he thought this was a good time to 'position his daughter for a run at higher office, once she had some experience.' "

"Why won't Neville help you?"

"Because he can't control me. All my relatives have good jobs, and I don't need anything rezoned. So nobody trusts me, or believes I love to fix things. I mean, even if I win, all I'll accomplish is gridlock."

"Somehow I suspect it would be more than that."

Hind smiled slightly. "Thank you."

"So how do you beat them?" asked Murphy.

"Outwork the bastards. Five o'clock in the morning, I'm at a train station, pumping hands. Then breakfast at the popular hangouts. The pro shop at Eisenhower. A craft fair in Glen Cove. Parades. Celebrations. You name it."

"Any money coming in?" asked Murphy.

"Besides my own? Some. Enough for a last-minute blitz. But Martin Daly's got a sign on every other corner in the county. He's busy right now spending two million bucks to keep his shitty job."

"Hell, his son will spend that much."

Hind chuckled. "Here's my beeper number. You find her, you call me first, okay?"

"Before her parents," said Murphy, "and her sister, even her beloved boss?"

"Nobody on earth loved her more. I guarantee it."

Murphy said good-bye and left Jackson Hind to his grief and worries. He raced back up Nassau Road to Mineola, parked behind police headquarters, and climbed the back stairs. "What do we got?" Murphy asked everyone who saluted him. "Any word?"

"We got bupkus," said Rocky Blair when they bumped into each other in the hallway outside Homicide. "No ransom demands, no claims from terrorist groups, no nothing."

"Come to my office, Rocky. Let's catch up."

Rocky nodded and followed Murphy, stopped short when Murphy braked to pick up his messages.

"How was lunch with El Jefe?" Annie Anderson asked as she handed up his stack. On the wall behind her was a picture of blond grandchildren splashing each other at Jones Beach. Each had her sunny grin, a dominant gene.

"Semi-informative," said Murphy. "What happened here? The basic fear and loathing?"

"That, plus a couple of women's groups called, wanting to know what you planned to do to protect them."

"Oh, boy."

"Alice called, too. You can call her back."

"Got it."

"Don Neville called."

"Screw him. Any coffee left?"

"I'll even get it for you."

Murphy and Rocky started into Murphy's office, then Frank stopped again. "Annie," he said, "when the pressure was building, and the press was hounding him, how did Cal Nash handle things?"

"Fire Island," she said, deadpan. "He'd hop a ferry to Kismet. Show everyone he wasn't concerned."

"You think that's what I ought to do?"

"Not really, Frank. Cal Nash got fired. You'll want Maude Fleming in there, too, I guess? Find out what's going on? I'll beep her."

chapter 10

ORMAN KELLER GOT WORD TO CALL HOME WHEN HE returned to Daly campaign headquarters after lunch with some of the staff, his only friends in the world. They had been talking up the kidnapping, guessing what had happened to Elizabeth Lucido, amazed at her betrayal of the party, wondering who would fill her multiple functions. Norman borrowed a superior's office, one of several along the long back wall. He sat behind an empty desk in a black leather chair, his pale hands sweating up the blotter.

"Hello?" said Nana.

"It's Norman, Nana. What's wrong?"

Nana told him about the visit from the cops.

"Did they say what they wanted?"

"Not exactly."

"Hold on." Norman got up and made sure the door was locked, then returned to the desk and picked up the phone. "Did they say where they were from?"

"Nassau County Homicide, the card says. Detective Maude Fleming."

"Jesus, Nana. That's the one they call Mother Murder." Norman's knees went weak, and his brow began to perspire. He stared at the portrait of Martin Daly on the far wall, a much younger looking Martin than the one to whom Norman would soon be groveling if this harassment continued. And as for any chance of advancement within the party ranks—he might as well drive one of the staked Daly lawn signs in the corner through his heart.

"You didn't let them in my room, did you?"

"How would I do that?"

"With a battering ram. The kind they usually carry in their trunks."

"They were really very nice, Norman. Detective Fleming is a pretty woman who wasn't wearing a wedding band. Her hair's too short, but—"

"Nana, please."

"Are any bigwigs there? You could ask them to nip this—"

"This isn't campaign crap, Nana. This is about that woman they said was kidnapped, the Deputy County Executive."

After a moment, Nana said, "The man cop looked mean, like a marine."

"Nana, you always told me the cops were my friends. Didn't you always tell me that?"

"You were young then," Nana said wistfully.

"ELIZABETH LUCIDO WAS A DOUBLE AGENT," FRANK MURPHY told his detectives that afternoon in his office. "She was sleeping with Jackson Hind . . . as recently as last night. And she was quote—helping Jackson with his strategy to unseat Martin—unquote."

"You don't say," said Maude. "Well, ain't love funny. How'd you find that out? He call when he heard she was missing?"

"Yes. But not before Martin Daly told me about them."

"Really."

"Call it a dead heat."

Rocky said, "That explains the soggy rubber."

"And perhaps a lot of other things," said Maude.

Murphy said, "Mr. Hind will be here with his lawyer at six, when almost everybody else has gone home. He says he'll give us everything we need."

"Good," Maude said. "Surprising, but good. He gonna lead us to a body?"

"I doubt it."

Rocky asked Murphy, "You think he did it?"

Murphy said, "Not really. Not at all, actually."

Rocky's shoulders slumped. "Oh."

"What else we got going?" asked Murphy.

Maude said, "We're checking her phone and bank records, mail, projects at work, talking to neighbors, friends, and enemies, yadda, yadda. Same dance we do for every case."

"You don't sound confident, Maude."

"I don't feel confident. Not yet."

"Anything we're not doing?"

Maude said they'd sent everything out that had to be sent out, all the notifications had been made, the all-points bulletins, a uniform cop stationed at her parents' house; they would await the lab reports and start ruling out available suspects, starting with Jackson Hind. They had enough people. "If her parents don't show by tonight, we should think about setting up a trace from the pole. When we talk to her folks, we'll see if they can offer a reward."

Murphy said, "Hit Daly up for a bundle."

"Be my pleasure," said Maude.

"God, I hate waiting," said Murphy.

"You and us both," said Rocky.

"She was always in such control of things," said Murphy. "Self-possessed. Have we gone through our occupied-dwelling-burglars-just-released-from-prison-list for alibis?"

"Being done by the day shift," said Maude.

"That's right," said Murphy, nodding. "You guys are left over from last night."

"No big deal," said Maude. "We're okay."

"No," said Murphy. "Fill in your reliefs and go home and get some sleep."

"First I'd like to—"

"It's not about the overtime cap, Maude. It's about having you sharp. Okay? If anything breaks we'll wake you up. And hand off your other files to the chief. You're working this and nothing else until we find her, just as soon as you get some sleep. And, oh yeah, Rocky, my man, Martin Daly is pretty pissed off at you."

"Yeah? Well, I'm pretty pissed off at him, too." Rocky said it so earnestly that Maude and Murphy laughed out loud. Rocky went on to angrily wonder why the nutless PBA always endorsed the fucking Republicans. Daly didn't deserve it. None of them did. "I felt like I was talking to a perp, not a witness."

Murphy's intercom buzzed. "Elizabeth Lucido's parents are here," said Annie. "They'd like to see you people."

ELIZABETH'S PARENTS WERE YOUNGER THAN MURPHY WOULD have expected, in their early fifties, and moderately wealthy from all appearances. They were respectful when they were ushered into the office, dignified in their terror. They had, they said, spent the day shopping and lunching at the Roosevelt Field Mall. They had first learned of their daughter's disappearance from the policeman parked outside their house when they returned.

"You check your answering machine?" asked Maude.

"Yes. The patrolman said to. No messages," said Benjamin Lucido. "Unfortunately." He was tall, wiry, shocked. His wife was blond-streaked and red-eyed.

"Nothing in the mail?"

"Nothing," said Dolly. "Was there any sign she was hurt?"

"Not so far," said Rocky.

"You're a close family?" asked Maude.

"Very."

Proudly they took turns interrupting each other, telling Frank Murphy and his homicide detectives that their Elizabeth had enjoyed an idyllic Long Island childhood, a happy and fulfilling adulthood, and throughout her life was the best damn daughter anybody could have had, attentive, loving, and just plain fun to be with.

They were both former Grumman workers, they said, the people who put men on the moon; and Elizabeth had been a soccer star, a saxophonist, sixth in her class at Columbia Law, a literacy volunteer, an avid skier. Then Dolly Lucido filled up with tears and fell against her husband, sobbing, the only sounds in the commissioner's office.

"Does Elizabeth have a lot of friends?" asked Maude.

Her father nodded. "In and out of the political arena. Everybody loved her."

"We'll need their names," said Maude.

"Of course. And you should talk to our youngest, Justine. She would know even better."

Rocky took down Justine's phone number and address in Manhattan, off York, on the Upper East Side.

"Elizabeth ever mention anyone stalking her, giving her trouble, that sort of thing?" asked Maude.

"No," said Dolly Lucido. "She would have handled that sort of thing herself, and quietly, too."

Murphy knew the mother was right. Elizabeth had never been a shrinking violet, never one to cower, or beg for protection. She took her shots and stood shoulder-to-shoulder with the best of them, ballsy to a fault. Murphy stared at the new pin-map behind Maude's desk, the Old Westbury scene labeled A, Elizabeth Lucido's house labeled B. There were red pins stabbed into the home addresses of Norman Keller and Jackson Hind.

"Did you know she was dating Jackson Hind?" asked Murphy.

"Yes, we did," said Dolly. "They told us about a month ago."

"Do you like him?" asked Maude.

"Very much."

"When was the last time you spoke to Elizabeth?"

"I left a message for her yesterday afternoon," said Dolly. "We actually spoke, I think, on Monday. She said she was entering Hell Week part ten, and planned on getting about five hours of sleep for the next five days. She told me things were coming to a head. I assumed she meant the campaign . . . both of them."

"For all we know, she did," said Murphy.

"Have we called in the FBI yet?" asked Ben Lucido.

"They stand ready to assist us in every way," said Murphy. "Out-of-state leads, experts, whatever we need, even though technically, all we have here is a Missing Person."

"What about offering a reward?"

"It never hurts," said Murphy.

"Do you believe there's any chance at all she's run away?" asked Rocky.

Ben Lucido's eyes narrowed. "Like a petulant child?"

"Or a confused adolescent?" asked Maude. "One with divided loyalties."

"Her loyalties weren't divided. They were taking Daly down."

Maude asked Dolly Lucido if she had some time to visit Elizabeth's house with her, to look through her daughter's jewelry, her personal property, to see if anything notable was missing.

"Of course. Right now?"

"If you don't mind. We want to start watching the pawn shops, in case there's something missing. You'd be surprised how many items turn up right away."

"That wouldn't necessarily be good news," said Dolly.

"It would depend," Maude said evenly.

Dolly Lucido bit her lip.

Maude said, "Detective Blair and your husband should get over to your house right away, get a crew working on the phones. I can bring you home later."

"Okay," she said.

"I'll handle Mr. Hind," said Murphy, as his cops and the Lucidos rose to leave.

"Good," said Maude. "Thanks."

"Tell him to call us," said Ben. "Tell him we love him."

chapter 11

T HE ONE-WAY EXTERIOR GLASS IN ALICE GETTINGS'S corner office window faced the Drive-In line and gave her frequent chances to study human beings who thought themselves unobserved. She routinely watched people tweeze chin hairs, pop zits, and worse. And then they want to borrow money?

Alice had been dating Frank Murphy for almost two years, and was engaged to marry him on her fortieth birthday, in February—two years from the day she had learned she could not have children. Alice Gettings had been surprised to find a man like Frank, who felt no need for his name or gene-code to travel past his lifetime. She had thought that a marvelous quality; and she had done her best to be worthy of him.

She thought she was succeeding.

But now, fighting the spread of dread through her stomach, she held in her shaking hands an unsigned fax that accused her fiancé of being more than friends with the missing public official, the lovely Elizabeth Lucido.

"So sorry," the transmittal ended, "but Frankie-Baby was fucking her. Just thought you should know before everybody else."

Her Frank—aka Frankie-Baby.

Alice could already hear her mother: "I told you he was too damn good to be true. Churchgoing phony." Commissioner Frankie-Baby. Who had not yet bothered to call her back.

Alice got up from her desk, gathered her briefcase and coat, and walked out of her office. "I'm leaving early," she told her secretary. "Have a good weekend."

"Is something wrong?" he asked.

"What could be wrong? My life is perfect."

ELIZABETH LUCIDO'S LIVING ROOM WAS OCCUPIED BY A SOLI-tary uniformed cop in a rocking chair. He was watching an afternoon talk show and scarfing down a meatball hero when Maude and Dolly walked inside unannounced. Maude Fleming gave him a withering look. "Any phone calls, rookie?"

The cop hastily rewrapped his sandwich, then checked his log. "Not a one, ma'am, except the precinct calling me once about my meal."

Maude nodded sternly, and would have ripped into the little Boy Scout had not Dolly Lucido looked around her daughter's perfect living room and gasped, then sat down quickly on the couch, hyperventilating.

The cop switched off the television and went to get her a glass of water.

"I know," said Maude, sitting next to Dolly, wrapping an arm around her quivering shoulders. "I'm sorry."

"Don't be sorry, Detective. Find her."

"I will. I promise. Was she always this neat?"

"She used to iron her doll's clothes."

Dolly and Maude linked arms like aged sisters and

slowly made for the bedroom, where Dolly saw the bare mattress and caught her breath again.

"Evidence," said Maude. "She wasn't hurt here."

Dolly carefully picked through the wooden jewelry box, ticking off the main pieces she knew would be there, finding them, holding them, and staring at them. Elizabeth's faux-mink was hanging in its garment bag in the closet, her stamp collection reposed in the box under the sheetless bed.

"Nothing good is missing, at least to my knowledge. Justine would know better."

"Okay. Worth a try," said Maude.

Dolly nodded, stunned, staring at the mattress.

Maude touched her elbow. "You ready to go?"

She hesitated. "Can I take one of her stuffed animals?"

"Sure," said Maude. "Of course."

From a bookshelf Dolly chose a ratty gray dog that looked thirty years old, hugged the toy for a moment, then tucked it in her pocketbook.

Maude rubbed Dolly's back. "Don't lose hope."

"I've never been so scared in all my life."

"I know."

The cop was on his feet by the door, like a Buckingham guard, the debris from his snack gone. Maude helped Dolly Lucido outside and into the squad car, then Maude returned to the house.

"Any nosy neighbors stop by?" asked Maude.

The cop shook his head. "No, ma'am."

"Any suspicious cars cruise by, maybe somebody wondering how we're making out here?"

He shrugged, reddening. "Sorry."

Maude punched his shoulder lightly. "Don't be sorry. Be good. You could even be the one to break the case. Maybe earn that fat paycheck."

"Sorry," he said again.

"Forget it."

JACKSON HIND'S ATTORNEY CALLED THE MAIN DESK AT NASSAU County Police Headquarters at six-forty that evening.

He explained to the switchboard operator that Mr. Jackson Hind was unable to respond as anticipated to headquarters that evening for an appointment with the commissioner. He was naturally very sorry for any inconvenience. *Ciao.* Click.

Frank Murphy sat at his desk and listened to a tape of the call, deciding it would be a mistake to overreact. Jackson Hind wasn't heading for the hills. The very notion was ludicrous. This unfortunate delay was political, not criminal, evasiveness. Even so, Murphy was grateful Martin Daly and his people had left for the day. They might not have seen it that way.

Murphy called Maude and filled her in.

"Asshole," she said.

"Maybe not."

"I want to use the choppers," she said. "Do an infrared sweep of our wooded areas. If she was dumped somewhere, and she's still alive . . ."

"Make the call," said Murphy, even though the operation would be costly and would no doubt turn up other time-consuming work, not the least of which would be all the houses glowing pink, growing pot.

"You never know," said Maude.

Murphy sent Annie Anderson home and locked up his office for the night. He left by the back stairs and cut through Detention unannounced, where, happily, no one was being abused. (During business hours it was hard for Murphy to retain the element of surprise. He wouldn't be halfway out his door before Jake would hit the phones: "Coming your way. Pass it on." Of course Murphy understood Jake's motivation. The world is full of two-way streets.)

It was dark out when he drove from Mineola to

Hempstead Turnpike, then turned east on perhaps the ugliest main drag in America, an over-signed visual sewer of commerce and concrete. Stores were dressed in their Halloween finery, and here and there Christmas lights were already going up.

It took him twenty-five minutes to travel six miles, to the county-owned Institute for Living in Bethpage. Murphy arrived with the cramped sensation that all Nassau's streets were crowded, not just Hempstead Turnpike. He locked his car and walked inside.

"Hey, Commissioner," said the captain of security at the front desk.

"What's happenin', Eddie?"

"Same shit, different day."

Eddie had retired as a detective sergeant five years ago, and already his pension wasn't enough. Or maybe it was that his second wife had thrown him out and his apartment was lonely. Probably, thought Murphy, it was both. Eddie reached under his desk and buzzed Murphy onto the locked ward.

Murphy popped a Tic-Tac and reminded himself to breathe through his mouth. Wally Murphy's bed was at the far end of the room, under his favorite screened window, next to an elderly black patient with the widest of smiles, always.

Wally Murphy was forty-five years old. He had been a perfectly normal three-year-old until he got German measles. His doctors gave him the wrong medicine and froze his brain. Now Wally was a skinny six feet tall, with thin gray hair and a long gray beard, and his favorite songs were the National Anthems of Canada and the United States. (Their father had been a rabid New York Ranger fan.)

Frank got Wally dressed in clean jeans and a red flannel shirt. He signed him out with the nurse, then Eddie, and walked him out of the stench through the electronic doors, hustled him into the unmarked car, buckled him into his seat belt, child-locked his door.

"Where to, little brother?" Frank asked as he slid behind the wheel.

Wally grunted, which Frank knew meant he didn't give a rat's ass as long as there was food and lots of it. Wally loved Burger King and McDonald's and Taco Bell and Pizza Hut, and the nice thing about Long Island was that you were never more than ten minutes from all of them.

They hit the drive-thru at the Route 110 McDonald's for a sack of burgers, fries, and Cokes; and Wally got right to work, feeding himself with both hands. After that, like on most nights, they went for an aimless cruise, hugging the hilly North Shore of Suffolk from Huntington to Fort Salonga, glimpsing moonlight on harbors here and there. Sometimes Wally would fold his fingers around the dashboard statue of St. Christopher and bow his head, one of countless instances when Frank would wonder if Wally knew what was going on, if he was signaling back from his limited world. Frank always talked to Wally as if he were the same bright little boy he had been before the doctors messed him up.

"A friend of mine was kidnapped last night, Wally. Or she flat walked out of her life. Which I seriously doubt. Married people do that. Single people are stuck with themselves."

Wally was munching french fries and looking out his window, absorbed in the scenery.

"You've heard me talk about her. Sexy chick, worked for Daly. Had the hots for me, and vice versa. Before Alice. We did the liquid lunch now and then."

Wally perked up at mention of Alice, who occasionally joined the Murphy men on their wanderings when she didn't have class or bowling or some other nocturnal endeavor. Of course Wally didn't know from hots or liquid lunches, so Frank dropped that angle.

Wally stripped the wrapper from another quarterpounder, slam-dunked half of it, grinned: His big brother had come for him, as he did most every night.

"I don't know," said Frank. "Maybe things got too damn complicated for her. That can happen to people. It's happened to me."

Wally pointed to the glove compartment.

Frank smiled, reached across to open it, handed Wally his favorite old picture of their parents, which Frank had laminated at work. Circa 1975, it showed a gray-haired Frank senior and a still redheaded Mary standing on a dock, with Lake George in the background. They were smiling, their arms around each other's waists. Wally stared at them and rocked faster, clutched the picture to his chest, humming.

An hour later they found their way back to the Institute. Frank got his Wally into clean pajamas and tucked into bed, packed his street clothes under his arm to be laundered. He bent over and kissed his brother's bearded cheek. "I love you, man."

Wally grunted and turned his face to his barred window, his view: the garish play of lights from Hempstead Turnpike merchants, two Martin Daly signs and one smaller one touting District Attorney Arthur Prefect as tough, honest, fighting for you!

Frank said good night to the staff and headed for home, one last bad move in a day chock-full of them; because when he got to his condo on Fairhaven Harbor, Alice was not home, just the fax she had received at the bank, curled up on the kitchen counter with the unopened mail, near the answering machine that was not blinking.

Frank read it twice while his stomach flipped, searched the condo as if it were a crime scene, then rode the elevator down to the garage to look for her car, hoping she was holed up in tears at a girlfriend's place on the second floor, wondering where else she might have gone, terrified.

He finally called her mother in Cranford, New Jersey, and learned that, yes, Alice was there, safe and blessedly asleep. "She said she would call you in the morning," Mrs. Gettings said coolly.

"Okay," said Murphy. "Thanks. And would you tell her for me that the message she got isn't true. That I love her."

"I can try . . . Frank." Click.

Murphy walked out to his dark balcony and searched the empty sky for his helicopters, then stared at the twinkling lights in the hills across the harbor, wondering if anyone over there was having a similarly shitty day.

He remembered Alice's advice not to give up his cozy spot teaching tactics at the Police Academy. "Why lay down with dogs?" she had said. "These people eat nice guys for breakfast." He had told her he would be cops' boss, beloved by all. And, if his vision of a worker's paradise failed, the one job where a man can goof off with his head held high is at the helm of a police department. Pretty much every day since that conversation Murphy had been glad he'd taken the job. Tonight he was not so sure.

Maybe the night shift would catch a break. Maybe the Air Bureau guys would get lucky.

Until Elizabeth was found dead there was hope, and he should not be the first one to lose it. He should be the last. He prayed that if she was alive she was not in pain, then he prayed that if she was dead it had come quickly, without terror, that she was with God.

He would have prayed for his own cause, too, but he did not want to sully the plea.

Saturday, Oct. 26

chapter 12

I T WAS SEVEN O'CLOCK SATURDAY MORNING, AND RAIN pecked Junior Daly's bedroom window, which meant his freebie golf game at Fresh Meadows was canceled, which meant Junior and last night's red-headed conquest—he believed her name began with J—could hang at his Mineola bachelor's pad and renew their acquaintance sober or, more accurately, hungover like dogs.

Junior could have lived with his father and Kym in the big house instead of this faux-Tudor singles pad within walking distance of the office and half the best bistros in Nassau: Dad's offer had been made with assurances there was plenty of space, they'd hardly know he was there.

Like that was something new.

Unless Dad wanted something done, thought Junior.

Then they'd know he was there; then life with Dad would turn his no-show job into abject slavery.

Junior might have been lazy, but Junior was not dumb. He had rampant good looks, and he had juice. Right now he did nothing to earn his salary; and he freely used his "reach" to score everything from discounts on homegrown to spicy debutantes like this little charmer. Why move under the microscope? His older sisters had fled Blue Landing as soon as they had graduated from college, something else Junior had failed to get around to yet. Junior could have had a roommate, but why leave witnesses walking around.

He rolled off the waterbed and locked himself in the tiny bathroom, sucked down three Advils and burned half a joint, blowing the smoke out the open window, trying to remember last night, having a little more success than he had remembering the night before that. He recalled he had slept late and then golfed Rockville Links with some carting executives yesterday afternoon, shot eighty-six fighting a slice, then played gin and lost, then drank some, then did some lines one of them had, in a Jaguar, then drank some more, and then met the girl . . . where?

He couldn't remember.

Anyway, he remembered wearing a condom.

So, good for him.

He brushed his wavy brown hair and gargled, splashed on Ralph Lauren cologne, then eased himself back into the waterbed, thinking he had to throttle back on the booze, maybe just smoke weed for a while, an occasional beer.

"Hey. You awake?"

The redhead did not move. Junior lobbed a leg over her warm thigh and nuzzled her neck.

"Hey, baby, how you doing?" He kissed her freckled cheek.

She opened her eyes and croaked a whiskey-fogged, "'Morning."

"I owe you one, I believe," he said.

"Yes, you do."

Junior wanted to last a while this time, so he thought of something else as he looked down on her, the day's schedule, figured when they were done jamming he'd tell her to split, then he'd shower, shave, and answer all those voice-mail messages, two of them from shit-for-brains Norman Keller, three from Dad, one from Charlie

Hotchkiss. Then he would crawl back into the rack until the college football action began. Junior liked Columbia over Yale at Baker Field, pick 'em.

What was he gonna tell Dad, anyway? Who was kidding who?

A day like yesterday, it was just as well he'd stayed out of the office. Why remind everyone he worked there? Why rile a prick like Charlie, who acted like every cent you made you stole from him?

Good God, his father was dumb. Like this Jane. Or Jean. A registered Blank with nice knockers and no dough.

Junior wondered what Norman Keller wanted, was amazed the party doofuss possessed the balls to call twice, like once wasn't enough. He could hear Norman now, begging for some dipshit job after election day, one where he got to wear a tie, whining: "When's it gonna be my turn? Hanh? I do all this work and for what?" The only white guy in Roosevelt, and they still almost gave his slot away.

"Junior? Stay hard, wouldya."

He stared at the wax inside her ear.

"And speed it up a little. I was like so almost there."

"Yeah, sure . . . And then I got to get up and get moving, okay, check in with the office and whatnot."

Jane or Jean froze first, like a bridge. "What about brunch?"

Junior, elbows locked in a push-up position, said, "I forgot I had to work today . . . this morning, actually."

"I thought you made your own hours."

He shook his head. "Not during the campaign, I don't. No one does. Not even my dad."

Her mouth twisted. "What kind of bullshit artist are you?"

Junior smiled ruefully, felt his arms begin to tremble. "The regular kind, I guess."

"Get off of me."

"I was kidding."

"I'll fucking scream," she threatened.

Junior rolled onto his side. "Don't scream. Just leave."

"Don't worry."

He sat up with his back against the headboard and lit a cigarette, watched his date angrily squeeze into her tight black dress and heels, suddenly remembered why he had cut her out of the herd. "Good-bye?" he asked good-naturedly when she got to the door.

"Fuck you."

Junior shook his head, thinking, She expected the truth? From a guy she boinks the night she meets him? Then he was thinking that some women get exactly what they deserve.

THE VIEW ACROSS FAIRHAVEN HARBOR FROM HIS FOURTH-FLOOR condo balcony was marred that morning by fog and heavy rain. Frank Murphy sat on a wrought-iron deck chair well back from the overhang, in a P.D. sweatsuit, contemplating the distance to the opposite shoreline, sipping his third cup of coffee. His gray-blond hair was damp from his shower, and his solid muscles ached pleasantly from his swim across the harbor—a habit begun in his youth. He loved the fitness swimming provided, but he did it for his sanity, never feeling fully alive unless he'd gotten wet and worked hard. As fatigue set in and the strokes grew tougher, he would always hear his first coach in his ear, guiding him, insisting on good form, pointing out that he wasn't sweating, that most poor people worked harder every day. Coach Nell had been a middle-aged Australian then. During World War II, as a young married woman, she and her husband were coast watchers, living on a small Pacific atoll, reporting the movement of Japanese ships off their beach. They were caught. They not so much refused to talk as didn't know anything valuable. Nevertheless, a Japanese naval officer had men tie her to a tree and sew her eyelids open, all the better to watch her husband's head sawed off. Coach Nell never mentioned this, but the other kids passed the story on. In any event, she was not a woman you complained to.

Murphy thought of something and dialed Homicide.

"Homicide, Fleming," said Maude.

"Me again," said Murphy. "We check late trains in and out of the area? The station's within walking distance for one of those criminal commuters they're always yapping about."

"Of course. Buses, too. And you don't want to know how many folks are growing pot. How was the water?"

"Thank God for wetsuits. Have we talked to her priest?"

"Somebody did," said Maude. "Relax."

"Am I driving you nuts?" asked Murphy.

"Not yet. You want to meet us at the parents' house? Justine Lucido is there now."

"Yes. Absolutely. Anything's better than sitting home."

Rocky picked up an extension and said, "I still say we hot-wire Dipstick Daly's office."

"Not funny, Rocky. Not helpful."

"Sorry."

"So what else we got on tap?"

Maude said, "Interview Norman Keller. Interview Hind, if he'll talk to us, which he'd be crazy not to. We got an informational roadblock set up for tonight in her neighborhood. Find the boyfriends in her life before Hind, besides Hind."

Murphy laughed grimly, imagining having to ask Alice to cover his backside. He hung up and stared at the phone, wishing she would call, knowing that when Alice was ready to talk they would talk, no sooner. She had his car phone number, his cell phone number.

She had his number, all right.

chapter 13

THE LUCIDO PARENTS TOOK A WALK DOWN TO THE beach, leaving Murphy and Maude alone with Justine, who was every bit as pretty as her older sister and apparently just as accomplished. She wore jeans and a blue silk blouse, real pearls, black high heels that matched Maude's. She told them she had a master's degree from the University of Chicago and worked on Wall Street, as an analyst. She detested politics. She was engaged to a painter whose work was shown around town. Her life was perfect. "Except now my big sister's been kidnapped."

She vowed to drop everything to search for Elizabeth. She had friends and money. They would fund a reward, post fliers, work the train stations like acolytes, whatever it took.

They sat at the kitchen table over coffee, and Justine talked about Elizabeth, her girlfriends, her relationship with Jackson Hind, and then Justine mentioned a few guys Elizabeth didn't talk about with her parents, all before meeting Jackson, losers she was sorry to have wasted time on. No names, probably other lawyers, Justine supposed. "Booze bangs," she called them.

She told them that Elizabeth had been thinking of leaving politics when she fell in love with Jackson Hind. She was sick of its slimy practitioners and wasted opportunities.

"And outside of work?" asked Murphy. "Any difficulties?"

"Elizabeth took a vacation last year with some college friends and returned most unhappy. I don't know what that was about."

"We'll need their names," said Murphy.

"Of course. The one man she truly feared was the chairman. That much I'm sure of. And that friend of his, that financier with the weird name . . . Baltusrol Vail. But if they're involved, you'll never find her . . . right?"

Murphy felt bile rise in his throat. "I wouldn't say that."

"Please find her. My sister doesn't deserve this."

"I SURE WISH JUNIOR HAD CALLED ME BACK," NORMAN SAID. "I mean, where the hell are these bastards when you need them."

"The hills," said Nana. "Your grandfather knew that. Always they head for the hills."

Norman jammed his hands in the pockets of his orange Young Republicans windbreaker and rocked forward, peered down the long hallway on the second floor of police headquarters.

"Relax," said Nana. "You're so nervous you look guilty."

"I can't believe you told them I came home late."

"I'm sorry."

"This is what I get for networking, Nana, for listening to you. I gave her my card. I told her I graduated in the top half of my class."

"Hush up, will ya," said Nana. "This hallway might be bugged."

Norman looked up, back and forth, his head on a swivel. "Oh, Jesus. Oh, shit." He might have tipped them to something, which could lead to something else, which could lead to his hobbies, which would ultimately embarrass everyone.

Nana Keller sat back and seemed to stare at nothing, then smiled expansively. "I remember when they built this place. Big party out on the lawn. Your grandfather held a banner."

Norman stared at her in amazement. "Who gives a shit, Nana? You know? Really."

"I'm sorry, Norman. I know you're nervous."

"Not nervous," said Norman. "Mad."

"These people are Nazis," said Nana. "You be careful what you tell them."

FRANK MURPHY FOUND THAT THE USUAL SWILL HAD ARRIVED IN his interoffice mail: a catalogue with hot models in body armor, a letter thanking Police Officer Whomever for bravely rescuing Citizen Whomever from a fire, a box containing a double-headed vibrator sent by an anonymous member of the rank and file. (It absolutely killed the guys, he knew, his frequent attendance at Mass, and some felt honor-bound to expand his horizons.) He was checking for batteries when Hind and his lawyer knocked on his open door.

"The latest in night sticks?" asked Hind.

Murphy said, "So that's what this is. Bejesus, I thought it was some kind of toothbrush."

Everybody laughed collegially and shook hands and sat down around the conference table. It was high time to "establish the parameters," as Hind's lawyer put it. Lofton Seals, a venerable senior partner in a New York firm, was there to save the Hind candidacy. Both visitors wore business suits to Murphy's Dockers and Crime Scene sweatshirt.

"Sorry about last night," said Hind. "I got sick to my stomach after you left."

No chance you needed time to think, thought Murphy. Or build an alibi. "You ready to do it now?"

"Whatever it takes, Frank. I don't want this police department wasting any more of its time on me. I want every available officer looking for Elizabeth."

Murphy's phone rang.

"Norman Keller's here," said Maude. "You want to watch me grill his chubby ass?"

"I have Mr. Hind and his attorney in my office right now. Why don't you and Rocky join us. Norman Keller can wait."

"My sentiments exactly."

For the next hour in Murphy's office Jackson Hind gave them more personal information than they had a right to ask for, enough to clear several men of many crimes. Lofton Seals never once cautioned silence. In front of cops who could only gain by arresting him, Jackson discussed his relationship with Elizabeth, from the beginning to the present. He spoke honestly of the thrills of sneaking around with the opposition's star.

"Was she seeing anybody when you met her?" asked Maude.

"No," said Hind. "I don't think so. She never said."

"Were you?" asked Murphy.

"No one."

Rocky Blair asked if he had ever met a Mrs. Babs Whitcomb.

"Never had the pleasure," said Hind. "She was from real money, Detective. What I have is chump change."

Hind's cell phone rang. He got permission to answer and took the call. "Hello, Charlie," he said, smiling. "Why yes, I'm in Commissioner Murphy's office right now, lending aid to the investigation. What can I do for you?" Hind listened and smiled, covered the mouthpiece, looked at the cops. "He wants to know what I think about intra-party dating . . . if I believe it's something that must ethically be disclosed to the public." Hind uncovered the phone. "The question is beneath you, Charlie. And I'll be glad to discuss ethics with you when we have Elizabeth back safe. You need to speak to Commissioner Murphy? No? Okay, then."

If Jackson Hind was the bad guy, thought Murphy, he was the slickest son of a bitch in town. You watched the man closely, he was a victim, too, but not a crybaby.

"Go with Detective Blair and give him what he wants," said Murphy. "Nothing you can do will help us more."

"For now," said Hind.

"Right."

The candidate and his lawyer left with Rocky Blair. Maude Fleming hung back. She leaned against Murphy's closed door. "What do you think? A possible?"

Murphy said, "Sure. Everybody is."

"He doesn't give me any vibes, but he is awful cute."

"Nice about it, too, considering this could mean the end of a promising career. He'd never beat Martin with criminal questions hanging over him."

"Quite a mess, eh?"

Murphy nodded, at that moment holding a dim view of human nature, including his own, unable to shake the feeling there was something he was not doing that he ought to, that he was in the middle of a big mistake. What made the feeling worse was that Frank Murphy almost never felt that way about his life.

"Let's talk to Keller," said Maude, "and pray to God he's a bed-wetting, fire-setting, pet-killing freak."

chapter 14

HELLO, NANA, MR. KELLER," MAUDE SAID. "THIS IS Police Commissioner Murphy. Won't you please come with us."

Norman and Nana and Murphy and Maude made their way through the bullpen to the homicide conference room, then sat at the gray metal table under flickering fluorescent light. Stale smoke fouled the air, despite NO SMOKING signs on the walls between charts of countywide phone extensions and sample homicide court informations.

"Coffee anybody?" asked Murphy.

Maude, Nana, and Norman said no, then Nana mentioned that her roof would surely be leaking with all this rain, and she wanted to get home, and Norman shushed her in a way that bothered Murphy, displayed a mean streak; he could suddenly see Norman Keller abusing his nana, consigning her to a nursing home, cheating her of her modest estate.

"What time did you get home Thursday night?" Maude asked Norman, starting in the middle.

"I got home maybe twelve-forty-five, one o'clock."

Nana coughed. "Make that more like one-thirty, Norman. I heard you rummaging in the fridge."

Norman blushed. "I ate half a chicken salad sandwich when I got home, and an apple. . . . The dinner at the restaurant got cold."

"What time'd you leave the restaurant?" said Maude.

"Around one?"

Murphy said, "Then how'd you get home at twelve-forty-five?"

"I mean, I guess around one, if we use Nana's estimate."

Maude said, "Why don't we use your recollection of the truth, Norman. That would be just as good."

"Twelve-forty-five to one."

"You go straight home?"

"Yes. Of course. It was late and I was tired."

"No stops at all?"

"No."

Maude handed Norman a photograph of Mrs. Babs Whitcomb, told him to look at it closely. "Ever see this woman before?"

His face showed puzzlement. "Sure . . . at party functions."

Maude said, "What time did Martin Daly leave the rally?"

"Before midnight, I think, but you'd have to ask him."

"And what did you do from the time Mr. Daly left until the time you left?"

Norman thought about this a second. "I helped collect and organize the sign-in sheets, and then take down the banners and whatnot. We reuse everything."

"How very environmental," said Maude. "But something's off kilter here, Norman. Like how long does it take to drive from Bellmore to Roosevelt? Ten minutes, maybe? You got some unwanted slack in your story."

Norman crossed his arms and lowered his chin to his chest. "That doesn't mean I did anything wrong."

Murphy believed that Elizabeth had been kidnapped sometime after Hind had left her, one-thirtyish, maybe two, which meant Norman would have had to sneak back out, which wouldn't be hard with only Nana to fool. "You go right to bed after your snack?"

"Yes. Like I said, I was tired."

Nana, Murphy noticed, was examining the wanted posters on the wall near the door, her face expressionless.

Maude stared hard at Norman. "You know Elizabeth Lucido well?"

"I've met her twice. Once last year at a press conference, and then I reminded her of that and gave her my card the other night at the fund-raiser. That is what this is about, right? My business card? She stuck it in her pocket with lots of other cards."

"No, Norman. Just yours. Ever been to her house?" asked Maude.

"Of course not."

Frank Murphy had, Frank Murphy remembered. Three or four times. Booze bangs, Elizabeth called them, him.

Maude chewed the end of her pen. "Ever been to Martin Daly's house?"

"No."

Murphy laughed. "Big player, huh, kid?"

Norman studied his hands. "I never said I was."

"His grandfather was," said Nana. "A Zone Leader, a—"

"Do you do any work for the county or are you strictly a party animal?"

"I work part-time for the county as well . . . in the County Attorney's office."

"Doing what?"

"Shuffling papers."

"You want to be a little more exact?"

"What I mean is, say someone comes in with a Freedom of Information request, which means they're looking for a smoking gun kind of document, one that could cause a problem? We have to show them everything, of course, but they can't take the stuff with them, and nothing says that documents can't be shuffled from file to file at the end of the day, the lunch hour, bathroom breaks, you know, placed where it would be difficult to find, like in a file they already looked at. That's my job."

"You're telling me you obstruct justice for the County Attorney?"

"Not just me. There's a team of us."

"What's with the private post office box?" asked Maude.

"Excuse me?" Norman was surprised by her change in tack.

"What's wrong with the mail going right to the house?"

"I wanted some privacy. Some security. If you hadn't noticed, we live in a very bad neighborhood."

"What kind of magazines do you subscribe to?"

"What?" Norman looked at Nana in shock, back at the detectives. "You can't ask me that."

Maude leaned close to Norman, almost forehead to forehead. "Sure I can, kid. Because I'm building a profile on you, seeing what makes you tick. I want your Internet bills, too. Know what I'm saying? You think this is a god-damn joke?"

Now Norman looked sufficiently scared. "No."

"You a freak, Norman? Tell me now."

"No."

"What else did you and Miss Lucido talk about Thursday night?"

"How good Martin Daly looked. His face-lift."

Maude looked at Murphy. "I didn't know about the face-lift."

"Just a tuck," said Murphy. "Park Avenue. He was bragging in the sauna last week."

Maude grinned and turned back to Norman. "She didn't mention anyone bothering her, giving her trouble?"

"No."

"You got a girlfriend, Norman?"

"No."

"You didn't follow the nice lady home, did you, Norman? You didn't watch her having sex with Jackson Hind?"

"No."

"Those footprints under her window sure better not match your shoes."

"They don't. Honest. I swear."

There had been no footprints discovered under the bedroom window, Murphy knew. Maude was probing for uncertainty, setting out bait.

"You sure?"

"No . . . I mean, yes, I'm sure."

Maude slammed her file closed. "Good. Then you won't mind giving us fingerprints, some blood and urine samples, just to clear up this cloud hovering over you."

"What cloud? Do I have to?"

Murphy walked behind Norman and patted him on the back, then squeezed the nerves in his shoulders, letting him know he could hurt him. "Not unless we get a warrant, Norman, which one of these days we'll probably get around to, especially since your alibi is dogshit."

Norman grimaced and whined, "I didn't say I *wouldn't* do it."

"Then why," Maude asked, "are you wasting our time?"

Murphy released his grip. "Yeah, Norman, why? Get with the program here. We're the good guys."

Norman turned to his nana. "Nana, what do you think? Should I do what they want?"

"I think your grandfather is spinning in his grave."

Maude walked the Kellers out, then returned and closed the door.

"What do you think?" Murphy said.

"That's a fucked-up young man. He draws a team."

chapter 15

A T THREE O'CLOCK THAT SATURDAY AFTERNOON FRANK Murphy picked up a couple of pepperoni pizzas for Eddie Black and the staff on Wally's floor at the Institute, then left them to their snacking and got Wally out of his bed at the end of a long row of beds filled with patients who never saw visitors. He dressed Wally quietly, so as not to wake George, who was asleep, a big grin on his dark face.

They ate a late lunch at Taco Bell, dessert at TCBY, then Frank dropped him back and went home, hoping to find Alice there, but maybe Alice didn't live there anymore.

He showered and shaved and put on a fresh suit in silence, thinking it was strange to be headed out without Alice by his side, chirping about this and that. Strange and lonely.

It was almost dusk when he left his building, and traffic remained heavy along the North Shore byways. His palms were sweating on the steering wheel as he plowed through the snarl of cars to Plainview in the rain, to the county-owned television station, where a telethon was being held.

He parked next to a fire hydrant and slipped inside, immediately joined the drink line. A large-screen overhead showed celebrity auctioneers, then shots of busy phone bank volunteers. Before he could get a Dewars, rocks, he was grabbed by a ponytailed producer and whisked onstage. Things were heating up, he was told. Bidding wars had erupted over junkets to Foxwood, foursomes at Shinnecock. A big thermometer showed the black ink of profit inching higher.

Murphy was handed his list of items to auction, lights blazing in his face. He scowled down at the first item: a boar's-hair brush, suggested bid of seventy-five dollars. Sweat dribbled down his left temple. Murphy smiled at the camera and said, "What do I hear for this genuine boar's-hair brush?" He held it up. "Let's open at seventy-five dollars."

A camera rolled in tight. The phones fell silent.

"A real beauty," said Murphy. "The kind they don't make anymore . . . donated by Wilma Carruthers of Mill Neck. Come on, folks, after the deduction you can own this fine brush for, say, forty bucks, depending on your bracket."

"Next item," said the producer.

Murphy paused while volunteers dollied a large, draped painting onto the stage. The portrait was unveiled, and Murphy got it: that he had been set up to look like a jackass. Yup, there was Martin grinning like a loon from the wings, and Seymour Cammeroli and his bodyguard near doubled-over in the back.

Murphy decided to foreswear his script. "Here we have a genuine Day-Glo painting of Abe Lincoln, Martin Luther King, and John Fitzgerald Kennedy, as they would have looked if they had all lived at the same time and hung around together. Say around 1962. Donated by Martin Daly, County Executive, from the family collection."

The audience giggled. The producer frowned.

Martin Daly, now joined in the wings by his wife, looked positively apoplectic. The station was his baby, his wife one of its stars. The audience noticed the byplay, and Martin smiled out at them with only his mouth. Then Murphy's cell phone rang in his jacket pocket. He flicked it out, turned his back on Daly.

Maude Fleming said, "It's me, boss. The Lucido parents just snuck out the back door with a suitcase."

"They get a phone call?"

"Nope."

"I'm on the way."

THE DRIZZLE WAS ENDING, AND THE EMERGENCY SERVICES COPS in the woods pulled down their hoods. To the east the thunder rolled away.

Frank Murphy crouched next to his Homicide detectives behind a hollowed-out log on a gentle hill overlooking the dark beach. The streetlights of Rye blinked on the far side of the Long Island Sound.

Maude Fleming said, "We got boats standing by, choppers in the air, sharpshooters in the treetops."

Murphy said, "So now all we need is our shithead to show."

"That's a roger."

"How long ago did they leave the house?"

"Thirty minutes," said Maude. "I called you right away."

Murphy checked his watch: It was just after nine. The air was thick with the smell of leaves and salt. Maude handed Murphy her night-sight binoculars.

She whispered, "By the end of the jetty. I guess they were told to walk back and forth."

"I got ya," said Murphy. "Still with the suitcase. I do hope Big Ben isn't packing heat."

"True story," said Maude.

Murphy remembered another true story, of a stakeout gone bad, outside a bank in Elmont. His stomach clenched and his skin crawled, and he was amazed at its power over him after all these years. People had insisted on dying that sunny morning. God, don't let anyone die tonight.

A shadow near the jetty moved. The sharpshooters above and behind Murphy tensed, swept the night for targets.

"Something's wrong," said Maude.

"What?" asked Murphy.

"This is not how you transfer ransom money, if you plan on spending any of it. Who we got watching the house?" Maude asked the Emergency Services lieutenant.

"A couple uniforms."

"In the house?"

"Car down the block."

"Rocky, get up there quick."

Rocky moved like a cat from the woods to the street. His footfalls could be heard as he jogged from sea level to the cul-de-sac above.

"Hit the floods," Maude said into her walkie-talkie.

The beach lit up like noon at the equator. The Lucidos were surrounded by the cops from the woods, two frogmen rising from the water. The Lucidos were saying they were sorry, they hadn't any choice, Ben had found a ransom demand tucked under their back door. "What would you people do? Tell me."

"Calm down," said Maude. "It's okay."

"With all due respect, Detective Fleming, I did what they said to do."

"We don't blame you," said Maude. "Really."

"They asked for fifty grand. They said to put it in a paper bag and leave it on our back porch and walk down here to the water with a suitcase. They said they would release Elizabeth in the morning."

Maude keyed her radio. "Rocky, the money's on the back porch. The Lucidos were a diversion. Repeat. The—"

". . . is Detective Blair, I'm in foot pursuit of a male white, carrying a bag, southbound, through the yards . . . he ditched the bag . . . he's wearing black pants and black hooded sweatshirt . . . wait . . . nevermind . . . I got the motherfucker."

By the time Murphy and Maude and the Lucidos scurried back to the house, Rocky was half-walking, half-dragging the suspect up the driveway. Rocky had the paper bag in his other hand, and his chest pumped out.

"Nice work, Rocky."

"Thank you, sir."

"You might hold off calling people motherfuckers on the air, though. Not everyone understands the thrill of the hunt."

Ben Lucido cried out, "James! Jesus!"

"You know him?" asked Murphy.

"James Crayton. He's a neighbor. James, why? Where is my Elizabeth?"

The man stared at the ground, saying nothing.

Ben Lucido grabbed the man's shirt. "Where is my Elizabeth?"

Crayton shook his head and said softly, "I don't know."

Murphy said, "Why don't you ask him, Rocky."

Rocky Blair pulled James Crayton eye-to-eye in such a

manner as to let him know a large measure of pain would accompany future interrogations. "Where is she, you stupid motherfucker? Before I break your fucking face."

"I don't know," said Crayton, shaking. "I didn't kidnap her. I heard about it on television and figured, maybe I . . ."

"Bullshit."

"I couldn't kidnap anyone," said Crayton. "I can't do anything right. My family is leaving me. I'm losing my house."

Rocky nodded and feigned sympathy, pulled him closer and kneed him in the crotch, lifting his feet clear off the ground. Crayton collapsed, then tried to crawl away. Rocky kicked his arms out from under him, sending him sprawling facefirst in the grass.

"That's enough," said Murphy.

"Really?" asked Rocky.

"Really."

Rocky straightened his jacket and dusted off his sleeves. "Okay, then, let's fucking try this again," Rocky said. "Elizabeth Lucido is where?"

"I don't know," Crayton said, cowering. "I saw all the cops at the house, and then I heard the news reports. I thought I could . . ."

Ten feet away Murphy heard Ben Lucido telling Maude, "He was laid off from Grumman a couple of years ago, in the first big wave. I knew he was having problems. He's been working at Caldor," said Ben. "They make him wear this little red vest."

Sunday, Oct. 27

chapter 16

DAYLIGHT SAVING TIME HAD ENDED THAT NIGHT, AND though Frank Murphy had reset his alarm clock when he got home, he need not have bothered. He was awake on his own at five writing Alice a love letter. He swam the harbor at first light, only a single clammer for company, got dressed, and mailed the letter. He made early Mass—at which Father Kukumbato implored the congregation to pray for Elizabeth Lucido—and still had time to snag bagels for the troops before signing in at headquarters at nine.

Murphy's end of the top floor was quiet, as he had expected it would be. He read the Sunday papers at his desk, hunting for mention of the opportunistic neighbor, finding only a synopsis of the official release and a different photo of Elizabeth than the one run in yesterday's editions. Twice Murphy poked his head into the Homicide section and found it empty. The coffee was mud, and the jelly doughnut he grabbed was stale.

Relax, he told himself. All the worker bees were out kicking tail. Everybody she worked with, played with, and quarreled with was being debriefed. Nevermind that the roadblock canvass had been a bust, nobody noticing nothing. Nevermind that the clock was relentlessly ticking away his friend's chances, her life, and all he could do was stalk his office. They had the resources they needed, unlimited overtime, the greenest of lights. Nothing more he could do, short of calling for Federal help, which wouldn't happen in Nassau County during an election year unless the Iranians were massing at the Cross Island Parkway, which, Murphy thought with a chuckle, they actually were.

He drove home at noon and sat on his balcony again, the portable phone by his side, staring across empty Fairhaven Harbor. He was bumbling badly, and he knew it. His entire life was infected with failure, not what he was used to, not at all. Frank Murphy had always had his fun, but Frank Murphy kept his shit squared away. Not this time, it seemed. This time his shit was ragged.

He pictured Alice at her mother's kitchen table, crying, and the shame he felt was painful. He got out his credit card and sent both women roses, then considered taking another swim, and then wondered if that would be excessive. Then he wondered if perhaps he was questioning himself excessively.

He prayed for the phone to ring, and finally it did. Only it was Martin Daly who found him on the couch in front of the Giants game.

"How goes the case?" asked Daly. "Any progress?"

"Not really."

"Damn shame."

"Right."

Daly suggested they duck out for a fast round of golf.

"This is kind of a bad time, Martin."

"It's not an optional appearance," he said. "Pick me up. Ten minutes."

Golf had become the game of choice among Nassau Republicans in recent years, as who in the dog-eat-dog nineties but a well-paid patronage appointee had the time and money to devote to this most difficult of games. What Frank Murphy found funny was how badly most of them played. He'd attended their outings. He'd seen those bent-armed, beer-bellied shanks.

Murphy left a second love letter for Alice by the answering machine, in case she returned, pleading with her not to jump to conclusions, swearing that he loved only her. Then he grabbed his trusty Staffs from the closet and rode the elevator downstairs to the parking lot.

He drove around the head of Fairhaven Harbor, hunched over the steering wheel of his county car, paying attention to the wooded, curvy roads. Martin lived on the tony eastern shore—once a safe haven for whaling captains and rumrunners. On the west side of the harbor—where Frank and Alice lived—homes were more reasonably sized and priced. Frank felt a twinge of jealousy as he rode up the winding driveway past the carriage house, and the duck pond, up to the white colonial that was larger than most churches.

He smelled the pine needles as he stepped from the car, felt the energy occasioned by the close proximity to wealth. Halyards clinked against the flagpole on the wide, sloping lawn, and a stone-and-mortar wishing well was tucked next to the woods. Behind the shoulder of the hill sparkled Fairhaven Harbor; and Frank realized that his condo enjoyed roughly the same view as Martin Daly's, if from smaller quarters and a different slant.

"Murphy!" cried Daly from an upstairs windows. "Grab my clubs from the garage."

"Yassuh, boss," Murphy said under his breath. "Loading the clubs now, boss."

Murphy slammed Martin Daly's monogrammed Mizumo golf bag into the trunk, then walked to the open front door and waited. Daly came jogging from the kitchen, smiling broadly, in kelly green pants and an off-white sweater. "Let's get out of here before she changes her mind," he said.

"Or wants to join us."

"Not funny, Frank," Daly said as he climbed into the

backseat. "Again. You got me? I don't think you're funny. And I don't like the way things are heading on this case, either. You know I get phone calls. I mean, these aren't crack-whores snatched off the street. People care about shit like this. Powerful people with wives and daughters. It makes them think they could be next."

Murphy said nothing, started the car, kept his eyes on the winding driveway. Artie Prefect was in Daly's ear again, that was sure. The D.A. was always sniping at Murphy, hoping to move one of his people into the police commissioner's job; have the whole thing covered.

"What's the story with this Norman Keller fellow?" Daly asked. "He's a committeeman, I'm told. Any reason we should dump him?"

"You sure don't want him talking about his part-time work for the county attorney."

Daly grimaced. "Right."

Seymour Cammeroli was waiting for them at the practice green of the Fairhaven Country Club. He wore white plus fours and his jet-black toupee, the biggest player in Nassau County, bar none. You wanted a county job, you saw Seymour. You wanted a contract, you saw Seymour. You wanted to be governor, you goddamn well better ask his permission. He was an old school pol, and he played rough. (Should a female Dem have appeared in her kindergarten play, she will be labeled by Seymour a known thespian; male liberals were said to favor homogenius rule.) Marsh Beinstock, a fiery, putter-throwing lawyer nicknamed Slingblade, was their fourth.

Seymour shook Frank Murphy's hand and said right away that he was a beginner, that he'd been taking lessons, a gift from his fourth wife. On the back of their golf cart stood six thousand bucks' worth of high-tech weaponry in tour bags Murphy doubted they could carry to the cars. "For some reason she likes to get me out of the house," he said. "Maybe you could give me some tips."

"Have her followed," said Murphy.

"Hah, that's funny," said Cammeroli. "Really fucking funny. You had a little action on the beach last night, I heard."

"False alarm. A desperate man trying to cash in."

Beinstock said, "Nice answer. Ever consider politics?"

Murphy smiled. "Good Lord, no."

Seymour Cammeroli looked sideways at him. "What? You think you're above this shit?"

"That's not what I meant."

"You like your job, Frank?"

"Most of the time . . . very much."

Cammeroli poked his finger at Murphy's chest. "I understand Hind pulled a fast one on you. Made you look like an amateur."

"I'd hardly call arranging counsel pulling a fast one."

"He a viable suspect?"

"No more so than your guy, Norman Keller."

"Horseshit, Murphy. And Keller's a douche-bag errand boy, not a candidate for county executive."

"Right now Hind's simply a very cooperative witness."

"No way, Frankie-Baby. Not when he's goose-stepping on my guy's testicles. What kind of leader would that make me?"

Frankie-Baby, thought Murphy. A nickname of his own gaining currency it seemed, at least in party circles.

Pulling on his golf glove, Marshall Beinstock said, "Really, Frank, I can't believe we're not making hay on this. Son of a bitch maybe kills our Elizabeth—"

"Huge fucking maybe," said Murphy. "And as we're all finding out, she was not exactly your Elizabeth."

"There's no gray area here, if only temporarily?" asked Beinstock. "It's almost Election Day. So I'm thinking something along the lines of 'Stonewall Jackson.'"

Murphy shook his head. "Not unless we want the department to be sued and deserve it."

Seymour settled in behind the wheel of his golf cart, frowning like a baby. "Hind won't hesitate to smear fucking Martin, he gets the chance. And there's no telling what Elizabeth whispered across the pillow."

Murphy said, "No, there isn't. So thank God everything's on the up-and-up."

"Don't get smug, Murphy. You knew her pretty goddamned well, yourself. All those quiet lunches in out-of-the-way places. Don't think this town didn't notice."

Murphy froze somewhere between anger and fear, staring down at the most powerful man in the county, contemplating kicking his fat little ass around the putting green. "You're wrong," said Murphy.

Then Marsh Beinstock remarked out of nowhere that he had heard rumblings of unrest, thought Frank ought to know. Tough town, Mineola. Short careers. "Before you know it, they'll be acting like you killed Elizabeth."

Beinstock's cell phone beeped. He snapped it open and listened, then covered it and turned to Seymour. "Don Neville needs to talk to you."

Seymour took the phone from Beinstock and snapped it shut. "Well, I don't need to talk to that fucking jerk."

Seymour and Beinstock laughed and slapped each other five, then drove up the path to first tee.

Martin Daly elbowed Murphy and said, "You see what I have to put up with? Every goddamn day? And they know everything, Frank. Beinstock's the best political operative alive, bar none. They only look like pussies."

chapter 17

T HAT SUNDAY AFTERNOON MAUDE SENT ROCKY HOME to get some sleep. He had run himself ragged all morning interviewing the girlfriends who had accompanied Elizabeth Lucido on her vacation to Bermuda, the trip from which Justine said Elizabeth had returned so unhappy. Two lived on Long Island. One in Jersey, one in New Rochelle. All had reported a wonderful experience.

Elizabeth's roommate at Castle Harbour, Dana Tunstall, was the only unavailable witness. A New York City corporate lawyer, she was taking depositions in Boston and was due back the middle of next week. Rocky had wrangled a phone number for her, at her hotel.

Maude looked at the twenty-four-hour clock, thought Sunday, noon, maybe, and dialed the number.

"Hello?"

"Dana Tunstall?"

"Who wants to know?"

Maude explained who she was and what she wanted.

"How do I know you're who you say you are?"

"Call me back at Nassau County police headquarters. Homicide. Get the number from Information."

Three minutes later the phone rang.

"Dana Tunstall. How can I help?"

Maude told her.

Dana backed up the other women's stories. "We had a ball, Detective. Beach all day, dance all night. With each other. And Elizabeth was so in love it was sickening. Jackson sent flowers to her room one night, champagne to all our rooms another."

"Wow," said Maude. "You don't see that everyday."

"No kidding, honey."

"Her sister, Justine, said she came home in an awful mood."

"Landing in New York can do that to a person."

Maybe, thought Maude. Maybe not. "Any reason for Justine to be less than forthcoming?"

"None. She worships Elizabeth."

"Elizabeth have any enemies left over from law school, or earlier, if you know?"

"Not to my knowledge. You people close to a resolution? I guess you're not if you're talking to me."

Dana Tunstall was right, Maude thought after hanging up. They were nowhere. And they were less likely to find Elizabeth with every passing second. For a moment Maude harbored the sad sensation that her body had been dumped at sea, weighed down with bricks on the bottom of the sound or the ocean. This time of year, with fewer baymen out there to run across a floating body part, that's what she would do with a corpse.

She picked up the phone and dialed the team watching Norman Keller. "What's he doing?" she asked the undercover cop.

"Believe it or not," said the cop, "he's standing right behind Artie Prefect at this bullshit press conference, waving a little flag. We're in Freeport, on the front steps of the library."

"Good size crowd?"

"You kidding?"

"Yes," said Maude. "I am."

She called Charlie Hotchkiss at home.

Maude said, "I need a tide chart and weather report for the day of the kidnapping. You got one lying around?"

"Why? What have you got?"

"Nothing. Why? What have you got?"

Charlie hesitated, perhaps as a tease. "The same."

"This isn't a race, Charlie, unless it's to save Elizabeth. If you can help me, you damn well better."

"I know that," he said indignantly.

"So what do you think? Both of us off the record, while it still might do Miss Lucido some good."

"You won't like what I think."

"Try me."

"I think political betrayal was dealt with swiftly and harshly."

"That's what you want to find, Charlie."

"These folks do not fuck around, Maude. You're dreaming if you think you'll find a body."

Maude nabbed a butterscotch ball from the middle drawer of her desk, popped it in her mouth. "You've been on the streets too long, Charlie. You're even more cynical than me."

"Got a better explanation?"

"Right now I've got dead ends and dilemmas."

"How's the new house?"

"Gorgeous, I hear."

"Go home and get some sleep, Maude. Tomorrow's another day, and that poor girl is gonna be dead for an awful long time."

"Stay in touch."

Maude left written instructions for the night shift and locked her desk. The boys on the front door wished her a safe trip home.

She found her red Honda Del Sol where she had parked it so many hours earlier and bent to unlock the door, suddenly rose up, glancing about. Someone, probably a card-carrying member of the Ancient Order of Homophobes, had key-scratched LESBO-COP on the driver's door in foot-high letters.

• • •

Frank Murphy watched the Yankee-Braves World Series seventh game at the Newport Grill in Garden City, where so many famous people were regulars he knew he would be left alone. Aside from the odd pat on the back as patrons passed behind him to pee, he was free to celebrate the Yankee win as if nothing in the world were wrong.

After the mound-wrestling and the praising of various lords, mullahs, wise men, and mothers, the American president was calling the Yankee locker-room and saying something about nice guys finishing first. Then the mayor of New York ruined everything, mugging Joe Torre on the podium and yakking on ad nauseam about the spirit of his city, as fascinating as the CEOs who hand beach-towel checks to Tiger Woods every week. Murphy was about to turn his back when he noticed Junior Daly hovering just offstage, but working his way closer. Junior was wearing a Yankee baseball cap with a price tag still attached, waving a cell phone at Joe Torre.

"Who is it now?" asked Torre, ducking a spray of champagne. "The pope?"

"Martin Daly, sir. A huge fan of yours and . . . George . . . Mr. Steinbrenn—"

Torre wrinkled his swarthy brow. "Who?"

"Martin Daly. From Nassau County . . . You guys played golf together once, as guests, at Rockville Links . . ."

Torre was lost, shaking his head.

"Anyway, he wants to congratulate you, and George, of course, and the team—"

Bernie Williams chose that moment to hose down everybody on the podium with champagne, ending any chance that Joe Torre would ever remember who the hell Martin Daly was, leaving not just the voters of Nassau County but all the Free World to imagine that Martin Daly was simply one more New York asshole cling-on.

There was a God, thought Murphy, and He had a wicked sense of humor and, it had to be noted, favored time-delay fuses on his doses of comeuppance. Every dog had his day, in every way, and Murphy knew his own was coming. He shoved aside his beer, left a ten-dollar tip, walked out, and drove home.

Alice Gettings's red Mustang convertible was parked near the gardens at the parking lot entrance, almost as if waiting to greet him. The relief he felt was palpable.

Frank rode up in the elevator, hopeful she was ready to believe his denials, his explanation.

The front door was double-locked so he used his keys, stashed his golf clubs in the hall closet, and hung up his windbreaker, knowing with Alice neatness counted. Her black-leather coat was thrown over the living room couch, not a sign she was sticking around. All the lights were on.

"Alice?"

"Back here."

No hello. No I love you. "Back here" meant the master bedroom. He leaned against the open door and knocked softly.

"You can come in."

Alice was packing a suitcase on the king-size bed. She was wearing black denim jeans and a man-tailored white shirt, and she had never looked prettier to him, particularly from the rear. She turned to face him, her jaw taut, her eyes red and swollen, as if she were in terrible pain.

"Hello, Alice."

"Hi, Frank. Or is it Frankie-Baby?"

"It's Frank, like always. Don't leave."

Alice exhaled loudly, put her hands on her hips. "Why not?"

"There's no reason to, none at all."

Alice turned to the dresser, tossed a handful of panties

into her suitcase. "I see you were so broken up you went golfing."

"I had to go golfing, Alice. Martin called."

"You had to play golf. Then you had to drink?"

"You know the drill."

"Now, I do."

This was going to be rough; Alice sometimes lacked the confidence expected of pretty women, sometimes saw herself as a spinster. When she felt left out, she got defensive as hell.

Frank said, "How's your mom?"

"She had a feeling all along you were too good to be true."

Frank folded his hands in prayer. "Look at me and listen, okay. You need to hear this, whether your mommy likes me or not, whether you're leaving me or not. I deserve at least that much, don't I?"

"I'm not sure what you deserve."

"Then give me the benefit of the doubt. Please?"

"Go ahead."

"Good. Now, I swear to you on my parents' graves that I never had sex with Elizabeth Lucido. You got that? Never. No sex."

"Hey, Frank," said Alice, "whoop-de-damn-doo. You had lunch with her, right? Dinner? Drinks?"

"So?"

That had been a mistake, to try to slough this off. Her eyes went wide, and the nostrils of her pointy nose flared.

"Business lunches," he said. "We shared intelligence."

"A good cop is never hungry, horny, cold, or wet. Didn't you always tell me that?"

"Come on, Alice," he said, "I'm madly in love with you."

"Sure, you're madly in love with me," she said. "Why wouldn't you be? You come and go as you please, I kiss your ass in public, make myself look like a goddamn fool." She slammed a sweater into the suitcase, a pair of blue jeans, a handful of skirts, her jewelry box.

"Don't let them do this to us."

Alice turned and cocked her head. "Who is them, Frank?"

"I don't know."

"See, that's what I don't get—that someone can drag you into the muck. And me, a quiet little banker with a solid reputation, not an enemy in the world. Here I am, after all these years, finally about to marry a really great guy, and then all of a sudden I find out he's a liar and—"

Murphy held up a hand and nodded. "I know."

"You know. But you have no explanation for this assault upon your character."

None you'd care to hear, he thought. "Maybe I have more political enemies than I suspected."

Alice sat down next to her suitcase, folded her hands between her legs. Her hair fell forward, hiding her face. "Lame."

"I know how this hurts."

She peered up at him. "Do you? Do you really know how it feels to get a letter like that?"

The truth was he did not. His heart had never truly been broken, not by a woman. Maybe that's what this was, part of his turn in the barrel—Karma for the crap he'd handed the ladies in his life before Alice. Marta would love this little scene; nasty little Robin would be cackling. Beth. Karen.

Alice said, "I have to go to work tomorrow. I have to look at that fax machine everyday from now on. Do you know how hard it will be for me to trust you? I mean, who watches the police commissioner? Are you really with Wally all those nights? Who can I ask? Wally?"

"You don't need anyone watching me."

"Says you."

He was foundering, wishing this would end, wishing he could hug her. Alice sat ramrod straight, unconvinced.

"Look," he said, "we've still got the Florida trip coming up. Wednesday, right? I'll make it up to you. A little sun, a little sand." He sat down next to Alice on the bed and put his arms around her trembling shoulders. "I'm innocent, I'm telling you."

He watched the decision-making play across her face. She wanted to believe in him; the happy ending she'd hoped for. She'd be nuts to believe him; who lied smoother than cops?

"Want help unpacking?" he asked.

"Don't push your luck, Frank."

"I don't have any luck."

"I'm finding it hard to feel sorry for you, know what I mean?"

Monday, Oct. 28

chapter 18

ONDAY MORNING IN MINEOLA USUALLY MEANT COM-
mittee reports and budget brawls to Frank
Murphy, all the busywork of a modern
municipality. Today it would be worse. At
nine o'clock Murphy sat in his office with Jake Posner,
rereading the Charlie Hotchkiss article in *Newsday*, with
Murphy rapidly gaining the impression that Charlie knew
a lot more than his cops. Hind was named as a possible
suspect in the headline: HIND ON HOT SEAT. His relationship
with the missing woman was examined, and roundly
deplored, by loyalists in both camps. And wasn't that cold-
hearted bastard Martin Daly already courting the sympathy vote, Murphy noticed, telling people that he was too
racked with grief to respond to Hind's latest personal
attacks. Maybe tomorrow, he said. Junior Daly, reached at
home, was quoted as saying, "My dad is naturally devas-
tated, as are all of us who proudly serve the citizens of
Nassau County."

Further down the page volunteer Lillian Paquet of the
Jackson Hind camp expressed outrage at the dirty politics and issued the usual denials regarding any criminal
activities. The story was spiced with a sidebar titled
NASSAU COUNTY: NO PLACE FOR A LADY, which contained an
anonymous quote from a "highly placed county insider":
"And yet Police Commissioner Francis Murphy remains
in charge, a man wholly unqualified for his position. A

man with files the police department refuses to release."
A photograph beside the article showed Frank Murphy,
Seymour Cammeroli, and Marsh Beinstock on a putting
green.

Murphy looked up at Jake. "Those bastards."

"Circa, say, 1983 or something?"

"Yesterday . . . at Fairhaven. Martin Daly was our
fourth."

Jake grimaced. "I notice he ain't in there."

"I noticed that, too."

Jake said, "And what's this shit about secret files?
Even I don't know about that, and I know everything in
this dump."

"Ancient history."

"About to be revisited," said Jake, "in spades."

Murphy said, "Seymour wants a piece of Jackson
Hind, and I won't fucking give it to him."

Jake said, "Then really, just once, couldn't he just come
out and say, 'Hey, Murph, help us cluster-fuck Hind or
we'll cut your bloody nuts off.' "

"Actually, he did. While they were taking this picture.
Yesterday."

Jake thought about this. "Now you know."

"Jackson Hind didn't kidnap Elizabeth. I'd bet my
pension on it, Jake."

"So who did? Any movement?"

"We don't know jack-shit, my man. Whoever did this
was very good or lucky as hell."

"Or both," said Jake.

"Thanks for cheering me up."

IT WAS SUNNY AND MILD THAT MORNING, ONE OF THE LAST PRE-
cious days before the frosts would slip out of the Catskills.
Martin Daly and his entourage were swarming a wood-
paneled meeting hall, working the Valley Stream Italian-
American Club, the Swamp Guidos Martin called them

when none of them were around. He was blustering his way through the good-natured joshing of those Italian-American Yankee fans who had remained with last night's telecast long enough to witness his embarrassment. (He had already scalded Junior, who had shifted the blame to an anonymous functionary, who was at that moment trading in his cell phone for a broom.)

The vacationing district attorney was present, Martin Daly noticed. The sniveling brown-nose was helping Bob Rankel hang a tricolor banner on stage. "Hey, Art," Daly snarled so everyone could hear him. "My signs are down again. What's up with that?"

"Where?"

"All over the fucking place."

Martin Daly turned to Junior, who was chatting with several assistant deputy commissioners of weight and measures. "Right, son? On Sunrise, Merrick, Jericho, Jerusalem . . . sounds like Israel, right?" His audience was warming up, loving this new subject, the Yankees' fiasco forgotten. Martin glared at Prefect again, for effect. "Where the hell were your people, Artie? Watching the game last night? When my signs are down, I look down. I never see none of Jack-off Hind's torn down."

"Now, that's not true," said Prefect, stepping closer and lowering his voice. "The boys have been out almost every night, except when it rains."

"Is that what the problem is? A little rain lately? Who don't want to go out, I want names. Now, take care of it! . . . Junior, take the fucking banner."

Junior replaced the downcast D.A., who then grabbed his black raincoat and fled the hall; and Martin Daly took delight in the sight of the top law enforcement officer in the county scampering off to obey his whims. It made him look cool in a crisis, ever in command. You couldn't pay for something like that.

Beat *Newsday* showing Murphy golfing while powerful women were vanishing.

Daly looked around for that asshole Frank Murphy,
and realized that the police commissioner was once
more absent from their little brigade, no doubt fuming,
no doubt with Elizabeth Lucido as an official excuse.
Phony bastard, thought Daly. Just like me, working his
end of the goodie bag. A fucking mistake he had been.

Elizabeth's choice, he recalled. Maybe he was in on
the coup as well, pretending to investigate these disappearances while the sand was running out of the Daly
hourglass. God knows it was a tactic his people frequently employed.

Then Martin spotted a couple of local committeemen
who had been less than energetic in his last campaign.
He gave them thumbs-up.

"Kick his ass, Marty."

"Consider it done."

"You the man."

"What's for lunch?" Daly asked.

"Lasagna, a nice salad, a little vino, whadyathink."

FRANK MURPHY, ROCKY BLAIR, AND MAUDE FLEMING SPENT
most of the morning in the Homicide conference room
with Lisa Tibaldi, who had served as Elizabeth's executive
assistant for the last two years. They were reconstructing
the past few months of Elizabeth's life from her office
records, her phone records, her photo album, her phone
book. They had pored over Elizabeth's business planner
from mid-February to the day she had disappeared,
which seemed to cover most of the hours of her life.
Elizabeth had used a code, a shorthand of initials; they
had been able to decipher stolen time with Jackson, visits with parents and sister. She had played racquetball
with friends now and then. Jogged alone and noted the
mileage. Worked like a dog.

"Who is BB?" asked Maude.

Lisa Tibaldi didn't know.

"Doesn't ring a bell," Rocky said without looking up from the victim's personal checking statements.

"Why, Maude?" said Murphy.

Maude said, "He—or she—is penciled in twice in the month preceding Jackson's appearance, once in Mineola, once in Albany, three weeks apart. And I mean penciled in. You can barely read it. Everything else she wrote in ink. Then Elizabeth meets Jackson in New Hampshire, and draws a heart around his initials and the date, and that's the last we see of BB."

"Barbara Bennett," said Rocky. "From payroll."

Murphy said, "She's sixty if she's a day, Rock."

"Just thinking of BBs I know. Beau Brummel, Bob Barker, Beetle Bailey, Bobby Bonilla, Bill Bratton."

"That hurts," Murphy said, "that you could even think of *him*."

Maude turned to a terminal and ran a simple search through the Nassau County payroll. The attempt failed to produce anyone even remotely related to Elizabeth in official duties with those initials. Certainly nobody who fit the target age and sex of the suspect. Young enough to be strong. Most likely male.

So maybe not a county employee, thought Murphy. Not this relatively closed business, but politics, a larger sample and an open gutter. Her involvement in the betrayal of Martin, as always, loomed large in any theories; but the thought of public officials resorting to murder to maintain primacy was hard to swallow.

Murphy got up and walked back to his office, knowing his people were lost, as far away as ever from the reveal-codes, the algebra of the explanations, behind this case.

Annie Anderson told him Jackson Hind had called, requesting an update.

"What'd you tell him?"

"That all the brave police were out catching bad guys. I said you would call him back when you had time."

"Always have a story ready, right, Annie?"

"Now, where'd I learn that?"

chapter 19

T HE AFTERNOON WIND WAS RAISING A SUDDEN, NASTY chill. Frank Murphy, who had arrived late for a rally across from the Great Neck train station, turned up the collar on his gray suit jacket and scanned the disappointing crowd, spotted Junior Daly smoking a cigarette behind the grandstand. He joined the handsome heir-apparent. "Junior," he said. "How you been? What'd I miss?"

"Everything, Frank. Actually. Nicely done. Again. Of course your golf buddy Seymour already boogied. He told Dad he didn't want to be associated with a 'less than successful' event."

"Good man in the trenches, that Seymour."

"Yeah. And now Daddy's all pissed off because Elections told him one of his oldest buddies just gave big money to Hind."

"Covering his bet," said Murphy. "Lot of that going around, I hear. Is there a fallback plan for Junior Daly?"

"Ireland. The Daly family farm. How about you? We gonna be neighbors?"

Murphy smiled. "Got a minute?"

"Sure."

Murphy pulled Junior into the shadows of the grandstand, stood close enough to smell the pot on his breath.

"You go straight home after the fund-raiser Thursday night?"

Junior eyed Murphy up and down, offended. "Yeah, why? I was drunk and went home."

"What time?"

"How the fuck would I know."

"Where were you all day Friday?"

"Sleeping it off. Those health insurance motherfuckers were buying me shots of Jaegermeister. What could I do?"

"Till when?"

"I slept until maybe three in the afternoon, I guess. Then I played golf."

Murphy stepped closer. "You know you stink of reefer, Junior?"

Junior sniffed his breath in his hand.

"You hate Dad so much, why not just go to work for Hind?"

Junior looked around, as if someone might be watching them. Murphy waited for a personal counterattack, perhaps mention of the *Newsday* piece. He didn't get one, he got a stupid shrug, so Murphy asked Junior about Norman Keller, expecting another stupid answer.

"Keller's a blow job," Junior said. "The last white Republican in Roosevelt."

"A player?"

"I just told you."

Murphy watched staffers begin breaking down the mobile bandstand. "You got blow jobs who are players," said Murphy.

"Not to hear Daddy tell it. Everyone in our camp is world class, top drawer, giants, except you and me, of course. We are mediocrities, compromises, sorry-ass losers dragged along—"

"Get help, Junior, really."

Junior grinned. "So what'd that loser Keller do?"

"Probably nothing."

Junior nodded.

"Anybody you know hate Elizabeth Lucido?"

"Hate's a pretty strong word."

"So's kidnapping."

Junior turned up the collar on his jacket. "Some people didn't like her style—which was pushy, as you may know. The gang at Stonehenge Investments didn't love her—some deal she squashed—but hate? Pissed off would be more accurate. Resentful. Lotta real Puerto Ricans didn't like her."

"No?"

"Too big for her britches."

"What about Baltusrol Vail? I understand Elizabeth hated his guts."

Junior leaned close and lowered his voice. "Do me a favor, Frank, okay, don't even mention that man's name. Okay? Fun is fun, and he's no fucking fun."

"Who, exactly, is Stonehenge?"

"Money management outfit in Westbury. Now there's some major players. Making everybody money: See Artie Prefect's new suits, Seymour's brand-new Range Rover with all the trimmings. Bastards strut around like Swiss bankers. Doing everybody's pension planning these days, except mine. Running IPOs. Real estate combines. Jeez, I hope the old man's not blowing my bundle."

"Figure Kym will do that," said Murphy.

Junior's eyes flashed first anger at Murphy, then respect. "You want to find out who took Elizabeth? Check her past. Before she came on board she used to run with a pretty fast crowd."

Which was horseshit, Murphy was thinking as he walked back to his car. Elizabeth Lucido never ran with a fast crowd in her life, unless we're talking academically, or the track team. Junior probably considered all Puerto Ricans criminals.

Murphy climbed behind the wheel, grabbed his cell phone off the dashboard, and checked in with Homicide. "What's up, Rocky?"

"Hind's hair and semen match up with the condom, as expected. He could still be our boy."

"Too easy."

"That's what Maude says."

"Listen to her."

"But according to Crime Scene, if there was a second visitor in her house that night, he left us nothing to work with. No trace evidence. Bupkus."

"Like this was all carefully planned and executed? Then sanitized?"

"Or she walked out willingly. Usually, a guy sneezes and we know what kind of car he drives."

"Pros?"

"Good ones."

"Where's our Maudie now?"

"If I told you I knew, I'd be lying."

"She looking at all hopeful to you lately?"

"Nope. Meanwhile, I'm digging through Hind's closets. Neighbors and friends. Ruling him out."

"You be discreet, you hear me?"

"Promise."

Murphy hung up, thinking: Pros. To take out a little girl. An unarmed, skinny little girl.

He started his car and headed from the parking lot. A uniformed cop waved him through the barrier and saluted.

" 'Night, sir."

"Thank you, Officer."

Murphy switched on the AM radio and listened to the evening news as he drove home, mostly a rehash of the *Newsday* articles naming Jackson Hind as a suspect, questioning his relationship with the victim, quoting unnamed sources, which Frank Murphy knew meant

Cammeroli, or one of his lackeys. Marsh Beinstock probably.

Fucking assholes didn't care if they endangered innocent people or emboldened a killer. It was all about points in a poll, and they were taking them.

Nice kid, that Elizabeth, they were saying.

Sure gonna miss her.

Tuesday, Oct. 29

THEY DESCENDED LIKE LOCUSTS THAT MORNING ON THE county legislature's monthly public safety meeting—usually a snoozefest, with seniors in wheelchairs, on crutches, heads wrapped in bandages, armed with complimentary brown-bag lunches from the Hind campaign, a highly orchestrated dramatization of the plight of crime victims in Nassau County since Frank Murphy took command of the police department. They carried pictures of lost property, sick children in hospital beds. They stood on line at the lectern and took turns slamming Murphy.

"We're losing the county to the element," the ancient ones said. "Crime gangs from Queens take the train here to work."

An elderly black woman shuffled to the lectern, the handle of a cardboard dagger protruding from her side. "Mr. Frank," she said, "last Thursday I was robbed leaving Bingo, and this is what coulda happened to me. And Mr. Frank, in Roosevelt we stay away from windows, sleep on the damn floor, get up and pick up the spent shells. This one young crack dealer swipes my lawn furniture and sets up shop in my driveway."

Murphy, trapped behind a microphone and water pitcher at the witness table, thought they were acting like he was pulling the jobs. He made eye contact with Jackson Hind, who was leaning against the wall in the back of the assembly hall, got back the blank stare of the assassin.

Martin Daly stepped to the table, covered Murphy's mike. "I'm ready to bolt when you are. We don't have to take this shit."

The concept of flight disconcerted Murphy, and he said nothing for a moment, stared into space.

"Did you hear what she said, Commissioner Murphy?" Jackson Hind called out from the peanut gallery. "One of the little people needs help . . . and the problem is not bunker shots—"

"The drug epidemic is a national problem," Murphy said, sliding onto autopilot. "It has its roots in—"

"We don't need a lecture on society's ills. These people have a message for you."

Murphy suffered silently through four more whippings until Daly finally called off the dogs. "The Police Commissioner understands your concerns and will address them. What else would you like?"

"A new commissioner," someone called out from the back of the crowded room. "A new county executive."

The crowd grew brave and cheered itself.

Daly said, "Doesn't anyone want to talk about the budget? We're considering historic reductions in the workforce."

"Reduce the workforce by two right now!"

Even Murphy had to smile at that, his cheeks aflame, his armpits soaked. Then the audience fell silent as Junior Daly helped a toothless old black man in a Mets jersey to the lectern.

"You got to respect the po-lice," the man said hoarsely. "Why, one time I ate too many peanut butter balls and almost died. Po-lice saved my ass. Officer Murphy right there."

No one got it, except Frank Murphy, that this was the best thing Junior could force anybody to say about him.

Legislators coughed, turned to their staffs. The audience laughed nervously.

"Phenylbarbital," Junior said helpfully. "He means he ate too many phenylbarbitals."

Which only made everyone laugh harder.

"Time out, everybody," said Hind, striding to the lectern, taking charge. "That's enough of the partisan crap—from both sides. We have serious business to do, here and elsewhere, like finding Elizabeth Lucido."

"We are looking for her as hard as we can," Murphy said.

"By golfing with the party bosses? I mean I know it was a Sunday, but if you were missing, wouldn't you want the cops—"

The crowd roared its approval, drowned out the rest of Hind's speech. Murphy watched Martin Daly and his entourage heading for the fire exit, glancing at their fat gold watches, looking worried, waving "no" at Charlie Hotchkiss and the horde, an act that said: Places to go, people to see, the sky is falling, the sky is falling.

Murphy stood up. "Like you said: I have work to do."

MAUDE FLEMING WAS LOCKED ON STONEHENGE INVESTMENTS. She began with a Dun and Bradstreet, then went to the New York State business records, and there found general filings had been made in April of the preceding year. Stonehenge was duly registered with Nassau County and Hempstead Town, doing business as financial advisors. Their lawyer of record was Marsh Beinstock.

New. And big. And influential. To the best of Maude Fleming's knowledge, that didn't come cheap in Nassau County.

And now, rummaging through the victim's office again, she was bothered that the file Elizabeth Lucido must certainly have grown for them was not to be found, not on any computer disks in the safe, nothing even close on the hard drive index.

Maude considered that perhaps it was filed under another name and made a note to check this oddity further, with Martin Daly. Perhaps there had been orders to hold Stonehenge at arm's length.

Maude started in on Elizabeth Lucido's overflowing IN box, and it wasn't long before the mountains of missives and columns of figures grew blurred and nonsensical. Her stomach growled and her back ached. She removed her reading glasses and rubbed her eyes, then put her head on the blotter, thinking she'd rest for just five minutes, no more, you had to pace yourself on a case like this.

She'd get back to it fresh then, and find Elizabeth, maybe tied up somewhere, hungry and scared but safe. A crummy motel room was where Maude liked to think of her as being held. She would find that dump and save her, in the nick of time. Yes. She would.

The telephone rang, three times. Maude sat up abruptly, picked up the receiver. "Miss Lucido's office."

"What's up, partner?"

Maude ran her hand over her close-cropped hair. "Not a thing, Rock."

Rocky said, "I talked to her parents before. They're ready to sell their house to up the reward."

Maude stared at the desktop picture of the Lucidos, knowing, as few people ever do, what they were going through. Lord knows she had seen it enough.

"We didn't find any connections at all between Elizabeth and Mrs. Whitcomb beside the Caucus?" Rocky asked.

Maude said, "They shopped a few of the same stores. That's it. Different clubs, different schools, different tax brackets. No close friends in common."

"We gonna check those stores, maybe their employees, their delivery boys?"

"You got it. Everybody, everything."

"Cool," said Rocky.

"The wolves are circling, partner. If we're gonna keep Frank Murphy around, we'd better solve this quick. Prominent victims at election time: Makes all the difference in the world."

IN AN ATTEMPT TO MITIGATE THE DAMAGE DONE THAT MORNING at the Legislature, Martin Daly ordered Frank Murphy to be the featured spin doctor on that week's *News of Nassau*, a cable talkie hosted by Kymberly Scallia-Daly.

"What if I get a question I can't answer?" asked Murphy.

"You won't," said Martin Daly. "I'm boffing the hostess."

While the station ran a promo for privatizing Nassau's parks, Kym joined them on the set. She wore a perky black cocktail dress, and she kissed her husband on the cheek, then patted Frank's clammy hand. "Just follow my lead," she said. "This isn't *60 Minutes*. Then we'll get lunch and some ice-cold Bloodys. I'm totally famished, I swear." A college girl in a peasant shirt wiped Frank down, miked his jacket, slipped offstage.

Kym smiled at camera one. "Welcome, everyone, to a show which I feel is both necessary and important, to answer recent charges questioning not only the efficiency of the Police Department but the character of its commissioner. Here to respond are County Executive Martin Daly and Police Commissioner Frank Murphy. Mr. Daly, maybe you can tell us what is going on here, vis-à-vis Frank Murphy and the disappearing women of Nassau County."

Martin Daly smiled benevolently at his wife. "I'd be glad to, Kym. What's going on here is nothing more than a malicious attack by Democrats on one very good police commissioner. Frank Murphy has innovated numerous community programs, raised the morale in the department, and shown enormous concern for the citizens. His efforts should be applauded, not derided."

"Hasn't the crime rate risen recently?"

"A statistical anomaly, Kym, opportunistically used by my opponents to avert attention from their own pessimistic, tax-and-spend policies of failure. Truly, I find it sad."

Kymberly turned to Frank. "What about the two missing women? Mrs. Whitcomb and Deputy—"

Murphy said, "We're not even sure the cases are connected. It's the media has them linked, not the Police Department."

"Are the charges of incompetence fair?"

"The charges," said Murphy, "are horse hockey."

Kym smiled. "Let's take some calls from our audience. Here's Edith, from Chicken Valley Road."

"Hi, Kymberly. Longtime viewer, first-time caller."

Murphy could have sworn he recognized the husky voice of District Attorney Prefect's wife.

"Welcome aboard," said Kym.

"I wanted to ask the commissioner about those secret files mentioned in *Newsday?* What's in them that he doesn't want known?"

Martin Daly said magnanimously, "Let me take that one." He pulled a piece of paper from his jacket pocket and began reading: "In 1976, Police Officer F. M. Murphy did confront two subjects who had just robbed a Franklin Square bank of six thousand dollars U.S. currency. Both subjects were carrying shotguns which extruded from raincoats they wore on a sunny day. Officer Murphy drew his weapon and attempted to place both subjects under arrest outside the bank. Subject Latice raised a weapon. Officer Murphy shot and killed both subjects. Officer Murphy's actions were in accordance with department rules and regulations, and the finest traditions of the Nassau County police."

Edith followed up. "So did they ever return Officer Murphy to street patrol?"

Frank leaned toward the camera. "There was quite an

uproar from the community, and it took me a while to get my bearings again. Shooting two people is not as easy as you think."

He could have gone on. Murphy had started attending daily mass after the shootings, to ease his guilt and to rid himself of frequent nightmares featuring the women he loved in coffins, hands folded, dead.

"And, of course," said Martin Daly, "you were promoted to sergeant shortly thereafter, so the question is moot."

Murphy said, "At least it was then."

IT WAS ALMOST DARK AS ROCKY AND MAUDE HEADED DOWN-stairs from the Homicide office, beat-tired and thoroughly discouraged. They had spent the early afternoon grilling local burglars just released on parole, the shank of the day interviewing more Friends and Family, each weeping citizen repeating the mantra: Elizabeth was steady, honest, no one would want to hurt her. This had to be random, the roll of the dice. Maude and Rocky had spent the early evening explaining their lack of progress to Murphy, whom they presumed was now explaining it to County Executive Martin Daly.

Maude hoped the night shift would take their messages accurately and recognize when something was important. She knew how fast a trail turned cold when critical evidence went uncollected, when follow-up questions went unasked.

Rocky offered to buy Maude a beer before she blew town, which she politely refused. She was late to have her hair trimmed, she explained, then meeting friends in Port Jefferson. "What are you gonna do?"

"A burger, that beer I mentioned. Snooze like hell."

"See you in the morning. Sixish okay?"

"Sure," said Rocky. "Why should we have a life?"

chapter 21

ARTIN DALY WAS IN THE LIMO WITH HIS STAFF when he caught the end of a Jackson Hind radio ad chiding him, Martin Daly, for projects that ran behind schedule, that fell apart before they were completed, reminding voters of a walkway at Nassau Community College that collapsed two weeks before it was to open for pedestrian traffic.

"He's fucking right," Martin said to his men. "Jack-off Hind is fucking right. Like when is the Victim's Center gonna be finished? I promised that last campaign, and people remember it."

His men looked out the windows of the limo. The sun was going down in an explosion of orange and red that even Martin paused to admire. He glanced at his only son, who sat next to him, drinking iced coffee and smoking a foul-smelling Marlboro like the idiot he was turning out to be. "What can you do to help here, Junior? Anything?"

"Huh?"

"You can dial a phone, right?"

"Touch-Tone and rotary."

Martin flipped through his pink-slip messages, sarcastically looking for something Junior could help with. "Hey, Beth Hopkins has a call in at long last. Finally made her mind up, I guess. You feel like boinking Legs for a larger contribution?"

Junior rolled his eyes. The phone rang, and Martin grabbed it.

Seymour Cammeroli yelled in his ear, perhaps to make himself heard above the pounding disco beat in the background: "How'd Maude Fleming find Stonehenge?"

"I don't know," said Martin. "I didn't know she had."

"Beinstock called. That bitch has been checking them out."

"Why?"

"I don't know why, Martin, because Stonehenge has nothing to do with nothing, ever. I thought you understood that."

"I do. I agree."

"So what could she know, Martin?"

"Nothing." Martin watched his useless henchmen watching him. "Routine."

"It goddamn well better be," Cammeroli said. "Or if it's more, you better come see me in person, you got it? And I want the traitor who flapped his gums."

"Understood."

Martin replaced the phone and stared out the window, boiling. He hated being spoken to in that tone of voice. Maybe a judgeship wouldn't be so bad. Then he'd only have to deal with these people and their ilk when they fucked up.

"Hungry, boss?" asked Rankel from up front.

"You trying to piss me off, Bob? My goddamn stomach's in a bloody fucking knot."

Rankel said, "Sorry."

"What'd Seesmore want?" asked Mike Barclay.

"None of your goddamn business."

Martin wondered angrily if the right people were on the Lucido case, from Frank Murphy down to Rocky Blair. From the beginning, everybody had said they were the best, Rocky and Maude. But maybe that wasn't good enough here. Maybe this case called for something else. "This detective Rocky," he said over the seat to Rankel. "A fucking asshole, or what?"

"Maude Fleming is so good it doesn't matter. They could pair her with a jackass."

"I'm telling you, it looks like they have. But I don't

see it, you know—this chick's alleged brilliance? Not yet, anyway."

Rankel said, "I'm telling you, boss, she knows her stuff."

Junior said, "You ask me, she thinks her shit don't stink."

Martin regarded his only son. "Finally, we agree. I think she's a full-of-shit lesbo-warrior who hates men, and I don't like where she's going. In fact, I think we probably need to keep tabs on what Rocky and Bulldagger are doing."

"Meaning?" asked Junior.

"Meaning from now on I want you to personally keep an eye on the investigation. See who they're talking to. Sort out what's going on. We owe that to Elizabeth, right? I mean, what the fuck, you're free most days, right? We've established that."

"Actually," said Junior, "I think that's a pretty good idea."

Martin Daly didn't know if it was a good idea or not, but it had come to his mind and he had said it out loud, so it must at least be okay. "Let's get a goddamn back-channel on this thing before it drags everybody down."

Rankel said, "We're here, boss."

"Where exactly is here, Bob?"

"Woodmere Jewish Center. Your six o'clock."

Martin knew by heart the speech he would give, his Yiddish-sprinkled tale of wealthy Jews who had helped make Nassau County great, folks just like them who gave and so they prospered, praise Moses . . . Robert Moses. He would state what he had done to keep the Palestinian hordes from Queens at bay, and close with his great love for Israel or a Jewish joke, depending on how it was going, the yawn factor.

Oh, how times have changed, thought Martin. He remembered when he couldn't buy a hat.

• • •

IT WAS HAPPY HOUR AT THE FAIRHAVEN GRILL, AND CHARLIE Hotchkiss occupied a corner booth, sipping a Coke and going over his notes on the afternoon's events: At twenty minutes to three he had observed Kym Scallia-Daly's red Miata convertible roll from the television station, top down, Kym at the wheel, auburn hair tucked under a white visor. Charlie had already confirmed with Kym's secretary that Kym was in a very important programming meeting and couldn't possibly be disturbed.

Charlie had followed her at a distance to a shopping center on 25A.

Kym parked in the fire lane, climbed out, left the top down, and casually wiggled into the dry cleaners, then the card store for lottery tickets, which she was scratching and tossing away as she walked back to her car. So I got her for a no-show job, illegal parking, and littering, thought Charlie, peering through his video camera, recording footage for his investigative piece.

Kym tossed an armload of men's suits into her tiny trunk and sat in the open car, fixing her hair, fiddling with her radio.

Waiting, Charlie realized. Looking at her watch.

She was all sex and rebellion, bristling. A bad girl, thought Charlie, married to a bully.

Kym picked up her cell phone and dialed someone angrily, listened for a time without speaking, then flipped the phone closed and drove to the far, empty corner of the lot.

Two minutes later a black pickup truck flying the stars-and-bars of the Confederacy parked next to her, and a fat blonde in Harley-wear climbed down from the cab.

Kym reached to open the passenger door of the Miata.

The truck-driving woman climbed in and passed Kym something palm to palm, accepted money in return, counted it, got out of the car, and hiked her fat butt back into her truck.

She was out of the parking lot before Kym got the convertible top up, before Kym disappeared below the dashboard, then came up wiping her face.

After that the First Lady of Nassau was off to the Jockey Club for drinks. She sat at the bar and talked only to the bartender. She had three vodka tonics and four cigarettes while she picked at a salad. She went to the ladies' room twice.

Then it was out to the car for a little more gearbox drug abuse, a lot more talking on the cell phone, finally arriving at an early Fairhaven Grill happy hour at five-fifteen.

The club was dark. Charlie, in a corner booth, set his gym bag/camera on the table, and watched Kym settle in at the bar.

The bartender obviously knew her. He gave her a ten-second French kiss over the bar. He was younger than her, maybe thirty, rock-hard, crew-cut. He mixed her a martini without her asking. She leaned over and French-kissed him again to show both her cleavage and thanks.

He brought her a wad of singles, and she pumped the jukebox full and picked a hundred songs before another customer could stumble into the darkness. She liked rough songs, Charlie noticed over the next thirty minutes: Melissa Etheridge, Springsteen, the Doors. She mouthed the lyrics without error.

Then Charlie got tape of her dancing with one of the working suits who filled the club. Her laugh was loud and bawdy as she rubbed her crotch on his thigh.

At seven-thirty Kym cashed out.

The bartender dried his hands on his apron and walked her to her car, then bent her over the hood for a long grope, which Kym returned with ardor, her leg circling his waist. When they broke apart she had his earlobe in her teeth. She drove home remarkably well, thought Charlie, for a woman who had partied all day.

Charlie watched her turn into her driveway, then he made a U-turn, heading for home, wondering if Martin was waiting for her, if he had any idea.

He almost felt sorry for the county executive.

And then Charlie was thinking what an easy target Kym Scallia-Daly would make, should there be a kidnapper picking off prominent Republican women who also happened to be beautiful.

That she was a bimbo might not be held against her.

"SOLLY GORDON, DEEP POCKETS. DR. IRV GOLD, ALWAYS GOOD for ten grand. Gary Steinberg . . ."

Junior Daly stood in the rear of the crowded synagogue, thinking his new duties could be a great way to impress his father, to repent for past blunders. He would follow the cops and figure out what they were doing, then solve the case a nanosecond before they did. Grab himself some face-time. It was never too early to position himself to inherit his father's job. In fact it was downright late.

And, he thought, smiling at the elderly Semites checking him out, he could borrow all the high-tech cop equipment he wanted. He could violate people's lives and civil rights. This was right up his alley, work one could perform stoned, with an outside chance to look as good as he had looked at the Pine Barrens wildfires, his handsome face streaked with soot as if he had personally rescued two dwarf pines and a chipmunk.

As his father got teary-eyed about the unbreakable bonds between Israel and Nassau County, Junior spun on his heel into the lobby, whipped out his cell phone.

"Hello?" said Norman Keller.

"Norman, it's Junior Daly. What do you want, kid?"

"Junior, I've been calling you and calling you. For days."

"Right. And now I'm calling you back." Junior read the bulletin board, announcements of services, reminders to tithe, a flier trumpeting Jackson Hind's equal time. "So, Norman, what do you need?"

"Nothing. I took care of it myself."

"Good boy. We like initiative. Say, listen, Norman, I need to meet with you, okay? I think I got a great opportunity for you." Junior ducked through the heavy doors and outside into the gentle October evening. He paced the empty sidewalk as he outlined the plan, watched Rankel sleeping behind the wheel of the limo, his head tipped back, his cap down low. "You'd be doing a great service for the county, and the party, most importantly, for me."

"I see," Norman said with rather insufficient enthusiasm.

"This puts you in with me at the ground floor, dipstick. You understand? My dad ain't gonna stay in office forever."

"But your father knows about this? We have his blessings?"

"While my father retains plausible deniability, he has in fact approved our mission. And hey, I never forget a friend. Neither does my dad. You know that. We'll meet tomorrow, get started right away."

"Thank you," said Norman, "for your trust in me."

Junior returned to the foyer in time to hear his father wrapping up, promising to be ever mindful of Hebrew concerns, ever vigilant at the barriers of hate, skipping the Jesse Jackson joke.

The crowd offered warm if not overwhelming applause; and Junior had the feeling things were taking a turn for the better. He told his father so when they were back in the limo. "Let's wait until we count the house," said Martin. "I didn't like the looks of those cheap motherfuckers."

Wednesday, Oct. 30

chapter 22

THE MORNING SUN FOUND JACKSON HIND READING the *Wall Street Journal* and eating cornflakes at his desk in the family house in Cold Spring Harbor. Over the stone fireplace behind his chair was a charcoal portrait of Elizabeth, sketched that summer by a SoHo street artist for fifty bucks. A bachelor's degree from Princeton hung next to credentials from law school at Washington and Lee.

His father had been a Federal judge. His mother's family was more accomplished, doctors and architects, mostly. They were in Palm Beach now, thank God, playing golf, afloat forever on stocks and bonds. They hadn't phoned home lately, which meant they didn't know of his difficulties, which meant the wire services had not picked up the story or his parents were truly disconnected from public life. He had never mentioned Elizabeth Lucido; now they would know her as a name linked to disaster.

For the last few years Jackson had lived alone in the big house, paying the taxes and utilities, the mortgage long ago retired. His few neighbors in this tony wooded enclave were cardiologists and stockbrokers, largely registered Republicans, though some had been kind enough to contribute. It wasn't about political philosophy on the local level, anyway. It was about money, and jobs—178,000 of them, working for Long Island's 968 taxing units. The Republicans were for the Good Old

Days. The Democrats other than Donald Neville and family were for Good Government. It was hard, Jackson knew, for the average voter to tell them apart. Now that he was a suspect in a crime, the issues would never get a hearing.

Now it was war. Murphy's spanking at the Legislative hearing had only been a warm-up. Jackson had plans to open a second front. Any losses he took, he would make them pay double; and he had already lost the woman he loved.

He heard brakes squeal at the end of his driveway, the whop of his *Newsday* hitting the concrete, and he walked outside into the quiet dawn. He picked up the newspaper and saw the front page held a series of photographs of Police Commissioner Murphy and an "unknown associate," drinking milk shakes in a diner, eating hot dogs in a diner, drinking coffee in a diner. The multiple headlines read: MURPHY'S LAW . . . COPS AT A LOSS.

He opened the paper and found three articles about Elizabeth. He stared at Elizabeth's head-and-shoulders photograph and doubled over in grief.

DOWN THE BLOCK, FRANK MURPHY SAT IN HIS POLICE CAR, watching Jackson Hind through binoculars, thinking: If this show of emotion was calculated, this bastard was the best actor ever born. Murphy rolled up as Hind headed back up the driveway. He tapped the horn.

Hind turned to look at the unmarked car, bent low to see who was driving. "Martin bust you back to the street?"

"You keep it up, he will."

Jackson shrugged. "This is a contact sport, you know?"

"Hey. Whatever. Can I come in?" asked Murphy. "Maybe for a cup of coffee?"

"Without a warrant?"

"Right. Just because I want to."

Hind looked up and down his block. "No."

Murphy stared at Jackson Hind, thinking, I don't blame you one little bit. Nevertheless, he was glad only he was present to witness the refusal. One could only imagine the mileage a man like, say, the district attorney, could make from such a response.

Murphy said, "For Elizabeth's sake."

Hind said, "What do you want to know about?"

"Your current impressions and suspicions. Also, Elizabeth's relationship to the Puerto Rican community. We're hearing she was not terribly popular. I'd like to talk about your political plans."

"She was generous and beautiful and very well known. She gave money and time to the Latino community. She showed her face, and she returned her phone calls. Wrong tree, Commissioner, but at least you're being thorough. Nobody from the barrio hated her. You've been lied to."

"Did Elizabeth ever mention Stonehenge Investments?"

"Sure," he said. "She said they were making people big money, fifty, sixty percent a year."

"The stock market hasn't been that good."

"They play more than stocks. Like real estate ventures, incubating law firms and engineering firms that miraculously get county business on monstrously inefficient projects. Now they want to build a monorail linking those projects."

"Did exposing them figure in your strategy?"

"Not really. They're not the only ones by any stretch of the imagination. Just the newest configuration of old names."

"Would Elizabeth keep a file on them?"

Hind said, "Sure."

"We can't find it anywhere. Not home or in her office."

"You've checked her car? The trunk. She kept work everywhere, in her glove compartment."

Murphy nodded. "We'll go through it again."

Across the street Hind's bathrobed neighbor was bending for his *Newsday*. He stayed that way to eye them over.

" 'Morning, Clarence."

"Jackson."

Neighbor Clarence headed back up his driveway, shaking his head.

"You know a guy named Baltusrol Vail?" asked Murphy.

"I've heard of him."

"What do you think?"

"I think he owns a lot of things. People, too."

"Look," said Murphy. "Maybe somebody in your organization knew of your romance and made a deal for themselves, or thought you were selling them out, maybe one of your closest people—"

"I think of it every night, Frank, for hours on end. Never fear. I'd turn in my own brother if I thought he'd hurt Elizabeth."

"I'm serious. Don't trust anybody."

"Said the police commissioner."

IT WASN'T YET EIGHT O'CLOCK THAT WEDNESDAY MORNING AND Frank Murphy, Maude Fleming, and Rocky Blair were in Murphy's office going over one more time what little they had learned: That Deputy County Executive Elizabeth Lucido had attended a fund-raiser in Bellmore on the night she disappeared. That she had talked to many people, including Seymour Cammeroli, Norman Keller, Martin Daly, Junior Daly, and God knows who else. The conversations were allegedly innocuous. She had arrived home around eleven o'clock. Her current boyfriend—and candidate for her boss's job—arrived within minutes. Jackson Hind, when interviewed, said he made love to Elizabeth and left her unharmed around one o'clock. A witness heard his car drive away. After that nobody on her block or the block behind her saw anybody come in or go out of the house. The next morning her front door was found ajar and she was gone. Dogs followed her scent through the backyard and out into the block behind her house, where the trail ended at the curb. The only ransom demand had been bogus.

She had to be dead, Murphy was thinking. Every day this was less a kidnap case than a full-blown homicide investigation.

"So far all the head-case burglars have alibis," said Rocky. "We're still using people from Vice to help, but the traditional stoolies ain't worth shit here. Our victim didn't have any bad habits."

"That we know about yet," said Murphy.

"Right."

Maude said, "Rocky got hold of Norman's rather substantial phone bills and AOL charges."

"He's a perve, right?" said Murphy.

"Massive monthly bill. So now we're talking to his neighbors, old teachers, people who'd know if he was capable of this."

"Teachers always know, don't they?" said Murphy.

Maude said, "Usually first."

"You want to keep following him?" asked Murphy.

"I don't know. According to the team, he doesn't act like a man with a deep dark secret. Let's give it another day."

"Fair enough. What else?"

Maude said, "I'm gonna see Cammeroli later this morning, see what he'll tell me about Stonehenge and Baltusrol Vail."

"Be tactful, Maude. And mention Jackson Hind as little as possible, or he'll call a bloody press conference before you're halfway back here."

"Got it."

Jake the Snack stuck his face in Murphy's office, followed up with the rest of his big round body. " 'Horse hockey'?" he said to Murphy. "What the hell is horse hockey? Excuse me, Maude."

"Something my mother used to say. You got the point."

"Seen today's rag yet?"

"Haven't had the pleasure," said Murphy.

Jake handed him the day's *Newsday*. "Check it out."

Murphy scanned the front page, saw himself and his brother guzzling hot dogs and milk shakes. In the article Charlie Hotchkiss revived memories of Long Island's unfortunate political history where diners were concerned.

Murphy flipped the paper open to a flurry of articles questioning the pace of the investigation. One of the articles quoted a grieving Mr. Whitcomb, who was wondering why Homicide hadn't called him lately. Then Mr. Whitcomb speculated on the chance there was a serial killer running loose, a killer with highbrow tastes.

"You call this Whitcomb asshole yet?" asked Murphy.

"Already blistered his staff," said Jake.

Murphy said, "Maude, Rocky, is there any chance we have a serial killer here, some clown with a grudge against powerful women? Should we be asking for FBI help? Am I a moron?"

Maude said, "Gut feel, they're different scenes."

"And I still say Babsie took a powder," said Rocky. "Asshole Whitcomb just can't deal."

Murphy said, "Maybe Babs Whitcomb was his fourth victim. Maybe Elizabeth is his fifth victim."

"I don't see it," said Maude. "Neither do the Feds. We got everybody monitoring all new Missing Persons cases as they come in. Troopers. Park Police. Macy's Security. Everybody."

"Okay. Keep plugging."

When they were gone Murphy called Alice at the bank, and they went over their itinerary for the police chiefs' conference in Florida. He felt guilty about leaving the county with Elizabeth Lucido missing, but his attendance was a political necessity, and he dare not whine about it to Alice. He had made arrangements to monitor the case by phone and fax, and Jake had agreed to take Wally out for chow a couple of nights.

Alice assured him she had everything else covered, the condo, the bills, her job, if he cared.

"Of course, I care. Is something else wrong?" asked Murphy.

"You mean besides today's newspaper?"

chapter 23

C HAIRMAN SEYMOUR CAMMEROLI SHARED HALF A nondescript, single-story office building with a printer, his cousin Benny. They were tucked away behind one of the really nice buildings at Mitchel Field. Maude Fleming knocked on the locked steel door, got buzzed inside. The lack of footprints on the lobby's freshly vacuumed beige carpet told her she was the first visitor through the front door so far that morning to a law office where no one practiced law. She flashed her badge at the Armani-suited man with the build of a stevedore sitting at the desk. The nameplate said Denny Dubois, but this brute was no receptionist.

Denny Dubois was polite enough and said Chairman Cammeroli knew she was there and would see her shortly. "In the meantime, youse could hang out wit' me."

"Why, t'ank you."

Denny stared at her, sizing her up. "You're from Homicide, right? Mother Murder?"

"Right."

"So who got whacked?"

These guys really did watch too many gangster movies. "The Deputy County Executive is missing."

"Oh, yeah, right," said Denny. "That Puerto Rican chick, right? A freaking shame."

"A freaking shame," Maude agreed.

Maude sat near the watercooler, taking note of the cheap pine paneling and tired colonial furniture, figuring Seymour Cammeroli saw no reason to spend money to impress people who had no choice but to do what he said. The thug working the desk was to let callers know that Seymour understood all forms of power, that no one was gonna shove Seymour around. Unless, thought Maude, the caller packed a gold detective's shield and a pearl-handled automatic. She told herself not to forget that, not to waver in front of this very powerful scumbag.

She said, "You look familiar, Denny."

"The Jets," Denny said after a moment. "Couple of preseason games. I tore up my knee just before the last cut."

"Sorry to hear that."

"Hey, whatever. I'm doing good here," said Denny. "Mr. Cammeroli is a hell of a guy. He loves you cops."

"Don't I know it," said Maude.

Just then the door to Seymour's office swung open and the music poured out. The little chairman was buttoning his suit jacket. He waved Maude inside.

"Hello, Mr. Chairman," said Maude. "Thanks for seeing me on such short notice."

"Like I had a choice," Seymour said jovially. "Like I had a choice. Such a funny girl. Denny, hold my calls."

Maude had been wrong about Seymour not spending money at the shop. The frills were located in Seymour's office: The Jacuzzi. The massage table. The NordicTrack.

Two large-screen TVs. Chairs you could sleep in. A desk you could ball on, if you swung that way. A stereo playing out-of-date disco at decibels favored by teens. This was Seymour's idea of discretion, hiding all the good shit in his office.

"Nice digs," shouted Maude. "Very Versailles."

"Nevermind me. How goes the hunt?"

"Little progress," said Maude.

"Pity. Pity. We miss her terribly."

"I won't take much time, sir," Maude said, sitting in one of the huge scoop chairs, leaning close so he could hear her. "I just need to ask you a couple of things."

"Shoot."

"What can you tell me about Stonehenge Investments?"

His face never flickered. "Brokerage house, in Old Westbury, I think. First-rate. Why? Come into some money?"

"Contributors of yours?"

"Fairly reliable contributors, I think."

"You think?"

He waved his hands, fussing away the details. "We have so many supporters. But why? What do you care?"

"I'm told they had a problem with Elizabeth. Some deal she squelched?"

Seymour knit his brow, then relaxed, as if a great fog had been swept from before his eyes. "Oh, I know what you're talking about. That was no big deal, Maude. A minor disagreement among people looking for financing. Happens all the time. . . . So who brought it to your attention?"

"A little birdie," said Maude. "So how'd it shake out?"

"Stonehenge went another way."

"What way?"

"An out-of-state bank, I think. You'd have to ask them."

Maude fought the inclination to tap her foot in time with the screeching lyric: "You should be dancing, yeah!"

sung over and over and over again. "And who is them?"

"Trade ya?" asked Seymour.

Maude smiled and shook her head. "Not when I can go to the damn phone book."

"Is the cheese-eater close to me?"

She thought about this. "I suspect you already know not to trust this person."

"How about if I guess the rat, you nod?"

"Nope."

Seymour gave up. "The main man at Stonehenge is Arch Collins. A hell of a nice guy."

"He your broker?"

Seymour laughed. "Honey, I got twenty brokers, calling every day. In fact, you find me a Nassau County broker that don't think he's my broker."

Maude smiled like she understood all about being chased with investment advice. The longer she sat with the man, the more her skin began to chill. She could easily imagine him whacking a traitor and then clutching for himself the noblest of motives: the party, the country, even God.

"Baltusrol Vail one of your brokers?"

Seymour's face went blank. "That's not Mr. Vail's line of work, so far as I know."

Maude wrote this down on her pad. "Would you do me a favor, sir? Would you call this Archie Collins guy and set me up an appointment?"

Seymour Cammeroli stared at Maude across the vast plain that was his desk, his lack of expression saying everything. "Love to. When are you free?"

"No time like the present."

"Wait outside, please."

Maude was happy to return to the silence of the waiting room and sat down with a *Penthouse* magazine. She marveled at how young the models were, if their bios could be trusted. A minute later Denny's phone rang.

He picked it up and nodded, then said to Maude, "Mr. Cammeroli said noon tomorrow, for lunch, the bar at Wheatly Knolls. You're buying."

Maude frowned. "Tell him we got a missing woman who might be dead by tomorrow."

Denny relayed this information, waited for a reply, then said to Maude, "That's the earliest, babe. Mr. Collins is out of town. Mr. Cammeroli said to say he knows what you look like . . . from the news."

"Right."

Back in her car, Maude phoned Homicide. "I want to go home, Rocky," she said, "and take a two-hour shower."

"Got slimed, eh?"

"The man's a skeeve. It was tough to share the air. Plus he plays his radio loud enough to split your skull, I guess so he can't be recorded."

Rocky told her to cheer up. "One of the Vice cops called in, Ellen Barohn. She said she found a possible on the Lucido case. A guy we missed on our first pass, don't ask me why. Fits our profile. On parole for burglary and sexual abuse since August. They're trying to find him now. He doesn't have a job, and no one is answering his phone."

"Tell me about him."

Richard Mitner's criminal record came close to what they were looking for: a career burglar, who had twice sexually assaulted female victims who surprised him in their homes. "One was twenty-five, a newlywed he groped as he forced her into a closet. The other was seventy. Her he raped. She just didn't want to testify. According to his parole officer, he's been straight since he got out, but of course he has to say that."

"Nothing on the various store employees?"

"Nice bunch of blue-hairs, wouldn't hurt a flea."

"This is pissing me off, Rocky, you don't know. And I hate dealing with these smarmy political bastards. I hate 'em all saying they don't know shit in a way that says not a motherfucking sparrow falls without their hand."

"Scum of the earth," agreed Rocky.

"Run me a background check on a Denny Dubois, male white, late twenties? Just for the hell of it."

"You got it."

"I'm exhausted, Rock."

"I hear ya."

"You think tagging Norman's a waste?"

"Yeah . . . I do. Use the manpower somewhere else."

"Okay."

"In fact, let's take the afternoon off and come back tonight. You don't have any plans, do you?"

"Nothing I can't change. Call me at dinnertime."

"Sleep tight."

"TIMES HAVE SURE CHANGED," SEYMOUR SAID AS THEY WATCHED on security cameras as Maude Fleming drove from their lot. "Back in the jungle, we could just tie a witch like that to the stake and move on."

"I hear ya."

"But why was she here, Denny? In the larger sense. Talking about things that are none of her business."

"Huh?"

Seymour shouted to make himself heard over the Spice Girls. "I'll tell you why. Because that lowlife Martin Daly couldn't run a lemonade stand, that's why."

Denny furrowed his muscular brow.

Seymour growled, feeling the same intestinal disgust toward Martin Daly that he felt when the family cat brought home a rabbit torn in half.

Seymour paced his office, getting his dander up, growing bolder. A fight was brewing—the kind he usually won. He remembered the rules as they had been taught to him by his predecessor—just before the great man was carted off to jail: "Help your friends and murder your enemies. Punish offenders swiftly and publicly. The public won't remember, and the party will never forget." His mentor had done his Federal stretch and was now living in Hamptonian splendor on the party's nickel, exhibit A when it came to the value of loyalty.

"You like Martin Daly?"

Denny lowered his head. "It's not my place to say, sir."

"I'm making it your place."

"A piece of shit, sir."

"And his kid?"

Denny waved a massive hand. "A fart in the wind."

"You like District Attorney Prefect?"

"What I seen of him. He's your brother-in-law, right?"

"Right."

"Good man."

"Something's got to change here, you know what I'm saying?"

Denny lolled his neck to stretch the muscles. "Your call, boss."

Seymour growled. "That's right. It is. Motherfuckers."

chapter 24

DANTE JOHNSON SPORTED RAIDER-WEAR AND OVER-sized jeans. His baseball cap, worn sideways, said X, and was not a part of his disguise. Driving a gray Hyundai that had been rented for him by the Friends of Jackson Hind, Dante had locked onto Junior Daly that day as he was leaving Mineola at the wheel of a funky black hippie van. Dante had followed him from the rear of police headquarters out to Old Country Road, then down the Meadowbrook

Parkway to the neighborhood where Dante lived. Dante Johnson had seen a lot of these vans cruising Roosevelt in his day, Grateful Dead bears line-dancing on the rear window, filled with Star Trek gizmos that beamed your ass to jail. It was the one county service the Republicans didn't mind providing.

He's gonna score, thought Dante suddenly, recalling rumors of Junior Daly's fondness for pharmaceuticals. And here I got a space-age video camera, right on my damn front seat. Now ain't that a Spike Lee bitch. Forget the smoking gun, we'll take the smoking son. Buy us a bag of rock, Junior. Then maybe Five-O could roll up, and he could film Junior telling them to get lost, go bother the spades, maybe show the piece to *60 Minutes*.

But Dante's heart sank as Junior passed through the Nassau Road buy-zones without so much as a glance at the sidewalk merchants on the stroll. Maybe he got a private dude, a house he goes to. Maybe he's scaring up some Brown Sugar voters. But Junior kept on rolling, like he was driving a tank. Past the high school Dante had attended sporadically, finally onto Dante's block, like Junior Daly was giving him some kind of Auto Club version of *This Is Your Life*.

He's here for me, Dante thought. To check me out. To bug my house. And lucky me, having the damn camera and everything. Just imagine the headlines: DEPUTY COUNTY EXECUTIVE ARRESTED FOR CRIMINAL TRESPASS. JACKSON HIND WINS LANDSLIDE. MR. DANTE JOHNSON APPOINTED COMMISSIONER OF PUBLIC WORKS. IMPROVEMENTS SLATED FOR ROOSEVELT, FREEPORT.

The daydream evaporated as the stealth van slowed but did not stop at the white split-level house Dante Johnson shared with his parents, Gertrude and John, who were at work. The van continued down the block and parked in the driveway of the neighborhood disgrace.

"Normy Keller," Dante said to himself. "What up wit' dat?"

Dante Johnson knew Norman Keller, ever since Norman's parents had ditched him in Dante's 'hood, maybe twenty years before.

Norman Keller was a geek, who even as a little turd bragged about who he knew, the strings his grandfather could pull. Of course that never did explain how come they was living in the 'hood.

Now Dante was wondering why Norman Keller had the Starship Enterprise parked in his garbage-strewn driveway. Hooked-up motherfucker must have bought it at auction, got an insider price. Bribed Junior to deliver it. Still worth the footage.

Dante parked in his own driveway and went into his house, watched the Keller dump through his living room window until Junior and Norman came out and closed the front door in his nana's face. When Junior started showing Norman the van, Dante got a can of beer from his refrigerator and placed it in a brown paper bag, took it for a stroll down the block.

"Hey, Norman. You a fucking cop now or what?"

Norman poked his head from the side of the van and nodded. "Yo, come here," he called. "Check out what this honey can do."

Dante leaned inside and sniffed. "You been smoking pot in here, Normy?"

Junior Daly, who was wearing jeans and a black sweatshirt, and sitting at the video console, explained that the van had been filled with drugs when seized, the smell had lingered.

Dante grinned and nodded. Cool. Junior thought Dante was a dumb-ass, drunken bum. Then Junior said he thought he knew Dante, or at least had seen him before.

"You ever in jail?" asked Dante.

Junior laughed and said, "Not yet, but I'm sure I've seen you before, and don't tell me all you black guys look alike."

"Wouldn't dream of it." Dante took a slug of beer, tried to look inside the van.

Norman said, "This is the deputy county executive. Martin Daly Junior."

Dante's eyes flew open. "And you hang with Norman?"

"Not really."

"Sometimes," said Norman.

Dante leaned closer and whispered, "Are you guys doing some Five-O shit? 'Cause we got some crack-dudes down the block, they always—"

"Can't talk about it," said Junior. "You'd better go."

Dante allowed himself to be dismissed and walked home. He called Jackson Hind from his basement extension, just in case the morons were checking *him* out now. "They desperate, boss. You gonna win. People can feel it. They be dancing in the streets like they did when Jimmy Carter won."

"I wish I could care."

"Come on, man, don't do this to us. You hear me? You know that's what they want."

JUNIOR'S BUZZ WAS WEARING THIN, AND HE WAS WISHING HE could sneak off and fire up another joint, not trusting Norman enough to party in his face, though it might come to that if this gig ran long. They had finally got rid of the nosy neighbor and now someone else had slipped in under their radar, was knocking on the closed side door of the van.

"Boys?" Nana said. "What are we doing in there?"

Norman slid open the door.

"Snack?" Nana held up a platter of bologna sandwiches and a bag of tortilla chips, apple juice in little boxes.

Norman looked aghast. "Nana, what are you doing?"

"This is a big responsibility," said Nana, "working for the county executive. You need to keep your strength up."

Junior Daly reached around Norman and took the food. "He'll do fine. Trust me."

And if he didn't, so fucking what? Truth be told, they were nonessential personnel on a nonessential mission, the best part of the assignment the option to honorably beg off the worst of the circuit, pick his spots, say, showing for the traditionally randy Businesswomen's Cocktail Reception, ditching the Roslyn Firemen.

"Did you know the missing woman well?" asked Nana.

"Who? Elizabeth Lucido? Too damn well. Mind if I take a leak?"

"Don't flush."

Their only bathroom was disgusting, the guest towels filthy, hair gathered like wool in the corners. Hey, you can be a gadfly asshole, but be clean, for Christ's sake. Junior thought of *The Munsters* as he zipped up and stepped into the hall.

Norman's bedroom door was ajar, a padlock hanging unlocked. Junior stuck his head inside and soaked up the atmosphere of the cluttered abbey, observed the dirty socks and briefs on the bare wood floor, the wall of electronics. He saw that Norman had pinched a computer from Accounting, a fax machine from GOP Headquarters. The television, VCR, and stereo were all stamped "Daly '93." What else you got here, Normy? You little sneak.

Junior opened the wooden box at the end of the bed. It held a stack of porno mags, a black leather mask, a studded leash, handcuffs, various gels.

"Jeez," said Junior, flinching. "This guy is fucking sick."

chapter 25

BETH HOPKINS, FORMER NASSAU COUNTY FEMALE Police Officer of the Year, and current legal counsel to the Nassau County Republican Women's Caucus, sat in her plush office at EAB Plaza, staring across Hempstead Turnpike at the Nassau Coliseum, wondering whether to send an additional thousand bucks to Seymour Cammeroli or directly to the Friends of Martin Daly. Word was, this year, send the money to Seymour, but she hated it to look as though she or the Caucus had abandoned Martin during a difficult race. In truth, she needed them both.

Beth Hopkins was a star on the rise. She was tall, blond, with a terrific pair of legs. She had made good use of those legs in a string of miniskirt ads she ran in local weeklies. Separated? Injured? Merely Disappointed? Call Beth Hopkins, the chick with great wheels. Get even with your tormentors, and at no additional charge imagine those thighs wrapped around your silly head. Nassau County men in growing numbers were choosing her to fight for their divorces. At thirty-six, she was the youngest partner at Beinstock, Bates, a firm that made the bulk of their money in court-assigned probate cases and consultant work for the county. Beth brought in her own business and knocked down three hundred K, not counting bonuses that arrived with stunning regularity.

She drove a black Lexus and owned a beach house on Dune Road in Westhampton Beach, a far cry from her days walking a footpost in Franklin Square. Her new friends were smart and rich. Her Rolodex contained the name, address, and phone number of every player in Nassau County.

Like many ex-cops, Beth liked to drink, tell war stories, and chase ass. Nevertheless, she had lately had trouble finding men who wanted anything more permanent than one-night stands, just men who promised adventure and delivered heartache. She blamed her long hours, she blamed the postfeminist age, she blamed her own age. Still, she had hope. She had time and money. She had those legs.

She turned from the window back to her mahogany desk and thought of calling her old boss, Frank Murphy. He would know which way this money was best spent. Then she could hear him laughing at her, telling her not to give these bloody bums a dime. That was the guy she should have married, she thought ruefully. They would have had a frigging ball.

She called Seymour Cammeroli, figuring that way she couldn't go wrong.

"Hang on to your money. There may be a change."

"Say what?"

"We got potential exposure problems, with Stonehenge."

With good reason, she thought. They had perhaps pushed the envelope a little too far this time: Moves she had argued against had been made nonetheless. There was a paper trail that could damage all concerned. Or there had been.

Seymour said, "Unless you can get your old boss to back the fuck off."

"You got a Plan B?"

"Actually, yes." Seymour outlined a scenario to make Arthur Prefect the next county executive, including write-ins by public employees and their families—and the rare party members who didn't hold jobs—and friendly businesses and all their employees. "We'll carry the paper ballots to seniors with fucking bundt cakes. We'll do the clubs, the rec centers. *Newsday* will spin it our way, most of the radio stations. So if Hind and Daly split the walk-up vote, I got Prefect winning by a nose."

Beth said, "You're not gonna leave the D.A.'s job wide open for Andrea Neville?"

"No, no, my dear. Perish the thought. There's gonna be two names on those write-in ballots, and now I'm thinking one of them should be a woman's name, they want to play that card. Maybe yours."

NORMAN WAS BORED. THEY HAD BEEN PARKED DOWN THE block from Rocky Blair's bayfront house in Long Beach for the better part of two hours, faithfully recording the late-afternoon comings and goings of various seagulls. Detective Fleming's house out in Suffolk County was next on the list. Maybe even the commissioner's condo that night.

The inside of the van was littered with the waste of stakeout takeout. Junior had already taken several walks and returned smelling of marijuana. Junior was presently snoring.

Norman, however, was brooding, concerned that Junior Daly had gone into his bedroom, scanned his collection. Even though dollars to doughnuts Junior Daly had a stash of his own. What single guy didn't? Married probably, too. Thankfully, the secret dresser drawer had not been disturbed, his special stock discovered. That would have been a disaster, Norman knew, a chance he should never take again.

He elbowed Junior. "Your father's gonna win again, right?"

"A Republican monkey could win," Junior said without moving.

"Where is he speaking tonight? Maybe we can catch—"

"Nowhere," said Junior. "The lazy slob's home with Kymypoo like he's up thirty points and fat with cash."

Then Norman said he didn't care for Jackson Hind. "A little too slick for me—speaking of fat with cash."

"A blue-blood fuck," Junior agreed. "You shoulda seen him at the tennis club when we were kids, Mr. Hotshot Champ of the ten-and-unders. Sucking up to adults, even then."

"People see through that shit. Your father has nothing to worry about. He's a great man, a great leader, a—"

Junior sat up with a start, eyes angry. "My father's a fucking asshole, Norman. Okay? He's a bully and a blowhard, with a bimbo wife leading him around by his dick. You don't know. I had to grow up with him. Always yelling. Always pointing out you don't measure up. Don't believe the hype. It'll get you every time."

Norman sat quietly for a moment, adding up the hours he had given to the cause of a bully and a blowhard, then said, "Who do we believe in, then?"

"Certainly not my daddy."

Just then a slinky blonde in an airline uniform parked her white Trans Am at the curb, got out and knocked on Rocky's door, was instantly admitted.

Junior said, "This is disgraceful. Poor Elizabeth's not cold in her grave, and the cops are taking pussy breaks."

Norman grinned at Junior, beginning to understand the bond street cops felt for each other, the cult of dirty secrets. Norman said, "Let's go do the lesbo, compare her chicks to Rocky's."

"You can do that after you drop me back at my car. I got a date tonight, and watching Rocky makes me want to keep it."

"You sure?"

"You're a sneaky fuck, aren't you, Norman? You're digging this."

"Same as anybody would."

• • •

"WE EACH HAVE OUR OWN BATHROOM," ALICE CRIED OUT. "AND mine has a bidet. Call over for champagne."

"Don't need to," Frank yelled from their villa's kitchenette, his voice muffled in the refrigerator. "This place is stocked for an army." He grabbed a bottle of beer and walked onto the screened deck, let the Florida sun bake his face. He chugged half the beer, wiped his mouth, and watched ladies in pink approaching in golf carts. On the blue horizon a line of thunderheads soared above the palm trees, like gods. Frankie-Baby, he thought, maybe you don't deserve this, but only an asshole would allow that to compromise his happiness. Then Alice joined him, slid her arm around his waist, and tugged him toward the bedroom.

"Wait," he said, grabbing their itinerary from the coffee table. "There's a clambake at four. That's only twenty minutes."

"You come with me now, and when we get to that clambake you can brag to your macho buddies that you already got laid."

"It's good to have you back, Alice."

"It's good to be back, Frank."

Thirty minutes later Frank Murphy realized that he was not the only high-ranking police official to have sex before the clambake. Ninety percent of the women under the big tent wore the legal minimum and spiked heels, looking not at all like the cop wives Frank knew. He felt himself the recipient of more than a couple of scowls. He considered removing his HI! I'M FRANK MURPHY name tag while Alice fought her way to the bar.

"Nice move, guy," said HI! I'M ALEX HAUPTMAN. Hauptman wore a red sombrero with handcuffs hanging from the brim. His T-shirt read BRUTALITY: THE FUN PART OF POLICE WORK. "No one told you this was stag?"

"I'm new."

"Cherry, I'd say."

Murphy said, "Maybe she hasn't caught on."

"Yeah, right."

"Where did these incredible women come from?"

"Somebody has a cousin in the escort business. We got the police discount."

"Looks like Tailhook."

From the direction of the spa Murphy could hear the macarena, punctuated by the squeals of fat men doing cannonballs, their wired young women getting splashed. A crowd was gathered around the hot tub, watching a village police chief bounce a hooker on his lap, her bare knockers slapping the surface.

Alice returned with Frank's beer, which she slammed against his chest, slurping half down the front of his golf shirt, chilling more than his heart. "Nice friends you got, Frankie-Baby. I'll see you back at the villa. On Sunday."

MAUDE FLEMING HEARD THE TELEPHONE RING AND RAN NAKED from her shower to the bedroom.

Dolly Lucido said, "I'm sorry to bother you at home, but you told me I could call you anytime."

"Yes, of course. Hang on a sec." Maude patted dry, then wrapped her towel around her slender torso. "What can I do for you?" she asked, sitting down on the bed.

"I did those things you told me to do, to feel like I was helping: put up signs and handed out fliers."

"Good. How's the reward fund?"

"Up to fifteen thousand already. We're finding out she had quite a few friends we didn't know. And thank you very much for your contribution."

"Outside of your family, Mrs. Lucido, I want to find her more than anyone."

"I've heard that about you . . . I've heard a lot about you. My husband had Jackson ask around."

Maude stood and opened her room-darkener blinds

and watched crows pick at her lawn, a cardinal in a tree at the rear of her yard. It was dusk, and the house was still because Renee was with her parents in Scarsdale for the week; her mother was having colon surgery, and her father was helpless.

"Do you believe in psychics, Detective Fleming?"

"I've never used one, if that's what you're asking. Some detectives do." Maude thought of Johnny Powell from her office, a dick who never solved anything, try as he might; or if he did make a collar, he lost it in court on some technicality or oversight or brilliant defense. He, of course, swore by psychics.

"Would you be averse to—"

"No. Not if you think it can help. Not at all."

"Can you come tonight? To my house? At eight? Alone. This particular psychic has trouble dealing with men."

Maude laughed. "So does this particular detective. I'll see you at eight."

"God bless you."

BETH HOPKINS LEFT HER OFFICE AT SEVEN O'CLOCK THAT evening and drove to the Regency Bar in Garden City. Like many career women, Beth knew the best happy hours, and at the Regency every Wednesday they had both a handsome professional crowd and a free buffet. Beth had work to do that night and no time to cook. She ate an apple on line, then made a lettuce and tomato sandwich to eat at the bar. She found a spot near the old-fashioned cash register and ordered a diet Coke from a muscle-bound hunk she knew as Rex. Waiting for her drink, she sized up the clientele.

Two lawyers she knew from the criminal courts held a corner table near the stock ticker. A police inspector huddled with his secretary at the bar. And there was Lieutenant Rankel at the far dark end of the bar, nursing an O'Doul's, which meant Martin Daly couldn't be far away. She didn't want to see Daly now, didn't want anything to show in her face.

She turned the other direction, feigning disinterest in her surroundings. She had hours of work to do, no time for men, no interest. . . . It took fifteen seconds for the shark to bite.

She didn't catch his name right off, but he was a seemingly nice young man in a boxy suit. He said he'd seen her ads, that he'd know her anywhere. "Do it myself, if I could," he said, "if I had your legs."

Beth looked him over closely and said in her huskiest voice, "Had them where, exactly?"

His grin told her everything. He looked at his watch.

Beth looked at her watch, saw it was seven-forty-one. She was nothing if not efficient.

IT WAS NEARLY DARK WHEN MAUDE PARKED IN FRONT OF THE Lucido house, behind an orange VW Beetle bearing a bumper sticker: "I used all my sick days so I called in DEAD."

Across the street the Crayton house was unlighted. A FOR SALE sign had been planted next to the mailbox.

Dolly Lucido came to the front door and gave Maude a quick, awkward hug in the foyer, then led Maude into the den, where she introduced her to a tanned young woman named Carla, a distant relative. They sat over hot tea and cookies while Ben Lucido politely excused himself.

"How do you think you can help?" Maude asked Carla when they were settled. "I mean, how does this work? Do you see things? Hear things?"

"You sound skeptical," Carla said without umbrage.

"Not at all."

"I don't see or hear anything, Detective. But at times I am a remarkably good guesser."

"I suppose you could say the same about me."

"I especially think I can help here because I've known Elizabeth all my life."

"I'm game."

Dolly dimmed the lights, handed Carla Elizabeth's stuffed dog. Carla closed her eyes and hugged the dog to her breast. There followed a long stretch of silence during which Maude closed her eyes and relaxed, allowed the tension to flow from her neck and shoulders. She hated to drive, she was thinking, especially at night. And Rocky loved the wheel, much as he'd deny it. A man who took the world literally, she wished he could see this. He'd be holding his sides.

"Would music help?" Dolly asked after a while.

"Does she have a favorite song?"

"Anything by the Eagles."

Carla held up her hand. "Wait . . . don't move . . . Elizabeth is alive," she said. "Alive but suffering. In the dark. Feverish. Shivering . . . Heat and cold, both at once. Maybe the trunk of a car, a big black car. Sometimes the trunk leaks, because she gets wet, the carpet smells."

"How do you know that?" asked Maude.

"I can sense very powerful disgust."

"Is she near or far? In Nassau County? New York City?"

"I don't know . . . near." Carla sat up straight and opened her eyes.

Dolly said, "Anything else?"

"She desperately wants to come home."

Dolly bit her lower lip and wept, and Carla held her and whispered that everything was going to be all right. After a while Ben returned, and Maude felt it was proper for her to leave.

She and Carla said good night to the Lucidos and walked outside together, stopped next to the orange Beetle.

"Have time for a drink?" asked Carla. "I know I could use one, or two."

"Sorry. But thanks."

"You're in love," said Carla.

"Yes."

"But lonely."

The wind off the sound stirred longing in Maude where she did not want it. "Thanks for helping us out."

Carla held out her hand. "I hope I have."

chapter 26

E LIZABETH LUCIDO REGAINED CONSCIOUSNESS IN TOTAL darkness, facedown on a dirty shag carpet. She blinked her eyes and scanned her staggered memory, at a loss as to where she was and how she got there. She was thirsty and sick to her stomach, and it felt like weeks of neglect had passed. A minute ticked by; nerve endings sprang to life. Her left cheekbone ached, and her hair was matted over her eyes; an itch tormented her ear. Her neck was killing her.

Think. Hard.

What had happened? The fund-raiser. She left early.

Her memory of events ended as she was driving past some pickets, grinning, flashing the peace sign. So maybe she'd had a one-car accident, and been thrown down an embankment. Maybe she was ten feet from the Meadowbrook Parkway and the cops just hadn't found her yet. Or maybe she was buried in a mountain of garbage.

Elizabeth tried to move her arms and legs and could not. She tried to roll over and could not. Tried again to remember what had happened, knew only that her neck was killing her, that her body felt as if it were shrouded in moss.

She got it then, that she was paralyzed, and her sudden helplessness overwhelmed her. "Oh, my dear God," she whispered. "Oh, my God. How can it be so dark?"

In her very first prayer Elizabeth told God she'd settle for the wheelchair, because life in a wheelchair was life, only in a wheelchair. She would still have her mind and heart. Or they could fix her, when they found her. If they found her.

"Help!" she croaked.

Her throat was parched, her lips cracked painfully.

"Help!"

They had to miss her by now, she thought, if it was Friday, payday in Mineola, the day after the night she couldn't remember.

They needed her for practically everything: contracts to settle, arguments to arbitrate. Lawsuits would not stop because she couldn't make it to the office. The chatter of tax-pacs would continue. Development deals would still be proposed, each more important than the last, each trailing strings. What was Martin Daly gonna tell these people? I'll get back to you when I know something? Like when? They needed her, they needed her, please, God, they needed her.

So half the Nassau County police force had to be out looking for her. Frank Murphy would certainly be canceling leaves and doubling manpower, calling out the dogs.

And Jackson would no doubt go public with their romance, make it a campaign issue to find her. The race would stop dead, on both sides. Nobody moves until we find Elizabeth.

She imagined her parents asking the public for help. Her sister Justine. Her friends. They must be thinking that she was a victim of some dastardly crime. They must be frantic.

"Is anybody there?" she called out in the darkness. "Please. Help me."

Then Elizabeth sensed someone watching her, coldly impassive, devoid of empathy, a dangerous plant. "Hello?" she called tentatively. "Is anybody there? I need help. I can't move."

Thursday, Oct. 31

chapter 27

J ACKSON HIND DRESSED DOWN THAT HALLOWEEN morning, in a tweed blazer, khaki slacks, white button-down shirt, no tie, not at all the look of a hard-charging candidate. He had spent most of last night thinking of throwing in the towel, focusing on the search for Elizabeth, the hunt for the criminal.

The phone rang, catching him in the kitchen, the call from an anonymous supporter, a male of limited education. "Beth Hopkins disappeared last night, just like Elizabeth. All the cops in town got their balls in an uproar."

"What? How?"

"Just remember, Mr. Hind, you got friends you ain't even met yet." The caller hung up.

Then Jackson's pager went off. He checked the number: Chairman Neville's private line. No fucking way. Jackson felt his blood thicken; his mind raced over the data until the phone rang again.

"Jackson, what the hell is going on?"

Jackson took a sip from his Princeton Tiger coffee mug. "Good morning to you, too, Father. How's the weather down there?"

"The weather's horrible. Now, what's going on up there? I just got a call from someone who remembers I wasn't such a bad guy."

Jackson briefed his father on the disappearances, how the story was playing in Mineola. His father listened like a lawyer, then said softly, "We're coming home tonight. I know how to fight this kind of fight."

"So do I," said Jackson, "from watching you."

"What I told you I did when you were little, and what I actually did, were two different things, son. There is your garden-variety political terrorism that goes on all the time, and there is all-out war."

"You think that's what I've got here?"

"I'm hoping for your sake, no. In any event, you need allies. And who can fuck folks better than a judge."

"I'm thinking of dropping out of the race, spend my time looking for Elizabeth."

"Why?"

"Because I love her, Dad. This didn't start as a palace coup."

"Stay in and fight. You can do more good from the pulpit."

"I'm not sure pressure from me is the answer. She is, after all, one of Them."

"You mean, she was," said his father, "before you turned her into their highest-ranking traitor . . . ever."

Jackson spared his father their history, that Elizabeth had hated Martin Daly and his scummy crew long before they had met. She knew they hired their mommies and daughters and aunts and bimbos, steered business to buddies, and took cash in brown paper bags. They drank and fucked while they campaigned for Zero Tolerance and Family Values, stood staunchly against welfare for anybody but themselves. God help you if you were poor or black or sick, or the child of someone thus afflicted. God help you if you challenged them. And it was more than just Martin you had to worry about, it was everyone who lived off the system, the wizards behind the curtain.

"You still got that Dante kid working for you?"

Jackson said, "Yes."

"Maybe have him start your car in the mornings."

• • •

ROCKY AND MAUDE HUDDLED WITH THE CRIME SCENE TECHS around Beth Hopkins's black Lexus on Seventh Street, which had been found by a Garden City traffic cop. It was parked in front of the Baskin-Robbins store, doors locked, alarm properly set. Under its driver's-side windshield wiper was a stack of parking summonses.

So far, Maude and Rocky were told, nothing had been touched.

"Okay," said Maude, "let's get busy, and let's do it right. Pop the trunk."

The Lexus was new-car clean and empty, but for a black leather briefcase on the floor in back. The interior smelled of perfume. Maude had the briefcase bagged and tagged for evidence. Then she leaned against the hood of their squad car and flipped through the pile of parking tickets, saw they began a little after 9 P.M.

The street would have been quiet then, this boulevard where men with NBA rings shopped side-by-side with best-selling authors and one frequently nominated daytime star. Here in Garden City, this flurry of police work was a barbarous anomaly.

Maude noticed few locals stopping to kibbitz, as opposed to street-crime-scenes in the ghetto, which invariably brought out the private detective in vast segments of the underemployed.

She realized this could be the end of the rope for Frank Murphy; and Maude suddenly found herself thinking how he had made the police department more tolerant, had immediately stood up to the outright PBA bigots—coaxed by Martin and Seymour—and switched the policy of "Don't Ask, Don't Tell," to "Don't Bask, Don't Yell," asking only that gays not flaunt their sexuality at work, just as he didn't want straight officers acting like horny dogs. Last month Maude brought Renee to the Homicide Dinner Dance, and no one raised an eyebrow. Now she feared for her boss's tenure. She felt she owed him a better end.

Maude nudged Rocky. "Look at their faces; the rich folks are appalled."

"Or scared shitless," said Rocky. "I mean, you'd think you were safe on Seventh Street."

The search dogs arrived then, and leaped out of their van, growling, reined in by jumpsuited officers. Maude expected they would find little of use, but she was using every tool, just in case. She said to Rocky, "Have someone from the Village come down and open the meter. Maybe we can count coins and figure out what time she parked."

"You got it."

"Then wake up last night's bartenders and get 'em down here to look at Beth's picture. See which joint she was in. If she left with anyone."

"Right."

Maude said, "I gotta go, okay? Stay with it."

"Will do."

"When you're finished here, catch a ride over to Beth's co-op with Crime Scene," she said, "in Roslyn. It's in the notes." Maude said she would catch up later. She promised to bring him a doggy bag and a stock tip from Archie Collins.

"Like I might trust one of those Stonehead fucks."

Maude slid behind the steering wheel and adjusted the seat and mirrors. She checked the stick-on calendar—courtesy of a Garden City bail bondsman—on the dashbord, and counted the days backward to Elizabeth's disappearance.

Six.

She counted the weeks backward from Elizabeth's disappearance to the day when Babs Whitcomb disappeared.

Six.

Maude had a queasy feeling about six hours from

now, or from the time Beth had actually disappeared, which would mean they might already have another victim, whose loss had yet to be discovered.

Maybe this would bring in the FBI full bore. Maybe it should. Maude considered for the very first time in her career the possibility that she could use the help.

CHARLIE HOTCHKISS ARRIVED ON SEVENTH STREET AS MAUDE Fleming drove away. He parked in the bus stop near the corner of Franklin, got out, leaned over the hood, and watched through binoculars the cops huddled around the Lexus, most of them shaking their heads and shrugging. Charlie scanned the storefronts and saw the owner of the Newport Grill watching the action from his doorway. He made his way down the block.

"Hey, Bernie, my man. Good to see you."

"Charlie."

"The cops been over to chat yet? What'd they say? Any buzz?"

"Give 'em time."

"I bet you'll hear plenty over lunch."

Bernie smiled and said nothing, as restaurant owners will. Charlie smiled back: no offense taken.

"Take care," Bernie said, turning back into his shop. "And come to dinner again, soon."

"I will. I'm saving up. . . . Hey, Rocky!" Charlie shouted across the street as Rocky Blair matched notes with the dog-handlers.

"Not now, Charlie," Rocky called back without looking at him. "Busy as hell."

"When?"

Rocky stared across the street at Charlie. "When Maude says so."

If Rocky was aware of how pussy-whipped he sounded, you couldn't tell it from the scowl on his military face. Rocky Blair was one tough bastard who didn't mind hiding behind one tough broad's skirts. So how tough is that? Better never to find out.

Charlie returned to his car, mumbling, reworking his theory, because this turn of events did not square with his original vision. This one did not compute: Beth Hopkins was nonessential personnel. Charlie had been almost certain the next victim, if there were to be one, would be Kymberly Scallia-Daly. His second guess would have been Alice Gettings.

Then he thought of possible headlines for tomorrow: BIMBO BARRISTER BEEMED UP. MURPHY JUNKETS WHILE WOMEN VANISH. NASSAU COUNTY WOMEN UNDER SEIGE.

THE THURSDAY BAR CROWD AT WHEATLY KNOLLS WAS MADE UP of corporate lizards and painted desperadoes, nevermind it was Halloween. No lesbians, though, Maude noticed. The girly-girls were drinking lunch down the road, at Squeeze, talking sex. At Wheatly Knolls the WASPS were talking missing women, buzzing with anxiety. Maude ordered a micro-brew and tried to guess the Stonehenge representative, then wondered if she would get Archie Collins in the flesh, or an underling.

"Detective Fleming? I'm Arch Collins."

Maude put her beer on the bar and shook his hand. He was barely more than a youngster, in a boxy gray suit with red suspenders. His hair was neatly trimmed and slicked back like a pit bull's. He smelled of Clubman Reserve. He smelled of arrogance.

When they were seated in the atrium, with a view of the parking lot, Arch Collins showed her his teeth and said, "How can I help you? What can you possibly think I might know?"

Maude said, "For starters you can tell me why you don't like Elizabeth Lucido."

"Who told you that?"

"Several sources."

"Detective, I disagreed with her once, on a business matter. It was nothing personal. Actually, I thought she was a beautiful and talented woman."

"You ever go out with her? Ask her out?"

"I'm married."

Maude nodded. "What sort of business matter?"

"A condominium development on the North Shore. It was a financing question. Nothing more."

"What was the name?"

Collins furrowed his sleek brow. "Project Ten, I think. We hadn't come up with a real name yet. Waiting for marketing to finish the heavy lifting," he added sarcastically.

"Gotcha. What was the problem? Why was Elizabeth opposed to the deal?"

"She said she didn't feel it was environmentally sound."

"I see. A pain-in-the-ass-do-gooder."

"No big whoop. There's a new deal every day." Collins picked up his knife and drummed its tip on the table, lightly. "So who dropped my name?"

"A friend."

"Of yours or mine?"

Maude laughed. "Mine, now."

"Oh, it is a dirty world."

"That's what I hear."

"What would it cost for a name, or don't people like you have a price?"

"Everybody has a price," said Maude. "And you can tell Seymour mine is equal pay for equal work, adequate child-care, reasonable maternity coverage, fair—"

"One of them, eh?" said Collins.

Maude rarely took personal offense during the course of her duties, but this guy made her skin crawl. She departed from her usual script. "One of them," said Maude. "And worse. Know what I'm getting at?"

Collins looked over both his shoulders, back at Maude.

"You're a fag, right? I heard. Let's get this over with quick. I'm a regular here, with a reputation."

Maude stood and grabbed her bag, shaking with rage. She leaned close and spoke into his ear. "Blow yourself, dipshit."

"You'd like that, wouldn't you?"

chapter 28

AFTER GRILLING THE ROUSED-FROM-BED BARTENDERS of Seventh Street, Rocky Blair caught a ride in the Crime Scene search van to Beth Hopkins's Roslyn co-op. The building superintendent took one look at Rocky's haircut and badge and handed him the key.

Rocky led his two-man team inside, and while the searchers got busy in the kitchen and living room of the very large apartment, Rocky strolled back to the master bedroom, onto the balcony overlooking a thin strip of forest the developers had missed.

Nice digs in a nice neighborhood, thought Rocky. Beth had always been a goer, one to trade up, dating only men higher in rank during her police department days. He hoped her climb hadn't ended badly. Rocky had liked Beth, what little he had seen and heard about her. Why shouldn't a woman make her way in the world? Why shouldn't she have some fun? Look at Maude, how they leaned on her when the fudge hit the fan.

He closed the bedroom door and opened Beth's chest of drawers, working from the bottom up, like a burglar. He found a black-leather photo album under her nighties in the second drawer. Between the covers was a loose, haphazard collection of Beth and her beaus, a who's who of Nassau County, including fucking Junior Daly, including on the last page a picture of Beth, topless, snuggling with Frank Murphy in a woodland hammock. Frank had a cigar in his mouth and a martini in his hand. He looked happier than Rocky had seen him look in months. The date on the back of that photograph was July, 1992. Rocky slid the picture into his blazer pocket, then called in the ferrets. "There's some funky pictures here you should catalogue, then I suggest you forget them."

The blue-boys joined Rocky in the bedroom and took a look, then snickered. "Thirteen assorted Polaroids," said one of them. "Second dresser drawer. Duly noted and forgotten, including the shots of Deputy County Executive Junior."

Maude arrived ten minutes later. Rocky took her out on the balcony and filled her in: "Beth stepped out by herself for a taste at the Regency Grill. Rex, the bartender, remembers she came in around seven and left like twenty minutes later with a young guy in a suit. This guy's been in there before, so he's local, we'll find him. We got a quick sketch."

"Let me see it."

Rocky handed her the artwork from his clipboard.

"Innocuous-looking fuck," said Maude. "What'd we find here?"

Rocky gave her the short version, then showed her the photo album.

"All these suspects," mused Maude. "All outranking us, even Junior. This is not what we needed . . . unless we get a chance to use it as leverage."

"How?" said Rocky.

"I'm not sure yet. But let's tell Murph what we got. He must be back from Florida by now."

"Let's hope so."

"Hey," said Maude. "At least *this* time he has an alibi."

• • •

AT TWO-FORTY-FIVE THAT AFTERNOON MAUDE FLEMING AND Rocky Blair were sitting in front of Frank Murphy, bringing him up to speed. They complimented his freshened tan and filled him in on the molehill of evidence gathered at Beth Hopkins's home and car, from her colleagues and friends. "She missed a breakfast meeting, is how they figured out she was missing," Maude said. "She didn't call in, didn't answer her beeper. Not like Beth at all. Her secretary called 911."

Murphy nodded, flipping through the pile of pink messages he had missed. Martin Daly. Martin Daly. Martin Daly. Seymour Cammeroli. Don Neville. It felt like he had never left; it looked like he had been gone for weeks. "We try the dogs again?"

Maude said, "Scent runs from her car to the bar. And then what?"

Murphy said he didn't know, he had been minding his business in Florida, a tactic that had proven highly ineffective. "Where was Jackson Hind last night?"

"Carle Place Rotary," Rocky said sadly, "in the plain view of hundreds of people."

Murphy said, "Cheer up, Rock. It was just a thought."

"And Norman Keller?"

Rocky said, "He says home. His nana backs him up. Now we're kinda sorry we terminated his tail."

Murphy said, "Weird dude, that Normy. But not a killer."

"It's not odd that someone picked Beth up in a bar, is it?" Rocky asked Murphy.

"—if we may speak indelicately," added Maude.

Murphy shook his head. He did not add that Beth Hopkins was great in the sack. Bad enough folks knew he'd boinked Elizabeth Lucido.

Maude handed him the photo album. Murphy flipped through it fast, felt a flood of relief to find he wasn't in it. "Where was this? Damn."

"Her dresser drawer."

"So Junior was nailing her, eh?"

Maude said, "Sure looks that way. I went through her phone logs for the last few days. Her secretary said Beth had handled a couple of clients in the office, nothing out of the ordinary. She had two calls out to Martin Daly's office, which had not been returned."

"What's that mean?"

"There's a race on, and she's a player," said Maude.

Rocky suddenly brightened and raised his hand. "You think this crazy fuck's got a thing for Elizabeths?"

Murphy looked at Rocky with concern.

Rocky said, "I mean, hey—you gotta consider everything."

"Maybe not everything," said Maude.

Murphy grimaced. "What else have I missed?"

"We also got back the Fingerprint ID list from the Lucido crime scene. It includes the usual contamination by public officials, including one Police Commissioner Francis Murphy, at the kitchen table."

"Downright embarrassing," said Murphy. "Sorry."

"We've of course got Jackson Hind, everywhere. And Junior Daly's prints, in the bedroom, on the bedpost. Neither one of them has been to the scene since we secured it."

Murphy cocked his head and said, "Junior Daly made it into Elizabeth Lucido's bedroom? That can't be."

Rocky said, "You don't think Junior could be the guy she wasn't proud of? I mean, in the dictionary next to shithead—"

Murphy laughed. "That's a big fucking club, people who aren't proud of Junior. But I'd be surprised as hell if Junior was ever with Elizabeth."

Rocky said, "Makes you wonder where Junior was that night, though, also last night, now that I think of it."

"Makes me wonder where damn near everybody connected to this case was last night. In fact, find out for us, and I mean everybody even remotely connected politically to Elizabeth or Beth, and that includes those Stonehenge schmucks. I don't like what I am thinking at all."

"Right, boss."

The detectives left Murphy's office, and Jake Posner checked in with the political temperature, which he described as chilly, turning to frost. "Women in high places are demanding protection. And some prostitutes went on cable last night, saying, Hey, what's the deal here, nobody gives a fuck when twenty hookers get slaughtered. Also, I issued your annual plea for Halloween sanity and fireproof costumes. You even suggested people give children money instead of candy or fruit, since that was now such a risky proposition in our dangerous age. Two weeklies covered me."

"That it?"

"The high points."

"And the low?"

"I took care of them for you."

"Honest?"

"Oh, there's a couple of brownnoses out of joint, a couple of asskissers in withdrawal. But other than this shit, the county's been quiet. Of course, MacLondon in Highway's been dying to show you some new way to bag speeders, but most of the adults understand what's important."

"What should I say to the press? I saw networks setting up alphabet city when I was sneaking in the back door."

"Not a thing, Frank. Stonewall 'em. Stay in here until they get sick of waiting or something bigger comes along. And dodge Mad Charlie at all costs."

"When I took this job I swore I'd never do that."

Jake laughed grimly. "Now you know."

• • •

GHOSTS AND GOBLINS TRAVELED IN PACKS THAT CHILLY AFTERnoon, as parents stood sentinel on the sidewalks, arms folded, watching everything, including the black sedan carrying the homicide detectives that parked at the curb in front of the tiny house they all feared most. The front lawn was knee-high weeds, Maude noticed as she climbed out of the squad car. Hedges had overgrown the first-floor windows. One corner of the rotted roof was covered by a navy-blue tarp. Trick-or-treaters crossed the street to pass on the other sidewalk.

"Think these folks know something we don't?" asked Rocky.

Maude grunted, remembering other houses neglected because their owners had embraced strange agendas. She knew there were three types of multiple killers: bad guys on a spree, avoiding capture; time bombs who massacre innocents in public places; and those who kill, let time elapse, then kill again . . . for fun. This house favored the third type, the sort who follows his crimes in the media, keeps scrapbooks, trophies, the kind of killer who cares about his public image.

Dick Mitner answered their third knock on the dirty white door, and Rocky and Maude could see right away that he was dying of something. His face was gaunt and gray; his pale neck above his black T-shirt was flaccid; he had purple sores on his wrists and forearms.

"Nassau County detectives, Dick," said Rocky. "We need a minute of your time."

"Only a minute? Well, what the hell. Usually you guys want years. Come in, come in, before you ruin my reputation."

Maude mumbled her thanks, and they stepped through the doorway into the squalid life of an unattended patient.

"AIDS," Mitner told them when they were settled in

his barren kitchen, facing each other over a rickety card table. "Got it up the ass in the showers at Attica."

Rocky said, "Jesus."

"Can you believe I'm thirty-four years old?"

"No," said Rocky. "I can't."

Maude thought he looked bad for sixty. The inside of the house looked worse. Garbage overflowed the black plastic pail. Newspapers were stacked against the walls. Mail lay on the filthy tile floor, unopened, bills to be settled by someone else.

"What do you want with me?"

Maude said, "Where were you last Thursday night?"

He hardly had to think. "The hospital."

"You sure?" said Maude. "We're gonna check."

"Look: I just got home from a month in there on Saturday. My doctor says I got a year, but he's so full of shit. So a six-month burglary-third gets a death sentence. You think the fucking state cares? Or the county?"

"Doubtful," said Rocky. "Knowing them as I do."

Anger filled Mitner's sunken eyes. "You ever make a really bad mistake in your life, Detective?"

Rocky thought about it. "Not really. No."

"Fucking don't."

chapter 29

THE NEWSPAPERS WERE CALLING HIM THE LADY-snatcher, and the cops had no clue.

He resisted the urge to gloat.

Commissioner Francis M. Murphy, who, it was reported, had returned immediately from Florida to deal with the latest attack, was again stumped. His best detectives were so far from an arrest that the District Attorney remained on vacation: and Arthur Prefect was not a man to give up walking a manacled killer into court.

The finest cops in America?

Not.

Outside a car honked.

The Ladysnatcher slammed down his newspaper and sidled up to the living room window. He pulled aside the curtain, checked the cars parked on both sides of the block, made sure he could account for the ownership of each.

A momentary sense of normalcy approached, receded.

That was dangerous, he thought, to expect smooth sailing so soon.

But this shit was taking years off his life, this heightened state of alert. And all because of her. This was her fault. She had opened the door on a shit-storm of trouble, the traitorous whore.

He had thought at the beginning they would walk right up to him—maybe at home, maybe at work—and slap on the handcuffs. He had thought at first that he had fooled no one.

And then they had come so close to the truth, to a link in a chain that could lead to the truth, he had almost panicked, almost given himself away. They had damn near had him, then mindlessly breezed on by, the brilliant homicide detective and her dogged partner, dumb as everybody else when all was said and done.

Beth Hopkins wasn't a bad person, but that had nothing to do with it. She had to go. Simple as that.

Now, he figured the cops were so far off track he could probably stop expecting that heavy-handed knock. But this was no time to get cocky. He needed to keep the game face on and both ears to the ground. Things could change in a hurry, as he well knew. Even though he figured he'd closed all the loopholes, one could never be sure, the prisons were full of guys who thought they had everything covered.

And really, each of the victims had asked for it in her own special way, so forget any chance that guilt might trip him up. Confession was good for the soul but bad for the body. Sure, he was sorry certain things had happened, but he couldn't change history.

Who doesn't have regrets?

He pulled back the curtain, looked outside again, rechecked the cars. Then the doorbell rang, and his heart leaped in his chest, and, Oh, God, he thought, the disgrace of it all, the media, court, jail. How dumb he had been. If he could only go back in time.

He steeled himself, opened the door. Three high school girls masquerading as Dallas Cowboy cheerleaders cried out, "Trick-or-treat!" and he thought, Oh, the possibilities.

chapter 30

FRANK MURPHY WANTED TO BE HOME ON THE COUCH with Alice, or cruising the hilly shoreline with his brother, but was instead that evening a prisoner of an emergency staff meeting in the County Executive's office, all the empty suits gathered around the conference table looking troubled.

Martin Daly had called the meeting to lay down the law. "I don't have to remind you boys that I am the public face of Nassau County, do I? I mean, you should have seen the Woodmere Jews the other night, staring at me like I was fucking shit . . . and they didn't go for spit when we passed the hat. Fucking peanuts."

Frank Murphy turned out the rant and recalled his

first meeting with this gang of municipal thieves, how they had assured him they stood ready to back him to the hilt in his war on crime. Certain he was in favor of the death penalty, the Sanitation Czar had gone so far as to say that it was a shame Murphy just couldn't go out and blast all the scumbags himself, like he had when he was a cop. First time Murphy had needed these bastards they were nowhere to be found. That was the last time Murphy had looked.

"The Victim's Center done yet?" Martin demanded.

"Tomorrow," said someone. "Day after, the latest, I swear to God."

"Damn well better be, even if we have to cut corners. Now, somebody tell me what's up with Project Downsize. I need shit to announce, ribbons to snip."

"We're still hiring staff. Expect the first reports in May."

"What about a zoo? People like zoos. Family values, that kinda shit."

Frank Murphy couldn't help but chuckle; and Martin Daly zeroed in on him, like he'd been waiting for an opening.

"Something amuse you, Frank?"

"No."

"We haven't got to your department yet, have we? You know, people are talking about you being in Florida with your girlfriend yesterday. That don't look too fucking good, you know. Bad judgment. A rudderless ship."

It looked, Murphy knew, like whatever Daly wanted it to look like.

"Fix it, Frank. All of it. Or you won't enjoy the support from me that you do now."

"Yes, sir."

Daly took his victory and turned abruptly to other matters. "Now," he said to Junior. "How we doing with the dinner dance? We pick a date yet?"

"Progress on that one. I'm still investigating options."

Murphy knew Junior wouldn't pick a date and place until his father put a gun to his head. Until then, Junior was no doubt milking this gig, dining around the county, scouting locations. Then Murphy's beeper went off, and he quietly excused himself.

"That's getting a little tired, too," said Martin just as Murphy reached the door. "Your beeper excuses . . . how fucking busy you are . . . how you don't have time for me."

"Right."

Murphy walked back to police headquarters and found Maude by the soda machine, smoking a cigarette by the open window.

"Here's the deal," she said. "Last night was an off night for most of the campaign staff. Martin Daly left his office at three-thirty in the afternoon. He played golf at the Brook Club, as a guest, then mooched dinner. On the way home he rented a video in Fairhaven at twenty-ten hours."

"What'd he rent?"

"Girls Who Wear Glasses. Rated X."

"And where, pray tell, was Junior last night?"

"Home, he says. Doesn't think anyone saw him."

Murphy smiled and shook his head. "I still want to know how he got his palm print on Elizabeth Lucido's bedpost."

"I asked him about that, assured him it was strictly routine. He said he had hand-delivered documents to Elizabeth two weeks ago, on a day she stayed home sick."

"You check the story? Sick records and all?"

"I did. It does."

Murphy said softly, "Time for the FBI here?"

"I got a call in to Quantico, just to talk scenarios. The guy I know there is off tonight but supposed to call me back in the morning. I know what he's gonna say, though. Where's the evidence a crime was committed?

Because, Hannibal Lecter notwithstanding, serial killers are shitheads and losers, not brilliant doctors. They make mistakes, leave trails. They usually don't know or care about local politics unless they have a specific grudge."

"Talk to him anyway. Maybe the species is evolving."

"Going backwards, you ask me."

Murphy fed the soda machine a dollar bill, punched the diet Coke button. "Suppose Beth Hopkins was somehow in on the revolution with Elizabeth . . . some kind of Martin's-Women-Getting-Even-With-Him thing. Suppose the big boys found out about it. How would they react?"

Maude said, "I can't imagine they'd use Junior Daly as a hit man. Can you? Unless they wanted to unload Junior, too. Good Lord, I've gotten cynical."

Murphy patted Maude on the back. "Me, too, kid, and I thank God for it every day."

"MAKES ME SICK I'M ON THEIR SIDE," SAID FRANK MURPHY. "Makes me wonder if anything is fair these days. Lord, Wally, it's dog eat dog out here. Worst I've ever seen it. Daly calling Hind a suspect. Jackson and his father acting like special prosecutors. And Jake says now there are people looking for any other decisions I've rendered which mighta backfired. Scumbags," said Frank. "All of them. I got merchants calling headquarters, screaming about losing the season. I mean, college professors are suggesting women of all classes unite against predatory males. All kinds of things are suddenly *my* fault."

They were driving that night near the old Grumman property, a relic from an era when Long Island was prosperous, and Frank felt sudden nostalgia for the Cold War, the good old Russians. They passed a playing field all lit up, and Frank circled back and parked. They sat for a while and watched a bar-league flag football game from a distance, Frank for some reason remembering

Ball Day at Yankee Stadium, circa 1965, his damaged little brother eating everything the vendors carried to the upper deck, finally throwing his complimentary baseball onto the field of play, which got everybody laughing. Some older men gave Wally their free balls, and he flung them out there, too. Then people in other sections got the idea, and despite the frantic waving of the umpires the crowd salted the diamond with souvenirs.

Frank had expected his father to be mad that day, but the tough old buzzard had laughed long and hard, until his eyes had filled with tears and his chest had heaved. Even so, Wally was never brought to a game again, not that Frank could remember.

Frank looked over at his brother, content in the darkness. "Alice is back," he said. "Not that she's happy."

Wally rocked and stared out the side window, showing Frank the matted gray hair on the back of his head, from a life spent largely in bed. Then Wally sang, "O say can you see . . ."

"Yes," said Frank softly. "They sang the anthem that day."

chapter 31

CHARLIE HOTCHKISS PARKED HIS TEN-YEAR-OLD BLACK Mercedes—which sported the decals of Chaminade and Wesleyan—under the streetlight across the street from his garden apartment.

The apartment, while clean, was a jumble of history and neglect. Charlie had been married for twenty minutes twenty years ago, and her out-of-date picture still sat on his desk. On the wall behind his chair was taped a

Day-Glo poster: All it takes for evil to triumph is for good men to do nothing. Charlie came from money, so he knew what to look for when poking through the mists of municipal skullduggery. And he loved history, the grand experiment of democracy.

What he hated were the waves of donor cash drowning the average citizen's voice, that campaign bribery was so commonplace as to be unremarkable. He often thought of those long rows of headstones outside his editor's window, of the warriors buried there, knowing this was not the government they had died for, that quietly, the very republic was under assault by our political parties. And Long Island was absolutely the worst, a political museum piece where one-party rule remained stubbornly in place, draining its citizens' blood. Until now. Maybe.

Two novels sat in his bottom desk drawer, one a murder-in-the-pressroom tale that had been politely rejected all over town, the other a literary work-in-progress about a lonely reporter who just cannot bring himself to grow up. Both manuscripts featured villainous politicians and jaded scribes. Neither sizzled like the best of his nonfiction work, even he was forced to admit. He had not looked at either since Babs Whitcomb had disappeared.

Charlie grabbed a diet Coke from his refrigerator and sat down at his computer. He typed in his password—DeScribe—and slipped onto the Net.

"You have mail," said his computer.

Which he did, sent by Anonymous, promising information on the Ladysnatcher case. All Charlie had to do was go to his office, a package would be waiting for him.

Charlie grabbed his windbreaker and headed out to his car, wondering how somebody had penetrated *Newsday*'s headquarters.

A lifelong paranoid, it didn't take much for Charlie to realize that he was being followed on Jericho Turnpike, by a black four-by-four with ear-splitting music pouring forth like battle anthems, a bass-line that altered Charlie's EKG when they idled side-by-side at the light. The driver was white, early twenties, goatee, in a T-shirt. He motioned for Charlie to pull over. Charlie waved him off, smiling to show his goodwill. The kid made a more insistent gesture.

Charlie shrugged: Why?

The kid mouthed, "Please." He held up an envelope.

Charlie pulled into a 7-Eleven parking lot and parked near the front door, staring at the thin brown man in the striped shirt behind the counter, who was perhaps going to be the only witness to his death. He hoped the security cameras were on.

The kid in the four-by-four jumped down and came up to Charlie's window. He was smiling idiotically, holding his hands behind his back. His shoulders looked like bowling balls.

"Mr. Hotchkiss?"

"Yes."

"*Newsday* dude, right?"

"Right."

The kid swung a beefy hand into the car and dropped the manila envelope into Charlie's lap, stunning his testicles. "I was told to tell you, trick or treat."

ON HER WAY HOME FROM WORK THAT NIGHT, MAUDE FLEMING stopped in Stony Brook at the We-Meet-By-Accident body shop for an estimate on the damage to her Honda. The owner was a retired Suffolk cop who cut law enforcement personnel a break. He was already home for the evening, so while the mechanic estimated the damage to her car, Maude waited in the office with the manager, Dave, who chewed toothpicks. She told him she was new to the area, that she and her girlfriend had just bought a house they couldn't afford.

"You need extra money?" he asked in a quiet voice.

"Who doesn't."

"There's a way," he said, shifting his eyes.

Maude sensed an offer to defraud the insurance company, and she felt sorry she was gonna have to bust the one good body-man that anyone could trust. But Dave closed the door, pulled a videotape from his desk drawer, and popped it into a VCR.

"Now keep an open mind," he said.

Maude was ready to slap Dave's filthy face, when a fully clothed man appeared on the screen. "Need extra cash? Consider the Amway life . . ."

"Interested?"

Maude smiled wearily. "No thanks."

The mechanic ducked his head into the office, said he had to special-order the paint, and asked when she could leave the car.

"I can drop it off Saturday morning; of course, then I've got to ride around with Lesbo-cop on my door for a couple more days."

"It's not a quick fix to do it right."

"Hey," she said, "what is? See you Saturday."

Ten minutes later she parked in her own driveway because their two-car garage was still filled with unopened boxes, some her stuff, some Renee's, as each had come equipped with one of everything.

Maude crawled into a gray sweat suit and stretched out on the living room couch. Before she could fall asleep the phone rang, and it was Ben Lucido's cousin Carla, with additional information, she said.

"On what?" asked Maude.

"It's about you, a feeling I had."

"Oh, yeah? Even though you know I'm attached?"

"Not that, al-though . . ."

"Carla."

"Be careful around water, okay?"

Maude waited for more.

"That's it. No vision. No details. Just general uneasiness."

"About water," said Maude.

"I wish I could do more."

I know, thought Maude. And I'm starting to wish you could. "Thanks for calling."

"My pleasure."

Oh, it was hard, Maude thought, to be a saint in the suburbs. She hung up and called Renee, who answered on the first ring, probably grabbed the phone next to her mother's bed.

"Hey," said Maude. "It's me. How's your mom?"

"Sleeping. What's up?"

"I miss you, kid. My life is all out of whack."

"Mine, too. How's the case?"

"Lousy. Nowhere. People think I'm so good at this, Renee, but maybe I'm not, you know? Maybe women are dying because of me. I don't know."

"You know that's not true," said Renee. "Who do they have better? Nobody, that's who."

Maude didn't reply.

"Murphy still a lamb?"

"He's trying."

"Hang in there. You'll get 'em."

"See you soon?" asked Maude.

"Not soon enough."

Bone-tired, Maude fell asleep in front of a black-and-white Alan Ladd movie. Then something made her wake up, a house sound she did not recognize; and she thought by now she knew the repertoire.

This was silly, she thought, sitting up on the couch, antennae tingling. She was a cop. She had a gun. Two guns. Strong's Neck was isolated, safe, only Dyke Road in and out, a joke Maude and Renee enjoyed. Be calm, she told herself. React appropriately.

Maude slid to the floor and used the remote to kill

the television. She worked her way around the cocktail table and crawled to the front bay window, got on her knees behind the curtain. She peered outside and saw a car she didn't know in the shade down the block, near Maple, the spine of the peninsula.

"Shit."

She dialed 911, listened to a recording, and waited, just like everybody else. Two long minutes later an operator came on. Maude explained who she was, reported the possibility of a prowler. "Send a patrol car quietly to Maple and Four Winds. Tell the officers an off-duty female detective is on the scene, in a gray sweat suit."

"What color hair?"

"Gray crew cut."

"Oh, yeah, I've heard of you. Okay, car 601 is on the way."

Maude belly-crawled down the bare wooden hallway to their bedroom, to get her gun and binoculars, then slipped on her black raincoat and sneakers and eased out the back screen door.

The night was dark and quiet. Stars but no moon above the trees. She would sneak down the block behind hers, and come at the strange car from Maple, maybe get a license plate for starters. Then she'd double back and watch her own house from the woods across the street. All those years in Homicide, she could outwait anyone. But halfway to Maple, Maude heard the footfalls of running shoes on her street, then a car start up and drive off. She froze against a tree, working the implications, none of them good.

A dog barked. Another answered.

Maude ran out to her street. The car was gone. She walked back to her house, thinking bomb, thinking: I should not be lazy here. I should call out the dogs and play it safe. If I open the front door and the house explodes, all anybody will remember about me was that

I was too fucking tired and lazy to have my house swept.

In the driveway she saw something stuffed under the windshield wiper of her Honda. She studied it a moment, then picked it free by the edges, saw it was an empty Nassau County interoffice envelope, folded over, on which someone had typed the word WATERWORKS.

| Friday, Nov. 1 |

chapter 32

THEY WERE ALL BACK AT NASSAU COUNTY POLICE Headquarters by twelve-thirty that morning. With cadaver dogs on loan from the N.Y.P.D., squads of Nassau cops on overtime fanned out and conducted an immediate, frantic, and ultimately uneventful search of all public water facilities in Nassau County.

Rookies from the police academy found three homeless men living in a Wantagh drainpipe, while Internal Affairs cops interrupted several Sands Point sodomies in progress, and Robbery dicks busted three college kids for smoking pot on a beach.

Around two-thirty that morning Maude looked across her desk at Frank Murphy and said, "Maybe it's something else. Maybe a private company."

"Maybe it's not even about this case."

"I've thought of that, too," said Maude. "I'll be in the library if you need me."

"I need to sleep," said Rocky.

"Go ahead," said Murphy. "I'll watch the phones."

Rocky got two hours and thirty-five minutes of sack-time in the back room before Frank Murphy gently shook him awake. Twenty minutes after that the squad car was headed south on Long Beach Road in a washed-out dawn. As they sat at a traffic light behind a garbage truck, Maude filled Rocky in on Waterworks, Inc., what she had learned from her check of public records.

"And this was the only privately held Waterworks?" asked Murphy.

Maude said, "In Nassau County."

Rocky said, "And no fingerprints on the envelope at your house?"

Maude said, "Not a one."

They slowed near the waterfront, found the red, gilt-lettered WATERWORKS sign, then bounced along a dirt road to a patch of verdant marshland in the shadow of the Oceanside landfill. They parked next to a turquoise trailer in a small clearing of flattened grass, got out, and immediately smelled the rancid accumulation of chemical waste at low tide. They covered their noses and coughed. Planes stacked over Kennedy Airport blinked down at them, growled.

"Let's do this quick," said Rocky. "I'd like my kids—should I ever be lucky enough to have any—with one head each."

The trailer was unlocked and empty, underneath it clear. They walked away from each other, probing the marsh with their flashlights, pressing through the shoulder-high grass. Just yards from a putrid canal, Murphy found the bodies facedown in the grass. They had been tied together at the waist with a rope and were as flat as if they had been run over by a road-grader.

"Hey, you guys," he called softly, after making the sign of the cross. "Over here . . . and watch where you step."

"CONGRESSMAN BALAN?" KYM SCALLIA-DALY ASKED, LOOKING up from the list of her husband's supporters on the table. It was eight o'clock in the morning, and outside the kitchen windows birds were singing autumnal farewells. On the sound a tanker rode high, it's rusty red waterline ten feet above the cold gray water.

Martin Daly sat across from her, frowning, adding up those he could count on for last-minute cash, hoping it would matter. "Of course the goddamned congressman. What the hell do you think?"

"Archie Collins?"

"Another no-brainer."

"Mike Mullin?"

Daly used his hand like an ax on the butcher-block table. "A useless drunk."

"But I like Janey so much."

"Hey, Kym, this is my fucking fund-raiser, not yours."

"All the more reason to be gracious."

"Fuck *that* noise," he said.

They ran quickly down the list until she said, "How about Commissioner Murphy and Date?"

"Chop that pompous bastard, too. . . . No, wait, on second thought, string him along."

Then campaign manager Mike Barclay called and ruined Martin's morning with news of bodies discovered on a South Shore property called Waterworks, which he believed belonged to a company known as Stonehenge, which he happened to know was a front for—

Martin blanched. "You're fucking kidding."

"I wish I were, Martin. You have no idea."

"Who are they? Not Elizabeth and—"

"I wish. They were fucking coke mules," Barclay said. "The cops say they fell from the wheelwell of a seven-four-seven from Cali. If it's any consolation, the M.E. said they froze to death before they were flattened."

"It's no consolation."

"Martin, you did not need something like this."

"I mean, of all the fucking luck. They can't splash down in Jamaica Bay? Help me here, Barclay. Say something."

"Maybe the cops won't bother to trace the real owner. It ain't his—your—our—fault."

"I should hold my breath and wish for that?"

"There's more, Martin: The numbers are rapidly going south. This race now is literally a dead heat, if Hind's not ahead."

"Then get the troops out there, goddamnit. This is no time to slack off. What do the polls say I should do? Do they like my zoo idea? Think of someone I can honor. How's the money?"

"Not where it should be."

"For just me, or the other races too?"

"Just you, near as I can tell."

"You say that like it's my fault, Mike."

"You say that like it's mine."

Martin gritted his teeth. "Didn't mean to, even though that's what everyone else will say when you're looking for your next job, right, Mike?"

"You suck, you know that?"

Martin Daly looked at Kym, who was staring back at him impassively, as if his political problems did not affect her in the least. If he could have reached her, he would have slapped her.

"This is because I wanted to be governor, isn't it, Mike? Because I wanted to improve myself and my family. Because Martin Daly dared to live large without asking permission. Right? I thought this was America, Mike. This is—"

"—exactly the way the game is played, and you've known it for years. Stop whining, Martin. It doesn't become you."

"Shit," cried out Daly. "Shit, piss, and corruption."

"Seymour won't actually let you lose. He just wants to make you sweat."

"Yeah? Well he keeps it up, I'll sink him *and* his fucking machine in quicksand, tell certain uptight people in Washington how things really work . . . and I mean all of it."

There was silence for a moment. "You do that, Martin, and no one you know will help you again, not even me. No one will ever invite you to golf or ski or eat. In fact, you'll wind up in a Dumpster, you do that. So I suggest you act like a man here. Which means: Think hard, and work hard, and turn this thing around before it eats you another asshole."

Martin slammed his fist on the table. "Fuck me!"

"No thanks, pal. But do swing by Green Acres on your way in. They're having a half-price sale. Work the escalators."

"Blow me, Mike, okay? Just blow me." Martin slammed down the phone and growled at Kym.

Honk-honk-honk.

"Rankel's here," Kym said happily, folding up the list, a pretty clear sign her efforts on his behalf were finished for the day. "Now, you keep your chin up and don't let these assholes scare you. You're an incumbent. You can't lose."

"It's hard to campaign from a jail cell, Kym. *Capice?* Of course, why would that bother you?"

MURPHY WAS OUTSIDE THE TEMPORARY COMMAND POST, BATTING away swamp bugs as Rocky and Maude passed the Waterworks bodies on to other Homicide dicks as fast as they were able, along with the home-delivered envelope tipping Maude off. No one on the case liked the idea of stoolies visiting homicide cops' driveways, but all agreed you took your breaks where you found them. Maude was locally famous, always walking bad guys into headquarters on the evening news: Dead bodies were her business. It made sense to drop a note on her windshield, thought Murphy. Who you gonna call but Mother Murder?

Maude and Rocky came out of the trailer and walked with Murphy to the squad car, going over Ladysnatcher scenarios, testing hypotheses, striking out. Murphy said, "So, to sum it up, we've now lost three members of the Caucus in about a month, and not a damn thing we can do about it."

"Six weeks," said Maude.

"Poof. They're gone. Not enough evidence left behind to fill a thimble. And we know that at least one of them had turned against Martin Daly."

Rocky nodded. "We should find out if Beth was in on helping Jackson, too."

"Right," said Murphy.

"And if Babs Whitcomb was."

"Jackson already said no to that."

Rocky said, "Maybe he's full of shit."

"What?" asked Murphy.

"Why'd Hind get a pass in the first place? He should be the most logical suspect. It's damn near always the boyfriend. Maybe this time it's tough because he's smart."

The tall grass behind them swayed in the early morning sea breeze. Murphy said, "Hind got a pass because I gave it to him."

Rocky stared at his feet. "Love stinks for the rich and famous, just like it does for everybody else."

"That's cynical, Rocky, and not completely true. And I still don't think he's involved in anything criminal," said Murphy. "But who knows? Anything's possible. Therefore, Maude, I'd like to set up some protection for you and Renee at the house."

Maude scoffed: "Not necessary, boss. Please."

"You're surer of that than I am."

"We'll get a dog."

Murphy folded his hands in prayer. "For me? For my peace of mind?"

"No."

"It's not nice to disobey your commissioner."

"It's not nice to embarrass Mother Murder."

Murphy sighed. "Okay, then, back on the Whitcomb-Lucido-Hopkins case. And let's make that the last hyphen we need."

Maude's cell phone rang, and she whipped it from her pocket. The task force had a possible business address for the guy Beth Hopkins had been seen with last. A grab-team from headquarters was rolling.

Ten minutes later, Frank Murphy, Rocky, and Maude were slumped low in the squad car, staking out the mir-rored office building where Beth Hopkins's last one-nighter was allegedly employed. Rex from the Regency had remembered the man coming in on other occasions. He had bragged about working in the latest fancy office building to rise at Mitchell Field. He had also mentioned something about off-roading upstate. "A real yuppie fuck," the bartender had concluded, "but that's what you get around here."

An undercover cop dressed in a UPS uniform had checked the lobby, the corporate listings for the building: four big law firms, one big HMO, the back office of a regional bank, two small financial advisors, and the Common Sense Society. The grab-team had scoured the lot for four-wheel-drive vehicles, found almost too many to keep watch over.

Nobody drove cars anymore, thought Murphy. Everybody thinks they need a truck for the bad times they sense coming. Suburban moms hovered over grilles capable of launching Scuds.

Maude taped the suspect's sketch on the dashboard and they spent the next twenty minutes watching smokers on break huddled against the breeze, fixing.

Maude sipped coffee from her container while Rocky drank his orange juice. Time dragged. Sleep beckoned. Murphy's eyelids felt like sandpaper.

"Hold it," said Rocky, sitting up. "Look. There."

Murphy shifted his gaze, and saw a red Jeep Cherokee turn down their aisle, roll past them, and park. A male white who matched their sketch climbed down with a briefcase in hand.

Maude said to Rocky, "Run the plate."

Rocky bent low and keyed the mike, whispered the tag numbers to headquarters.

From the suspect's physical carriage, Murphy guessed the man was not worried about being observed. A yuppie fuck, the bartender had said. One who worked for himself, or had a very lenient boss.

Maude keyed her walkie-talkie. "Take him."

Task force members appeared among the parked cars as if from nowhere and casually surrounded the suspect as he sauntered up to the building, just a few fellow tardy employees, only they were suddenly holding weapons on him. Over the man's indignant protests they cuffed him and led him to a black sedan, guided his head into the backseat, and slammed the door.

"Task Force to Homicide."

Maude picked up the radio. "Come in."

"I like your odds," said the sergeant. "Your boy here shit his pants when he saw my shield. I mean, talk about black-and-white fever."

Rocky looked at Maude and smiled tentatively. "That's a good sign for us, right? When a guy craps in his drawers?"

Murphy said, "I've always thought so, God forgive me, but he did just get surrounded by a SWAT team."

The sergeant said, "We'll get a hook on his Jeep, tow it in for you."

"You guys are the best."

Her radio crackled. ". . . 1998 Jeep Cherokee, registered to a Tucker, Robert J., D.O.B. of 2/21/55, residing at . . ."

"Please," said Maude, looking heavenward, then back at Murphy. "Let this be over."

CHARLIE HOTCHKISS WAS LOCKED IN THE *NEWSDAY* VIDEO ROOM, rereading the cover letter that had accompanied his new information on practically everybody:

Dear Charlie:
If you're serious about exposing corruption in Nassau County, I suggest you speak to people on the attached list of former and current disgruntled public employees, clergy, contractors, and activists. These people can tell of illegal sandmines, mob garbage contracts, and health care swindles, the real story behind the LIPA/LILCO bailout. Land grabs. Zoning scams. Baltusrol Vail. The crimes they commit to keep the system intact. Disappearing cases in D.A. Prefect's office, where his Special Investigations Unit is best known for tipping off targets. Ask about Police Commissioner Frank Murphy's sexual relationship to the missing women. Then try to guess why no one can find them. We are drowning in filth. Help.

Charlie folded the letter and the long list of names back into the manila envelope, then loaded the tape that accompanied the letter into the video machine and turned it on. The first few images were blurry, then sharpened enough for Charlie to see the tape was of a meeting in a diner parking lot on a street like Hempstead Turnpike or Jericho Turnpike. Seymour Cammeroli, Baltusrol Vail, and Denny the Goon were sitting in Seymour's Blazer. A moment later Booby Marrocci arrived on his custom-blue Harley and joined them in the truck. In the time it took Booby Marrocci to smoke a cigarette, the meeting was concluded and all then went their separate ways. The tape ended there.

Charlie turned on the lights and took a deep breath.

Some brave soul had captured Baltusrol Vail on video-tape, nevermind Seymour meeting with the Mafia. And then they had sent the evidence to him.

Charlie scrolled up Vail's file and read what little there was of it. An All-American linebacker at Duke in the early sixties. Military Intelligence in Vietnam. A junk-bond wizard during the early eighties. Rumored to have escaped Federal prosecution by the slimmest of margins when a key witness disappeared. Now a municipal bond consultant, with vast holdings of his own. Rich, generous, mysterious, and feared in a way few men truly are.

Charlie unlocked the door and walked back to his desk, where the phone was ringing like the bells of hell.

"Charlie Hotchkiss."

"They got the wrong guy today," said a woman's voice he did not recognize.

"Who? What guy?"

"Homicide."

"How do you know that? Who is this?"

Charlie began to motion to a colleague to set up a trace, but the phone in his ear went dead.

chapter 33

RAINWATER HAD POOLED UNDER ELIZABETH'S CHIN, and by twisting her neck painfully she could get the side of her mouth flat enough to get a drink; and from time to time she filled her belly with the foul brew. It was daytime, she realized, because a slice of sunlight was seeping down on her from somewhere.

She bent her neck as far down as it would go again

and observed her bloodstained hands, saw they were not restrained, as was true for her pale bare feet. She saw a broken fingernail on the third finger of her right hand that looked as if it ought to be quite painful and was not. The air reeked of excrement.

"Hello?" she cried. "Is anybody there? Help!"

The silence mocked her, and Elizabeth came to a chilling if accurate conclusion: No one had been where she was for years, no one would be there for years to come. This was no accident. Why else had she been left untethered? Whoever left her here could not have known she was paralyzed. So that person thought she was dead.

There was no reason to return if she was dead. The work was finished. She had been left for dead, and she was not dead, and might not be dead for quite some time to come.

It wasn't a kidnapping: She had no money to pay a ransom, not like some of her law school chums. Her parents were not wealthy or well known. Her life had been a steady climb, good things arriving, things she had earned. And then Jackson.

She imagined his face, as it was that day in New Hampshire, last winter. Of course they had seen each other around Mineola before—what woman in local government didn't know who the hunky blond was—but they had never had the opportunity to speak. They had almost collided at a big red Manchester mailbox, two Long Island politicos loyally working the northern wings. Jackson had recognized her first and turned to his local companion, saying, "And here, believe it or not, we find the lovely Miss Lucido, rising star of the Nassau County machine, a delicate flower far from home."

She had recognized him inside his woolly hood, and she had blushed, and he had seen it and pressed on recklessly.

"Well?" he said. "Speak up, woman."

The snowflakes flew around them, and their breaths mingled, and the next thing she knew they had ditched their escorts, their fliers, and were sipping brandy in front of a stone fireplace in a cozy inn far away from their own motels. He told her Hillary stories and made her laugh, made her comfortable, acted like he was comfortable everywhere. She remembered their first kiss, which came after dinner, under hard-frozen stars, leaning back against her ice-cold Prelude, her knees weak. Somehow she had resisted his plea to take a room. But that had been the last time she had refused him anything. She wondered if Jackson was still thinking of her as alive, if anyone was, or if they had already given up.

She loved life too much to die. She was interested in too many things: politics, people, the stock market, the Knicks, film, and children, she wanted children, grandchildren.

"Hello?" she called. "Please! Is anybody there?"

Elizabeth tried to remember that last night, the fundraiser. Jackson came over after. No drinks, no snacks. Little talk. Straight to bed. Then ice cream. She remembered him leaving soon after, remembered walking him to the front door with her feelings slightly hurt, her wearing just a T-shirt, his T-shirt. Then nothing.

This was payback; they had been caught. Seymour and Martin had probably known from the beginning. You couldn't keep something like that quiet. After the Stonehenge deal she had wanted to carry in the suicide bomb that rocked the house, and they had nailed her outside the gate. That thought reverberated in her mind as she looked at her bloody hand and tried to lift it again, realized that she already had, moved it at least an inch from where it had been.

The thought sunk in: There was movement, hope.

Elizabeth closed her eyes and prayed without planning what she would say: "Please, Blessed Mother. Give me more pain. Let the man who loves me save me. Let the man who loves me—"

A door creaked open, and a wash of sunlight flowed down from above. She heard heavy breathing, the grunts of labor. Someone was coming for her. She was saved by accident, or her attacker was back to finish her off. She was clearing her throat to cry out when an occupied body bag landed in a heap across her legs. Elizabeth bit her lip and froze, closed her eyes and played dead.

There were more grunts from above, the sound of a door closing, its lock clicking. Footfalls departing, then nothing.

In the momentary light she had seen her tomb, and its earthen walls and artifacts: a chest of drawers, a stack of magazines against one wall, and, sitting up in a chair, a naked mannequin with bright red nipples. In the corner nearest the light source she had spied a pyramid of canned goods, perhaps soup. And a stepladder, on its side. It had only been a moment, but she had seen it. She tried to drag herself from under the bag, to reach that corner, but she succeeded only in moving her right hand an inch.

Her fingers bumped into something round on the ground, like a doorknob broken off and fallen, no, she thought, clutching it, a yo-yo.

A butterfly yo-yo.

So she shouldn't be bored.

chapter 34

M ARTIN DALY ANSWERED HIS OFFICE HOT LINE LATE that morning expecting to hear more bad news, or, God forbid, a question about his real estate investments. But it was only Junior, saying, "Dad, listen, I just got a call from my people across the street."

"From your apartment?"

"From the office, Dad, even though I am not yet physically there. The task force picked up the Snatcher. Some guy named Tucker. They brought him in under the radar."

"You have people at police headquarters? Who? Custodians?"

"So don't thank me."

Martin realized he had hurt his son's feelings. "This guy the bad guy on both cases?"

"It's possible."

"And the custodians know before I do," said Martin. "Something is very fucking wrong here."

"Like I said, anything I can do to help."

"Finding these women alive now would help. I mean, forget selling the concept that I am evolving into a gentler political life-form. All anybody knows these days is that rich women are vanishing and my cops are fucking up." Daly spun in his chair and stared across the parking lot at police headquarters. "But maybe not, eh. Maybe we got ourselves a November Surprise for Hind, poor man thinks he just pulled ahead. Maybe Detective Fleming *is* Agatha-fucking-Christie. A couple of shots of me beside grateful, rescued women ought to put an end to this fucking farce."

Junior said, "You're welcome," and hung up.

Martin could only wonder at his son's complete lack of ambition. One would have thought Elizabeth's disappearance would have spurred him to increase his participation, not hide out more than ever. He was truly his mother's child, God rest her soul.

Martin walked to his valet and examined his ruddy face in the mirror, then splashed on an English aftershave. He combed and sprayed his curls, grown rigid and thick with dye. He decided the POLICE flak jacket would be wrong for this occasion; it could backfire like that helmet did on Dukakis—and might even lead to the press pointing out that *his* wife also drank like a fish. The executive look was what we wanted here, the image of a CEO leading an efficient operation. He straightened his tie, checked his teeth.

There was capital to be made here, a chance to quash the rumors of incompetency and end the race with Jackson Hind—just when everyone was starting to think this old dog had lost his bite.

Nobody was better at this, he told himself, rolling his shoulders like a prizefighter. Not Seymour. Not Jackson Hind. Twelve years he had ruled Nassau County, and pretty goddamn benevolently. And if anyone thought he was really gonna change, they could kiss his Irish ass.

He hit the speed-dialer, to call his wife with the news of their resurrection. As usual, he got her machine. He could beep her, but why bother. Why ruin the mood? Let her hear what was happening just like everybody else. She'd call to suggest dinner at one of the hot restaurants, show the beautiful people it was safe to come out again and bask in the limelight, safe to be seen with him. He'd put her on hold, tell her he was busy, let her know she had worked her way back to the B-list.

MURPHY AND MAUDE WATCHED THROUGH THE DIRTY ONE-WAY glass as Robert Tucker paced the otherwise unoccupied interview room. Maude said, "Rocky told him not to sit for fear he'll ruin the chair."

Murphy said, "That Rocky's a damn good man, thinking budget first. You think this is our boy?"

Maude frowned. "He's the kind of guy I love to hate: single, white, the right age, and he's a tobacco lobbyist for an outfit called, get this, the Common Sense Society."

"We're gonna need more than that to string him up."

Maude chuckled grimly. "His story, and I've only heard it start-to-finish twice, is that they met at the Regency Bar, downed drinks, and sprinted to his apartment for your basic zipless fuck. They made it on the living room carpet, her on top. When they were done, he hit the bathroom, Beth got dressed. He offered her a ride home; she told him her car was just down the block. They made vague plans to do it again. Beth said she might be real busy, running for the district attorney's job. They kissed good night. Last he saw of her, she was stepping into the elevator."

"Wow. What else'd they talk about? He say?"

"Her career, her connections. How she could help him."

"Weird," said Murphy.

"This sound like Beth Hopkins?"

Murphy said, "Other than the district attorney bullshit. Beth doesn't have to brag to get laid. This guy got priors?"

Maude said, "A coke bust in New York City, early eighties."

"Who doesn't? Any connection to the other women?"

"What? You think I'm a miracle worker?"

"Yes," said Murphy. "Sometimes I truly do."

"Don't bet the ranch."

Murphy bumped into Arthur Prefect in the men's room outside the Homicide office. The District Attorney gave Murphy barely room to urinate, then cornered him near the sink. "I understand you've got the guy?" he said. "Is it time for us to step in?"

Murphy said, "You mean take over and fuck it up?"

"Now, there's no call for that."

"Who called you?"

"Who didn't?" said Prefect. "They got the Ladysnatcher. They got the Ladysnatcher. . . . So what's going on? What's going down? We do still work together, don't we?"

"I thought you were on vacation."

"Always ready to serve my county, Frank. You know that."

"Yeah? Well, then hand me some paper towels."

Prefect did, ignoring the insult. He folded his hands in front of his crotch as if waiting for a tip.

Murphy couldn't help himself. "Let me give you the inside poop on something, Arthur, okay? There will never be a County Executive Prefect. There will be a County Executive Junior before that happy day. I don't care who you married."

"Why?"

"The little thing in your past—I'll bet other people know about it, too. Which might finally explain to everybody—including the Feds—how few real investigations you launch on your own."

"What little thing?" said Prefect indignantly.

Murphy had not the faintest idea. Prefect was known largely by the public for his ill-advised arrest of a county worker burning a Nassau County flag outside labor negotiations. Murphy was simply guessing. "Come on, Artie, we're gentlemen here. Ever hear of Stonehenge?"

"You can't threaten—"

Murphy tossed his paper towels in the basket. "Look, forget I said a word. Just tell Martin not to announce jack-shit until I say so. This might not be the guy, and if it is the guy, Art, let's not blow any chance we have to save the women. In addition to which, nobody is stealing the credit from my cops. That about cover it?"

"Share would be more the word," said Prefect.

"Mooch. Glom. Filch. Swipe."

Prefect offered his hand. "Comrades?"

"In a pig's eye."

Murphy left Prefect to examine his conscience.

Inside the Homicide office he found Robert Tucker examining his conscience, standing glumly in front of Rocky Blair. He was your garden-variety yuppie, no great shakes in the looks department, which only meant that Beth hadn't changed her standards much. Murphy looked at the lawyer sitting next to Tucker and raised an eyebrow. "Got himself the A-team, I see."

Rocky said, "He just got here. Ain't that great news."

The defense lawyer, Dick Neubauer, smiled at Frank Murphy and stood to shake his hand. "Hello, Frank. Nice to see you again." Dick Neubauer was one of the few very fine defense attorneys in Nassau County. He was straight and smart and tough. "Embarrassed my client here a little, didn't we?"

"Didn't mean to."

"At the very least he's fired for coming in late."

"I'd say that's his own damn fault."

Neubauer sat back in his chair and put a well-shod foot on the edge of the conference table. He loosened his tie. "Look, we are as disturbed as you are about these disappearances. We understand the pressure you're under. We would like to help. Nevertheless—"

Maude said, "Elizabeth Lucido is in his telephone book, with three stars next to her listing."

Tucker began to say something, and Neubauer put a hand on his forearm. "Because she was a very powerful Republican, Maude. Do your homework here, people. Tobacco, Republican, ring a bell?"

"Then he's boinking Beth Hopkins?"

Neubauer arched his considerable brow. "I think you've been wildly premature."

Murphy said, "You wouldn't if you were one of these women."

"He'll cooperate, unless I think you're going fishing. If I don't want him to answer, he won't."

"Fine," said Maude.

She asked Tucker a few innocuous questions, probed without success any connection to Babs Whitcomb, then Murphy called a halt to the questioning and asked his cops out to the hallway.

"Go slow, okay," he said. "I want to stall them a bit while we check out the Jeep."

"Will do."

At the end of the corridor the press had gathered like vultures who had smelled something dying.

"Can you get rid of them?" asked Maude.

"You sound like Martin. Come on. Let's have coffee down at my office. Let everybody stew."

"Good idea."

Ten minutes later Murphy, Maude, and Rocky returned to the interview room.

"Got your strategy worked out?" asked Neubauer.

Murphy feigned hurt feelings. "Dick."

"How was the sex?" Maude asked Tucker out of the blue.

He thought about it a moment. "Great."

"All-time top ten?"

Tucker winced. "Besides being uninhibited, Beth has a great body, Detective. She works out, she said. In fact that's one of the other things we talked about."

"When Beth left your apartment, she wasn't particularly scared or apprehensive?"

"Walking on air, was the phrase I believe she used."

The room filled with leaden silence, and Murphy felt his stomach tighten into a knot. They had nothing on this guy who got unlucky. Ungats. Bupkus. Shinola.

"Speaking of walking," said Neubauer.

Murphy looked at Maude, who shrugged, at Rocky, who shrugged, at Neubauer. "You'll probably want to use the back door."

"No, Frank. Not really."

chapter 35

THE STEPS WERE JAMMED WITH PLAYERS AS MURPHY and the cops escorted Robert Tucker and Dick Neubauer out the front door of headquarters, Murphy hoping to minimize the molecular disturbances when entourages collided on the steps.

"You did the right thing here, Frank," Neubauer whispered in his ear as cameras clicked and questions ricocheted. "That kid's no killer. And knocking a piece off Beth Hopkins doesn't make you a bad guy, now, does it?"

He said it in such a friendly tone that Frank did not get angry. For a moment he could see Beth. Her on top, of course, the way she liked it. Her narrow breasts pressed together. Then the twisted furrow of Elizabeth Lucido's spine as she looked back over her shoulder at him.

"If I ever get in trouble," Murphy said, "you're the guy I'm calling."

"I'd be honored. Now smile."

Martin and Junior Daly appeared dumbstruck as the cops walked Rob Tucker to freedom.

"That's it?" Martin Daly cried out. "He skates?"

Murphy turned and leveled a glare at Daly. "No comment."

"I'm not a damn reporter, Murphy. I'm your boss, and I'm asking if you think he's connected to Elizabeth or Beth or Babs?"

"I don't know, Martin. What do you think?"

"I'm not paid to think, Murphy. You got that?"

"Then you're certainly earning your money."

Daly stared at Murphy with all the hate he could muster, then turned to the cameras and said that he believed this incident moved the case to another level, whether the police commissioner did or not. "I find it sad that—"

Charlie called out: "What about the Waterworks bodies?"

Martin turned to leave, hastily.

"Martin?"

"Look, I'm really busy right now."

"Not that busy, believe me."

"I don't know anything about any bodies in any waterfall, or whatever you just said. Now, please."

Daly and company fled across the street, so Charlie grabbed Maude and Murphy as they tried to make their way back into headquarters. Murphy held up his hand. "We can't talk yet either, Charlie, about anything. Please."

"But you can listen."

Everyone stopped short. Murphy said, "Go on."

Charlie said, "Waterworks, Inc., is a dummy corporation held by a private group of investors known as Stonehenge, which is actually a front for several prominent Republicans, including but not limited to Martin Daly. The company bought what is arguably marshland on the South Shore. The asking price was four million dollars. The sale price was two-point-one. Then Waterworks scrapped its original plans for a seaside golf course and applied for an emergency reclassification to heavy industrial last month."

"Yeah?" said Murphy "Why?"

"The place belongs on the Superfund list. But it's still worth a fortune if the new owners can switch the zoning. And if anyone can get something rezoned around here—"

"I've already talked to Stonehenge," said Maude.

"Maybe without all the information you needed," said Murphy.

Charlie's eyebrows flew up, and he waited for more but got nothing. "Anyway, I got my best nerds checking the available corporate records, working through the dodges, but they're thinking, bottom line, when the smoke clears, Martin and Kymberly own the place."

Murphy leaned close to Charlie. "Who sang, Charlie? Who left the envelope on your windshield?"

Charlie smiled coyly and said, "Do I rat out my people any more than you do?"

"No. You don't. And I respect you for that."

Maude said, "Any chance you're talking to a killer, Charlie, or just a whistle-blower piling on?"

"I don't know who I'm talking to, actually, but so far the facts check out."

Murphy punched Charlie in the arm. "You've been waiting for this a long time, haven't you?"

"Who around here hasn't?"

Murphy regarded the dogged reporter, his wrinkled flannel shirt and dirty khaki Dockers, his black running shoes, no socks. A true believer, he was, God love him. Nothing in his life but the news.

Maude said, "So why go to you? This isn't like ratting out a no-show job or something. If you know someone heavy's involved in kidnappings, or murders, you come to us, toot sweet. Game over."

"If you believe the cops can be trusted," said Charlie. "They already know the D.A.'s no frigging good."

Murphy nodded and said, "Is this the dirtiest government you've ever seen, or what?"

"Third-World corrupt," said Charlie.

"Stay in touch, Charlie," said Murphy. "We're on the side of the angels, too."

Murphy watched Charlie heading for his Volvo, jogging past a black van parked near to the curb. The white guy sitting behind the wheel of the van had binoculars pressed to his face and was looking directly at Murphy.

Murphy recognized the van and waved.

The guy behind the wheel ducked down.

"Fucking rookies," Murphy muttered. "Goddamn embarrassing sometimes."

FRANK MURPHY CORNERED MARTIN DALY IN HIS OFFICE. "SIR," Murphy said. "If you could, would you drop your daily planners for the last year by my office today? We need to match them up with Elizabeth's."

Martin Daly's face turned from angry red to terrified pale. "Excuse me?"

"Maybe we can find something to jog your memory. Like you said, anything we can do is worth a shot."

His entourage watched uneasily, some perhaps expecting to see handcuffs next.

"We'll need Junior's, too, if you'll notify him. We can never seem to get in touch with him."

Martin blundered into a long-winded rebuke of his effrontery, insisting loudly that the proper way to refer to his son was as Deputy County Executive Daly.

"Whatever," said Murphy. "Tell him we want it right away. Also, any possibility Beth Hopkins was in on screwing you, too, in the political sense? We'll find it if she was."

"I'm sure you will, and then we'll all know."

"We'll find out if you knew about it, too."

Martin Daly said, "Good-bye, Commissioner. And enjoy it while you can."

Murphy left the office knowing he had stung Martin,

hard, showing him his limits in the starkest terms. Murphy had no doubt Martin Daly would find a way to make him pay.

KYM SCALLIA-DALY SPENT THE MORNING AT HER GYM, SURVIVing a hangover by dreaming of sex in the sauna with the towel boy, Marco. Any actual exercise would have killed her, so she begged out of dance class. After a shower and a rubdown, she got dressed in a low-cut sweater and jeans and breezed from the locker room.

She climbed into her Miata, needing an icy cocktail in the worst way. There was a one-woman cooler on the floor next to her, and she dug a premixed Bloody Mary out of the ice, swallowed a third in one gulp, gasping at the relief. Then she picked up her car phone and started down her list of pals, hoping someone was free to come out and play.

chapter 36

M AUDE AND ROCKY WERE IN THE SQUAD LOUNGE, whose once-white walls were covered with dirty-joke faxes and wanted posters, purple fliers for Holy Name bus trips to Atlantic City, blue fliers for a preseason Knicks game at the Coliseum, the sign-up sheet for the Homicide golf outing, distractions Maude would concern herself with when things got back to normal.

Bone-tired, she stretched out on the cot next to the wall phone and watched Rocky strip to his T-shirt and boxers, the man, she realized, next to whom she had been sleeping during emergencies now for years, the

man, other than her brother, for whom she felt the
greatest affection. She watched his hairy back and burly
shoulders as he hung his clothes over the back of the
chair.

"I told them to wake us in two," she said.

"Well, aren't you a goddamn Girl Scout."

Rocky pulled down the only shade and killed the
overhead fluorescent lights, turned on the television set
that showed a reporter speculating on the latest theory
that Nassau Republican Chairman Seymour Cammeroli
was moving away from Martin because he thought
Martin had something to do with the missing women.

Thirty minutes later the door opened and light filled
the lounge. Bob Rankel was in the doorway, with
Martin and Junior Daly's Weekly Planning Books for the
periods requested. "Here's what you wanted. What's all
this about?"

Rocky propped himself on one elbow and rubbed his
face. "Hi, lou. What's up?"

Maude said, "Just churning the crap around, lou,
hoping for a break. Where'd you find Junior?"

"Actually, the Boy Wonder rolled in on his own. The
oddest thing."

Maude sat up and swung her stockinged feet onto the
tile. "Martin pissed off?"

"He'll never forget this, guys. In fact, if I were you
two, I'd find me a set of crooked steps and fall down
them. Retire wealthy."

"We think about it every day."

THE LOGS WERE LAUGHABLE, FRANK MURPHY SAW RIGHT AWAY,
containing among other items of municipal interest: a
recipe for a cocktail, The Tranquilizer, fast horses to bet,
primo tee times, circles around paydays. Martin Daly
really did do nothing but party at public expense. And
Junior's set of books were incomprehensible, incomplete,

and in pencil, proving only that Martin should rate country clubs for *Golf Digest* and Junior should finish fifth grade.

Flipping back to last winter, Maude showed Murphy a day on which Martin was actually present at work when Elizabeth saw "BB" at night.

Murphy picked up his phone.

"Martin Senior is out of touch at the moment," said Daly's secretary. "Can Martin Junior help?"

Murphy said, "Dubious. Just tell Martin I want to show him a certain list when he has a moment."

"I'd be glad to . . . Listen: Is Mr. Daly on this list? He's gonna ask right away."

"Tell him he's gonna be on mine if he doesn't call."

LATE THAT AFTERNOON FRANK MURPHY, ROCKY, AND MAUDE interviewed Beth Hopkins's parents in the Homicide conference room.

Her father had flown in from Northern California. The mother lived in SoHo. They had bickered about everything from the moment they laid eyes on each other.

Unfortunately, neither had seen much of their daughter in the last few years. "First the police department and law school," her mother said. "Then her practice, those crooks she signed on with."

"Her first abortion," added Dad.

"Nice, Herb."

"Fuck you, Karen."

Maude stood up and said, "Look, I want you to know that finding Beth has the top priority around here."

Her father asked, "Higher than finding a deputy county executive?"

"Sir, I know Beth from the Fifth Precinct. We worked adjoining sectors while she was going to law school. I'm looking for her like I'd look for my sister. Okay?"

Rocky said, "You people know Junior Daly?"

Karen Hopkins said, "I know who he is."

"A friend of Beth's?" asked Mr. Hopkins.

"Not really," said Karen Hopkins. "She said he was a jackass, to quote her directly. She mentioned you a lot, Commissioner."

"We're friends," Murphy allowed.

Maude asked, "Did Beth ever say anything about anyone following her lately?"

Herb scoffed. "Beth could handle something like that."

"So then where is she?" asked Karen.

They looked at Murphy. He didn't have an answer.

Herb did. "She's dead, Karen, and the sooner we accept it the better."

BACK IN HIS OFFICE, MURPHY DRANK HOT BLACK COFFEE AND stared at his empty IN box, which was normally a cluttered reminder of his failure to keep the paper flowing. He buzzed Annie Anderson. "Annie, has my mail fallen off lately?"

"I was kind of enjoying it, after that spate of hate mail."

"Anything come today?"

"Just one, from the IRS."

Annie brought Frank a letter advising him that according to an 1199 filed by Frank Murphy Security, Inc. (which did not exist), he had failed to report fifteen thousand dollars' income the previous tax year. As a result, he was required to appear in Holtsville, New York, on November fifteenth at noon. He was to bring all documentation for the three preceding tax years. He was free to bring professional assistance, at his own expense.

Murphy got on the horn to Martin Daly's office, was told he was still unavailable.

"Beep him."

"His beeper is broken."

"Then beep Bob Rankel for me. He is still one of my cops."

"Bob goes home early on Fridays."

"Just like everybody else over there."

Maude and Rocky barged in as Murphy slammed down the phone.

Maude said, "Daly still ducking us?"

Murphy said, "Something the big hump's very good at."

"What an asshole," said Rocky.

"Lotta assholes in this town. Truckloads of them. But I want to make sure we got our guns on Martin because of good police procedure, not because we think he's a douche-bag and it would be fun to fuck up his campaign."

Maude said, "We'd be remiss in not checking him and the people at Stonehenge out, whether it's fun or not."

"Okay, then . . . Thank you. Keep plugging."

"Wild horses," promised Maude.

Murphy nodded, noticing how tired and gray Maude looked, that she had not bothered with makeup today, or earrings. "Tell me the truth, Maude. You can't sleep if you're sitting by the window with a gun."

"Do I look that bad?"

Murphy had never thought of Maude Fleming as being concerned with her appearance, unforgivably doing her the injustice of forgetting that she was a lady, besides a very good cop. "This one's wearing us all out."

"Forget it. No guards."

Murphy looked at Rocky. "You doing anything tonight? Got a date?"

Rocky shook his head.

Murphy dug in his pocket and pulled out his wad, handed Rocky a fifty-dollar bill, and said, "I'm buying dinner. Then you sleep at Maudie's. Okay?"

"Sure."

Murphy turned to Maude. "Okay?"

"Whatever. . . . Thank you."

"Now, get out of here, both of you."

chapter 37

ELIZABETH LUCIDO DREAMED SHE WAS ON THE cashier's line at a Friendly's, where she had eaten breakfast and had no money to pay. Her mouth was stuffed full of bacon when holdup men burst inside.

Suddenly Jackson was shooting at her. Frank Murphy was shooting at Jackson. Her high school bandleader placed her in a straitjacket and dragged her down the steps of the County Executive building, to the parking lot, and left her there for dead. Then Martin was driving a John Deere over her bones.

She woke up gagging on the stench of decomposition, with just enough light now seeping down to see around her chamber.

There was a glorious throbbing springing up from her fingernail to her shoulder, and she thought, Please, Blessed Mother, give me torrents of pain, waves of sensation. What else hurt? Her neck, her shoulder. Her right ear. Nothing below the waist. Yet.

She had regained the strength and dexterity to zip open the bag, she realized, if she wanted to.

If she knew who it was, it might help her figure out who had dumped them here. Then even if she died here, she could scratch his name in the earth.

It took what felt like thirty minutes of circuit training, but Elizabeth finally worked the zipper open from the feet to the head, thinking she had never endured such agony to win such tiny victories.

In the dim light of the dungeon the dead woman looked ice-cold, her skin a ghostly white. Her skirt had ridden up, her ankles were bound.

She had a bullethole in her forehead, the skin puffy and black around the exterior.

Beth Hopkins, Elizabeth realized.

One of Martin's old girls.

Martin, who had partners below the line who depended on his continuing influence, partners who could reach out and crush the opposition. She had threatened them, and the world had fallen in on her. None of this should surprise her. This had Baltusrol Vail all over it.

Elizabeth curled her lip and snarled, worked the zipper closed. She eyed the stepladder on its side against the wall and set out on a journey of one hundred inches.

If she lived, she vowed, if she could drag herself to that ladder, she would crawl out of this hole, and she would find the people who had done this, and she would get even in ways not seen since the Spanish Inquisition.

Her enemies were not infallible. They had made mistakes. For one, they had left her alive.

chapter 38

A T THE ROCKVILLE CENTRE BOWLING ALLEY, TEN lanes were in use by an early league. The participants were of all genders and races, getting along as if they had all been Skull and Bones together at Yale. Jackson Hind, without his entourage, moved from end to end, working the peaceable crowd as they unwound from the labors of their day. He complimented strikes, picked up splits, while munching fries and pressing flesh. He promised his programs would deliver jobs beyond fast-food counters, hope for their children, freedom from the burden of supporting the machine. One man offered him a chance to roll a few, and Jackson, in stockinged feet, went spare-spare-strike, then knew enough to put his shoes and blazer back on.

He was eyeing the exit, thinking of the next stop, when Charlie Hotchkiss entered the alley, obviously looking for him, which might or might not be good news.

Jackson buttonholed Charlie to the side, near lockers that smelled like feet. "Any word on the girls?" Jackson refused to call the disappearances the Ladysnatcher case. He refused to believe Elizabeth was dead.

Charlie shook his head. "And don't pin your hopes on that Tucker guy, either. He's already suing Martin for libel."

"Not the cops?"

"Nope. Mr. Tucker said they were professional, if aggressive. He understands what they are up against."

Charlie asked, "Where's Dante?"

"Special assignment."

"No doubt planning some November surprise?"

Jackson didn't bite. On the wall behind the reporter a poster promoted Cosmic Midnight Bowling—including strobe lights, jelly-shots, and rock and roll, and he thought with regret how everything had to be jacked-up these days, tweaked beyond recognition.

"And the rest of the True Believers?" asked Charlie.

"Eating dinner with their families."

Charlie said, "You, know, if Martin Daly had half your energy—"

"—he'd still be an asshole."

Charlie bowed to concede the point, however professionally bound he was not to verbally agree.

Jackson said, "What can I do for you? Need a headline?"

"You hear anything about a write-in campaign for Artie Prefect?"

"He's already on the ballot. What's the point?"

"Not for county executive."

Hind threw his head back and laughed. "That's a new one on me. I'd have thought it would be Seymour himself, looking for a piece of the limelight."

"It's plausible if you do the math."

"Really?"

"It's that close. Also I wanted to let you know Martin's using the back-channel to link you to Beth Hopkins, planting the seed with my less ethical brethren. I got called by the *Daily News* for a fact-check, since everybody seems to think I'm in your pocket."

"What did you tell them?"

"I said I doubted it."

Jackson bit his lip. "Of course, this link is strictly professional."

Charlie laughed. "They're talking about some racy photo album the cops found, supposed to have you in it. Any truth to it?"

"No."

"Doesn't matter. You'll see the innuendos."

Jackson looked over at his curious new fans, at all the work he had to do merely to save his good name, never mind getting elected. "You know what, Charlie? I almost don't care."

"Keep this in mind, kid: The winner rewrites history. Daly wins, none of this ever happened."

"Right."

"Don't quit, man. Waterworks is about to explode in Martin's face."

"How?"

Charlie grinned. "I've already said too much."

Charlie headed for the exit like he had a school board meeting to cover, stopping just once to look back and wink.

Jackson said his good-byes down the lanes, urging everyone to vote and bring a friend. Outside the alley, Jackson sat in the dark in his Le Baron and pondered what to do next, with the opposition headed for the gutter. Their continued assault deserved a response, he decided, one large enough to deter further personal attacks. He pulled out his cell phone and called his dad at the house.

Dad listened without comment to the latest development.

Jackson expected tough questions, lawyer's questions.

His father said, "Do nothing. While your enemy is destroying himself, don't interrupt him."

"This isn't about the race anymore. This is about my good name. Our good name." Jackson peered through his windshield at the parked cars and trucks of people with outwardly placid lives, time for bowling.

"I'm telling you: Let it be. If you don't bite, Martin can't use it. Then, in a day or so, I'll call up that phony cocksucker and remind him that some of us still remember the boom-boom room, before he met Kiki."

"Kym."

"Before Kym there was a Kiki, rest assured. That funky town was Babylon during the seventies and eighties, don't tell your mother."

Jackson waited a moment. "Okay . . . Thank you."

"You're welcome. Any word on Elizabeth?"

"No. But thanks for asking."

ALICE GETTINGS WAS PERCHED ON THE EDGE OF THE LIVING ROOM couch when Frank got home. She was in her overcoat, her cheeks stained with teary mascara, two suitcases by her feet. "We had a run on the bank," she said without preamble.

Frank stopped short. "Bad loans?"

"Withdrawals," said Alice. "Because of you, we had county workers in droves, closing their accounts, telling my tellers they didn't trust their money with me anymore, since I was gonna marry a bum like you. Two big developers and half a dozen contractors transferred their funds. I've got a meeting tomorrow with the chairman of the board. I suspect I'm being fired, but nicely."

Frank simply said, "Oh, Jesus."

"You had to see them standing in line, smirking when they thought I wasn't watching. I wanted to cry right there, but I didn't want anyone to see. I worked hard for that job."

Frank tried to put his arms around her, but she held him off. "Alice, I never thought my—"

"You should have checked with me before you took on Martin. I could have told you what it would cost."

Murphy stared at his feet. "I might have done it anyway."

"Yes," said Alice, "I know. Which is why I have to go . . . at least for now. Until I come first."

"I still love you," he said, knowing it no longer mattered.

"Only when you want to, Frank. Not all the time."

"You don't know that."

"Don't insult me."

EVEN THOUGH THE MISSION WAS THRILLING, AND THE VALUE OF their exercise unquestioned, as Norman Keller thought back over the last few days he realized that Junior Daly was fast losing interest in their assignment, at least in the long stakeouts. And this in spite of progress they could be proud of: He had witnessed the Tucker pickup and put the word out in a timely fashion. He had earlier this evening witnessed Alice Gettings throwing two suitcases into the trunk of her Mustang and driving off at what he would characterize as a high rate of speed.

What a putz, he had thought, watching Frank Murphy slink back inside his lobby, a beaten man. What an amateur, thinking he could go against the wishes of the party.

Junior was missing out on something big here, too, but that, thought Norman, was the story of Junior's life.

Norman didn't mind being alone. He was used to it. Norman's parents had left him alone virtually since birth. But that had been his fault, according to them. Now, Norman was alone again, parked in a handicapped parking spot at the Garden City train station, which was his legal, if not moral, right. Norman Keller was indeed handicapped, had the paperwork to prove it, but the handicap had nothing to do with the distance he could cover from car to store. Sometimes he took advantage of his classification, sometimes he didn't. It depended on how he was feeling at that moment, about other people mostly, how they were reacting to him, what he could glean from their faces, their body language.

Tonight it wasn't personal. Tonight Norman was bent low in the window, watching through his video camera the outdoor pay phone near the tracks, where he had moments earlier taped to the glass a Polaroid close-up of his penis.

The late Friday night trains from Manhattan came and went, and Norman happily recorded close-ups of harried strangers reacting to his penis in various ways, until a white-haired man in a hound'stooth blazer stuffed the snapshot into his breast pocket and, looking both ways, walked away.

Private stock, Norman thought, an obsession he knew all about.

| Saturday, Nov. 2 |

chapter 39

JACKSON HIND'S RAPID RESPONSE TEAM WORKED throughout the night. While Martin and his minions slept, Jackson Hind, Irwin Gold, Dante Johnson, and all the other worker bees were chugging coffee, running here, there, Judge Hind watching over their efforts, often expressing amazement at how many things could be done at a Kinko's in the dead of night. Some things, he admitted, *had* changed since his retirement.

When the crew was finished, and the new commercial's final cut had been delivered to *News 12*, they all drove up to the Hind house in Cold Spring Harbor for breakfast beers and chili in front of the big-screen television.

DAYBREAK FOUND CHARLIE HOTCHKISS AT HOME, STILL SEARCHing for a link to Seymour Cammeroli, some evil motive or as yet invisible alliance to explain the series of disappearances. He knew it was there. He had watched the man pull strings for over a decade, and there was always a hidden agenda, almost as a point of pride. And if you wanted to understand Seymour, you kept an eye on his mother.

In the beginning he had situated Mama in the Surrogate Court, that she might oversee the division of lucrative probate work to that particular school of half-assed lawyers dependent on same, legal seagulls who could then be counted upon to attend funky fund-raisers and crowded golf outings, in addition to making large cash donations to the party chairman. Five years into the program, Mama suddenly moved on.

To please her only son she accepted a raise, a promotion, and a Jeep Grand Cherokee to park herself on the zoning board of appeals. Stalled projects got moving. Concrete got poured. In those days Seymour was still selling the hype that he was a benevolent boss, and after he took his cut, he shared the swag with everybody, even the unions. Who was gonna complain? Not the leading Democrats, whom he had co-opted with a smattering of public jobs wholly dependent upon his goddamn say-so. Not the similarly neutered Independents. Pretty much any other critics they painted as fringe and ignored. Charlie's own newspaper even looked the other way sometimes. For certain people, the editors insisted the story be airtight, then wrapped with a big red bow. No bow, no go. A reporter pushed it, *he* was labeled fringe.

Then real estate tumbled. Stores stood empty, on good streets and bad. Fingers got pointed as debt piled up. It was time to circle the wagons. Stay alive till 'ninety-five, was the slogan. Protect assets. Mama Cammeroli moved again.

Actually Buildings and Grounds sent a crew to cart her and her files across the parking lot to the office of the district attorney, where her son-in-law, Arthur Prefect, was busy backhanding into the crapper cases against their most prominent benefactors. Mama made sure the game remained the same.

Seymour loved his mama, and Mama loved her son, an American success story, Charlie thought ruefully, you could look it up, right in his very own paper. She had been widowed at twenty-six and raised her two kids all alone. What was always left out of the story was that she had raised them to be cruel.

Mama could write a book, thought Charlie. His book. But Mama wouldn't talk with a gun to her head.

Charlie fixed a second cup of instant coffee and sat down at his computer to edit his piece for Sunday, "Will Waterworks Drown Daly?" He finally had the opening right when his fax bell rang and a surprise edition of the *Grunt* curled out of his hardware.

This was rare, he thought, to get another so soon, off the apparent schedule. Charlie was jealous of the *Grunt*, and would kill to find the insider who kept scooping him.

One small article criticized Commissioner Murphy for not trusting his key people, for micromanaging the Ladysnatcher case and leaving other duties unattended, a softball piece considering what could have been written.

There was a story on open-ended contracts dating back thirty years. An embarrassing family tree of jobs and perks. And a mock-letter from District Attorney Arthur Prefect, which said that he and his wife were enjoying their "annual ass-licking tour of good old Nassau County, U.S.A."

Charlie was still chuckling when another fax curled up from his machine, a fax that said only: Turn on *News 12*.

SOMEONE HAD SCRATCHED "ASSHOLE" ON MURPHY'S POLICE car during the night and quick-glued both door locks. Murphy gave up jamming his key in them and stormed back into the condo. Upstairs, he called Jake to come get him on his way in to work.

"I wasn't going to work today."

"Sure you were."

"It's Saturday, Frank."

"Don't wimp out on me now."

Frank sat on the balcony and waited, wondering if Alice had nuked his car, or if it was someone else who currently hated his guts. Jake Posner was wearing clothes suitable for housepainting when he arrived at Murphy's condo fifteen minutes later. He handed Murphy the latest *Grunt.*

"I'm a nice guy, right?" asked Murphy, reading as they were riding down in the elevator.

"Would I be here on my precious day off if you weren't the all-time motherfucking best?"

"Not a micromanager?"

"Hell, no."

"So why am I being screwed with? You can tell me."

"Martin put the word out. The slide, as they say, has been greased. I've seen it before. It's like at the pistol range: Now everywhere you look, a bad guy pops up."

They walked out into the parking lot and stood beside Murphy's car like mourners at a grave.

"So what should I do?"

Jake said, "Call the county garage, I guess."

JAKE HUNG UP MURPHY'S OFFICE HOT LINE, STRUGGLED TO HIS feet, and turned on the television in the corner. Murphy looked up from the spread-out paperwork on the Lady-snatcher case.

"What now?"

Jake said, "A new Hind commercial. I hear we're not gonna believe it."

Anchorman Greg Cergol opened the morning show with national reports, then local briefs, then a quickie weather report—increasing clouds, periods of rain—before a highly polished political commercial began.

The television audience watched several clips of Junior Daly and Norman Keller riding in a black van while the sound track featured the ominous pounding of a distant bass drum. The voice-over artist said gravely, "Send the children from the room, citizens of voting age, because what you are about to see will shock and disturb them. Witness a day in the life of Deputy County Executive

Martin Daly, Jr., and his trusty assistant, Republican staffer Norman Keller." Amateur video footage showed Norman and Junior videotaping busy Homicide detectives, the police commissioner, political candidates, and pretty girls. The targets were each identified on the bottom of the screen. A sequence followed of Norman and Junior eating Big Macs, then Junior Daly sneaking away from the van, ducking behind a Long Beach Dumpster, squatting low and stoking up a joint, holding the hit, his face blown up like a pumpkin's.

"Well, I am shocked," said Jake.

"Ever smell Junior's breath?" Murphy asked Jake.

"Haven't had the pleasure."

The tape jump-cut to Norman Keller entering a phone booth at the Garden City train station, surreptitiously looking around like he was some kind of pervert, then taping to the wall what—with magnificent magnification—appeared to be a photograph of an erect white penis.

"Ever smell Norman's dick?" asked Jake.

"I thought it was a lousy picture of Martin."

Mercifully, the commercial concluded with Norman Keller in the driver's seat, his head tossed back and his eyes half-closed. A slow fade replaced Norman's face with an unflattering shot of County Executive Martin Daly.

Murphy said, "Was Normy Keller actually jerking off?"

Jake said, "That's pretty much what I look like over the bathroom sink."

The voice-over artist concluded, "Do we really need four more years of Martin Daly's family and friends running the show?"

The image of Martin's scowl faded to black.

"Damn," said Murphy. "You don't see that everyday."

"Martin just could lose this thing," said Jake.

"A notion," said Murphy, "that two months ago was unthinkable. Of course we'd be talking chaos. Locusts. Indictments. One hundred years of—"

The phone rang.

Jake picked it up, listened, looked at Murphy, covered the phone. "Charlie Hotchkiss wants to know why you authorized the use of that police van for political purposes."

"I didn't."

Jake smiled. "Junior stole it?"

Murphy said, "Have Charlie ask Junior's daddy."

Jake said, "How about, No comment, Frank? It's worked before."

"Come on, Jake. You want to cover for people like that?"

"No."

"Tell me the truth. You've wanted to sink that pompous fuck since the first day you met him."

"I didn't necessarily want to do it this morning."

"You know what? Sometimes we don't get to choose the when. Tell Charlie the fucking truth."

MARTIN DALY STARED DOWN UPON FAIRHAVEN HARBOR, THE kitchen phone to his ear, dying a slow death. Charlie Hotchkiss was on the other end of the line, waiting for a reaction.

"Jake the Snack told you that?"

Hotchkiss said he had confirmed certain information through Captain Posner.

"Good Lord, I made that fat fuck, pinned his damn bars on. Why is everyone turning on me?"

"I'd blame Junior, I was you."

"You talk to him yet?"

"Junior hasn't called back."

"When you find him, tell him I'd like a word as well."

Then Martin steadfastly denied Norman Keller. He had no knowledge, he claimed. He was ignorant. A political campaign was a vast, unorganized beast—questionable actions were sometimes taken on his behalf, he was shocked, outraged, it was obvious the killer hated Republicans, was perhaps an anarchist, foreign-born, possibly swarthy, of Middle-Eastern origin—

"So what's the problem, Martin? Why snoop in the first place? You don't trust Murphy's cops to solve the Ladysnatcher case?"

"No comment."

"You know how that sounds, don't you?"

Martin thought about it. "I know how it sounds."

Charlie laughed. "And you know that Jackson Hind suddenly has money pouring in, from Dems, Independents, even some of your people. Any comment on that?"

"This is America. People are free to make mistakes. I, of course, am free to remember them."

"You always were quotable, Martin. I'm actually gonna miss you."

Daly hung up and called Mike Barclay directly, demanded he explain the sudden surge to Jackson Hind.

"You mean besides the Junior Daly Comedy Hour?"

"It did seem like an hour, didn't it," said Daly.

"At least."

"Give it to me straight: How bad did he hurt me?"

"We're still finding out. But remember, also, Jackson's good at this shit. He's got that face. A silver tongue." Barclay said he had seen a list of large contributors. "A lot of big-shot women are already on there."

"Yeah? Friends of Elizabeth Lucido?"

"And maybe some husbands got their arms twisted, and there's the girls who think he's beautiful. But your numbers with women have always been lousy. They perceive you as arrogant. I haven't the fogglest idea why."

Martin stared out at the harbor. "Can't we use Kym to help?"

"Don't be dumb, Martin. People hate Kym more than you."

Daly mentally scanned his list of devoted supporters. "Where are my unions? Where are—"

"The unions say your office is inattentive to their needs unless, of course, you want something back. They say you don't return their calls anymore."

"Sure I do. Elizabeth did."

"Not lately. And I'm talking before she disappeared. Massively inattentive, was a phrase I heard. Downright rude."

"That fucking bitch!"

"I didn't hear that. What I did hear was a rumor knocking you off the ticket for health reasons, going with a write-in for Arthur Prefect, who, of course, will graciously accept the call to higher office."

"I wouldn't step aside for him if I was dead."

"I think they know that."

In an absolute panic, Martin dialed through the party roster, in short order learning that Elizabeth Lucido had been freezing out his biggest supporters since July, dumping phone calls, holding up goodies, double-crossing valued friends. Key people were pissed off at him at a time when he needed them to be positively fucking thrilled. If he had to say, "I'm sorry, my old friend, I didn't know," one more time that morning he thought he would scream.

Oh, yeah, Elizabeth had fucked him good.

He put down the sweaty phone and walked to the base of the staircase. "Honey? You want to get up now? I need some help. People are trying to bury me alive."

His phone rang again, and he raced to it: his man at the zoning board.

"The board delayed decision on Waterworks. Lots of backstroking by everybody."

"Murphy did this to me, with that fucking dyke."

He called Seymour, who could not or would not come to the phone, and he didn't dare call that big fuck

Denny a liar. "He's off today, Mr. Daly. Like most people. He did see your son on television, though."

Martin hung up, gut-sick at the Mineola Freeze-Out, a tactic he had used on so many others. Nobody knows you. Nobody calls you back. Identity is a trick. After all these years in office, he thought, all those favors, hell, all those crimes, he had earned no more true and dependable friends than he had when he was a kid, when he was Farty Marty, and the Berezuk twins down the block de-pantsed him just for laughs.

Martin pictured the three missing women at a political command post somewhere, in a bunker, plotting his overthrow, loving his confusion. All to be forgiven by Cammeroli and Prefect when the last vote was tallied.

Impossible?

Nothing was impossible on Long Island.

Read the brochures.

chapter 40

THE LADYSNATCHER SAT IN HIS CAR TWENTY-FIVE yards down the tree-lined street from Martin's home. He was flipping through *Newsday*, waiting patiently, unafraid of being caught, because he had an infinitely plausible story ready, just in case. He stared through the drizzle and the trees up at the big white house. Don't think I only do broads, you donkey prick. Don't think for one moment you or yours are safe.

Fuck me, my man?

Oh, no. Fuck you.

The Ladysnatcher heard the guttural throb of a Porsche from high up on the hill, and he slunk low in his seat, waiting.

chapter 41

HE BOXSTER FLEW THROUGH THE GATES AT THE END of the driveway. Martin caught a glimpse of a vehicle parked halfway up his neighbor's driveway, and thought of the recent burglaries in the area, then dismissed it. He ground gears and burned rubber on the three-mile course to the Fairhaven Country Club. He ignored the valets at the bag-drop and parked at the front door.

His so-called friends were in the Grill Room, under portraits of past swells and favorite hunting dogs. Seymour Cammeroli, Archie Collins, Judge Abner Hoffmann, and that scumbag Slingblade Beinstock were rolling dice to pay for the Bass Ale they were drinking from pilsner glasses. There was one empty chair at the table, a cigar burning in an ashtray.

"No golf?" asked Martin.

"You looked outside?" asked Beinstock. "That wet stuff is rain."

"Funny."

Seymour said, "What do you want? We're playing a game here."

"I want to bounce those two detectives."

"No," said Seymour. "That will signal panic."

"I don't think you understand. They found Waterworks, Seymour. We're fucked."

"Not we, Martin. You. You are fucked."

Martin stared at Seymour, failing to comprehend the message.

Archie Collins said, "Answer your calls."

"What do you mean?" asked Daly.

"We're out of Waterworks, ten minutes after that dyke dick left Seymour's office. I called everybody, you included."

"Who bought your shares?"

"Your blind trust."

Martin got it, hard, in the pit of his stomach.

"You guys fucked me."

Collins said, "Like I said, answer your phone calls."

Seymour spread his hands, palms up, and said, "Sorry, buddy."

"I've been a little busy, you know? Broads disappearing. Cops fucking up. Answer my phone calls. Well, don't that beat—"

Seymour slammed down the dice. "And don't hire dip-shits like Norman Keller, either. His father was an asshole, his grandfather, too. I have never been so fucking embarrassed in my life."

"That was Junior's idea."

"It's always Junior's fault, isn't it. Or Kym's. It was always Elizabeth's fault, when she was still around. What do you say when I'm not in the room, you motherfucking prick. It's Seymour's fault, I'll bet."

"Never."

"After the election, unless you manage to lose the fucking thing, you and me better come to a different agreement. You undertstand?"

"What are you doing to me? You're acting like I have something to do with these broads. Like it's gonna explode in our faces. Is that why I'm hearing fucking Prefect's name?"

A heavy hand wrapped around his neck and roughly moved him aside. "Jump in my grave that fast, Martin?"

Martin glared up into the handsome face of Baltusrol Vail. "Who the— Mr. Vail, I'm sorry. I didn't realize. I—" Martin had not seen Vail in at least two years, and not from lack of trying. Any rumors he was ill were clearly ridiculous; a more fit, tanned, All-American male you never saw. He wore white trousers and a white sweater, gold on his fingers and wrists. His shoulders were as wide as a dashboard. "Good to see you, Baltusrol, it's been a long—"

"You're not a member here, are you?"

Daly swallowed and looked at the boys around the table, who had all taken that moment to study their knuckles. "Fine. Sorry. I read you loud and clear."

Vail said, "I doubt it. We'll see you around."

Not without effort did Martin hold his head high as he walked out of the Fairhaven clubhouse. He squeezed into his Boxster, and patched out, made it as far as the stone gates of the club before he skidded to a stop, opened his door, leaned out, and threw up in the flower bed.

He had never been so frightened in his life, not even when he found his first wife overdosed in the basement at Blue Landing, and he was forced to contemplate raising his children on his own.

MAUDE KNOCKED ON HIS OFFICE DOOR AND CAME IN. "LOOK, I really do need to talk to Martin again."

Murphy said, "Where's this heading?"

"You're not gonna like it."

"Junior?" asked Murphy.

Maude shrugged. "They were rivals. He's a fuck-up. She was sabotaging his father's campaign."

"Like he'd care," said Murphy.

"His alibis suck, all three times. He knew them all. We got his prints in Lucido's bedroom."

"How does it feel in your gut?"

"Empty."

"You think we should be following him?"

"I don't know. Maybe we should work him over first."

Murphy found her indecision troubling. "What else is going on?"

"Detectives from the Robbery squad spent the morning with the bar crowd from the Regency the night Beth disappeared, interviewing several folks who shouldn't have been there. So far no one linked to our cast of characters was present."

"Too bad. Keep trying. . . . Maude, am I a micromanager?"

"Not at all, boss. And the *Grunt* ain't always right. We're glad to have you around. I promise."

"Okay. I'll talk to you later."

Frank figured Maude was just being nice, that it was a good time to hit the highway by himself. Give his cops a little air. He called down to the garage. "My new wheels gassed and ready?"

"Yes, sir."

"You get the pot smell out of it?"

"Did the best we could."

"I'm on my way."

"I'll wake everyone up."

"You're a pisser, Capriotti."

Five minutes behind the wheel of the black Grateful Dead van and Murphy felt almost young again. A part of him had dearly missed the blasts of adrenaline, the constant edge particular to police life, at the mercy of fate, or any asshole with a quarter. Listening to radio runs, he felt it all coming back to him, the tension, the rush. Not all of it, actually, because the dispatchers would not be sending him to horrific auto accidents or family fights, he would not be fishing swollen bodies from reservoirs or searching for stolen bikes. He would not be rolling on a sidewalk, fighting for his gun. One of the lies cops told

themselves was that the job was different every day,
when it wasn't, not at all. It was the same sad story, time
and again.

Murphy parked the van in his condo garage for
safety, locked it tight, walked into the lobby to check his
mailbox.

Jackson Hind, wearing mirrored sunglasses and a
Reggae Sunsplash baseball cap, was waiting for him, reading the *New York Times*.

Murphy double-clutched, his reverie of increased
capacity broken.

"Hey, Murphy, got a minute?" Jackson smiled his
winning smile. "Sorry to bother you on a weekend."

"We're a twenty-four, seven operation. You know that."

"I hear we've got something in common."

"Yeah?"

"Our fiancées are missing."

Murphy couldn't help but like this guy; he could see
why his followers were passionate. He warned himself
not to fall for the schmooze. "She said I didn't consider
her feelings enough."

"You're not the first man to hear that."

Murphy punched the elevator button. "How'd you
know?"

"Not many secrets around here, are there?"

"There's too damn many, Jackson," said Murphy.
"Let's fix that, what do you say? Feel like a beer?"

"I'm parched."

The doors slid open.

Five minutes later they were on Murphy's balcony,
solemnly toasting Elizabeth's health and staring out at
the harbor, at the trees on its jagged shoreline.

Jackson admitted: "This has been bloody hell."

"I'm sure it has."

"The campaign was cake. I had it on cruise-control
and was holding up like a stallion."

"You were scaring the hell out of them. Still are."

Jackson nodded. "Good. But it doesn't keep me warm."

"Tell me what you know about Beth Hopkins."

Hind admitted he knew Beth Hopkins from the Mineola power-swirl. She had never given to his campaign. They had flirted as adversaries but had never been lovers, despite current rumors regarding a certain photo album.

Murphy did not mention that he wished he could say the same. "She's not in on the palace coup?"

"Negative."

"Babs Whitcomb?"

"I've already answered that. No."

"How'd you hear about Beth's photo album?"

"Charlie Hotchkiss."

Hind was right about secrets in Mineola; they were rare as good ideas. "How long did you have someone tailing Junior?"

"On and off for the last year. Pretty steadily since Labor Day. You'll agree it finally paid off?"

"You have someone on him the night Elizabeth disappeared?"

"No."

"Beth Hopkins?"

"Yes, I did. He rode around with that Norman character until around six o'clock in the evening, then they split up behind the Executive Building. Junior got in his car and drove off to wherever. My man stayed with Norman, figuring he would eventually head home to Roosevelt, which is where my man also lives. An unfortunate coincidence, I'm afraid."

"And, of course, Norman Keller wasn't busy snatching Beth, was he?"

"Nope. Sorry. But just between us kids, was that not funny or what?"

"As good as Tommy Gulotta in his Islander pajamas,

climbing into bed with John Spano." Murphy fondly remembered how a fraudulent amateur had damn near fleeced the wolves, you want to talk about backstroking and head-ducking. "Martin lives right over there, you know," Murphy said, pointing in the direction of Blue Landing. "Quite a spread."

"I'm thinking of quitting."

"Aw, no. Don't quit. You can take him."

Hind gave Murphy a quizzical look. "I'd have to fire you, Frank, and from what I hear, you're a damn good commissioner."

"Be worth it," said Murphy, "just to watch them suffer."

THAT SATURDAY AFTERNOON JUNIOR SPENT PARTYING IN NEW York City, allowing the taxpayers of Nassau County to fund an eight-ball of coke for him, while they still could. He wore crummy chinos and a Budweiser sweatshirt; there was no chance someone would recognize him, no chance he'd be starring in a second Hind commercial.

He had taken the train to Penn Station and then worked his way north and east across Manhattan, zigzagging his way to the river, winding up in a bar on First Avenue, where the patrons were watching Notre Dame football. The station ran the Norman and Junior commercial at halftime, but no one at the bar recognized him, good-looking guys a dime a dozen in New York. Watching through cocaine's detachment, even he had to join in the laughter, particularly when Norman's eyes rolled back in his head.

Three drinks later Junior had grown balls enough to squeeze into a phone booth in the back and use his cell phone to check his answering machine.

He listened to three nasty messages from Maude Fleming, one from Norman, and one from dear old dad. Taking the path of least resistance, Junior dialed Norman, to see how he was making out.

"Not too fucking good," Norman whined. Norman said he was no longer needed in the campaign, that when he went down there they told him to get lost. His gloating black neighbors were mocking him, the little kids calling him short-stroke.

"Don't worry, my man. (Sniff) I'm getting even for both of us," said Junior.

"Please," said Norman, "don't do me any favors. Someday people will forget this, and I'll be able to get a job raking leaves."

"And those will be Nassau County leaves, if I have anything to say about it." (Sniff)

Norman hung up on him.

Junior momentarily considered calling his father and apologizing, decided against it. Maude Fleming had no shot.

He thought about doing more lines, then getting laid in a big way, so he ducked into the bathroom, did the lines right off the top of the toilet tank. He left the bartender a tip and stumbled outside and down the street, figuring he would grab a cab to the Lower West Side, now that Disney'd forced the working girls from Times Square.

Or, fuck it, he could go to a nice midtown hotel and use his county credit card, get some broads he'd actually touch if he wasn't on a blast. His expense report would reflect his attendance at a seminar. For the good of the people.

They'd find him then, he thought, from the credit card. He'd seen that in movies. Fuck. What now?

Junior was standing midblock on First, yellow cabs whizzing by him, paralyzed by sexual indecision and coke, looking like a midwesterner, trying to light a cigarette.

A white man in a New Jersey Devils' cap stepped forward with a lighter flaming. Junior leaned into the fire and sucked, until the man slugged Junior hard in his unsuspecting belly and shoved him into the alley.

Junior couldn't draw the breath to say who he was, what he could offer, as if that would have helped.

chapter 42

ROCKY BLAIR SAT AT A SPARE DESK IN THE REAR OF THE Records Bureau, ignoring the deadpan, prying eyes of lifers. He was flipping through a foothigh stack of documents, but he was worrying about the photograph of Beth Hopkins with Frank Murphy, which was still in his jacket pocket, where it very much shouldn't be. He was dreading the man-to-man questions he would soon have to ask the best boss he had ever worked for. He was dreading telling Maude.

Going through Beth's police department files, expecting to find glowing recommendations from Frank Murphy, Rocky discovered that Beth Hopkins had once worked a summer job for the Village of Fairhaven, one of many breeding swamps for Nassau County politicians. She had been eighteen at the time. Her duties were described as special assistant to the Director of Citizen's Affairs. Her tenure had continued after high school, through night college, until she left to join the Nassau County Police. The mayor of Fairhaven at the time had been Martin Daly. The recommendation given Beth by the Director of Citizen's Affairs, her immediate superior, was first-rate. It was signed by Martin Daly, Jr.

Junior, thought Rocky, recommended someone for something? What a joke. Rocky pulled out his cell phone and turned his back on the fossils. He called

Maude at the Homicide office, told her what he'd found.

"Really," said Maude. "Nobody volunteered any of that. Jesus, how old was he then? Nineteen, maybe?"

"Now we're getting somewheres," he said. "Right?"

"Maybe," said Maude. "But tread lightly there, my brother. Don't talk about it to anybody. And don't start looking like you're enjoying yourself."

"There's a couple of other things I should check at Fairhaven Village Hall."

"Fuck that noise," said Maude. "Slip what you can down the front of your pants and then act like you didn't find shit. Put on your coat and say thanks to the dinosaurs."

Still holding the phone to his ear, Rocky loaded his blazer pockets with the forms he needed, then spun around and faced the crew, two of whom were definitely straining to hear his end of the conversation. "Right. I hear ya," he said. "Good enough for government work. You want fries with that burger?"

MURPHY, ROCKY, AND MAUDE OPENED JUNIOR'S OFFICE WITH A key from Janitorial Services. The air inside was foul with smoke and mildew, the furniture filthy, the carpet covered with dust balls.

"Looks like he keeps housekeeping out of here," said Maude.

"Because no one can do the job like he can," said Murphy.

Cobwebs draped the computer.

Rolling papers and condoms filled his bottom drawer.

His out box contained a Sony Discman and twenty assorted rock and roll discs, heavy on Pink Floyd and U2. It might as well have been a dormitory room, thought Murphy.

"This hump makes more money than all of us," said Rocky. "Is life unfair or what."

Maude opened a cabinet and stood flipping through the few files there while Murphy checked the clothes closet and Rocky scanned the *Penthouse* magazines he found in the bottom desk drawer. The closet held a softball uniform on a hanger, two putters, and a case of Pindar merlot, shy four bottles.

Maude held up a manila envelope. "I got a file here on that sexual harassment suit they settled against Junior last year."

Murphy remembered the case: Junior, drunk, had dropped trou at a retirement party for a clerk in Public Information, then tried to get one of the younger secretaries to record a farewell wish into his bone-o-phone. Lots of laughs, Murphy had heard, until the offended sought counseling. The matter was settled quietly. Your tax dollars at work.

"None of this means nothing," said Murphy. "Just a boy misbehaving."

"Give me time," said Maude, "and maybe not much."

chapter 43

E LIZABETH REACHED THE PYRAMID OF CAMPBELL'S chicken noodle soup at four o'clock that afternoon, ready to gnaw through the side of the cans. The dresser drawers were stuck, and she was weak, but she heaved and pulled and finally yanked one free. A tray of silverware and two plastic walkie-talkies clattered onto her legs.

She found a rusty church key on the ground, opened a can and, lying on her side, she drank and wept. She spilled as much as she swallowed, but what went into her mouth was good enough, cool and wet, her first nourishment other than muddy water for over a week.

She rested then, flat on her back, staring up at the crack in the door above her. It was bigger today than yesterday. It would be bigger still tomorrow, after nocturnal animals spent another night scratching at it.

Elizabeth devoured a second can of soup and gave thanks to her God.

A second drawer held a child's sleeping bag, and she covered herself as best she could.

She would survive, she promised herself. Nothing would stop her. She would have her revenge.

She remembered them all in the car somewhere in Glen Cove last year, before she met Jackson. They had an hour to kill. Martin had called up to Rankel, "I need a blow job. Who are we near?"

And Rankel had provided a woman's name, the happy news that they were less than a mile away. The lucky woman was, of course, home, and Elizabeth and Bob Rankel waited outside in the car while the king paid a visit to his subject. That was when she knew what he truly thought of her.

Elizabeth's mind wandered to Seymour, the only one who could set this in motion. That little bastard wrecked folks willy-nilly, for sport.

Elizabeth had questioned the logistics of the Waterworks deal, the chances of discovery by a less than understanding press. She had been told to mind her own business in the harshest terms. She had enough on her plate. Don't get pushy. Did she have to run everything? Look at the power you've got, he would say, what I can take away.

What I can take away.

The light from the crack above grew weaker as night drew on.

Elizabeth decided it was time to see what she could do with that ladder.

chapter 44

F RANK MURPHY ATTENDED A JACKSON HIND FUND-
raiser that evening at the Brookville horse
farm of Yvonne and Marco Stratford, local
stars of stage and screen, who were, sadly, no-
shows at their own house. In fact, you couldn't even see
the main house, so far away had the striped tent been
situated.

Nice Portosans, though, thought Murphy. Plenty of
floodlights. And real nice stables for ten very lucky
horses. You could hardly smell them. The fence that
ringed these meadows cost more than his condo.

Under the big tent there was food he couldn't name,
so Murphy sipped scotch on the rocks and studied the
faces of politicians who won as often as the Washington
Generals. Don Neville was there, of course, shaking
hands and slapping backs, giving aid and comfort to
only his daughter, pretending bravely to lead the loyal
opposition; but anyone who knew anything knew he
was bogus, a front man. He had no cash to give to
Jackson's campaign, few workers at his disposal. Just
like everybody else, he called Seymour Cammeroli when
he needed something done and hoped he got a call
back. He was consulted on key issues about as often as
Junior.

Neville stood at the mike and got everyone's attention only by tapping three-by-five cards against it loudly.
He read aloud a telegram of support for his daughter's
candidacy from Alex Baldwin.

• • • •

MURPHY ROAMED THE BACK OF THE TENT, NOTING THE BODY-guards, which you don't see every day, thinking you knew you were out of your element when Charlie Hotchkiss looked like good company.

"Hello, Commissioner. Notice there ain't any unescorted big-shot broads here tonight?"

Murphy grimaced. "That's not how I would put it."

"I can clean up the prose later. But you know what I mean. The Ladysnatcher's doing wonders for the personal security industry."

"If you suggest an atmosphere of unease grips this party I shall wring your bloody neck."

Charlie stroked his jaw and stared at the crowd. "Think the Ladysnatcher's here?"

"I don't know."

"I still like the Stonehenge connection," said Charlie. "Beth Hopkins doing their legal work."

Murphy kept his surprise from showing, aided by a sudden commotion near the main tent as security personnel moved temporary fencing to allow the Reverend Jeremiah Dartmouth to pull up close in his Lexus. Murphy watched the cable-television guru climb out and shake hands and hug women, then refuse all worldly sustenance as he stepped to the mircrophone. He said something comforting about democracy and the higher calling of politics. Then he checked his Rolex and cut short the Benediction. Another function, he apologized. His flock was large and widely scattered. Charlie moved off to grab a word with him, but he was gone in a blink, trailing a cloud of floodlit dust between the rows of shiny cars.

Boy, had times changed. Murphy remembered when men of the cloth embraced poverty and drove Volks-wagen vans, stayed around endlessly to break bread and drink wine. His parents had not given him and Wally much, but they had given them a relationship with God, the comforts and constraints of religion. "Takes all the wondering out of it," his father liked to say. "God said it and I believe it. End of fucking story."

Murphy walked from the tent, out past the last parked car, ten yards farther over the uneven turf of the dark field. He pulled out his phone and called Maude at her home. "Rocky there?"

"Yes, Daddy. We're all tucked in."

"Beth Hopkins was in on Stonehenge, for Slingblade Beinstock."

"That means Arch Collins knew both women. I'll have to ask him again if he knew Babs Whitcomb. Where'd you get that little tidbit?"

"Charlie."

"God love him."

"Why didn't we have it?" asked Murphy.

"I don't know, boss. People who should have volunteered it, didn't."

"I really don't like having to lean on Charlie for breaks, you know what I mean?"

"Sorry."

"Don't be sorry. I know how much digging is involved." It was clear from her tone he had hurt her feelings. "What's Rocky think?"

"Rocky thinks it's Junior."

"At least he's off Jackson Hind."

"Rocky adores suspects he already dislikes."

"Who doesn't?"

After a moment Maude said, "You okay?"

"I'm tired, and frustrated, and I'm sorry if I was short with you," said Murphy. "I'm going to see my little brother, then I'm going home. Then I'm going to call Alice and beg her for the umpteenth time to come back."

"You tried roses?" asked Maude.

"And candy. And a tennis bracelet."

"Maybe try leaving her alone for a while."

"That's what got me into this mess."

"Perhaps."

THE NURSING STAFF AT THE INSTITUTE WAS REMARKABLY BUSY when Murphy strolled in, their serious faces buried in charts, their helping hands digging in drawers, punching phone numbers. Nobody said hello. Nobody said thanks for the sack of White Castle burgers he plopped on the counter.

As Murphy walked toward Wally's window, ignoring the ward stench, he heard his brother grunting from the middle row of beds, and he got it, the point of the cold shoulders, the lengths his new enemies were willing to go to settle scores.

Wally had been moved away from his window, his buddy George.

Wally was a weeping, sweaty mess, fighting his restraints, his eyes wide, tortured, pleading.

"He's taken a turn for the worse," said the nurse who suddenly eased up next to Murphy. "At least that's what the doctor said. They wanted him closer to the nursing station."

"Baloney. This is bloody goddamn politics."

The nurse studied her shoes. "I didn't see nothing wrong with him myself till they moved him down here."

"He lives for that window. And Laughing George there."

"And visits from you."

"Where's Dr. Kantrop?" snarled Murphy.

"On a Saturday? Probably Vermont."

"Can you fix this by yourself?"

"Not without getting jammed up."

"Then get Wally's discharge papers ready."

"But who's gonna—"

"But nothing, dear. And make sure to tell Kantrop I'll be back."

Half an hour later Wally was tucked into Frank's big bed, watching television as if he'd never seen one.

Frank was on the phone in the spare bedroom next door, Alice's home-office, hunting the clinic administrator down, and on the verge of threatening the owner of the answering service with arrest, when the fax beeped, and a single paper curled into the tray. It was a special edition of the *Grunt;* and he read it expecting a beating.

Oddly enough, he didn't get one.

The stories were largely about grant money lost because Martin Daly's staff failed to file for them on time. The "We're Related" column was a cartoon of a dope-smoking Junior and a masturbating Norman Keller that had to have been done by a professional. The caption said: THE JERKY BOYS. JOINT OPERATION.

Frank tossed the *Grunt* in the trash and closed up the spare room. He put on pajamas and climbed into bed with Wally.

"Good night, my man."

Wally looked at Frank and smiled so widely Frank's heart near burst. Frank patted Wally's hand, rolled over, and buried his face in the pillow, hoping his mother was smiling down on them; because having his little brother in the Institute had loomed over the whole of Frank's life, as a constant threat and a guilty blessing. He often wondered at what he had missed without Wally around, if he would have been more selfish or generous, dependent or brash, how Wally's lack of a normal life had shaped his own. Sure, he had learned to appreciate his life, and to remember other folks hauled around loads you couldn't see. But he had also discovered that, sometimes, taking nothing for granted could wear a person out.

He hoped his father could see them together, see how real men treated the wounded. It wasn't necessary to hide your unfortunate ones. Not everybody was born perfect, or remained perfect.

Families stuck together.

Sunday, Nov. 3

chapter 45

URPHY AND MAUDE FLASHED THEIR TINS AND BUL-
lied their way past security into the hallowed
confines of Beinstock, Bates at seven-thirty-
nine that Sunday morning.

Beth Hopkins's office was spare, modern, with a view
of the Coliseum. It had been thoroughly cleaned out,
the wastepaper basket emptied, files dumped; whatever
papers she'd left out on the desk or credenza had been
put away. Dust outlined where her terminal had sat.

"I'm surprised someone hasn't moved in already,"
said Maude, sitting behind Beth's desk, soaking up the
ambience.

"Cold, ain't it."

"Hey wait," said Maude. "Come here."

She pointed to Beth's blotter, which had not been
removed. Handwritten in ink across the bottom right
corner were the words: DISTRICT ATTORNEY ELIZABETH HOP-
KINS. Below that, D.A. HOPKINS. "Maybe she wasn't blowing smoke. If they can write in Prefect for Daly's job, they
gotta write in somebody for Prefect's job, too, right?"

Murphy said, "They sure do."

"Let's keep digging."

They left Beth's office and shooed from the file room
a flustered young male associate they caught playing
solitaire. Murphy locked the steel door behind them and
looked around. Even in here, the wainscoted walls held

portraits of clipper ships, hunting dogs, and partners. They spoke a promise: Every partner was a king; every client a gentleman.

"Don't waste time," said Murphy. "The sharks should be here soon."

Maude got busy going through Beth Hopkins's files, while Murphy flipped through other drawers, looking unsuccessfully for files on Baltusrol Vail, Seymour Cammeroli, Barbara "Babs" Whitcomb III. They had twenty-two minutes before the first knock landed on the door.

"Hell-o-o? Excuse me?"

Maude glanced at the door, flipped faster through papers.

"Commissioner Murphy? Marsh Beinstock here."

"Good morning," Murphy yelled with good cheer.

"Are you kidding me, Frank? Are you out of your goddamn mind? Our clients expect confidentiality, not a squad of cops pouring over their deepest secrets."

"Coming, Marsh. Relax." Murphy started toward the door, slowly, looking at Maude, waiting for the go-ahead.

She finally looked up at him, exasperated. "Fuck it. I need hours."

Murphy unlocked and opened the door.

Marsh Beinstock stood in the doorway in a yellow golf ensemble, holding a court order sealing the law firm records. Beinstock handed the order to Murphy, who saw it had been signed fifteen minutes earlier, no doubt on the Fairhaven putting green.

"There's a better way to do this," Murphy said, "us being big golfing buddies and everything."

"No, there is not."

"Maybe you'd get to see your missing partner again."

"We doubt it."

"Oh, you do?"

"Unhappily, yes. Turn the page."

"Nice."

"I will tell you this, for when you run out of leads. She was a gambler—with a sizable debt run up at two casinos. We talked to her about it in a partners' meeting last month. Perhaps you might . . ."

Maude growled. "You know what this makes you guys look like, right?"

"Nobody cares, Detective Fleming, or at least not for long. And I'll take that file, please."

Maude handed him the Stonehenge file without comment.

Murphy glared at Beinstock. "Good Lord, isn't anybody straight?"

"The world is not black or white, Commissioner. You know that. The straight are mowed down."

"Or kidnapped?" asked Maude.

"Be very careful, Detective. Your star is sinking fast."

Murphy asked Maude, "You seen enough?"

"Sure did," said Maude. "Let's rock."

THE PHONE CALL MARTIN HAD BEEN DREADING CAME FROM A former congresswoman, keynote speaker, and current perky-mom, calling on behalf of the state committee. Martin could not have been more unsettled by a French kiss from a Mafia don. He sat up in bed and swung his feet onto the hardwood floor. "Susan. Good to hear from you. How's your dad?"

"Pissed off. Just like the governor, the senator . . ."

"Seymour's holding me at arm's length, he, he . . ."

Susan said nothing, which said volumes.

Martin did not roll out his résumé, nor break into one of his stump speeches. He begged for his political life, or failing that, a judgeship.

She scoffed at his weakness. "We haven't lost Nassau since the Stone Age. Since Nickerson. But you might."

"I can fix this. I swear it. Have Pataki give me thirty minutes outside LILCO—a totally controlled photo op—

no chance of questions. Susan, I'm in trouble here."

"Withdraw. Step down. Go away. You're bad news."

Martin hung up and stared out the window like a man with a date with the electric chair. Out on the distant gray water a red-and-white tanker blew its foghorn; closer to the shoreline a clam boat chugged past. The air smelled fresh, earthy, full of life.

Why me? he thought. Why are all worlds beautiful except mine?

Then he thought of someone else whose world suddenly wasn't so beautiful, either, hit the speed-dialer, woke his only son and told him who had called, and why.

Junior coughed up a hair ball. "Fuck that dopehead phony. What time is it anyway? Ow, my aching head."

"Noon, asshole . . . and the dope joke is funny, coming from you. What's the matter with your head?"

Junior groaned and said, "I got rolled, Dad, on the fucking East Side, in broad fucking daylight. By a *white* guy. I woke up in an alley, without my wallet or my watch. I had to walk to Penn Station, looking like a bum."

"You are a bum."

"Like how many times can I say I'm sorry?"

"I'll let you know."

"Hey, you want me to quit? Say the word. Only how will it look if even I turn on you?"

"I suggest you read today's newspaper before you threaten me with your alleged clout. Charlie-boy fucked you, kid, top editorial. Let me read you the best parts: 'Much blame lies with Junior' . . . yada, yada, here we go, 'a well-dressed, handsome nitwit. The family embarrassment. Flunked out Hofstra, Adelphi, Post, NCC . . . a record of dis-achievement in lofty positions that would be laughable were it not so sad . . . For Martin Daly to deserve a vote, he must fire his son. Let's see this new Nassau.' "

Junior said, "Who gives a shit, as long as I get paid."

"Seymour won't pay you, and I can't pay you. You'll be riding a bike again, and living up here with me."

After a moment Junior said, "Okay. I'm coming."

"Straight here, son, no stops, no detours. And don't come in here stinking of pot. I've fucking had it."

BARBARA LASCH LIT A CIGARETTE AND BLEW THE SMOKE AWAY from Charlie. Reluctantly, she said, she had come to the decision to back Charlie off, even after seeing evidence that Kym Daly was an open book of scandalous behavior. The slam-job on Junior was enough, she said. "Let them breathe."

"But this is Family Dysfunctional, and they're running the goddamn show."

"You gonna demand he divorce her? Lighten up."

Charlie crossed his arms and frowned. He did not like to be accused of being overly righteous, and that's exactly what his editor was saying.

Barbara Lasch said, "I don't like to bash Kym because I feel sorry for her, for being dumb enough to marry Martin in the first place. She wasn't such a loser way back when."

"And because you dine with her at the Long Island Women in Media luncheons. And—"

"Careful, Charlie. She's not the animal you imagine."

"No?"

"She told me once what it was like in her family growing up. Not pretty, let me tell you. Her father used to deliberately cause trouble in restaurants, getting loud about something right after they'd packed away their dinners, so that most restaurateurs ate the bills just to get them out of the building. She said it haunts her to this day."

"How *does* she carry on?"

"That's cold, Charlie."

"I don't get paid for warm and fuzzy."

"Point taken."

Charlie explained a setup he had in mind, a plan to trap several honchos at once. "They'll be tripping over their dicks to get in on this."

Lasch stubbed out her cigarette, half-smoked. "Let me think about it."

"Why?"

"Because that's the kind of world we live in, Charlie, okay?"

JUNIOR FOUND THE FAMILY MANSE ON WARTIME FOOTING. DAD wore a tie and sat at the head of the kitchen table, working the phone. Kym had actually toasted English muffins, and the coffee was fresh.

When Dad hung up, Junior smiled painfully across the table at him and said, "So, what's the problem?"

"Besides you?"

Junior put his muffin down. "You know, these personal attacks really are counterproductive. I'm a human being, okay? You did this to Mom. One day you'll do it to Kym."

"He goddamned well better not do it to me," said Kym, spinning from the counter with a butter knife in her hand.

Martin slammed his palm on the table. "Listen, you two, focus! I'm down six points and losing ground, Seymour's talking about writing in that asshole Arthur Prefect, the state committee's taking a hike, the cops are fucking up, and now it's supposed to rain on Tuesday. . . ."

"Why, Dad?" said Junior. "How did this onslaught of bullshit happen to us?"

"I'll tell you how. It began when some back-stabbing assholes told Charlie Hotchkiss about Stonehenge and Waterworks, maybe about everything else. Then there was your movie with Keller."

Junior wrinkled his brow and looked at Kym. "What is this Waterworks thing I keep hearing about?"

"You honestly don't know, do you?" said Dad.

"Du-uh."

"It's our retirement account, son, the one no one ever needed to know about. We really should talk more often."

Junior sullenly buttered another muffin while Martin explained Waterworks in layman's terms, that it was a potentially priceless property bought dirt cheap. The previous owners were given lifelong no-show county jobs to sweeten up the deal; the new owners had expected quiet rezoning and massive profit.

"It was brilliant," said Martin. "We were gonna multiply our money by ten in two years, risk-free, tax-free."

Like these guys ever paid their taxes, thought Junior, who had years ago figured out that it was all about money. You getting enough? Not pussy, cash. "Jackson Hind's fucking right," Junior said. "You really are the Darth Vadar of Nassau County."

"Don't go soft on me now, kid. Your inheritance was in there, too."

"Kym's money, you mean."

Martin sat back and covered his heart. "I can't believe you can say that to me."

"What was I thinking? Jeez."

Dad said, "In any event, I'm not going down without a fight. Okay? Got my life thrown into this. So I'm thinking a full-tilt sprint to the middle, and I'm spending every last dime I can get my hands on. We'll get Don Neville and some Democrats to come out for me. Change the whole paradigm. We'll need to put on new spinmasters, of course, maybe fly-ins from Washington. And I'm thinking Murphy has to be the fall guy."

Junior said, "It's too late."

"We can still win this."

"I don't think so, Dad. Not without the party."

"And who are you? Don Imus?"

"I'm just saying maybe we should stop throwing the family fortune away. Let Prefect have the fucking job. Take a fucking judgeship and get lost. I'll take the Medical Center, or something."

"You'll take the Medical Center. I love it. Have you called Maude Fleming back yet, by the way? She'd like to measure you for stripes."

"She's on my list."

"Move her up to next. And I want to listen in."

Kym looked up from her nails and said, though no one had asked her, "I agree. This game's gotten too damn nasty for my taste."

Martin said, "I don't believe you two."

Junior said, "Look, I'm not quitting on you, Dad. I just want you to know that my spirit is damn near broken."

On the sound a foghorn moaned, and Martin hoped it was not the death knell of his career. "Sorry to hear that, but quitting is just not what we are about. You think Jackson Hind is the good-government candidate? Well, you ain't seen nothing yet. These scumbags want a New Nassau? They're fucking getting it. Meaning from now on, we tell the people the truth."

"Dad, they'll boil us in oil."

"I don't think so. In fact, I think the people long for a breath of fresh air."

"Good Lord, you've gone nuts."

"Watch me."

Martin picked up the phone and called Democratic Party Chairman Donald Neville, thinking there was more than one way to skin this particular cat.

Don Neville's wife said, "I'm sorry, but Donny's at church. Can I have him return your call?"

"Please do. Tell him it's of the utmost urgency."

chapter 46

C HARLIE HOTCHKISS HAD NOT BEEN ON THE ADELPHI campus in Garden City since the Diamond-opoulus controversy, and he remembered fondly the warring factions, their signs and chants. Now the university was in the middle of a full-body makeover, attempting to recapture its good name. A new board member had gotten the bright idea of hosting a political debate, as a way of raising the level of discourse on campus. Others felt the school would be better served hosting a conference on the Life and Times of Howard Stern. As per the norm in the academic world, the minority packed the court and carried the day.

Charlie Hotchkiss decided he would use the scheduling disagreement for his opening, trusting conflict to hook his readers.

He closed his notebook and got out of his Volvo, feeling as he always did on college campuses: dwarfed by the magnitude of all he did not know, inconsequential, an intellectual fraud. He envied the undergraduates tossing Frisbees on the quad, who apparently already knew it all.

How fast it all flies by, he thought. How little of it registers. We don't vote. We don't say our prayers. We piss away our freedoms. The list goes on.

The sun was ducking behind fast-moving clouds as a crowd of hippified faculty types filed into the auditorium and took seats up close, not a few of them carrying Jackson Hind signs.

Charlie found himself a spot on press row between two women who owned North Shore weeklies and did not speak to each other.

Jackson Hind took the lectern first and got everybody

stoked without raising a sweat. These people loved him and sympathized with his underdog status, and they loved what he could do for them if he won. If John F. Kennedy, Jr., wouldn't run, at least they had Jackson. Charlie could see it: Daly was done. He just didn't know it yet.

Martin Daly assumed the stage next and stood tall, boomed his address in defiance. "Forget the polls, what you read in the newspapers, and hear me out . . . I think you owe me that . . . No longer will my New Nassau be shortchanged by the policies of exclusion and patronage. No longer will the party come first when it comes to pork. Times have changed! And I have changed! Jackson Hind is right: The people deserve better, and I'm just the guy to give it to them. Now, I refuse to stand up here and insult you people. Things are not good in Nassau County. Not good at all. We Republicans need to do better. For instance, we need to improve our police department, we need to free our men and women in blue from the shackles of political interference and micromanaging."

The stunned crowd stared up at him.

Martin shook his fist down at them. "Where the Ladysnatcher is concerned, I promise you: no justice, no peace."

Charlie Hotchkiss nudged his neighbor on the left. "Do you believe this crap?"

But damn if it wasn't working. You could see it on their faces. There was suddenly something admirable in Martin.

Good Lord, thought Charlie, not now. He stood and yelled, "What about the sport trucks for everybody and their uncles?"

Martin nodded bravely at the question, the questioner. "To that I say, it's time to put feet on the street."

"The cell phones?"

"They can carry quarters."

"The expense accounts?"

"History."

Jackson Hind tapped his mike. "And the no-show jobs with the lucrative pensions?"

"There is no place for waste in my New Nassau."

"What about the open-ended contracts?"

"I say tear 'em up."

Jackson leaned toward his mike and said, "Well, hell, Martin, if you'd done all this earlier, I wouldn't have had to run. You could have saved us all considerable time and trouble."

Martin bowed magnanimously.

Jackson said, "Seymour know about this?"

"Who?"

Charlie cried out, "Martin? . . . Are you feeling okay?"

The crowd laughed and Daly smiled. "You media people are always so negative."

Charlie said, "And you paint smiles on dung piles."

"It's a new dawn, Charlie. Get with the program. Now, on a personal note, my son has asked me to announce that he is signing himself in for some much needed rehabilitation and rest. And you reporters can write down in your stories that I said that it is never easy to be the son of a powerful man, and for that, I have offered my son my apologies."

John Devine from the *Times* stood up and asked what everyone else was thinking: "Hey, Jackson, should we believe him?"

Hind squinted across the stage at Martin Daly. "Aye," he said, "there's the rub."

JUNIOR DALY KNEW HE LOOKED SILLY WALKING FOG-BOUND Nassau Beach in a business suit, like a politician at a disaster site, pretending to be useful. Sugar-fine South Shore sand poured into his wingtips and filled his cuffs; the lousy traction provided a slippery slope.

The surf was roaring. Two children and a mother in sweatshirts and rolled-up jeans watched waves crash on the jetty.

Seymour's bodyguard stood outside the biggest cabana, the one with the satellite dish. Paranoid motherfucker's probably got motion sensors and a periscope, Junior figured. He nodded at Denny and knocked on the open wooden door.

"Come on in, kid," called Seymour Cammeroli. "It was only a matter of time."

Seymour was lounging in his robe, looking like Jabba the Hutt. He was not wearing his toupee. A woman, not his wife, was slipping through a door to the tiny back room. None of this seemed to embarrass the chairman.

"Your father's crazy, you know," Seymour said.

"You're telling me?"

Seymour fixed a scotch on the rocks from the bar for himself and handed Junior a beer from the ice bucket. He relaxed on the county-owned couch and offered Junior a county-owned deck chair. "So what can you do for me, kid?"

Junior pointed out that he'd been around a while, people talked to him, that he knew—

"You don't know your ass from a hole in the ground. And people think you're a fucking idiot."

Junior smiled sheepishly. "I know a few things about you."

Seymour reached down between the folds of his robe and scratched his nuts. "Look . . . kid. I can walk. You can walk. I want this thing we have in common to go on. So if you came here to threaten me—"

Junior blinked. "No! Jesus. No threat. I meant you'd been around the block. You're the man. The only man."

"That better be all you meant."

"Honest."

Seymour nodded, accepting his apology. "I want you to know, my thing with your father is strictly business."

"Because of the governor thing?"

Seymour wasn't saying. Gulls outside were crying hungrily; and Seymour was now unwrapping a big cigar for himself. Junior struck a match, lit it for him. Seymour blew the smoke away from Junior.

"You should have come to me sooner, kid, when you still had value, before the whole world got to watch you smoke reefer with that dickie-waving freak." Seymour ran his hand over his bald head, seemed to notice for the first time that he was sans toupee. "What I think now is, there's no way to finesse it."

"How about I drop out of sight for a while, get myself together. Then I come back in something really fucking easy but important sounding. I swear I'm there to reclaim the family mantle, all of that shit. It'll be beautiful. Only you and me will always know that all I'll ever want is that easy fucking job."

Seymour wrinkled his brow. "Even the garbage man dreams of punching a button at the landfill. That's how America works. Ambition."

"Or loyalty to the right guy."

Seymour punched Junior's shoulder, then gave him a brief round of applause. "And people say you don't pay attention."

"Elizabeth Lucido started that rumor, not me."

"Do me a favor? Don't mention that pain in the ass."

"Done."

"Okay, kid, here's what I want: the thing that makes your dad step aside without a fight. Now, I know it's there."

"He drove my mom to an overdose. That's not enough?"

"Nope."

Junior looked both ways and nodded. "I'm on the case."

• • •

AT FIVE THAT AFTERNOON FRANK MURPHY AND MAUDE Fleming got on the speakerphone in Murphy's office and called Martin Daly in his car, to demand an immediate meeting with Junior.

"Junior's a suspect?"

"Yes."

"You gotta be shitting me." Daly's voice crackled; he was also using the speakerphone, letting unknown others listen in.

Murphy said, "He's made himself a suspect. In fact, he's begged for it."

"Well, why don't you just shoot me in the balls, Frank?"

"Maybe when this is over."

The cops heard muffled voices arguing, then Martin again: "You and I both know Junior's got nothing to do with those women."

"Sorry. Your son's got means and opportunity for at least two of the victims. And his alibis are horseshit."

"His alibis have always been horseshit," said Martin.

"He should probably bring a lawyer when he comes in to talk to us. Even you must realize that."

They could hear Daly say to Lieutenant Rankel, "Bob, get them to back the fuck off."

Murphy said, "Yeah, Bob. Go ahead and try."

Rankel said, "Call Junior and have him take this meeting, boss. If you ever in your life listen to me, this is it."

"And he better tell the truth, sir," said Maude. "This isn't a campaign speech. We're gonna verify."

Martin said he'd arrange a meeting as soon as possible. He again tried to assure them that Junior was seeking help on his own, that while self-destructive, Junior would never hurt anybody else. "He just checked into Brunswick, admitting a long-term cross-addiction to coke and alcohol. What more do you want? His political career is over."

"As it should be," said Murphy.

Jake and Wally came into the office and flounced on the couch. Wally's eyes were drawn, and his hair a windblown mess. His jacket was buttoned to the neck.

After a moment Daly said, "I'll have him call you."

"You really think Junior Daly's a brilliant serial killer?" Jake asked skeptically when the speaker signaled a disconnect.

"I don't know what I think. How's Wally?"

"Bored, like me."

"Seriously."

"I am being serious. He's not having fun."

Murphy smiled at Wally. "Sorry, kid. None of us are."

Wally looked at his hands and rocked.

Jake said, "Say, did you see what Cammeroli told *Newsday?* The patronizing bastard. 'Sometimes Martin gets ahead of himself. Everyone knows campaigns are kept aloft with hot air.' I can see the billboards already: PREFECT WOULD BE PERFECT."

Maude said, "And Seymour will rule the world as we know it, without anyone having ever voted for him."

"Hey," said Jake. "It's only right."

"What can I do to blow up their plans?" Murphy asked.

Jake thought a moment. "Keep doing what you're doing."

"Which is what?"

"Drawing the fire away from Maude?"

Murphy said, "In other words, not much?"

Maude said, "That's your opinion, not mine."

Murphy said, "The worst part is, this is no longer about Elizabeth or Beth Hopkins. Goddamned Martin doesn't care. Seymour doesn't care. Only Jackson cares. And us."

Jake chuckled grimly. "Now you know."

chapter 47

THE LIGHT INSIDE HER TOMB WAS FAILING FAST, another day coming to an end. The body bag oozed a sickening stench.

Elizabeth's fevers were wildly gyrating: under the sleeping bag she was sweating, she was shivering. Her head and neck and shoulders had screamed with agony as she situated the ladder for a climb to the trapdoor, a climb she feared she was now too weak to make.

Her throat and lips were too dry to pray.

She knew she was dying, that if she was ever gonna get out, the time was now.

Elizabeth struggled into a sitting position at the base of the ladder, and said a small prayer as her hands gripped the sides and she pulled.

She barely moved. She had grown too weak, she realized. Malnutrition had overtaken her recovery from trauma, her temporary paralysis. She thought of the feral nails scratching at the door last night and tried again.

This time she made torturous progress, grabbing the ladder rungs as she got to them, using her knees for support.

At the fourth rung from the top, she stopped to rest, and held on for dear life, even though her palms and her arms burned with effort. Resting was worse, she decided after a moment, sapping her strength. She took a deep, determined breath and pulled again.

The next rung snapped, and wood was ripped through her hands as she slid down the ladder.

She struck her jaw on a rung halfway down and was mercifully unconscious when her body hit the ground.

Monday, Nov. 4

chapter 48

A DEMONSTRATION WAS HELD IN DRIZZLE ON THE front steps of Police Headquarters that morning, by a group demanding Frank Murphy's resignation.

Charlie Hotchkiss recognized old-guard Daly loyalists with town jobs holding the hastily painted signs. Charlie watched Conor McLaughlin, a retired Cove Neck Chief, grab a bullhorn and plead for help from FBI profilers. "Francis Murphy's overmatched. His own girlfriend has fled the county in fear."

Charlie knew Conor McLaughlin had commanded a six-man constable job in a sleepy Gold Coast village, and had less actual police experience than your basic Fortunoff security guard. Inflation had swallowed McLaughlin's pension and he needed a job, possibly Murphy's job. Charlie had also heard Bo Deitel was in the running, and Bill Bratton's résumé was always on file. As for the FBI jumping in, Charlie knew they required evidence of a violent crime, or that someone had fled across state lines, and to date, there was none. Their lone contribution to this wicked mess thus far other than running down out-of-state leads had been to pass on an unsubstantiated rumor that Barbara "Babs" Whitcomb III had been seen in Stuttgart, Germany, in late September, happily riding a tour bus.

Demonize and destroy, thought Charlie. Frank Murphy didn't deserve it, but he was clearly the scapegoat on the Ladysnatcher case. Charlie thought that was a shame. While Murphy tended to readily excuse his cops' mistakes, you knew what side he was on. He'd been going to church long before anyone was watching.

The gentle rain turned hard, and the demonstrators tucked their signs away and wandered from the steps. The press had their story: it was time to wash up.

But before the cameras could break down, Jackson Hind squealed to the curb in his black LeBaron and leaped out. "Where's everybody going?" he called to the demonstrators. "How's about some equal time?" he called to the press.

People froze where they were, watching Hind, ignoring the rain. Cameras were switched back on. "This is my woman who's missing. You understand? The woman I love. And I'm not the least bit unhappy with Frank Murphy. So why are these Fairhaven Village highway workers upset? What do they know about the case? I think the police are getting somewhere, and fast. In fact, I wouldn't be surprised if Elizabeth and Beth are rescued at any moment. . . . You people ought to be ashamed of yourselves," he said. "You're playing *de*fense on the cops."

No one said a word.

The demonstrators turned as one and hurried away.

Jackson faced the cameras. "Now, on a personal note: I would like to wish Deputy County Executive Martin Daly Junior well. One can only wonder how someone with so unfortunate a drug problem wasn't noticed sooner in the halls of government."

MARTIN DALY WATCHED THE DEMONSTRATION BREAK UP FROM his own office window across the street. "Where the fuck are they going?" he asked Mike Barclay. "And what the fuck is Hind saying?"

Barclay said, "They're going home. Or back to work."

"Why?"

"Du-uh. It's raining?"

Martin saw two, maybe three drops on his window. "It's fucking drizzling. I told them bust nuts till noon. Look at them scatter. This is treason!"

"You got what you needed."

"Bullshit. What I need is blood on the streets. Don Neville call us back yet?"

"Nope."

"Do you believe the fucking nerve?"

"Seymour probably told him not to. How much nerve does that take?"

Martin nodded out the window at his cowardly tempo-troops. "Give 'em fifteen minutes to get back to work, and then call their fucking bosses."

"What makes you think their bosses'll be there? And why piss off people who might actually vote for you?"

Daly fumed, watching the cowards climbing into their cars in groups.

"Maybe they don't want Hind to recognize them, just in case he wins."

"You know what, Mike? You're fired."

"You know what, Martin? I'm glad."

Daly stormed past Mike Barclay and his own secretaries and into Bob Rankel's denlike office, grabbed the remote, and shut off the television.

Rankel sat up on the couch. "What happened?"

"Mike Barclay quit on me. Pussy never had the stomach for a fight."

"Who's gonna replace him?"

"I don't know. Maybe you?"

Rankel furrowed his brow as he scanned his comfortable office. "You know, boss. I've been quiet up till now."

"And?"

"Maybe it's time we packed it in."

Martin stared at Rankel's shaved head and wondered at the sloth entombed inside. "Go get the car," said Martin. "Or maybe you think I should be driving myself."

"No, sir. Sorry, sir."

HURRICANE JESSICA WAS ROILING THE ATLANTIC ONE HUNDRED miles northeast of Wilmington, North Carolina. On Long Island, an adventurous surfer had already drowned at Long Beach. Frank Murphy was in the headquarters press room, taking blame for the storm.

"Is Jessica gonna hit us directly?" wondered the fool from the Associated Press.

"As I said, we don't know yet. We're expecting quite a storm surge either way."

"Will the South Shore flood?"

Murphy smiled wearily.

Then that Wolf guy from CNN asked, "Is it true your fiancée has left Nassau County until the Ladysnatcher is caught?"

"No. That's not why she left at all. Is it true your real name is Leslie?"

"What about—"

"Good day, people, and I use the term loosely."

He walked upstairs, gritting his teeth.

In the crowded Homicide office Maude told him she had gone over Junior's answers in detail and found windows of opportunity where Junior would prefer there be none. Still, it was not nearly enough.

Rocky said he'd been across the street in the Executive Building, nosing around some secretaries he'd dated. He told Murphy: "Junior knew Babs Whitcomb good. One of his duties was liaison to the Caucus."

"This is getting really weird," said Murphy.

"Roger that."

"Let's go back even further," said Maude. "Cover Junior from the cradle to now."

"Gotcha."

Rocky threw on his blazer and left.

Murphy listened quietly on another extension while Maude called Archie Collins at Stonehenge. "How well did you know Babs Whitcomb?"

"I didn't hear you."

"The really rich woman who disappeared, the kind of woman a bottom-feeder like you would have noticed."

"Hardly knew her at all."

"Are you lying again?"

"Excuse me, Detective?"

"The other day you withheld information I could have used. And that North Shore development that needed financing turned out to be on the South Shore."

"When you asked me those questions the information was different."

"Oh, really?"

"Just like you, Detective. I do as I'm told."

"No," said Maude. "Not just like me."

"Hey," he said, "you had your chance for clarification, but you threw a hissy fit and walked out. You got any other questions, you talk to my lawyer."

"And who might that be?"

"Marsh Beinstock."

Maude hung up.

Murphy said, "Okay, if it was Junior, how'd he do it, never mind the why. How'd he make these women disappear without a trace? The man can't find his ass with both hands."

Maude shook her head and studied the Lucido photopack one more time.

"Think you missed something?" asked Murphy.

"I must have."

chapter 49

S QUATTERS' SHACKS ON THE LAWN OUTSIDE FAIR-haven Village Hall filled the air with cooking smells; a renegade judge had enjoined the village from removing this longtime housing protest. What His Honor had called "The Bros. Garden." Seagulls worked chained-down trash cans for leftovers. At the far end of the park a Long Island Railroad train rumbled by, the 12:12 out of Penn Station.

Rocky Blair pulled his overcoat closed and shuddered, stepped inside the ornate lobby, which resembled what banks used to look like, high-ceilinged, rich in tradition and trust. He told the receptionist what he wanted.

"Do you have an appointment with the Director of Citizen's Affairs?"

"Not exactly."

Her expression told Rocky what she thought of people who did not exactly have an appointment. Grudgingly a call was made. Then Rocky was directed to the back of the building, where he met an ancient receptionist with a dime-sized brown mole on her forehead.

A gray-suited member of the politburo came out to talk to him. Rocky had seen this particular commissar before, in the newspaper, a disbarred lawyer who knew the location of so many skeletons they called him Boot Hill.

"Citizen's Affairs?" asked Rocky, examining the business card Boot Hill handed him. "What's that make the rest of this place?"

"None of their fucking business. Just like helping you break Martin's balls is none of mine. You rank-and-file people ought to let Murphy fight his own battles."

Rocky felt the heat rising in his head. "Say what?"

"Do your job, is what I'm saying, nothing more, which is exactly what I'm saying: nothing more. You want to question me, get a subpoena."

Boot Hill turned and disappeared behind the oak door from whence he had come.

"Psst."

The old lady with the mole on her forehead crooked her finger at him. She was sixty-five if a day, illegally smoking a cigarette and knitting at her desk. "You want to know about the Hopkins girl and those lowlife scumbag Dalys?"

"Yeah."

"Have a seat, Detective. How do you like your coffee?"

"Light and sweet, just like me."

She picked up a phone and barked orders. "And bring the doughnuts from that brunch they had before. Get the jelly ones."

Rocky sat down across from her and admired the pretty pink sweater she had crafted that morning on taxpayer time.

"It's not like I'm busy, or anything."

"How long have you worked here?" asked Rocky.

"Thirty-one years."

"Good for you."

"Not really."

"No. What I mean is: Your employment covers the years we're examining."

"Gotcha."

"Basically, what I want to know is: Did Martin Daly or Martin Daly Junior have more than a professional relationship with Beth Hopkins while they were working here?"

She folded her hands and sat up straight. "Both of them did. Senior and Junior. Sick bastards. You know, you look at Junior Daly long enough, he reminds you of that preppy murderer they let get away with it. No remorse about anything."

Rocky nodded and scribbled in his memo book while the woman went on and on about Junior.

Rocky looked up. "What'd he ever do to you?"

The woman looked at her hands. "Gave me my nick-name."

Rocky waited.

"Behind my back they call me Mahatma, even after all these years."

THAT AFTERNOON MAUDE CAME TO MURPHY AND SAID, "I think Junior Daly might be worthy of twenty-four-hour surveillance. Just to be on the safe side."

Murphy tipped his swivel-chair and put his wingtips on the desk. "Make the case for me."

"He's an habitual failure who openly hates his father, who feels Dad's philandering drove his mom to her death. He has his own very public drug problem. The booze problem. His access to all three victims. No good alibis for any of the times of occurrence. A wealth of possible motives. His prints in Elizabeth's bedroom. His picture in Beth's album."

Murphy, who also fell into a few of those categories, said, "I want more."

"I've thought all along it was either a pro, or some-one these women would never think would cause them harm, a description that fits Junior quite nicely. Even I didn't look at him earlier because he's such a fucking putz."

Murphy said, "Okay, I agree he's worth a closer look. But make sure, Maude, of everything. Cover the bases. This is all just a little too convenient for my taste."

"Step by step," said Maude, "just like always."

After she left. Frank Murphy called Martin Daly's car

and got Bob Rankel, who said Martin was away from the car.

"He's an asshole, Bob, you know that, right?"

"Frank, what are you doing? You and Martin, this is stupid politics—"

"I really don't need your advice, Lieutenant."

"Hey," said Rankel. "Forget it. I just drive the car."

"Try to remember that, and maybe I will too."

Murphy hung up and put on his jacket and straightened his tie, grabbed his keys and cell phone. "I'm out of the building for a while," he told Annie. "Where are Wally and Jake?"

"Where else?"

Frank found them in the cafeteria, at a table near the window.

"Good," said Jake. "I'm glad you're here. I think Wally's sick."

Jake was right: Wally was staring out the window, shivering, his eyes unfocused; he wept when he saw his brother.

Murphy and Jake helped him up and walked him back up to Murphy's office, helped him lie down on the couch. Annie covered him with a blanket. Wally curled up and closed his eyes.

"Do we have a thermometer?" Murphy asked her.

"We got a first-aid kit that has everything. Don't you worry. You go do what you have to do. I'll look after Wally."

"Thanks, Annie. You're the best."

"No," she said. "You are—and I've been here a long time."

"Thank you."

The sky was gray and blowing hard as Murphy battled traffic on his way to party central. More than a couple of Martin Daly's signs were down, and not because legions of pacifists were out in pickup trucks, stomping them.

Murphy parked outside Seymour's office and walked into the reception area. The lights were on, and he could smell coffee, but the desk with the Denny Dubois nameplate was vacant.

Murphy knocked on Seymour's door.

"Who is it?"

"Frank Murphy."

The door swung open; the music poured out, Steve Miller's "Fly Like an Eagle."

"Come in, Chief," yelled Seymour. "What's shaking?"

"Plain and simple," Murphy said when they faced each other over Seymour's desk. "I want my little brother taken care of, without interruption, for the rest of his natural life."

Seymour said, "I want a lot of things, too, Frank. That's why I work so hard."

Murphy glanced over at the exercise equipment. "Pumping iron, lately?"

"Denny uses that shit."

"So what do you want from me?"

Seymour cracked his knuckles, thinking. "Well, here's what we got, Murphy: Even with most people telling him you're an okay police commissioner, I happen to know that Martin would like you to quit. He knows he'd get a five-point boost by showing any signs of leadership at all."

"Fuck Martin. What do you want? I'm tired of trying to read smoke signals."

Seymour smiled. Steve Miller segued into poor dead Otis Redding's "Sitting on the Dock of the Bay."

"I'd like you to stay, Frank. And, of course, I'd like you to find out what happened to those women. It would be especially nice if it happened before Election Day and made Martin look like a total dick."

"I was hoping to do just those things anyway."

"Then we're on the same page. Happily."

"I thought the deal would be tougher."

"I'm a pussycat, Frank. You know that. You can owe me."

"Why tank your own man?" asked Murphy. Outside the window, behind Seymour, it was raining sideways.

"All politics are local, Frank. You know that. I can't let no one fuck with me. I got a mother to worry about, a sister."

"My brother gets his window back."

Seymour showed Murphy his palms as if he were surrendering. "I really don't know what happened there, Frank, but I can certainly fucking fix it. You know I don't play that crap. Families are everything to me."

"I was just thinking that."

"Anything else?"

"I want Dr. Kantrop castrated."

"Easy there, Frank. Maybe he had no choice."

"He's a doctor," said Murphy.

"So what?"

CHARLIE TOOK THE NEWS HARD—THAT BARBARA LASCH HAD suddenly quit and gone off to Cleveland, to a similar position at the *Plain Dealer*, another *Times-Mirror* paper— which he found highly suspicious.

Nobody made a lateral move to Cleveland, not even participants in the Federal Witness Protection Program, not chronic complainers like Barbara Lasch. Moline, Kennebunkport, anywhere but Cleveland.

Charlie's temporary boss was now Katherine Carpenter-Whitney, from corporate, a relic from the days of the *Long Island Press* wars.

Charlie tried to catch her up on the Ladysnatcher case, but she didn't want to hear it. She raised a withered hand and peeled off her bifocals. "Save your breath, Charlie."

"Barb ran this thing by you before she left?"

"What thing?"

"The part about Daly's wife?"

Katherine sighed. "Charlie, listen to me. I want you to cover the recent string of pit bull bitings in ghetto neighborhoods. Make it scary. Do it deep. You've done enough for now on Martin. Let it rest."

"But—"

"Soldier on, Charlie. That's an order."

Charlie felt his chest grow tight, and his blood pounded in his ears. "They got to us, didn't they? I always wondered how you survived all these years here."

"Have the photographer get close-ups of the wounds and some snarl-shots."

"Get 'em yourself, Katherine," said Charlie. "I quit."

chapter 50

W HAT LOYALISTS REMAINED ON MARTIN DALY'S TEAM were gathered in the atrium lobby of the Victim's Center for the ribbon cutting. They stood in a line behind him, wearing hard hats and raincoats, as if they had just finished pounding the last nail. This was a big day for Martin, a first step on the road to redemption, a chance to show folks all he had done for them. He was holding forth from the lectern, extolling the virtues of private-public cooperation under his able leadership. He was halfway through his remarks when the roof began to leak: ". . . And thus this hallowed ground which we consecrate today will forever comfort all who have been oppressed or hurt or denied or ignored, whether from Racial Discrimination or Breast Cancer or Domestic Violence or DWI."

Martin knew the roof was leaking because a tiny white wad of wet plaster plopped like birdshit on the three-by-five file card he was holding.

He looked out at his audience and saw the heads and shoulders of donors and dignitaries similarly spackled.

He picked up the pace. "Maybe someone called you the N-word once, or a kike. . . ."

Rusty water was suddenly streaming down the marble wall behind Daly, flooding the floor, flowing around his feet and soaking the toes of high-heeled ladies in the audience. Embarrassed aides shuffled from the stage to get buckets and mops. Umbrellas popped open. Reporters giggled.

"Say your husband abuses you. . . ."

A late arrival opened the lobby side door, and the wind rushed in, and the floor-to-ceiling windows on the other side of the lobby hummed a mournful tune, causing Martin to stop speaking and watch with awe. The windows bowed out, then shattered.

People panicked, uncertain where to run, the emergency exit lighting being one of the corners cut. The crowd buzzed and wrestled itself. A woman in a mink tried to cut behind Martin and fell hard, then lay screaming as if she had broken her hip.

Martin saw a way to turn this disaster around. He plucked the microphone from its holder and held it near his mouth as he kneeled next to the victim, offering aid and comfort. Cold water soaked his trousers. "Are you okay?" he asked the woman. "Is there anything I can do?"

She stared up at him coolly, then pulled the mike from him and spoke into it. "Get the roof fixed, Martin. I plan on owning this place."

Then Bob Rankel picked Martin up by the elbows and hurried him through the revolving doors that were now spraying water like a car wash. Charlie Hotchkiss was waiting outside like a sniper, blocking their path but giving way, walking backward toward the limo, smirking and scribbling. "I'd say that went well, eh, Martin? What'd we pay for this baby? Who's the contractor here? One of Seymour's boys?"

Bob Rankel tried to protect Martin, shielding him with his thick body and angry scowl. "He don't have to talk to you, Charlie. You don't work for *Newsday* anymore."

"That's right. Now I work for the *Voice*. Martin? It may be your last chance."

Martin heard the ring of truth in Charlie's warning and pulled up short. "You know what, Charlie, it's not really funny, what they're doing to me and my family. It's not American."

"Not only that. It's totally unprecedented."

"Never buck the boss, my friend."

"Talk," said Charlie. "Get it on the record, while people still give a shit. After you've lost, it's sour grapes."

"Charlie, I hate you, and you hate me."

"But I'm fair."

The crowd of new victims was closing fast, and Martin had the feeling some of the men had gone looking for a rope. "The hell you are."

"Be a hero," said Charlie. "Not a flop. Just once."

Charlie was right, thought Martin. Now or never. "Out of the county somewhere."

"Huntington Village," said Charlie. "Heckscher Park, near the museum."

Martin ducked into the backseat. "In this weather?"

"You want to be alone, right?"

"Right."

The crowd surrounded the limo, calling for his scalp. The last thing Martin heard as the door slammed shut was: "You're an asshole, Daly." They rocketed away from the curb, scattering advocates and press with equal abandon.

"Jesus," said Martin. "What the fuck."

"Not good," said Rankel.

"Ya think? . . . Just drive."

On the ride east to Huntington the radio announcers were saying Hurricane Jessica, previously expected to make landfall at Myrtle Beach, South Carolina, had turned hard north. A state of readiness had been declared for the eastern seaboard from Delaware to Cape Cod. Evacuation plans were in effect for coastal and low-lying areas.

"That means huge rain," Daly said. "If Seymour tries a write-in, we're fucked."

"That's an awful lot of write-ins, boss."

"There's an awful lot of pawns, Bob. Me and Hind split the voting machines, you just don't know."

"I got more bad news, came in while you were giving your speech. Junior walked out of Brunswick rehab."

Martin threw his head back and stared up at the rain-bombs exploding on the moonroof. "My life is in a goddamn shambles, Bob. You know that? My son is a murder suspect. My wife is a drunk. My campaign's down the shitter, and I got a hurricane roaring up my ass. Just watch me get blamed when those waves roll in. Motherfuckers . . . You know. I could be unemployed by tomorrow night, and believe me, I'm not as rich as I look."

"You're gonna win, sir. I know it in my bones."

The one thing Martin Daly hated was false cheer coming from someone else. "Yeah?" he said as he slid the partition on Rankel closed. "And what the fuck do you know?"

THE RAIN THAT HAD RUINED THE PHOTO OP AT THE VICTIM'S Center suddenly stopped as they rolled down prosperous Main Street in Huntington, past old white churches and the hillside graves of patriots. The limo turned north on Prime Street and pulled to the curb in front of the Heckscher art museum.

Martin got out of the car, accepted the umbrella, then told Rankel to get lost for twenty minutes, to get coffee and Danish.

"You sure?"

"I'm sure."

Charlie Hotchkiss parked behind the limo and climbed out of his Volvo. They nodded at each other and walked in silence down a path to the duck pond and sat on a bench. Across the pond, two old men in yellow slickers were sailing miniature clipper ships. Overhead, more clouds piled up, growing dark, yellow-tinged, the sky set for another blow.

"Late in the year for us to get hit with a hurricane," Martin observed. "Just another chunk of bad luck."

"You think what just happened back there was luck?"

"What do you mean?"

"Martin, the Empire State Building was thrown up in a year, during the goddamn Jazz Age, in the middle of Manhattan. You can't build a leak-free quonset hut in a decade."

Martin waved his hand dismissively and said, "You act like *I* did the tile work, Charlie. I'm not the only one to blame."

"So let's spread it around. Names, dates, and amounts. That's what it's all about. You'll go down a statesman."

"Come on, Charlie. I'll go down a flaming asshole. The first question everyone will ask—including the Feds—is why didn't I do something sooner."

"So you saw the light a little late. At least you saw it. What do I know? You were out of the loop? It's not beyond the pale, given your vigorous golf schedule."

Martin stared down at his wingtips. "What do you want to know?"

Charlie got right down to it, asking first about a list of political appointments that had no rhyme or reason unless you saw the family trees of the original owners of the Waterworks property, unless you realized how far undermarket the Stonehenge offer was. Going right for the jugular, as usual, thought Martin. Mine.

"I don't know much about that. A blind trust. Slingblade Marsh and the boys . . ."

"I'm telling you, Martin. The hands-off reputation could really pay off. I mean, I heard about your day-books."

Martin smiled bitterly, thinking it had come to this, pleading incompetence, buffoonery, like his son. It no longer mattered, he realized. The people would remember Junior smoking pot, Norman pounding pud, himself amid the ruins of the Victim's Center.

"Have you tried to make peace with Seymour?"

"He doesn't want to hear it, and frankly, I'm all done begging. Don Neville doesn't return my calls these days."

Charlie opened his jacket and pulled out his notebook. "Well, that is rock bottom, Martin. So go on. Get even."

Martin swallowed hard and started at the beginning, in the Village of Fairhaven, then the Town of North Hempstead, his coronation by Seymour as county executive, then some of what he had to do to keep the job. For the next twenty minutes he gave up friends, allies, and associates, enough to collapse the machine from within. Names. Dates. Cash. Trips. Prizes. Pussy. The death of his first wife. The embarrassment of Junior. Some capers Charlie smugly said he knew about. Some things Charlie had missed. Martin got into it, tossing one shocker on top of the other. When Martin finally stopped talking, Charlie closed his notebook and sighed contentedly. "And it's been like this for years, right?"

"Long before I wandered by. And you don't have to look too happy about it."

"You can provide documents?"

"I wish I couldn't."

Charlie stared into Martin's eyes. "After all this time, I can't believe I'm gonna say this to you: You're a brave man, Martin Daly."

Martin did, in fact, feel a lightening in his chest, the temporary peace of the confessional, a sense of gratitude for Charlie's understanding of the human condition. "Try to remember that when you write my obituary."

"You have my word."

They smiled and nodded at each other, then stood and shook hands, and Martin suddenly felt vindicated, understood on some deeper level. Charlie shuddered and fell forward into his arms, draped his chin over Martin's shoulder, as if they were slow-dancing, and Martin wondered if perhaps Charlie wasn't taking their newfound brotherhood too far. Then Charlie slid heavily through Martin's arms and crumpled to the sidewalk.

Martin stared down at the blood on his hands.

chapter 51

SUFFOLK COUNTY POLICE CARS FILLED THE PARK. Overhead, the wind howled through hundred-year-old trees.

"This was a place of peace, a mingling of life and art, and now it is an obscenity."

Hap Jankowski, the Suffolk County detective trying to interview Martin Daly, told the monstrously unhappy museum director at his side to stop interrupting, to calm down, get a grip.

The angry director pointed a long red fingernail at the grassy knoll behind her museum from where, presumably, the fatal shot had been fired. "How can I walk back there now? How can anyone?"

Martin said with all the charm he could muster, "Lady, a friend of mine has just died. Could you please give it a rest."

The director humphed and strode away.

"Bitch," muttered the detective.

Martin said nothing, as the director was the least of his problems. If he wasn't mistaken, there was a black guy in the mob of reporters behind the sawhorses who sure as hell looked like Bernard Kalb. Assassination attempts can do that, Martin mused, draw the heavyweights back to the streets. And he had no one to prep him, no clue as to spin.

Thank God Bob Rankel had come back with the coffee and seen what was going on. Martin had been terrified, hiding behind the bench, fully expecting further carnage. Rankel had drawn his weapon and run to him across the line of fire, had covered Martin's body with his own, waited out those awful seconds of exposure with him, then dusted him off and calmly done what was needed to get Suffolk County started on the murder of Charlie Hotchkiss.

Maybe Bob Rankel would be keeping his job.

Martin had given Jankowski a fast statement, filled with white lies, half-truths, and obfuscations. He had then begged Rankel to get him out of there. There was a sniper on the loose, sure. But worse, he had ten pages from Charlie's bloody notebook crammed in his jacket pocket.

"Can't we go now?" asked Daly. "I'm really shook up."

"Not yet," said Jankowski. "You want a doctor?"

"I want to go home and take a shower."

"Soon. I promise. Why don't you wait in your car."

Back in the limo, Daly told Rankel to get on the phone. "Get me a support team out here before these country bumpkins fuck things up beyond repair."

"You got it, boss."

"Lieutenant Rankel?"

Rankel's bald head swung around. "Yes?"

"How does Captain Rankel sound?"

Rankel's muscular face broke into a grin. "Pretty damn good, sir."

MURPHY, MAUDE, AND ROCKY ARRIVED AT HECKSCHER PARK within an hour of the call for help, and for once, Murphy noted, Martin Daly seemed genuinely glad to see them, jumping from the back of his limo and waving like a fraternity buddy.

"Murphy, Maude, thank God you people are here. These hicks don't get it, what this means. The ramifications. We had just sat down to talk, and my God, my God . . ."

Murphy asked, "Why here, Martin, with Charlie of all people? Why now?"

"Haven't you heard? I got religion. Me and Charlie were gonna be friends. We had just got here, and then Bob went off for coffee."

Murphy gazed down the path to the Suffolk County cop-crowd around the waterside bench. "Dangerous to be your friend, isn't it, Martin?"

"You trying to make me feel worse?"

"What were you gonna tell Charlie?"

"Stuff about Hind."

"You're a liar."

Martin grabbed Murphy's arm and walked him ten feet up the sidewalk. "Sorry, Frank. They raised the stakes. Whatever message their sending, I'm getting."

"Who?"

Daly shook his head.

Murphy looked back at the limo, where Maude was answering her cell phone. She listened, nodded, disconnected.

Daly said to Rocky, "How come nobody ever calls *you?* Doesn't that ever piss you off?"

"Now wouldn't that be kinda dumb?"

Maude said, "Junior's at Blue Landing, shitfaced, asking for his daddy. He apparently walked out of Brunswick sometime this morning."

"So I heard. Okay to meet you there?" asked Martin wearily.

"Sure, Martin," said Murphy. "Whatever's convenient."

chapter 52

S HE SUSPECTED SHE HAD BROKEN HER LEG NEAR THE ankle, from the angle at which it lay, but all in all Elizabeth was surprised to be alive, amazed at what the body could endure. She lay on her back, breathing bad air, staring up at the crack in the door, as anger overwhelmed her, frustration at her inability to perform once-simple tasks.

And what the hell were the cops doing? Why didn't they find her? The words, *Back Burner,* invaded her hope. And where were the angels she so fervently believed in? When would they come for her? When, O God, would her punishment end?

They would be through it tonight, she knew. The animals. They would leap down on her. Possums, coons, a hungry dog: It didn't matter. She would be dead by then, or she would be gone.

She had decided: If she didn't make it out by nightfall she was ending her life with a can opener.

She stared at the stack of magazines. The animals had clawed away enough wood over the past several nights for her to read the label on the July 1978 *Playboy.*

It had been mailed to subscriber Martin Daly, of Fairhaven, New York.

Goddamn Martin had buried her on his own estate, figuring rightly it would be the last place the cops would look. And he had fucked up even that simple task.

He couldn't even kill a girl, the gutless turd.

Rung by rung, fueled by hate and growling with effort, Elizabeth dragged herself halfway up the ladder, then rested, then tried again for the top.

She got her hand within an inch of the doorknob above her. Then she was fighting to hold her place, then slipping, just a little, then some more, then the rest of the way down, slowly, fighting it, not with a bang this time, but a whimper.

chapter 53

YOU'RE KILLING ME," MARTIN DALY SAID IN THE SPAcious, booklined living room at Blue Landing. "There is no way on God's green earth my son is a killer. I thought Norman Keller was a suspect."

Murphy said, "Norman Keller can't jerk off without getting caught."

Maude said, "Two of the women are old girlfriends of his."

"Beth Hopkins was. Never Elizabeth."

"No?"

"Junior's got no alibi for Charlie Hotchkiss, either, by the way, except he told your wife he was drinking with some black guy all day. A friend of Norman Keller's."

"That's highly possible, if the black guy was buying."

Then Junior limped down the front circular stairs in his black silk pajamas, scratching his head and rubbing his eyes, handsome even now, and Murphy thought, If this kid could only remember his lines, he'd make one hell of a leading man.

Junior took one astonished look at his father and the cops and got the setup, that his ass was in a sling. He froze on the bottom step and loudly protested his innocence of all crimes anywhere, then his disdain for Maude Fleming and Rocky Blair and any of the other morons who had worked on the Ladysnatcher case. "Like I told Kym, I was with Norman Keller's neighbor. How could you people think I'm a killer?"

His father said, "Look at you, son, you got a dickie-waver's neighbor for an alibi."

"Norman didn't actually wave his dick at anyone, Dad."

Maude's cell phone rang. She walked to a corner of the living room, then turned back to the men. "Junior's alibi is standing in the squad room right now. Guy name of Dante Johnson, works for Jackson Hind."

"Bingo. *My man.* Well, thank you, Jesus," said Junior.

"Jesus has got nothing to do with it," said Murphy.

Murphy asked for the phone from Maude and listened as Detective Bobby Buchmann laid it out: "According to Johnson here, Junior borrowed a doctor's slicker and boogied from Brunswick. He's getting drunk in a Freeport gin mill. Dante befriends him. Junior tells Dante he's very angry at daddy. Life ain't fair, that shit. Dante puts him in cab and sends him home, right around the time Charlie Hotchkiss went down."

"Thanks, Bobby."

Murphy hung up and scowled at Junior.

Junior said, "What have I done? I mean, really. Didn't steal nothing. Didn't hurt nobody. Just got high. That's all."

Martin said, "Stayed high, is what it looked like."

"There's no fucking need for this hospital shit. I'm no more fucked-up than half my friends."

Murphy said, "Good day, Martin. Please do what I said, okay? Have Rankel keep watch here tonight. And I'll have a team outside."

"Yes, I will. And thanks for thinking of me. And Murphy? Today in that God-forsaken park, Bob Rankel was magnificent. A credit to the force."

"So noted."

"You, too."

"Don't go soft and mushy on me now, Martin."

Out in front of the Daly mansion the rain was steady, the winds bending trees. Leaves flew past as they squeezed into the squad car and got on the phone to Suffolk again. No luck, they were told. No witnesses, no shell casings, no footprints, no evidence at all.

"Just a shot in the park," Rocky said grimly. "Our boy is very fucking good."

WHEN MURPHY GOT BACK TO HIS OFFICE, ANNIE ANDERSON told him that during the early afternoon Captain Posner had been suspended from duty by the head of the Internal Affairs Division. In addition, Jake was being brought up on criminal charges by District Attorney Prefect, all for baby-sitting Wally on company time.

"Where's Wally?"

She cocked her head at his office door. "Asleep."

"What did he think of all the commotion?"

"He heard Jake yelling and he cried, of course."

"Keep an eye on him?"

"Of course."

Murphy literally ran to the Personnel office.

Arthur Prefect was there with two IAD cops, supervising Jake's removal from duty, collecting his gun and shield. "He's meat, Frank. Let him go."

"Why, you sniveling sack of shit," said Murphy, advancing on the district attorney.

"No!" said Jake, looking up from loading boxes. "Don't make it easy for him, Frank. Every dog has his day, don't you worry. His is coming. Then I'll be back running things, and he'll still be married to the Frito bandito."

"Is that supposed to be an insult?" asked Prefect.

"Du-uh."

"You're on drugs." Prefect turned to IAD cops. "Walk him out."

"One second, *mein Herr*," said Jake.

"What?"

Jake bent over his computer and tapped several keys. A second later, all around the office, printers started printing and faxes started faxing. From every device the new *Nassau County Grunt* appeared simultaneously, not only in the Personnel bullpen but around the county, at Task Force 2000, 2001, Pre-Planning, the courthouse, the jailhouse, the county executive's office, the spare room at Murphy's condo.

The headline, in bold letters, read: MARTIN DALY OBSTRUCTS LUCIDO INVESTIGATION. PREFECT HAS NO CLUE. JUN-IOR DALY TOP SUSPECT. The "We're Related" cartoon showed ten clones of a joint-smoking Junior Daly, relaxing in hammocks. It was titled, simply, The "Future." The editorial was a heartfelt farewell to Charlie Hotchkiss, of the *Long Island Voice*, which closed by calling Charlie "a brother, a mentor, and a true American hero."

Arthur Prefect jammed a copy of the *Grunt* into his pocket and stared at Jake Posner with hate, this removal chore now a labor of revenge, a pleasure. " 'Ass-licking tour,' eh?"

Jake grinned at Murphy. "So I'm free to watch Wally, whenever you need me."

"Thanks, Jake. I'll talk to you tonight. And you're right, you will be back."

"Like hell he will," said Prefect. "And the *Nassau County Grunt* is dead and buried."

DURING A BREAK IN THE WEATHER, DISTRICT ATTORNEY ARTHUR Prefect held a news conference on the steps outside his office, announcing his own widening probe of a scandal at police headquarters, the crisis in public safety management, he called it. He told the hastily assembled reporters he was cutting short his vacation to assist the overstressed police department in the Ladysnatcher case, bringing the full resources of his office to bear. "We will not rest until we have closure!"

Search dogs had been assembled for the photo-op, old lawyers in neckties and flak jackets arrayed behind him. Murphy stood in his raincoat at the back of the crowd, fighting his hate. All the while the press was checking him out, to see if he was on board, none daring to ask.

Bob Rankel slipped up next to him, obviously on a spy mission for his master. "Commissioner," he said officiously. "Do you believe this fucking snake?"

"I want to remember this, what it looked like and felt like, when it's time to consider Prefect's plea for mercy."

Rankel smiled as if he were in on the joke. "What's Jake gonna do?"

"Write for *Newsday*, probably. What do you care?"

Rankel looked around to see if anyone had heard.

Murphy stared at the lieutenant's thick neck and wondered at the kind of man who would rather drive the boss than row his own boat. "What are *you* gonna do when Martin gets dumped?"

Rankel said he planned to return to regular police duty. "What the hell. I could use the rest."

Murphy dreamed of shitty assignments for Rankel, something with evening hours and weekends, weather.

"So you guys thought Junior whacked Charlie?"

"That has such a nice ring to it: whacked Charlie. Go away, Bob, before you really piss me off."

Murphy burned as he watched Rankel slink to the other side of the crowd and buddy up to other cops, thinking he could play both sides. Now there was a place to cut costs, should anybody actually give a fuck.

The crowd began clapping as Arthur Prefect promised swift and certain justice. "Prefect would be Perfect—write it in," they chanted. "Prefect would be Perfect—write it in."

Then the conference broke up, and people streamed for their cars.

Arthur Prefect, however, took his time on the front steps, shaking hands and tossing quips with the papparazzi, making a point of hanging close to the cops, even as more rain began to fall.

Murphy watched him shake Bob Rankel's hand, chatting casually with his opponent's bodyguard as if, truly, they were all on the same side. Then one of the police dogs behind them made a big deal out of sniffing Bob Rankel's crotch, whining, tugging on his leash. Prefect said, "You want to give your ass an extra wipe next time, there, Bob?" and everybody laughed, everybody loved him. Then Prefect and his entourage squeezed into limos and headed off.

Murphy remained on the sidewalk, watching them, abandoned but for his K-9 cops. "Amateur hour, eh, boss?" said a K-9 cop named Wilson, the one whose dog had developed a fondness for Bob Rankel's balls. "What'd Snack do to piss them off?"

"Stood by me," said Murphy, "through thick and thin."

"He was the freaking *Grunt*, huh? Damn. I'll bet next they say you were in on it."

"It's already come up, matter of fact. That's a nice dog you got there. What's his name?"

"Justice."

"Really?"

Wilson patted the dog's head. "My kids named him."

"Around here it would take a kid. You work the Ladysnatcher crime scenes?"

"Yes, sir, we did."

"What do *you* think happened?" asked Murphy.

"Nothing."

"Nothing?"

"That's what the evidence says. Nothing happened. They up and walked out of the machine."

chapter 54

JUNIOR DALY STOOD AT THE KITCHEN WINDOW AND watched the thinnest trees near the shore bend over, giving up their last leaves, then stand straight, denuded, waiting for the next blast. New Jersey was now Hurricane Jessica's prime target, with landfall expected at Asbury Park sometime during the next forty-eight hours, according to the FM radio.

"You can almost hear the Springsteen benefit," said Junior, before taking a big hit on a fat joint and turning to hand it to Kym.

She put down her Bloody Mary and toked like an expert.

"I love fucking Bruce," Junior said when he'd exhaled. "Now, there's a real Boss. Seymour Cammeroli ain't no Boss. Just a fat little sneak with roadkill on his dome."

Kym spit smoke and laughed. "Seymour's a putz. He wants to fuck me in the worst way."

"They're all putzes. Dad included. World-class, top-drawer, blue-ribbon putzes. And they all want to fuck you."

"You want another drink?" Kym asked, nodding at Junior's empty glass.

One more drink, thought Junior, and he'd tell her what he really wanted.

"Who's it gonna hurt?" she asked.

"Sure. Why not."

He studied her buns as she shook up another Mary, thinking she was only six years older than him, thinking he'd had far worse and loved it. And it wasn't like his father deserved his loyalty.

He could see it maybe happening, later, when they were drunk, isolated by the storm. She would want to change outfits, to get comfortable . . . he would offer to help unzip and unsnap things. They would—

The door from the garage flew open, and his father glared down at them through the pot smoke. "Good God almighty."

"What?" said Junior, though it was plain that Dad had returned to his bunker for solace and found his troops in open rebellion.

"Well, look at this."

"What?" Junior said again, open-mouthed.

"Start packing, son," Martin said through clenched teeth. "First thing tomorrow, you're getting help in the finest hospital Ireland has to offer."

"Oh, give him a break, willya?" Kym slurred.

"No more breaks. For anybody."

Kym lit a cigarette, ignoring him.

Martin said, "I'll deal with you later."

"Oh, boy, am I scared."

THE PIN-MAP ON THE WALL HAD BEEN EXPANDED BY MAUDE to include the adjoining town of Huntington, Heckscher

Park, and the death of Charlie Hotchkiss. Progress of a sort, Murphy thought ruefully.

"I don't care what anybody says. Junior doesn't sing to me," said Maude. "Not one note."

Murphy looked at his best detective and said, "Me neither. In fact, I think we've been led by the nose to him."

"For political purposes?" she asked.

"Maybe." They were alone in the Homicide bullpen, and Murphy had a hunch he wanted to talk out. He got up and closed the door to the hallway. "Maybe not. Bear with me a minute, and if you think I'm crazy, promise never to repeat this."

"What's on your mind?"

"I may be way off base here, but let's talk about Bob Rankel for a minute."

Maude closed the file on her desk and cocked her head to one side. "Okay. Why?"

"These crimes all took place when Junior was alone, right? Except for Charlie Hotchkiss."

"Except for Charlie."

"Right. So now I'm thinking, who would know that? His dad? What about his dad's driver?"

"Go on."

"Rankel also knew Junior was AWOL from Brunswick before Charlie was actually shot. He just didn't know Junior was alibied up."

"Okay," said Maude, leaning forward, interested. "But that didn't make you think of him as a killer."

"Nope. A dog named Justice did that."

"Say again," said Maude.

"One of our K-9s kept sniffing Rankel at Prefect's press conference. Prefect made a bad joke about it, of course, but I checked after they left: Chris Wilson, the K-9 cop, said the dog worked the Lucido scene and the Hopkins scene."

"Probably all the dogs did," said Maude. "And still that ain't much to go on. Maybe Rankel got laid on the way to work."

Murphy smiled and nodded. "He was always a swordsman, hair or no hair. That was one of the reasons Daly picked him, a *compañero* with no conscience. So I'm thinking he might have had a thing with one of these women, or all of them."

"Maybe. Might. Still not near enough," said Maude. She opened her pocketbook and pulled out a cigarette, lit up.

"I checked with Ben Lucido this morning. Rankel made a hundred-dollar donation to the reward fund. With two kids in college, I'd have thought twenty-five if at all."

"Interesting. An attempt to mitigate guilt?"

Murphy said, "It's more than we got on Junior. Right?"

"I don't know. We want to see if Rankel has alibis or a motive. Go over his involvement, at every juncture. See if he had his own reasons to do this, or did it for someone else . . . Damn."

"He's the only guy we never checked."

"You're absolutely right," said Maude, "because he's one of us, like so much furniture . . . Damn, boss. You might have something here."

She opened her top drawer and selected a red-headed pin. She walked to the ever-changing map and slowly drove the pin into the heart of the county seat. "Where does asshole live?" she asked.

"Bellmore, I think. A garden apartment."

"What time'd he drop Martin and Kym off that Thursday night after the party?"

"We never asked, but Martin told me it was midnight."

Maude got another red pin and stabbed Bellmore, on the South Shore, stood back, and stared at the map.

"You play connect-the-dots," said Murphy, "and he could have done it easy."

"He could have come down New Hyde Park Road, and parked on the block behind her. Son of a bitch."

Murphy's stomach tightened. "Do this very quietly, Maude. Verify any statements he made to anybody, quietly. We spook him, and we've got a problem. We're wrong, and he'll never forget it."

"Check."

"I'll be back. I'm gonna go check his time sheet for the night Beth disappeared."

"Grab his file, too."

"You got it."

MURPHY POKED HIS HEAD INTO HOMICIDE.

"He signed out that night at 1700 hours, even though Martin knocked off at noon."

Maude grinned. "He still had plenty of time to nail Beth, even if he did beat you for some overtime."

Murphy opened his briefcase and took out Robert Rankel's personnel folder, went over it quickly for Maude. There were holes, Murphy pointed out, in Rankel's career, unexplained demotions, years of sick leave abuse followed by years of perfect attendance. He was in, out. Then he was in for good. Which might explain those holes. The last dozen years made for a most impressive résumé, never-mind he was usually driving Martin Daly hither and yon. When he wasn't behind the wheel, Bob Rankel had been an attendee—at county expense—of every professional seminar known to American law enforcement. Lieutenant Rankel took Barricaded Suspects in Phoenix; Electronic Surveillance in Los Angeles; Radar in Rome, New York; and the entire FBI course at Quantico.

"Nice scam," said Maude. "All on overtime."

"There's one more thing. There's a memo notation that his ex-wife, Arlene, filed a complaint with Internal

Affairs last year. I don't know what it's about, but I'm sure we can't follow that line inside without tipping him off."

"I'll talk to her."

"Good."

"So the big prick only looks like a chauffeur," said Maude, sitting back, blowing a stream of smoke over her shoulder.

"In real life he's the best trained cop from here to fucking Montauk, even if he slept half through these seminars."

"And he damn near got away with this . . . if it's him."

"If it's him, we seriously want to take him from behind. And be iron-clad right."

"Got it," said Maude.

"What else have I missed?"

"Not much," she said. "You've done good for a boss."

"Give it to me straight."

"Where they are, for starters. Must we really waste time going over it now?"

"Sorry," said Murphy. "You're right. Get busy."

Maude said, "I'm gonna talk to Suffolk County again. I'm thinking maybe we need to expand our canvass out there. And then I'm gonna sit here and just think for a while."

"Let's talk every hour."

MAUDE CALLED HAP JANKOWSKI, HER OPPOSITE NUMBER IN Suffolk Homicide, told him Martin Daly's driver might be a suspect, that for all she knew the target could have been either man. "Please, quietly check Rankel's statement for veracity. He said he was buying coffee at a deli when the shooting took place, let's find out. You remember what he looks like?"

"Kojak, right?"

"Right. What else you got?"

"Nothing but trouble. I swear to God I saw Peter Jennings in our parking lot this afternoon."

"Get used to it. Call me back."

What if, Maude wondered, Bob Rankel had done this for Seymour or Baltusrol Vail? What if he had been Seymour's back-channel on Martin for all those years, phoning intelligence back to party headquarters. Nobody visited Seymour in person. Hell, she remembered making the first set of footprints on the carpet that day, just like the first cop on the scene of Elizabeth's house had done.

Maude sat up straight and stared at the plants on her desk that needed water, the pile of administrative paperwork she'd left untouched. She opened up the box of case records by her feet and pulled out the Crime Scene photos from Elizabeth's living room, saw again the first cop's single set of footprints on the recently vacuumed carpet. They had been made when no one answered his knock and he walked inside to look for her.

There were no other footprints on that smooth beige carpet, not even the victim's. Maude remembered assuming Elizabeth's living room was a showplace, never used unless she was entertaining. She had done her work in the kitchen that night, slept with Jackson in her bedroom.

The photos of the living room showed scalloped edges along the wall near the front hallway: a hand-held vacuum had been used on the carpet, not your basic turbo-charged Electrolux.

A Dustbuster. A Dirt Devil.

Maude called the uniformed cop stationed at Elizabeth's house, and held on while he checked the closets.

"No Dustbuster in the house," he said after a few minutes.

"Not on the inventory list?"

"Negative."

Maude grabbed her raincoat and crossed the street to the county garage. She schmoozed the grease-streaked maintenance foreman for five minutes, then asked if she could check over the backup executive limo, the use of which Elizabeth Lucido had refused and Junior never been offered.

"Sure."

"I'm thinking of buying one."

"Must be a lot of money in murder, eh?"

"Not enough."

The foreman produced a ring of keys from his desk drawer, and unlocked the limo's doors for her. "It sits idle most days. We use it when Land-Force One breaks down."

"Pop the trunk for me?"

"Don't want to sit behind the wheel?"

"In a minute."

"You're looking for a body, aren't you?"

"I'm always looking for a body."

There was a spare tire, a jack, a bag of salt, a six CD changer, and a Dustbuster in the cavernous trunk. The Dustbuster was shrink-wrapped in its original cellophane.

"Nothing, hanh?" he asked.

"Nope."

"Thank God."

Rocky Blair called on the cell phone as Maude was walking back to headquarters. Rocky was back at the office, after talking to Beth's secretary. The woman didn't know about the calls Beth made to Martin Daly's office on the day of her disappearance.

"Where was Mr. Beinstock when you asked her this?"

"Hovering over her shoulder. So I couldn't ask about Rankel."

"Too bad."

chapter 55

MAUDE DROVE DIRECTLY TO HEMPSTEAD AND parked in front of the white split-level occupied by Bob Rankel's ex-wife, Arlene.

"Internal Affairs," Maude said when Arlene Rankel opened the front door. Maude held up her shield.

"Where you been, babe? I called months ago."

Mrs. Rankel was tall, thin, a weary blonde nearing fifty.

"I'm new to the unit," said Maude. "Maybe you can catch me up on what's been happening."

"What's the point? He moved out. Good riddance."

"Well, I still have this report I gotta fill out."

"Well, then come on in. By all means. What the hell. Got to keep the paperwork straight. Goddamn police department."

They had lived together for twenty-five years, Arlene Rankel said when they were seated in the living room, whose pale walls bore the tracings of plaques and citations Bob Rankel had removed. She said they had separated early last winter, because he was in love with someone else, someone at work, a younger woman. His one true love, the middle-aged jackass.

"What about you?"

"Bob said it wasn't anything I'd done, just a quarter-century with anyone was too much to take. He hadn't planned on falling in love. It just happened. And anyway, the kids are almost grown."

"Nice," said Maude. "Original."

"Then I think she dumped him . . . God, I hope she dumped him. The bastard actually called me for a reconciliation. Said he'd come to his senses. I was his oldest friend, the mother of his kids. I was tempted, God help me. Then I realized I was happier with him gone. I told him, 'Fuck off.' "

"How are the kids?"

"Glad they're at college."

Maude took a chance. "His lawyer's Beth Hopkins?"

"The barracuda herself, not that I wanted anything like this to happen to her."

"Of course not. Doesn't have anything to do with it. Bob have a temper?"

Arlene snorted. She rolled up her sleeve and showed Maude where the doctors had put the pin in her arm.

"Good Lord. Bob did that?"

Arlene said, "All my life I was brainwashed by that bastard. Never be a rat. Never rat out a cop. Stick together . . . Yeah, Bob did that. Big fucking deal."

Maude stared at her pad, as if she were ashamed. "Like I said, I'm new."

"I don't mean to be cruel, honey, but you don't look new."

THE AFTERNOON RUSH WAS BUILDING, FRUSTRATING.

On her ride back to the Homicide office, Maude called Justine Lucido and asked her how Elizabeth got home from Kennedy Airport after her Bermuda vacation.

"Martin Daly sent a car."

Son of a bitch, she thought, idling in traffic in Hempstead, watching a black woman push a double-stroller around the crowd outside a liquor store. "Do you know what she thought of Bob Rankel?"

"Martin's driver? Probably nothing. Why?"

"No reason."

Maude pulled to the side of the road near the Jack in the Box and flipped open her copy of Rankel's file. A thirty-eight Colt service revolver was registered. The off-duty weapons box said: None. She checked over his first job application, which had been filed with Nassau County in July 1970. He'd had no criminal record when he came on the job, not even a parking ticket, nothing but the highest recommendations from teachers and former employers. He was six-foot-six, two hundred twenty pounds. Blood type O negative. Right-handed. His hair had been brown. His eyes were brown. His middle name was James. His nickname, typed in the appropriate box, was Big Bob.

"Well, I'll be a son of a bitch."

Now Maude was sure they had their boy, her mind snapping closed equations too long left hanging. Beth Hopkins was his divorce lawyer. He had probably talked about the affair, bragged about nailing Elizabeth. Beth Hopkins was an ex-cop, who might have got to wondering, a loose end he couldn't leave. Whether Beth was onto him or not, her telephone messages to Martin Daly might have got him thinking, got her missing.

Charlie Hotchkiss was closing fast, which got him dead.

Maude told herself to forget from now on that Rankel was a cop, due no regard from her. He would kill her if she stood in his way, so she better be ready to kill him first.

She dialed Murphy's office and told him what she'd learned from Arlene, and the file, what she surmised.

"BB. Damn. We got him yet?"

"Not quite."

"But you love him, don't you?"

"A lot."

Murphy said, "He should have mentioned that Beth was his lawyer. But 'I just drive the car,' is all he says. I'll bet he killed Charlie, too, doubled back on those boys and plugged that leak."

"Yup."

A county bus rolled by and blasted her with soot.

Murphy said, "So Elizabeth had a booze bang with our man Bob."

"Hey, maybe he's a good listener. He's sure not my type, but then none of you are . . . We should tail him, boss. Maybe he'll lead us to the women."

"I was thinking that, then I thought, hey, we already got the county executive watching his every move, at least for the next twenty-four. Any more surveillance than that, I'm guessing he'd spook. He gets lawyered up and makes bail, we'll never see him or those women again. Let's have him buried first. The night after the election he'll be free as a bird. Then . . ."

"We gonna put Martin Daly wise? I'd say he's at some considerable risk."

"Nope."

"Really?"

"If Rankel wanted Daly dead, he could have had him any time, like at the park."

Maude said, "Lot of variables in there, boss. I'm glad it's not my call."

"You think Daly could keep a straight face?"

"He'd be pissing in his pants."

FRANK MURPHY REACHED MARTIN DALY BY PHONE AT HIS CAM-paign headquarters, where the county executive was, he confessed, "sucking every last ass I can lock my lips on."

Murphy gave him the disturbing news that there had been a fairly credible threat against his life, not counting all the other routine oaths of vengeance. "Given what happened in Huntington," Murphy said, "I think—"

"Goddamn it, Frank!" Daly screamed into Murphy's ear. "I'm ready to just quit, you know it? Just plain let the sharks take over. I was warned this crusade could cost me my life."

"Look, Martin, we'll put more guys on your security detail tonight and tomorrow, for as long as it takes. Plus have Bob Rankel stay over again tonight and earn his fucking paycheck. Tell him I've authorized the overtime. And then I'll add a second team no one can see on the perimeter."

"A good team," said Martin after a moment. "The best team."

"Invisible," said Murphy. "I promise."

AT FIVE-FIFTEEN THAT DARK AND WINDY AFTERNOON ALICE Gettings left a job interview at a savings bank in Cranford, New Jersey.

She thought they had liked her, that perhaps they'd make an offer. Anyone who came out for a job interview on a windy, rainy day like this had to be motivated. And her experience spoke for itself.

Of course, she didn't know if she would take the job if offered. She didn't yet know if she was breaking up with Frank. She missed him, sure enough. Her eyes still filled with tears several times every day.

Thus distracted as she was by her tumultuous love life and the horrible weather, Alice Gettings never realized she was being followed, all the way from the parking lot of the bank to the driveway of her mother's house.

Alice got out of the Mustang and ran back to check the mailbox. A big pink envelope had arrived along with the catalogues and circulars of the season. Alice opened the card, read it, shook her head sadly, then walked up the driveway and dropped it in the trash can by the side of the house.

He could beg all he liked, she thought. She wasn't gonna sit in the condo while he hunted for his girlfriends. Uh-uh. Not gonna happen.

Tuesday, Nov. 5

AS THE HARBOR WAS FAR TOO ROUGH TO SWIM THAT stormy morning, Frank Murphy stayed in bed until almost sunrise, then scrambled eggs for his overnight guests. While Wally and Jake were diving into their food, Frank sat at the head of the kitchen table with just coffee and read the morning paper.

Newsday led off their Election Day coverage with a cover shot of poor Charlie Hotchkiss facedown on the ground near the bench. The headline read: A LINE OF DUTY DEATH. Pages two and three carried all the no comments, no clues, the vows of revenge, sidebars on other murdered reporters from Arizona to Argentina.

Page eight had a shot of Martin Daly trotting in disgrace from the Victim's Center, followed closely by snarling rich people. The headline read: DALY DROWNS AT VICTIM'S CENTER. LAWSUITS LOOM.

On page nine there was an update on the Ladysnatcher case. According to District Attorney Arthur Prefect, the governor was now involved; as of midnight last night he had called on the Feds to assist. A crack team was being assembled at Quantico.

"We're out," Murphy said, looking across breakfast at Jake. "According to the ass-rag, Governor Goofball is coming down to solve this himself."

Jake was reading Part 2, checking out the daytime

television schedule. "Appleknocker," he said. "Ichabod Crane."

Murphy said, "Seems a crying shame Giuliani's not free."

The editorial page was devoted to candidate endorsements. Murphy ran down the page, finding no surprises. At the bottom of the page, to Murphy's disgust, *Newsday*, after much soul-searching by the editorial staff on a "real tight" call, endorsed the incumbent, Martin Daly, for Nassau County Executive. Although the challenger, Jackson Hind, showed promise and put up a valiant fight, Daly's experience and savvy has earned him another chance, it said.

Wally grunted unhappily at his empty plate.

Jake refilled it with eggs, but Wally grunted again.

"Wally, baby, what's wrong?" asked Jake.

Wally looked at Frank and grunted again.

Frank said, "He wants to go for a ride."

Jake put down his fork and wiped his mouth. "I know you're real busy today, Frank, but if we could somehow arrange it, I really need to sneak into my office for an hour."

"You think that's smart?"

"Smart or not, we got a backlog of favors people still expect you're doing for them."

"Sorry, Jake, we're out of the favor business, at least temporarily."

Jake tapped his fork on the plate, then nodded. "Fair enough. So me and Wally'll take a ride. Then we'll eat some more. Then my arteries will explode."

Wally heard his name and put his head on the table next to his plate, moaning.

"What's the matter, Wally?" asked Frank, not expecting an answer.

"This happened yesterday, too," said Jake. "I couldn't snap him out of it."

"You feeding him enough?"

"Does the pope wear a beanie?"

Murphy said, "What do you think the problem is?"

"The truth?"

"Just like always, Jake."

"I figure little brother wants to go home."

Frank wanted to tell Jake that Wally *was* home, as long as they were together. He remembered the tiny living room they had played in as boys, the smell of pot roast in the air, waiting for Dad to come home from his footpost in midtown, hoping he was sober. Waiting. Waiting. Hoping.

"The Institute, Frank," said Jake. "It's where he lives. Alice Gettings lives here with you. Remember?"

Murphy grimaced. "You act like I have Alzheimer's."

"You ain't the sharpest knife in the drawer."

SEYMOUR CAMMEROLI AND HIS STAFF MOVED INTO THE TOP floor of the Marriott at seven-thirty that morning.

Party workers flung open the Presidential Suite and laid in provisions fit for a sheik and his harem. Flowers in crystal vases adorned end tables. A porno flick was already running in living room A.

Artie Prefect sat in his raincoat with his back to Seymour's television, waiting to learn his future.

As the music got faster and the breathing on TV got louder and lustier, Seymour yanked the remote from Denny and flicked on the Weather Channel, where in short order they learned that Hurricane Jessica had turned hard northeast and was now expected to miss the American coast altogether. Heavy wind and rain were expected until midnight, flooding in the low-lying areas, particularly on the high tides.

Nobody reacted.

Everyone stared at Seymour, waiting; what they had heard was only bad news if Seymour said so.

Seymour looked down at Artie Prefect on the couch. "I don't know, kid. This is cutting it kinda close. We get the hurricane square, it's doable. This way. . . ."

"Heavy rain will still affect the vote," said Artie. "Massively, I'd say. Flooding in the low-lying areas, you heard him. I think we can trust the machine to prevail. What time is high tide?"

"I don't know," Seymour said, and he wasn't talking about the tides. He gazed across the long room at his faithful zone leaders, all bright-eyed and bushy-tailed, waiting for the word, poised to order the rank-and-file troops to man phone banks, drive buses, roll wheelchairs, carry cripples, raise the dead if necessary. Thug poll-watchers had already been dispersed about the county, to challenge undesirables, and intimidate minorities, no matter which pawn Seymour decided to back.

Near the main door of the suite several six-foot stacks of write-in ballots had been readied.

Trucks idled behind the hotel.

Seymour kneeled next to Prefect and whispered in his ear, "A Jackson Hind administration puts people in jail. You realize that, right? He's a vengeful motherfucker."

"We can whip them both. I know it. Ten o'clock tonight, we'll open champagne."

Seymour smiled and shook his head, laid his hand upon Prefect's bony shoulder, and used him for a crutch. "Another time, Art. Okay? Work with me here. A solid front, and all that."

"Please?"

Seymour faced his leadership corps. "Today we work for Martin Daly, like our motherfucking lives depended on it. Everybody got that? I don't want to hear about no communications glitches. We're putting Martin Daly back in office."

His people agreed as one: "Good idea." "The right move." "Let's kick some pinko ass." "You the man!"

They crowded close to pat Seymour's back and assure him of his wisdom while Arthur Prefect slipped out the door.

Seymour turned to Denny, who had already switched back to the smut. "Get Martin Daly on the horn. Tell him he owes me huge. And have somebody burn those fucking ballots. Then call that douche-bag Neville and tell him it's Daly, so get busy."

FRANK MURPHY STARED AT THE PICTURE OF KYM SCALLIA-DALY on the campaign flier that had come in yesterday's office mail. She was sitting by the family hearth at Blue Landing with what had to be a borrowed golden—Murphy had never heard mention of a dog—and she was dressed in gingham like somebody's grandmother, hands folded in her lap, smiling warmly. "Please," her message to Nassau County voters began, "stay the course. Don't fall for hollow promises from a pretty face. Don't abandon my Martin's principles. Nassau County can't afford it."

Murphy was wondering what exactly those principles were when his Homicide detectives knocked at his door.

"Terrible news," Murphy told Maude and Rocky. "The Feds can't fly in today. Maybe by nightfall. Maybe even tomorrow."

"So then it's just us incompetents today?" said Maude.

"Till tonight. Been thinking?"

"Yup," Maude said. "All damn night. And the way I see it is, we can wait until we're sure, or we can scoop him up now and sweat him, thereby looking like we're trying to sabotage an election if we're wrong . . . But if *I* was one of those missing women, I'd sure as hell vote for now. And, hey, if somehow we're wrong, at least we had good hearts."

"I'd bet my condo we're not wrong," said Murphy.

Rocky said, "You think there's any chance he knows we're on to him?"

"No way of knowing," said Murphy.

"He might have got a heads-up from someone we brushed yesterday. The longer we wait, the more we risk another incident. He driving Martin right now?"

Murphy said, "According to Daly's office, they're at the Merrick train station, together right now like Batman and Robin."

"Okay. Now where the hell did he hide the bodies?"

Murphy scratched his head. "It was me, I'd dump 'em in the drink."

Maude looked at her watch. "You know what, Frank. We don't have time for this crap."

"What do you mean?"

"We don't have time for search warrants. We don't have time for wiretaps. If *I* was one of those women, I'd want you and me and Rocky to get off our asses and commit a couple of crimes."

Murphy looked at her and realized what she was saying. He smiled. "If I was in trouble, I'd want you guys coming to the rescue."

They piled into the Homicide squad car and sped over to Rankel's garden apartment in Bellmore, off Jerusalem Avenue, Rocky driving like a Russian cabby. They separated outside the complex and knocked on doors until Maude found an elderly neighbor willing to express to them his concern that he had not seen his friend Bob Rankel lately.

"Not all day yesterday?" asked Maude. "Or last night?"

Richard Calhoun stroked his grizzled, neighborly jaw. "Not once."

"Or the day before?"

"It's been a while."

"And that worries you," Maude suggested, knitting her brow.

"I guess so. Should it?"

Maude nodded grimly as Rocky and Murphy joined her.

"Foul play?" the neighbor asked the men.

"Only one way to find out," said Murphy. "You ask us to look inside."

"Could you do that?"

"Absolutely. I'm the police commissioner. Stand back."

They used a pry to gain entry, then told Mr. Calhoun to wait back in his own apartment.

"You want me to call for backup?" he asked.

"Not necessary."

Rankel's small studio had a view of the street. Police plaques covered the whitewashed walls, pictures of Bob Rankel hobknobbing with the upper crust, never a hint that Bob was there to drive them. The queen-sized bed was unmade.

The coffee table was covered with Ladysnatcher articles.

On the bedside table was a timeline on graph paper, the sort used by Homicide detectives to track the movements of multiple suspects.

"Look at this," said Maude. "He's made notes. What he was supposed to know. When he was supposed to know it. Here: Junior drunk, alone. Jackson Hind in picture. Stonehenge revisited."

"Okay, folks," said Murphy. "Dig deep."

"But neat," said Maude. "Let's not lose evidence on a bad search."

"Good Lord," said Murphy, "I can't wait to see that bastard in cuffs."

Maude picked through the clothes closets while Murphy checked the desk. In the top drawer he found a folder of compromising photos of Junior Daly, taken since the boy was in his teens. Smoking pot. Skinny-dipping on the beach with other neighborhood kids. There were shots of a VW microbus seriously crumpled around a tree. Copies of two canceled checks in the amount of five thousand each. A cryptic disciplinary report from

Junior's brief stint at Lasalle Military Academy that suggested he may have had unauthorized sex with a female employee at the school. A check for ten thousand. Murphy realized that Bob Rankel had been planning on framing Junior for something, anything, for years. The dopey kid was his insurance policy. Now a claim had been filed.

Murphy said, "Beep Junior."

Rocky pulled his head from Rankel's refrigerator and said, "You got it."

Junior called back within a minute. Rocky handed Murphy the phone.

"Commissioner Murphy here."

"Junior Daly. What do you want?"

"Where are you?"

"Kennedy Airport. Why?"

"Take a look at the departures board, kid. Any of them say canceled?"

"Yeah. And postponed. So what?"

"Never mind. I need your expertise."

"What expertise?"

Murphy let him slide. "If you were going to hide bodies, where would you put them so no one could ever find them? Think hard."

"I don't have to think hard. That's an easy one," Junior said.

"Really?"

"Blue Landing. My fort."

"What?"

Junior told Murphy how he had dug it almost ten feet deep by himself and furnished it, installed shag carpeting, then laid flat across the top an old wooden wall with a door, left over from a renovation. He had covered the wall with dirt and leaves. He told Murphy how to get there, using the path by the wishing well.

Murphy asked, "Dad know about this fort?"

"Sure. When he couldn't find me around the house, he'd send Rankel up to get me."

"When was the last time you were actually in the fort?"

"Maybe fifteen years ago. Before I started driving. Why?"

Murphy said, "I found some pictures of you fucking up . . . Okay, a lot of pictures of you fucking up. I'm gonna destroy them for you, Junior. Give you a chance to make a clean start."

"At what? What are you talking about?"

"There's gonna be an opening on your father's staff, and I think you'd be just perfect for the job."

"You're a madman, Murphy. Quit talking in riddles."

"Kiss the Blarney Stone for me, kid."

Murphy hung up and filled in the others.

"I like it," said Maude. "A lot."

"You two check it out, quietly. Meanwhile, I'll find out where Martin is. Then we'll talk about picking Rankel up—without getting Martin's stupid head blown off."

"Or ours," said Rocky.

"Amen to that," said Murphy.

AT THE MARRIOTT, UPSTAIRS IN THE PRESIDENTIAL SUITE, EARLY exit polls showed the county executive race was still too close to call.

Seymour Cammeroli carried his lucky Dick Nixon coffee mug to the huge picture window and gazed heavenward. "Keep pissing, Big Fellow. Don't fuck with us now. Keep those shiftless Dems home, watching *All My Children*."

Behind him, Seymour's entourage laughed wildly, as entourages will. Some were already drinking, chatting on the extra phones, inviting friends to join the party.

Room service arrived with a sumptuous brunch, set it up and departed.

The buzzer rang again, and Denny hit the intercom. "Who is it?"

"Martin Daly."

Denny looked at Seymour, who put down his knife and fork and wiped his mouth, then nodded.

Denny opened the door to Martin Daly and Bob Rankel.

"Gentlemen," Martin said grandly to everyone. "My brothers and sisters. How we doing?"

The party-puppets froze while Seymour did his blank-face and Denny Dubois and Bob Rankel stared each other down.

Martin opened his raincoat and waited for Rankel to help him take it off.

But Rankel was busy in a turf war of his own.

For a moment the only sound in the suite was Carol Silva on the television, giving an update on the weather. "High winds continue to batter Long Island . . ."

Eyeballs clicked back and forth, from Martin to Seymour, Rankel to Denny. The awkward moment ended when Seymour cracked a wide smile, stood up, and opened his arms in Martin's direction. "What can I tell you, Martin," said Seymour. "You da man!"

Seymour and Martin hugged to the crowd's warm applause. Grown men cheered: "Hoot, there it is, hoot, there it is."

"Welcome home, Martin," Seymour whispered up into Martin's ear during the wolf-whistling. "That bad taste in your mouth is my shit. Don't forget it."

"Right," Daly whispered back.

"Now could you please do us a favor and shut your fucking mouth. That New Nassau of yours sounded to me like a lot of my friends were gonna be out of work."

"Like you said, hot air. Campaign rhetoric. I had to

stop Hind. Only now how do we get around those promises?"

"Oh," said Seymour. "*That.* I guess the same way we always do, you dopey bastard."

"Mr. Vail okay with all this?"

"As long as you never do it again."

Martin leaned back and said loudly, affectionately, "You had me going there for a while, boss."

"In your pants, I had you going. Right? Right?"

"It's still a close race," Martin said.

"Yeah, and whose fault is that?"

Martin said nothing, just smiled a little smile, grateful that nothing had really changed.

chapter 57

THERE WAS ENOUGH RAINWATER IN THE PIT NOW to drown herself and end her misery. The idea came to her because Elizabeth was sure she was dying, and she was lying on the ground in a daze, water seeping into her mouth as she combed through the few regrets of her short, productive life, among them a dalliance with Big Bob Rankel, the drunken mistake of her career. She clenched her fists.

Big Bob Rankel.

If a human being's cells were totally replaced in seven years, someday she could say she had never touched him. If she lived that long.

Big Bob Rankel.

Not Martin.

She recalled she had opened the front door to him

that night without looking outside, thinking Jackson had forgotten something.

She remembered his face screwed up in rage, him calling her a no-good bitch? A cunt? Something from his wide vocabulary. She remembered his knobby fist approaching at warp speed. The explosion in her brain.

Bob Rankel had actually had the nerve to consider himself betrayed. Imagine that.

Elizabeth looked up at the light diving down through the widening crack in the door.

One last time, she thought. One last chance to get even.

She grabbed the bottom rung of the ladder and started up, using her knees like feet on the slippery rungs, ignoring the agony.

Throughout her torturous ascent she thought of how she had spent the last days of her life. When she was ready to quit and slide back to the ground, she pictured Rankel kissing her, and her fury drove her upward, her knee on a higher rung, twisting to reach the knob, turning it, finally getting her back against the wood, one more rung.

Push.

Open.

Wind and rain tore the door off its hinges and whipped her damaged face. Another rung and she flopped sideways onto the soaked earth, shivering with effort, unable to call for help. Then she rolled onto her back and stared up at the fierce clouds racing over the trees, weeping uncontrollably with a joy she could never have imagined.

chapter 58

L OCAL ROADS WERE FLOODING FAST AS BLOWN-DOWN leaves clogged storm drains and sewers.

Maude and Rocky fought their way north across Long Island through the blinding rain, getting trapped in a particularly noxious traffic jam caused by county highway workers—using a full array of orange cones and yellow flashing sawhorses—tearing Jackson Hind signs from telephone poles.

At last they turned onto Shore Road in Fairhaven and drove past the gates at Blue Landing.

There was a security guard in his private car parked halfway up the driveway, so Rocky and Maude parked their squad car near the end of Shore Road. They got out and put on their raincoats and jumped the low stone fence at the corner of the property, then headed up the grassy hill along the edge of the woods, stepping carefully over downed limbs, holding their coats closed.

The overgrown path by the wishing well was blocked by an uprooted maple.

"Jesus," said Rocky. "Don't mess with Mother Nature."

Maude aimed her flashlight down the well.

Nothing but wet leaves.

According to Junior the underground fort was twenty yards into the woods, and sure enough, as they turned one last corner they saw an old wooden door opened up from the earth.

"Oh, no," Rocky whispered. "You smell that?"

Maude did, and it almost made her cry.

They stepped to the edge, shined their lights into the pit, saw the body bag at the bottom.

Only one.

Rocky took off his raincoat and handed it to Maude. He tucked his flashlight in his back pocket and started down the ladder. A rung broke under his weight, then the next one, and he slid slowly down the ladder, splitting it in half.

"You okay?" asked Maude, shining the light down.

"Other than the goddamn splinters in my hands. Damn."

Maude directed the beam about the subterranean chamber, finding the opened cans of soup, the silverware, the mannequin, the piles of excrement, the magazines.

"Open the bag."

Rocky yanked open the zipper and recoiled in disgust. "It's Beth Hopkins, I think. And it sure looks like there was more than one body down here. The residue in these cans ain't been sitting here fifteen years."

A limb cracked loudly overhead. Maude said, "The son of a bitch moved 'em, and maybe not too long ago."

"Looks that way. You think he's coming back for this one?"

"Not until after tonight. If you're thinking stakeout, forget it," said Maude.

Rocky looked up at Maude, then back down at Beth. "So does Bob Rankel hate the fucking Dalys, or what?"

"Or just found them terribly convenient."

Rocky climbed onto the chest of drawers and took Maude's outstretched hand. She hauled him out of the pit, filthy with mud, looking like a coal miner.

"Looks like you need a new blazer," said Maude.

"My guy can get this clean."

They found the security guard in the driveway fast asleep.

"Jesus Christ, who are you?"

They flashed their badges.

"How'd you get so dirty?"

"Never you fucking mind," said Rocky.

The guard hadn't seen anything. It was his first day. A disciplinary transfer from Goals 2002.

"Seen anybody come or go?"

"No."

"Who's up in the house?"

"Nobody."

Maude and Rocky walked away from the guard's car.

Maude said, "We swear the kid to absolute, total secrecy, how long will it take for Rankel to hear this?"

"Ten minutes, if that."

She had to balance the risk to Martin Daly against the remote possibility that Elizabeth was still alive. Think. Elizabeth had been taken first. Or second, if Babs Whitcomb had also once inhabited that hole. Maybe this was a staging area. A decomposition chamber. Odds were, she realized, Rankel was busy moving bones.

"Scare the living shit out of him, Rocky, as only you can, then we're driving to the Marriott. Those other women are alive until we tag the toes."

chapter 59

RANK MURPHY SAT AT THE SWITCHED ON CONSOLE in the back of the snoop van and contemplated the fleet of county vehicles in the hotel parking lot, the cookie-cutter thugs on the doors.

The press camp had set up their satellite city on the west side of the building, adjacent to the Coliseum parking lot. In spite of the horizontal rain, protestors and counterprotestors were gathering on the sidewalk near the Hempstead Turnpike entrance, all in foul-weather gear, wrestling laminated signs, ready to do their utmost for God and country.

Land Force One was parked by the hotel's front door, in flagrant defiance of Nassau County fire codes.

It was three o'clock in the afternoon, and the hotel was filling up. In two more hours, Murphy knew, this place would be crawling with innocent bystanders, the worst place possible to capture a dangerous man.

His cell phone rang. "What?"

Maude spoke in code. "We need to arrest BB immediately."

"Everybody's at the hotel. It's gettin' on party time."

"We're responding forthwith," said Maude. "Time is of the essence."

Murphy wondered if that meant the victims were still alive. "That's good?"

"It's significant."

Murphy said, "I'll be snorkeling about the lobby. Unless circumstances change."

"On the way."

Murphy shut down the console and climbed out of the back of the van. He bent his head into the wind, fought his way through the lot, and joined the rain-blasted crowd in the lobby.

They were shaking out coats and umbrellas, moaning over fallen hairdos. One fat woman was scolding her husband for skipping the valet service. "I mean, how freaking cheap can you get, Vinnie?"

Murphy glanced into the cocktail bar, just off the main lobby. A couple of A-team hookers made eye contact with him, climbed down from their stools, and collected their huge pocketbooks.

"Ladies," he said as he walked in.

"Commissioner," they said as they walked out.

His cell phone went off again, and Murphy wandered to the end of the bar.

"Hello, Frank."

It was Alice.

Frank said, "I'm in the middle of something here, honey. Can I call you back?"

"Fine. Whenever you can squeeze me in."

"Don't be like that."

"No. Really. I understand. I don't count."

"Alice."

"I just wanted to tell you that I finally caught on that I'm being followed. And I don't appreciate it one little bit."

Murphy's heart stopped. They were wrong about Rankel, wrong about everything. This was his nightmare and no one else's. "It's not me, if you're right about the tail."

"Sure it's not, Frankie-Baby."

"Are you sure you're right?"

"Of course not. I'm a blonde. What do I know? By the way, I got a job offer today."

"Alice, Jesus—"

"Look, call me at my mother's tonight, okay? I have to go."

Murphy stared at the dead phone in his hand, thinking he didn't even know where she had called from, he couldn't even call her back.

Thinking . . .

He stuffed his phone in his pocket and headed back through the lobby for the front doors, arrived outside in time to see Maude and Rocky roll up, splashing the shins of two uniformed valets who were standing near the curb.

Murphy jumped into their backseat.

They told him what they had found in Junior's fort.

"Good God in heaven, poor Beth," said Murphy. "How?"

"Took one right between the eyes, it looked like," said Rocky.

Murphy stared at his hands while his insides collapsed. "You trust the security guard to keep his mouth shut?"

"He doesn't know what we found, but he knows we were there."

Murphy said, "How long, after we call it in, will everyone in this building know about it?"

"Fifteen minutes," Maude guessed. "No more."

The side windows were steaming up. A car behind them honked twice.

Murphy's watch said two-twenty-five. "Do it."

Maude grabbed the mike from the dashboard and made the necessary radio notifications for the crime scene in Martin Daly's woods.

"Repeat that address?" said the radio operator.

"You heard me. Martin Daly's house. Blue Landing. Fairhaven."

"You want to call me on a land-line?"

"Negative," said Maude. "Send the fleet."

Maude hung up the microphone.

"You think we need numbers here?" Murphy asked, wiping steam off his window and staring up at the big hotel.

Maude said, "Better off without 'em."

Rocky said, "Of course, they'll crucify us if we're wrong."

MURPHY, MAUDE, AND ROCKY FOUND MARTIN DALY UPSTAIRS, alone in his personal suite, a great man pondering his brush with sudden unemployment.

"What now?" Daly asked the cops, waving them inside before anyone saw them.

Daly had been watching CNBC, Murphy saw, keeping tabs on his portfolio, perhaps wondering if he could afford to retire.

"Where's Bob Rankel?" Murphy asked.

"How the hell do I know? And what the hell is going on at my house? I just got a phone call from my office that police cars—"

Maude said, "Sir, we think Bob Rankel murdered Beth Hopkins and Elizabeth Lucido and almost certainly Charlie Hotchkiss."

"No fucking way."

They told him Beth Hopkins was found dead in his son's underground fort. Elizabeth Lucido had possibly also been there, for quite some time. Her body had yet to be found.

Martin put down his drink. "This is a joke, right? A practical joke. Jesus Christ, people, the fucking polls aren't closed. Does Jackson Hind have this?"

Murphy said, "Frankly, we don't give a fuck."

"Well, I give a fuck, Murphy. Okay? If I still have a job, I can get another driver."

"We're here to save your life, Martin. The least you could do is say thank-you to Maude and Rocky."

Daly growled, paced the suite, finally turned and allowed a conciliatory grunt to escape his compressed lips.

"You're welcome," said Maude. "Now we need you to get Rankel down here without tipping him off."

Martin seemed to be stuck in the damage-assessment mode. "Jesus . . . Jesus. Beth Hopkins."

Murphy said, "You either help us make the grab or you're in on the escape, you understand?"

"You think he'll run?"

"Don't you?"

Though it was obviously difficult for Martin to weigh options without benefit of staff, he got it right this time. "Seymour brought up a string of broads. My guess is Rankel's there, getting his rocks off."

"Great," said Maude.

"So maybe just wait till he comes back here. He's supposed to check in every half hour or so—in case I need something."

Murphy looked at his triathlete watch. "Sorry, Martin. In about five more minutes everybody in this hotel is gonna know a body was found at your house. We'd like him in custody by then, if it's okay with you. What's he wearing?"

"His basic funeral suit. His driving gloves."

"And a gun," said Rocky.

"At least one," said Martin. "Maybe more."

JUNIOR DALY WAS ON HIS THIRD BLOODY MARY IN THE International departures bar, watching fellow travelers stroll the concourse. Some of them recognized him and smiled. A few flashed him the two-fingered peace sign from an era long past. "You da man!" said a third.

Damn, Junior thought, he was a fucking celebrity, albeit of the seminotorious variety. He stood out at an airport bar. Junior knew in his bones why his father liked it so much, why he suffered such indignities to remain on the stage. He took a long, spicy swallow and thought: It would be a colossal waste to run away and give this up. He should stick around and play this hand.

Maybe.

His shrink said he was reckless when drinking and sorry when sober.

Well, hell, who wasn't?

Junior glanced across the concourse at the rain power-washing the windows and figured that if not for the storm, he would already be airborne, his decision made.

He nudged Kym and told her he had to piss, to get him another Bloody Mary. "Dad's buying."

"It's his privilege."

On his way to the men's room Junior's beeper went off, and he saw it was the phone number of his best marijuana connection, a man he needed stroked if he planned on staying in town. He found an empty booth at a vacant gate and returned the call.

"Yo, Junior," his man whispered, "Dude, I'm on a security gig at your old man's house. The homicide cops were like just here. Now some other cops are here. I mean way plenty of them. I heard them saying there's a dead chick in some fallout shelter in your woods. So I said, Yo, what up wit dis?"

Junior hung up, thinking no wonder everybody thinks I'm an asshole. Maybe better wait for that plane. Then it gnawed on him that he'd been set up again, that the public persona of Junior Daly as a jackass had been a team effort from Day One, starting with his fucking name. Junior. Might as well have named him Butt-Boy. Or Dipshit.

Enough was enough.

Junior walked directly to the rent-a-car counter with his Nassau County credit card in hand. "I want a Jeep, loaded," he said. "Something that can handle this storm. And I want it now."

"Yes, sir," said the salesman, checking boxes and circling numbers on a form. "And how long will you be needing the vehicle?"

"I'll let you know."

"You want the extra insurance coverage?"

"Fuck no. What a rip-off."

Riding the start-and-stop shuttle bus to the rent-a-car lot, Junior didn't feel the least bit guilty about leaving Kym behind with his carry-on bag and two Bloody Marys.

The lady knew what to do at a bar by herself.

chapter 60

B OB RANKEL HAD THE OVERDOSED HOOKER ACROSS his shoulder as he headed down the back-stairs. He banged her head off the wall as he pushed through the side door into the wind-driven rain.

The taxi he had arranged was waiting. The cabby held the back door open while Rankel poured the hooker inside.

"Here's twenty bucks," Rankel shouted. "Dump her at the Hempstead train station."

"That's thirty . . . because of the weather."

Rankel peeled another ten off his roll, then went back inside and upstairs to the third floor.

He ducked into the Seaford suite, where he was warmly welcomed and fitted with a beer.

The Seaford leader assured him the race was in the bag, a big day for Martin. But someone else had heard earlier that exit polls were less than encouraging, and the crowd in the suite stood facing a television, waiting for more.

Rankel couldn't imagine a Martin Daly concession speech, or him having to move out of his lounge, for that matter. Life would go on as it should.

Then *News 12* flashed a special report bar across the bottom of the screen while showing stock aerial shots of Blue Landing as if it were Monticello, then someone was talking about Martin Daly, and a land-based camera with a rain-spotted lens zoomed in on a cavalcade of cop cars in his driveway, a cop stringing yellow tape from tree to tree, then closer still on the wishing well.

"The body of missing attorney Beth Hopkins was dis-covered today—"

"Shush," said the zone leader. "Turn up the volume."

Everybody watched, everybody said, "Holy shit."

They turned as one to Bob Rankel for some explanation.

But Big Bob was already in the wind, headed down the back stairs again, blaming everybody else but himself for his problems, wondering if he had the strength to bluff his way through this. "Hey," he would say to anyone who asked, "I'm just the fucking driver. Who knows what sick shit rich people do. Junior Daly always was a weird little dude."

He ran past linen closets and laundry carts until he found an empty office in the basement near the boilers, and he hid inside, lights off, needing just a moment to gather his thoughts.

This was her fault.

All of it.

He had lost his wife over Elizabeth, and the love and respect of his children. Even though he had kept their liaison secret, even though he felt like shouting it to the world, even though he felt like a lovesick fool. She had flicked him off like a booger, a fuckup.

The pain in his heart festered.

She didn't even notice his moping. She didn't notice him at all. In fact, they had not spoken more than five friendly words until the night of the fund-raiser, when he had sensed a thaw, a touch of the old camaraderie. With the Dalys home drunk so early, he had figured a house call might not be a bad idea.

As on his prior visit, he had parked in the dark spot on the block behind her house and slipped through the rear yard, damn near running smack into Jackson Hind as that bastard strolled out the front door, practically zipping up his fly.

Rankel had pressed himself against a bush, knowing what she thought of him, of Martin, of everything they stood for.

He waited till Hind drove away, fuming, then played it cool on her doorstep, pretending county business had brought him there so late.

She let him in, and they argued.

He lost it, like any man would, hitting her harder than he intended, not that it mattered now.

From that point on he was into damage-control, sanitizing the scene, clipping loose ends.

He remembered he had bragged to Beth Hopkins about banging the boss-lady. Lawyer or not, Beth would have figured it out. So he took her out, right off the street.

Lucky, he had been damn lucky.

When he felt the cops circling he had given them Junior and a full pack of motives, telling himself that since Junior didn't do it, they'd never be able to convict him.

But that motive was shot to shit when Junior got alibied on Charlie Hotchkiss.

Still, bodies in the playpen could place Junior front and center again.

Sitting in the dark basement office, listening to the whir and click of the elevators, the suction of fans, Bob Rankel failed to convince even himself.

He had overplayed his hand, fell in love with his scenario.

So what could they know? What could they have? A witness? New evidence? How did they find the bodies? he wondered, when no one knew where they were but him.

Maude, he thought ruefully.

A fucking fag had figured it out.

Thank God he had planned for this shift in fortune, planned extensively, as well-trained cops are known to do.

chapter 61

URPHY AND HIS HOMICIDE DETECTIVES, WITH
Martin Daly in tow, went suite to suite, starting at Seymour's, knocking on doors, ignoring shouted questions, finally knocking on
the Seaford door and learning Bob Rankel had been
there maybe ten minutes earlier, seen the shocking
news, and abruptly left.

"We all thought that was a little strange," said the
zone leader.

"Did he say where he was going?" asked Murphy.

"Not a peep." The zone leader shook his head and
looked at Martin. "What's going on, Martin?"

Daly stared at him. "You mean, what does this mean
for you, don't you, you selfish little shit?"

"There's a dead body hidden in your woods, Martin.
I'm not allowed to question that?"

"No."

Murphy turned his back on the squabbling pols and
pulled out his walkie-talkie. "Close up the perimeter,
folks. We got us a runner. Okay, everybody, we're looking for Lieutenant Robert Rankel, from our job, wanted
for homicide. Male white, shaved head, six-foot-three,
two hundred fifteen pounds, in a black suit, white shirt,
black tie, no doubt a clip-on. He's an expert in everything, and he's armed. Use the utmost caution."

BOB RANKEL LAY FLAT ON THE ROOF OF THE HOTEL, LISTENING
to his walkie-talkie and watching the circle of police
cars—marked and unmarked—settling in around the
hotel, closing down the obvious automotive exits.

Inside, he knew, they were searching the rooms for

him, painstakingly rousting lovers and other strangers.

They wouldn't want to take him in the lobby, putting countless innocents at risk. They would wait for him to walk out to the limo, fat, dumb, and happy.

He could always steal a car, of course, and make a break for it, but there were tools in the limo he preferred to have along, particularly if he was never coming back, a possibility he had to face.

The wind tore at his ill-fitting valet's uniform, drenching him.

He made up his mind, for better or worse: anything but jail.

He duck-walked back across the roof and inside to the service elevator door, which he rode down to the main floor. He pulled his cap low and stepped into the lobby.

FRANK MURPHY STOOD IN THE WILD WIND ON A THIRD-FLOOR balcony, watching over the hurried comings and goings below.

Blazer-loads of the faithful were pouring in, women dressed for the evening in the afternoon. Men in bad sport coats, with tiny flag medallions pinned to their lapels. Sheep, thought Murphy, as he turned his attention back to the search for the wolf.

Then a valet tried to move Martin Daly's car from the curb, apparently to accommodate the arrival of a swarm of six black limos flying the flag of the State of New York. The valet hesitated a moment to let a pedestrian pass and got blocked in by a tour bus.

Maude called in from her spot watching the back doors. "Nothing doing."

Rocky reported that he was leaving the main kitchen, heading for the service bar, then the basement.

"Anything up front?" asked Maude.

"No, Maude. Nobody leaving. Everybody coming in."

"He's not getting laid, Frank. He knows we know," she said.

"I know."

Three minutes passed like hours, Murphy alternately sure Rankel was getting away, or long gone, laughing at them.

Murphy scanned the parking lot and spotted a bald man trotting down an aisle, headed for the main driveway. Murphy held his breath, the walkie-talkie to his mouth.

The man bowed his head into the wind and turned in the direction of the hotel.

JUNIOR LOWERED WINDOWS TO AIR THE POT SMELL OUT OF THE rented Jeep as he swerved around the governor's fleet and parked behind the tour bus.

A uniformed valet opened the car door for him.

Junior said, "Leave it here, Parking Dude. I might have to split now and then."

"Yes, sir."

Junior held out a ten-dollar bill.

The valet grabbed Junior around the throat and shoved him back behind the steering wheel, then yanked open the back door and climbed into the seat behind Junior.

"Hey!"

"Shut up."

The valet mashed a pistol in Junior's right earlobe.

In the rearview mirror, Junior saw who it was.

"You? Why?"

"None of your fucking business, asshole. Now drive on out of here. Casually. Like there's nothing wrong."

"Fuck you, Kojak. Run that tough-guy shit by someone else."

"Wrong again, kid."

Rankel smacked him hard with the gun, opening a

gash on the side of his head above his ear, leaving Junior woozy, but far more ready to cooperate.

"Drive good, or die bad, kid. Your call . . . I never liked you anyway."

FROM THE BALCONY FRANK MURPHY SAW THE VALET STUFFING Junior back into his seat, jamming a gun against his head.

"Maude. Rocky. Front entrance. He's got Junior Daly. They're in a gray Grand Cherokee, heading for the south exit from the lot, slowly, caught behind a bus . . . now onto Hempstead Turnpike heading west. Perimeter team, you copy? Follow but do not intercept. He's got a hostage."

Murphy stuffed the walkie-talkie in his raincoat and ran down the crowded stairs to join his team in the lobby.

They flew out the front doors, saw the homicide car was blocked by the governor's staff cars.

"I got the van," said Murphy. "Come on."

They splashed through the puddles and piled into the van, Murphy behind the wheel. He grabbed the mike off the dash. "You see 'em?" Murphy asked the perimeter supervisor.

"Yes, sir. West on the turnpike to the Hofstra arch, then they jumped the center divider through a break in traffic and made a U-turn, you copy? They are now headed east on Hempstead Turnpike. I'm guessing for the Meadowbrook Parkway. Repeating . . . suspect Rankel eastbound . . ."

The van squealed from the parking lot.

"They're northbound on the Meadowbrook," said the supervisor. "Going fast."

Murphy stomped the accelerator, whipping the top-heavy van through an illegal turn, cutting off a Budweiser truck.

Rocky grabbed his shoulder from the back. "You okay there, Murphy?"

"What, you think I'm too old for this? Have a little faith."

The van tilted wildly as it wheeled around another tight corner and screeched toward the parkway. With the siren wailing, cars were suddenly weaving in front of Murphy, or worse, stopping right in their lanes, testing his reflexes, again and again. He would always remember their confused looks as he drove past, Rocky flipping them the finger.

"We lost him," said the supervisor. "Going by Roosevelt Field. Maybe on Ring Road."

Murphy swiveled his head about, checking side roads, squinting to see through the wind-flung water on his windshield.

"Anybody got him?" Maude asked on the air.

Nothing.

Martin leaned his head between Murphy and Maude and said, "Murphy, I can't lose my son. You understand that? Forget about the race. I want my son back."

Rocky called up from the back of the van, "I'm reading his file, boss. Rankel's good at bugging things, defensive driving, hostage negotiations, marksmanship, seamanship, search and seizure, deadly physical force."

Seamanship. Murphy remembered that before Bob Rankel drove Martin he was a Marine Bureau cop, the second best job in the department. "Where's he keep his boat, Martin?"

"Freeport. Woodcleft Canal. Just down from McQuade's."

"Ocean capable?"

"Oh, yeah. Real nice boat."

"On a day like this?"

"I wouldn't take out the Port Jeff ferry on a day like this."

"You're not wanted for murder."

Murphy jumped three lanes of oncoming traffic and the grassy median, then turned onto the shortcut to the Meadowbrook southbound. He was standing on the gas as they crested the first stone overpass.

"There he is!" cried Maude. "Way up on the right. They must have circled the mall."

"Got him," said Murphy, shutting down the siren and the lights. "The no-good prick. Should we notify the Coast Guard?"

Maude said, "I don't think they'd want to send a crew out just now. And we'd tip him off. He's got to be monitoring us, right, Martin?"

"Bet on it."

"Explosives," continued Rocky, "protecting your CEO, field interrogations, traffic stops—"

Murphy said, "Get Rankel on the radio?"

Maude said, "I don't see why not."

"Do it."

Maude keyed the mike. "Bob, it's Maude Fleming. What do you say we talk?"

No answer.

Silence in the van, but for the swish of high speed on wet roads.

"Are you monitoring, Bob? Sure you are."

Silence.

"Nothing's ever as bad as we make it, Bob. You talk to your lawyer, come up with a plan, bail. Hell, you'll be going to Giants games again in a couple of weeks . . . Come on, Bob, this is no way for cops to treat each other. Where'd you go?"

"Back off, bitch," Rankel finally answered. "You hear me? The last thing in the world I want to do is hurt another cop. Man, you don't know how close you already came."

Murphy keyed his mike and said, "Uh, Bob? By the way, you're fucking fired."

"Better check that with Martin."

Daly grabbed Maude's hand and keyed her mike: "You give me back my son, and you can have anything you want."

"Like you fucking care about Junior. Wait. What? Is this being taped?" Rankel laughed bitterly. "This is me you're talking to, remember. I know everything."

"You hurt my son, and I'll see you in hell."

Murphy said, "You've got things to trade, Bob. Use your head. There's never been a better time to make a deal. Hell, we can patch in Artie Prefect if we need to. Do a little one-stop shopping."

"Sorry, Murphy. Sometimes things don't work out. Nice knowing you, though."

The van was half a mile back of the Jeep. If Rankel could see their headlights and identify them, if he had any idea they were following in the van, he'd have been better than human.

"He thinks he's home free," Murphy said off the air.

"Maybe," said Maude.

Murphy got back on the air and asked brusquely, "Where'd you put Babs Whitcomb?"

"Good God, are you a donkey-Irish dope . . . I don't have nothing to do with Babs, never did. Her own old man waxed her, you want an ex-cop's opinion."

Maude keyed her mike. "Where's Elizabeth?"

"What do you mean, where's Elizabeth? Do I look like a fucking idiot?"

"Say again?" said Maude.

"No more talk," said Rankel. "Adios."

"Rankel!" cried Murphy. "Talk to me."

Silence.

"Shut off all the radios for a second," said Maude.

Murphy flipped the dashboard toggle switch.

"He thinks we found Elizabeth," said Maude. "In Junior's little fort. Right?" She looked back at her partner.

"Sure sounded like that," said Rocky.

Maude said, "Frank, go to a secure channel and get our people at Blue Landing to spread out their search, including the woods, the waterfront."

"You got it."

Murphy made the notifications, then settled in the middle lane, following the red dots on the horizon he knew to be the taillights of the Jeep.

Martin's cell phone rang, and he snapped it open like a switchblade. "Yes?"

"Martin . . . Don Neville here. Sorry I took so long getting back to you . . ."

JUNIOR WAS GETTING STRAIGHTER BY THE MILE, ENJOYING THE luck of drunks and babies as he whizzed south on Guy Lombardo Avenue through the crowded Freeport neighborhoods south of Merrick Road, dodging puddles and falling tree limbs.

It was almost dark out now, and the oncoming headlights were blinding him. By Atlantic Avenue the puddles had turned to ponds, then small lakes, with whitecaps.

"Slow down," said Rankel. "Ten miles an hour. I want to see if we're being followed. Okay, pull over here and wait."

Junior parked the Jeep at the curb just south of Ray Street and checked his rearview mirror. He turned and looked over his shoulder at Rankel. "That van back there a few blocks. It just stopped, too."

Rankel stared at Junior. "You really don't recognize it, do you?"

Junior looked a little closer. "Well, I'll be damned."

Rankel placed the gun against Junior's head. "Drive. Fast. Make a right on Front Street."

Junior nailed it.

Two blocks back, the van did too.

"Cute, that Maude," said Rankel. "Acting lost."

Power lines were down in Randall Park, a tree uprooted, leaning on the backstop. Two cars with occupants were stalled in the middle of Lombardo and Front, like ships stranded at sea.

Junior snaked around them, swamping them, though he doubted whether even so fine a machine as the Jeep could navigate the knee-deep flood at the intersection of Woodcleft and Front.

"End of the line," he called back to Rankel. "Now what?"

"Gun it."

"We'll stall. Hell, we'll drown."

"Like I give a shit."

"I'm serious. We'll break our necks."

"You should be so lucky."

Junior felt the gun behind his ear, closed his eyes, and floored the Jeep. They made thirty miles an hour before they hit the six-foot-deep lake.

The next thing Junior knew his airbag had gone off in his face and his shoes and pants were getting wet, then Rankel was cursing at him, hitting him upside the head with the gun.

chapter 62

STRONG, WARM HANDS SHOOK HER AWAKE.

Voices called to her from the storm, not comprehending her fatigue. They knew her name.

She was sheltered, wiped dry, and swaddled in warm blankets. "Hang in there, Miss Lucido. Just a few minutes more."

She watched naked tree limbs passing overhead as they carried her from the woods to the ambulance, as if back from a foreign land.

The last time she had seen trees they had been in full fall color.

"You're gonna be okay," somebody told her as a warm light burned before her face, and blessed heat enveloped her.

The doors closed and the ambulance rocked as it rolled.

"Elizabeth? Can you hear me? You're gonna be fine, do you understand? We're going to the hospital now."

Elizabeth opened her eyes again, and nodded weakly at the ambulance technician. "Yes. Thank you."

"What hurts?" he asked.

"Everything . . . Nothing. I'm thirsty."

He held a cup of cool clean water to her lips, and she drank.

"What day is it?" she asked.

"Tuesday," he said. "Election Day."

"Wow."

He smiled. "An overtime day."

"Yes, it is. I remember that . . . You get time and a half, plus meal money and mileage."

"And worth every dime of it," he said. "Don't you think?"

"Absolutely."

"Do you remember what happened to you?"

"Oh, yes, like it was yesterday. Lieutenant Rankel did this."

The tech wrote the name on his pad. "The cops said they'd meet you at the hospital."

"Good." Elizabeth closed her eyes, then opened them. "Could we swing by my polling place?" she asked. "I'm gonna vote in this fucking race if it kills me."

The tech patted her wrist as he stabbed an IV into the

back of her hand. "Sure, ma'am," he said. "Whatever you need."

Then the world was a warm and lovely place, as sleep dragged her under. She had missed everybody so much, and from the looks of things they had got along fine without her.

"Hey," she said. "Don't let Rankel get away with it."

"You have my word."

chapter 63

MURPHY BRAKED SHORT OF THE FLOOD, FORTY YARDS from the disabled Jeep.

Whitecapped waves hurled themselves out of the canal and clear across Woodcleft Avenue, between telephone poles and abandoned cars, restaurants, fish stores, and gin mills, a scene from a disaster movie, so different from the summer months when a person hungry for seafood and thirsty for beer can find no finer South Shore destination. During a hurricane, it's the last place one might recommend.

Bob Rankel, gun in hand, was out of the Jeep in the waist-high water, dragging an unconscious Junior half out of his seat belt, then leave him hanging from the harness, facedown in the foamy water. Rankel looked back at them once, quickly, then waded down the street into the higher water, holding the pistol and fanny pack over his head.

"Let's get wet," Murphy said. "Martin, you get Junior."

"Right."

Murphy, Maude, and Rocky ran for the water like kids at the beach, and they followed Rankel gamely through the surf roiling Woodcleft Avenue, falling, getting knocked backward by waves, dodging a thirty-foot cabin cruiser broken free from its slip.

"Where'd he go?" asked Murphy, clinging to the side of a bayman's pickup truck.

"I don't see him," said Rocky.

"Head for the docks," said Maude. "Watch for an ambush."

The bullet caught Rocky high in the shoulder.

"Awgh! Shit!" "How'd he do that?"

Murphy ducked behind the truck and saw blood spurting from the collar of Rocky's raincoat. Rocky's face screwed up in pain.

"You okay?" asked Murphy.

Rocky was clutching his forearm to his stomach. "Oh, God, does that burn. . . . The motherfucker's shooting cops. I don't believe it."

Murphy said, "Rocky, can you make it back okay?"

"Go get that bastard. Don't worry about me."

"What do you think?" Murphy asked Maude.

Maude looked up at Murphy and said coolly, "I think now I'm gonna kill him."

"JUNIOR. PLEASE. BREATHE."

Martin had Junior propped back up in the driver's seat of the Jeep and was slapping him, then staring into his son's face for signs of life, marveling at how much he looked like his mother when they had found her in the basement.

"Junior . . . Son. I love you. Wake up."

"Huh?"

"Are you okay?"

Junior belched booze into Martin's face.

Martin said, "Take deep breaths."

Junior's face was ashen, his stubbled chin striped with blood.

"Junior."

"What?" Junior mumbled.

"I'm sorry."

"Un-huh."

"I'll change."

"Okay."

MURPHY AND MAUDE FOUND DECENT COVER ON THE HIGHER ground of a loading dock behind a commercial fishery, and from there they peered through the storm at the chaos in the canal. A riot of vessels large and small had piled up against the bulkheads, and the waterway was frothy with debris, all the way to the bay.

"There," said Maude, pointing south, seaward.

Bob Rankel was on the dock, behind the Sea Dog Pub, holding the guide ropes for support with one arm. He had a red-headed teenage waitress in a headlock with the other.

Murphy and Maude jumped from their perch and started after him, spreading apart as they went.

Rankel raised his weapon over the waitress's head and fired at Maude, shattering the windshield of the speedboat to her left, then hitting the water three feet behind her before she dove behind a piling.

Murphy, who was working his way along the backs of the stores, saw that Rankel had Maude pinned down. He held his fire, pressing onward through the waves, hoping to draw Rankel's fire.

Rankel saw Murphy and swung his pistol around. Murphy dove behind a Dumpster, felt the blast of the rounds hitting steel, heard the pinging. He peeked over the top in time to see Rankel hurl the waitress into the canal.

A wave crashed her helplessly against the bulkhead, then swept her out into the middle.

Murphy tucked his gun in his belt and gave up his

cover. He stumbled to the bulkhead, dove into the violent water, and discovered that all the long-distance swimming in the world was no preparation for the suck and pull of a raging sea. He was bounced this way and that during his frantic search, and he found the unconscious woman as much by accident of physics as any great skill. He grabbed her around her neck, and tried to speak to her, swallowed a bucket of the cold salt water as he desperately treaded water, bobbing up and down with the woman limp in his left arm, sliding in the direction of open water.

Murphy heard twin engines roar to life and looked around for the exhaust. Forty yards away, Bob Rankel was at the wheel of his speedboat.

IF HE COULD JUST MAKE OPEN SEA, THOUGHT RANKEL, AND RIDE out the storm, he had a chance to disappear. A great chance. He untied the stern line, thinking his backup identity was waiting for him on Fire Island, transportation from there arranged, everything ready to be assumed and enjoyed. He could be in Boston by noon tomorrow. Toronto the next day.

This did not have to be the end of his life.

The storm would clear, the waters would calm. Night would fall, and the stars would come out, and they would never, ever find him.

He pointed the heaving bow in the direction of Frank Murphy, and behind him, freedom.

He rammed the throttle from idle speed to wicked fast.

The last Bob Rankel saw of Frank Murphy, the poor police commissioner was trying to haul the waitress back under with him, looking like he wasn't going to make it.

SWIMMING STRAIGHT DOWN AND MAKING LITTLE HEADWAY, Frank Murphy thought mostly of Wally, alone in the world, and who would care for him; how he had failed. He thought of Armand and Buster, dying on the sidewalk outside that bank. He thought of Alice, and then sensed his good friend Jake would act as her umbrella, through his funeral and beyond.

His ears were ringing and his chest was burning, but he held his breath and kicked as long and hard as he could, which wasn't long, not with all the energy he'd expended, not with the waitress in his arm.

There are some events you cannot train for.

Ultimately, he went back up for air.

MAUDE FLEMING LAY FLAT ON HER BELLY ON THE HEAVING dock, trying her damndest to draw a bead on Bullet Bob. But the target was moving and she was moving, and the wind was howling, and the stakes were so high.

Then she saw Murphy foundering in the path of the onrushing speedboat, the waitress in his arms, and Maude experienced a moment's clarity; she saw the dotted line to Rankel's chest and pulled the trigger of her nine-millimeter fast, until all she could hear was click, click, click, click, instead of boom, boom, boom, boom. . . .

Ten yards from Murphy the speedboat swerved hard to port and crashed nosefirst into the bulkhead behind the private homes on Guy Lombardo Avenue.

Half a beat later, the boat exploded, launching Rankel's body like a rocket over the canal, lighting up the night.

Flame and debris rained down upon the water, and Maude couldn't find Murphy or the woman, couldn't even tell if they were still together.

The worst moment of her life finally ended when she saw the two heads pop into view in the middle of the canal.

• • •

AN HOUR HAD GONE BY, THE WIND WAS DYING OFF, AND THE specialists of disaster were still arriving: ambulances for Junior and Rocky and the waitress, detectives and reporters, divers to hunt for Rankel's body. A salvage vessel.

The governor was allegedly due at any moment, to make a statement.

Murphy left the temporary command post and found Maude inside the Sea Dog, sitting at the dark, empty bar. He sat on the stool next to her and draped his arm around her shivering shoulders.

"Thanks," he said. "We were meat."

"No sweat."

"You okay?"

"Sure."

After a moment Maude got off her stool and faced the jukebox, digging some quarters out of her pocket, feeding the machine.

Murphy said, "They found Elizabeth in the woods near the beach, Maude, alive, heading the wrong direction. She thanks you, too."

"Thank God," said Maude, staring at the play list. "She all right?"

"I wouldn't say that."

"And Babs?"

"Not a trace."

Maude said nothing.

Murphy walked over to her and gave her a hug from behind, then turned her and held her as if they were about to waltz. "Pick a song?"

"Nothing here I like."

Frank nodded. "You okay?"

"Sure," she said. "Just cold. Tired."

"Right."

She looked up at him, as if he were her father, and the corner of her mouth curled up in hard-won wisdom Murphy recognized immediately.

She said, "So, that about how it's done?"

He knew "it" meant watching your bullets end another person's life. "You were magnificent, Maude. As always. Only now comes the hard part."

Her eyes misted over. "The guilt?"

"For me it was fighting back the pride."

chapter 64

D R. TUFO REPORTED THAT HE AND HIS STAFF AT NORTH Shore Hospital had saved Elizabeth Lucido's life by only the thinnest of margins. She had arrived severely dehydrated and malnourished, with a spinal cord injury, and a broken ankle, running a fever of 104.3. Chicken soup or no chicken soup, all agreed that twenty-four hours more in the elements and she'd have died. Jackson Hind was with her, he said, and she was resting comfortably.

At 10 P.M. Martin Daly told the press corps assembled under the hospital portico that he was tired but of course relieved that the Ladysnatcher case was solved, and grateful that he and his son had enjoyed some small part in capturing a very bad man.

He did not mention that man had been his close friend and confidant for the last fifteen years.

Regarding his narrow victory over Jackson Hind, he said only, "The people of Nassau County have spoken, and we have heard them loud and clear. We will stay the course. Let the healing begin."

He led aides and reporters in the Pledge of Allegiance.

Then things fell back into line for Martin Daly: Kym called him and agreed to meet him back at the Marriott for a victory romp. Then Joe Torre called while they were jamming in a locked back bedroom in his suite, but some arrogant campaign underling refused to put him through.

Naturally, Don Neville was turned away at the door.

FRANK MURPHY GOT BACK TO HIS OWN OFFICE THAT NIGHT AFTER everyone was safely tucked into bed at the hospital.

He found a message from Jackson Hind on his voice mail, saying only, "Thank you for everything," and a second message, from Alice, saying: "Figures Frank Murphy saves the waitress. Anyway, you're my hero."

He walked to his window and stared at the dark Executive Building across the street, imagining the soap opera that would be going on right now if Martin Daly had lost. The shredding. The disk deletions. The raids on discretionary accounts. All that bloodshed avoided, for now. Possibly forever.

A damn shame.

Around eleven-thirty Jake and Wally arrived with pizza and beer for the hard-typing troops in the Homicide bullpen. Then the Murphy brothers left headquarters in an unmarked car via the garage, and after a Jericho Turnpike burger-cruise Wally was going back to the Institute, to his window, and the safety of his routine. But they would have their sleepovers again, and often.

"Rankel panicked," said Frank. "He flipped out, and he whacked her. With those stupid sap-gloves. He thought he killed her, and he freaked. Then he covered that mistake and made more . . . like a lot of us."

His cell phone rang, and it was Jake, with word that Alice was outside their condo, with luggage.

"And how do you know that?"

"The surveillance team I've had on her."

"Really, Jake? Since when?"

"Not to spy, to keep her safe. Who knew *what* the fuck was going on?"

"How'd you manage that without me knowing?"

"A lot of people owed you favors. Fans of the *Grunt*."

Murphy said, "She's not cleaning me out, is she?"

"A great friggin' catch like you? Get real."

AFTER ELECTION DAY THINGS FELL PRETTY MUCH BACK into place in Nassau County. Lard was ladled to the loyal; fence-sitters were fired. Critics condemned.

In a flurry of government activity promotions were handed out, new job titles invented, new initiatives proposed. Failed projects were renamed and restarted. Investigations were dropped.

A budget gap was revealed and a tax hike passed without fanfare, because no matter what the people were paying for their government, it clearly wasn't enough.

Democratic Chairman Don Neville was allowed to trade his Lincoln Town Car for a Range Rover, which he needed for his no-show job at the Board of Elections. His daughter joined the law firm of Beinstock, Bates. A disappointed Arthur Prefect remained despised and dangerous, waiting in the wings.

Martin Daly began to think about his legacy. He began to talk about it. His aides began to talk about it. Pressure built for some grand civic gesture in his name, other than the Victim's Center, which remained closed, under what Daly aides call "retro-fit."

Junior came up with it—the grand Daly gesture—upon his return from two weeks of rehab at an undisclosed location in Florida: The county would clear out one of its last precious parcels of open space and build a wildlife attraction, with an aquatic stadium with corporate skyboxes, a tourist attraction that would eventually be a stop on a monorail being planned. Beinstock, Bates was retained to expedite the project, The Daly Domain.

Newsday turned its investigative guns on some disabled cops they caught bowling.

Jackson and Elizabeth eloped.

Dante went back to college, sadder but wiser. Norman Keller stayed home.

During the third week of December, Police Commissioner Frank Murphy received a Christmas card at his office. It had been mailed from the Tryall Club, Montego Bay, Jamaica, West Indies, exactly two weeks prior. Inside the angel-shaped card was typed the following message:

THE ONLY ONE I MISS IS YOU

Murphy made the sign of the cross.

Warmth spread from Murphy's heart to his face. He picked up his phone and hit the speed-dialer.

"Homicide. Fleming."

"It's me. Tell Rocky he was right about Babs Whitcomb."

"She walked, didn't she?" said Maude. "That bitch."

"Yup."

"You have proof?"

"I think that's safe to say."

"Except publicly, right?"

Murphy looked across the parking lot at the Executive Building, the twinkling lights of tiny Christmas trees in the office windows. "Be rather a sticky situation for her hubby, who, of course, has well-connected friends who will bring all manner of pressure to bear, and yada, yada . . ."

"Merry Christmas, Frank. Peace on Earth."

"All any good cop can ask for."

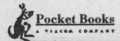

Visit
❖ **Pocket Books** ❖
online at

www.SimonSays.com

Keep up on the latest new
releases from your favorite
authors, as well as author
appearances, news, chats,
special offers and more.

SIMON & SCHUSTER
A VIACOM COMPANY
www.SimonSays.com

Pocket
Books